THE
IRON
DRAGON'S
MOTHER

THE
IRON
DRAGON'S
MOTHER

Michael Swanwick

TOR

A Tom Doherty Associates Book

New York

THE IRON DRAGON'S MOTHER

Edited by Jen Gunnels

A Tor Book
Published by Tom Doherty Associates
175 Fifth Avenue
New York, NY 10010

www.tor-forge.com

Tor® is a registered trademark of Macmillan Publishing Group, LLC.

The Library of Congress Cataloging-in-Publication Data is available upon request.

ISBN 978-1-250-19825-9 (hardcover)
ISBN 978-1-250-19826-6 (ebook)

Our books may be purchased in bulk for promotional, educational, or business use. Please contact your local bookseller or the Macmillan Corporate and Premium Sales Department at 1-800-221-7945, extension 5442, or by email at MacmillanSpecialMarkets@macmillan.com.

First Edition: June 2019

Printed in the United States of America

0 9 8 7 6 5 4 3 2 1

For Millie, Mary Ann, Evangeline, Pat, Marianne, Barbie, Lucy, Alicia, and their mothers and their mothers' mothers, all the way back to Eve.

ACKNOWLEDGMENTS

I am grateful to the (alas) late Lucius Shepard for giving me permission to quote from "The Scalehunter's Beautiful Daughter." To Byron Tetrick for flight protocols. To Tom Purdom for the culture of military life. To Anatoly Belilovsky for the nomenclature of Russian megalizards. To Bill Gibson for once again providing a character with the wristwatch *juste*. To Marcin Pągowski for help with the Polish language. To Kevin Bolz for help with Breton naming. To Ellen Kushner for Satie's *Gnossiennes*. To Barbara Frost for the banker's calculator. To my son Sean for Faerie realpolitik and for choreographing the dragon-fight. To Barbara Weitbrecht for marine creatures. To Tom Doyle for supplying the motto of the Dragon Corps and to Mario Rups for Latinate grammatical antecedents. To Janis Ian for permission to quote from "Jesse." To the late and sorely missed Gardner Dozois for teaching me how to write in the first place. And to the M. C. Porter Endowment for the Arts for life, love, and everything else.

Quotation from "The Locomotive," a short story in the collection *Art in Nature* by Tove Jansson (1978, Sort of Books, 2012; translated by Thomas Teal), reproduced here by permission of Sort of Books.

Excerpt from "Averno" from *Poems 1962–2012* by Louise Glück, copyright © 2012 by Louise Glück, reprinted by permission of Farrar, Straus and Giroux.

THE
IRON
DRAGON'S
MOTHER

Once upon a time there was a little girl—and now my story's begun.

She grew up, she grew old, and then she died. And now my story is done.

—Helen V., notebooks

DYING IS A DREARY BUSINESS. HELEN V. LEARNED THAT lesson early in the process, when she was first coming to grips with the fact that not only would she never get better but that nothing she did in the time remaining to her was going to matter in the least. For a ninety-something-old woman whose thoughts and actions had always, ultimately, mattered, it was a bitter pill to swallow. As was not having anything to look forward to but the final hammerblow to the back of her neck at the end of the slaughterhouse chute.

She didn't know that the dragons were coming for her.

"And how are we today, lovely lady?" The day nurse came dancing into the room, inexplicably chipper as always. At least he wasn't whistling. Some days he whistled.

There were a dozen leads attached at one end to various parts of Helen's body and at the other to a rank of monitors, all of them like little children, prone to demanding attention for no reason that made any sense to Helen. One had been beeping away for half an hour valiantly trying to alert an uncaring world that her blood pressure was high. Well, of course it was, and would remain so, too, until somebody switched the damned thing off.

It hurt to turn her head, but Helen made the sacrifice so she could move her glare from the monitors to the nurse on the far side of the jungle of plastic vines that moved fluids in and out of the desiccated sack of flesh that had once given her so much pleasure. "We are dying."

"Oh piffle. Just listen to yourself—you're being so negative! How are you ever going to get better with an attitude like that?"

"I'm not."

"Well, I'm glad that you see my point at least." The day nurse briskly yanked tubes from catheters and swapped out plastic bags on their chrome rack. He locked a gurney to the side of the bed and with a tug and a shove rolled Helen onto it. Then he changed the sheets, rolled her back again, and made the gurney go away. Finally, he tapped the weeping monitor, silencing it, and said, "Your blood pressure is high."

"Fancy that."

"Whatever happened to those lovely flowers you had?" Without waiting to hear that Helen had commanded they be thrown out because she did not care for hollow gestures from distant relations she barely knew existed and would not recognize on the street, the day nurse picked up the remote and switched on the television. A crackly roar of laughter flooded the room. Least jolly sound in the universe. Still, she had to concede that it was doing its best to hide the profound silence of her life dwindling away.

"Either that television goes or I do," Helen said. "Oscar Wilde. November 30, 1900."

"What?"

"Nobody ever gets my jokes." Helen closed her eyes. "Story of my life." Which was true. Yet she was unable to refrain from making them. She was stuffed so full of cultural trivia that she could no longer hold it all in; it seeped from every orifice and psychic wound in humiliating little dribbles and oozes. "This is slow work," she said, and lapsed into what previously she might have mistaken for sleep but was now merely and at best the negation of consciousness.

When she came to, it was night.

Early in her career, when she was a mere scribbler, Helen had learned that every scene should be anchored by at least three evocations of the senses. A short-order cook in a diner hears the sizzle of eggs frying, smells the half-burnt coffee in the percolator, and leans a hand on a countertop that's ever so slightly slick with grease. That's all you need. But it couldn't be done here. Everything jarring, unclean, or worth looking at had been smoothed away or removed. There were no sharp corners. All the sounds were hushed: distant, emotionless voices, the unhurried squeak of soft shoes on linoleum in the hallway. The colors were all some variant of grayish off-white: eggshell, taupe, cream, cornsilk, pearl, latte, gainsboro, beige. Worst of all were the smells: bland, anodyne hospital smells. Now that all the unpleasant things had been made to go away, she found she missed them.

I am like an old dog, she thought, deprived of interesting stinks and stenches.

A hospital was a place of elimination. It was where you went to eliminate pains, diseases, waste products, blood specimens, wrappings, bandages, smells, sensations, internal organs, and, ultimately, one's self.

"You are headed straight for Hell," the night nurse said with absolute conviction. Apparently she'd woken up in the middle of a conversation. These things happened.

"Papist nonsense," Helen retorted. She'd expected better

from a good Baptist lady like the night nurse. Next thing you knew, she would be elevating the Host and praying novenas for the salvation of Helen's soul. Helen felt a twinge of pain and tried hard to ignore it.

The night nurse began unclipping tubes and unhooking drained plastic sacks so they could be replaced with plump new ones. She never talked when she did so; she gave the task her full attention. Admirable, one supposed. "I am no more than a device. For transferring fluids. From one bag to another," Helen declared. "In the most expensive manner possible."

Her work done, the night nurse said, "You make a joke of everything."

"You have me there. That's exactly what I do."

"You are standing at the edge of the abyss, and still you laugh. You are about to fall right over into the flames and you're giggling like a madwoman. Lord Jesus has his hand out to pull you back. You need only accept his grace in order to be saved. But what do you do? You pretend that life is nothing but chuckles and smirks. Out of pride and arrogance, you are laughing yourself right into eternal damnation."

The night nurse preached a righteous sermon. Direct, no nonsense, straight from the heart. But did she hear an amen? She did not. Not from Helen, anyway. Helen V. felt nothing inside her but the growing insistence of a not at all spiritual pain. Anyway, it would be hypocritical for her to pretend to believe in a God who, the nuns of her distant childhood had all agreed, hates hypocrites.

"What's this you're reading?" The night nurse picked up her paperback book from the nightstand.

"Words, words, words," Helen said wearily, hoping the night nurse would put it down without pursuing the matter any further. The pain twisted, making her gasp.

"Some kind of pagan trash," the night nurse decided, insightful as ever. She put the book back, face down.

"I need a painkiller."

"Mmm-hmm." The night nurse was filling out some damned form or other.

"I really need that painkiller."

"You'll get it. Just hold your horses."

"This is a power play. Isn't it?" She could well imagine how a woman who had never gone scuba-diving in the Maldives or found herself inexplicably judging an air guitar competition in an unlicensed slum bar in Johannesburg or spent a summer trying to convert a rusty old Ferrari to run on vegetable oil because she'd fallen in love with a boy who wanted to save the world might resent her. The night nurse had probably led a hard life. One could understand her withholding drugs from extremely annoying old women just because that was the only power she had. Not that Helen, in her final days, was extremely anything. She liked to think of herself as the Nemesis of Nurses, the Terror of the Tenth Ward. But probably the people charged with ushering her into the next world with as little fuss as possible thought of her only as the difficult old lady in room 402. Well within the normal range of human rudeness. "God, if there is a God, will forgive you. For finding me a pill. If there is no God. Then the goddamned zeitgeist. Of our collective unconscious. Will forgive you."

"You got all these big words. But they don't actually *say* anything." The night nurse went away, leaving Helen weeping with pain and hating herself for it almost as much as she hated the night nurse for doing this to her. The petty, petty, petty . . .

The monitor began to beep again.

Then the night nurse was back. There was a ripping noise of plastic being removed from packaging. Small fiddling sounds as she did something with the tubes and plastic bags. Finally she said, "I put some Demerol in your drip. Be patient, it'll take effect soon."

"I like you," Helen managed to say. "Really. Thank you. I really do like you."

That cut no mustard with the night nurse. "And you tell me any damn-fool thought that enters your head. It don't matter who you like. Only whether you love God more than you do the sound of your own smart mouth. You better think about that. You better think about that long and hard."

Amen, sister, Helen thought. In assisted living, she had expended a great deal of energy pretending to work on her memoirs, *Writ in Water*. Well, now the time had come to admit that not only was she never going to finish them but she had never really intended to make a proper start. Life was for the living, memoirs were for those who had something to say, and she had been a failure on both fronts for a very long time.

The night nurse silenced the monitor. "Your blood pressure is high."

"Is it? I can't imagine why."

⁎⁎

"Oh, those two," the evening nurse said in an easy, good-humored way. Once again, it seemed, Helen had been awake and talking for some time. Emily was a little dumpling of a woman with a round, pink face and thin blond hair. She was also, or so Helen V. believed—and her judgment was acute in such matters—genuinely kind. She must have known a lot of pain in her life. "I don't know how you put up with them."

"I'm enjoying them both. I could do a show about either one." Helen was feeling unaccountably expansive. Must be her second wind. Her last wind, rather. Not that her breathing was any the easier for it. *"Nurse Sunshine*—about an RN. Who infuriates everybody without realizing it. Chirpy, positive, upbeat. A sit-com, of course. Female, it goes without saying. God forbid a man should be cast as such a ditz. That's a fight I've lost too many times. The pilot writes itself. Starring whomever the head of network programming. Is screwing this season.

"*The Night Nurse*, though . . . That could be made interest-ing. A rigidly moral woman. Who takes it upon herself to con-vert her charges. But here's the hook. Knowing what backsliders human beings are. Whenever she does save one. The night nurse immediately kills them. So they'll die in a state of grace. You see. And go straight to Heaven. Every time a patient begins to rise up. From the Slough of Despond. To feel hope again. The audience will quail with dread. Here it comes. Oh God, here it comes. Great suspense. Complex character. With the right ac-tress, it could be a hit."

"That's right, you used to be a writer, didn't you?"

"Not a bit of it. I was a producer. I made things happen." Helen said it nicely, though, careful not to offend. She liked Emily because she'd let Helen take the conversation anywhere she wanted. It was rare luck to find a good listener here of all places. "Writers are like bedpans. Necessary, perhaps. But you wouldn't take one out to dinner."

The evening nurse laughed. "You know what, Helen? I am going to miss you. You're not like other people, are you?"

"No. Thank goodness. One of me is more than enough."

But now Emily was tidying things up, and Helen knew what that meant. She didn't have any material prepared to keep the evening nurse from leaving, so there was no choice but to fall back on the truth. "I've got an escape plan," she said.

"Oh?"

"I'm going to bust out of this joint." She waited until the eve-ning nurse opened her mouth to assure her that this was out of the question and said, "That paperback is *The Tibetan Book of the*

Dead. Annotated. I've been studying it. In the instant of death. There's an instant of freedom. If you try to hang on to your life. You just spiral back down into samsara and rebirth. More of the same. But there's that one instant. In which you can take a leap into the unknown. Into a better world. I'm taking that leap."

"I didn't know you were a Buddhist."

"I'm not. Opiate of the people. Crap and nonsense. Still, escape is escape. Right? When somebody bakes you a cake. With a file in it. You don't care what brand file."

"I don't think I'm following you."

"Okay. This book maps out what happens after you die. Nobody else, no other religion, does that in any kind of detail. Well, Dante, but forget him. Maybe they're on to something. Somebody came back from death. And blabbed. And the monks wrote it down. And it became religion. But maybe it's not properly religion at all. Maybe it's just stone-cold fact. Think about it. It's worth a . . ."

But Emily was heading for the door now. A smile and a wave and she would disappear into the past, a fading memory, a minor regret.

"I could build a show around you too," Helen said to make her audience stay.

She could, too. Helen was sure of it. A hospital was an ordinary place where the drama of life and death played out in the most ordinary way imaginable. Grand themes reduced to small gestures. At the center of which . . . an ordinary woman, of ordinary goodness. One who never faces down a terrorist or talks an ailing presidential candidate into changing his health care policy or a teenage pop star out of committing suicide. But does what she can for her charges, takes the night shift for a friend—no, not even a friend, a colleague—who wants to see her daughter sing in the school play . . .

Emily was gone.

Just as well. Even Helen V. could never sell such a show. There just weren't the numbers for something that thoughtful and intelligent. Maybe there had been once, in the fifties, but not today. Today, she was simply sorry that she had said her escape plan out loud. Once spoken, it sounded suspect. Let's not mince words, it sounded stupid. Still, it was all she had. "I am perplexed," she said. "Aleister Crowley. December 1, 1947." Another day, she supposed, was over. Helen closed her eyes and let the darkness carry her downstream.

A sudden shuddering noise rose up from the machine that periodically inflated the sleeves that had been Velcroed around Helen's legs, and the miserable things began squeezing and releasing, first right, then left, as if she were walking. It was supposed to keep her blood from clotting, and it was timed so that it came on just when she'd managed to forget about it. She supposed she was awake. Somebody was whistling.

"Wakey-risey, pretty lady. What a beautiful day. Makes you glad you're alive, doesn't it?" The day nurse began unhooking and rehooking bags. Then he did the thing with the gurney so he could roll her out of the way and change the sheets.

"No," she said. "It doesn't."

"Oh, you. You're incorrigible." He rolled her back onto the bed.

Out of boredom more than anything else, Helen said, "I've been wondering. Do you have a name?"

"Oh, now you've hurt my feelings." The day nurse put his hands on his hips and, smiling, scowled. "It's Charles. I've told you often enough."

"Chuck. Got it." Helen turned her head to stare at the row of monitors and then, because she could not help it, turned back to face him again. "Tell me, Chuck. Why are you always so goddamned happy?"

"Now, stop that." Incredibly, a note of genuine annoyance entered the man's voice. It seemed she had punctured his armor of fatuousness. "Just because you're not well doesn't give you license to treat people like fools and idiots."

"Oh, Chuck, Chuck, Chuck. Didn't you ever see Fellini's *The Clowns*? You're a fool. I'm a fool. The whole damn planet is. A ship of fools. That's why we're here. To give God a giggle. If you can't laugh at idiots, what can you? When you're tired of idiots. You're tired of life."

"Incorrigible. Simply incorrigible." The day nurse was smiling again.

"I am not tired of life," Helen said. Then, because it didn't sound very convincing, "I'm not."

The day nurse switched on the television. "Whatever happened to those lovely flowers you had?" he asked. Then, whistling, he walked out the door.

✳✳

Wakey-risey, pretty lady—and don't forget you're going to Hell. This was the way time passed. All too slowly, and all too swiftly toward its appointed and inevitable end. Excruciating either way. How many decades had she been here? A month? Nine hours?

Hating herself for it, Helen began to cry.

No, no, no, she thought—that's not me crying, it's just my body. But she was lying to herself and she knew it. She was as weak of spirit as she was of flesh. She was afraid of being alone with her thoughts. It was night again and the nurse was nowhere near. The halls were silent as death. Appropriately enough. Come back, she prayed, and I'll let you convert me. Alleluia. I swear.

Nothing.

A blackness profound and deep was gathering at the edges

of the room. Or had it always been there, waiting, and only now was Helen become aware of it? Slowly, it crept from the corners of the ceiling and beneath the bed, like fog gathering in a moonless sky, growing thicker and darker until there was nothing around her but blackness. Like a cheap lens-based special effect in a bad horror flick. She'd been responsible for her share of those too in her time.

All the monitors were crying now. Peace, my children, she wanted to say. A week from now you'll have forgotten me entirely.

In some far province of her mind, Helen was aware of hurrying footsteps, of people crowding into the room, jerking the bed around, doing urgent medical things. But when she tried to focus on them they faded into unreality, the fantasies of a dying mind. "So there it goes at last, the extinguished thing," she murmured. "Henry James . . ."

Abruptly, she could say no more. Not the last words she would have chosen had there been an audience. But there was no audience. Story of her life.

Her little machine daughters were really putting on a show, hopping up and down, hysterically weeping and wailing and for all she knew blinking too. Well, they'd simply have to learn to get along without her, for the darkness was closing about Helen like a cocoon. Squeezing the light from the room. Slowly but inexorably compressing it until there was only a fuzzy circle of the stuff dissolving in the distance. Which reminded her that there was something she was supposed to do. Something . . .

Then Helen remembered her escape plan. But there was no time! The light was dwindling, dying, it was only a spark.

All in a panic, she concentrated her thoughts on the distant speck of light and *leaped*.

She didn't know that the dragons had come for her.

Nor did they.

There are no accidents in the sky.

—Pygmy song

SHE DIDN'T KNOW . . .
I—what? No, please. Let me just. This isn't. Did somebody—? Keep those wing flaps level. Where was it? Don't. Voices like seagulls babbling swarmed up in her ears and overwhelmed her senses. Oh, you are in trouble now. Daughter of Night pray for me. But how? Over there. Stat. No! Am I going to die? Stop that.

She didn't know . . .

Oh, please. This is not. Where's the ground? The voices blended together in a timeless instant of dizziness and white noise in which she thought in panic: Who am I? What am I doing here? Hit the afterburners and close your eyes. Oh shit no. Bury her in a warrior's grave. There's no way out.

. . . who she was.

Then, in a sudden and terrible burst of clarity, she realized that she was not where she had thought she was, that she was in the cockpit of a dragon, that the dragon was in the air, that there were other dragons in the sky about her, that therefore she must be flying a mission, and that she was gods-knew-where doing who-knew-what and had apparently lost control of one of the most powerful and dangerous war machines ever built.

But Caitlin's hands, though sweaty, were steady on the rubber grips at the ends of the armrests, and the interface needles were set deep in her wrists. She could smell cold iron and feel the great beast's engines grumbling, and just below the surface of her own thought was the roiling oceanic vastness of its mind, seething with hatred! anger! battle lust! yet obedient to her will. She called up infrared and ultraviolet overlays to the true-color imaging display, purpling the sky and spangling it with stars she could not otherwise have seen in daytime. Then she summoned a map of the constellations. Matching stars to sigils put her above Ultima Thule, somewhere to the north of her base. With a thought, she dismissed the camera wraparounds. The cockpit was all chromed steel, optical glass, and ebony-slick surfaces. The pilot's couch—dark crimson leather with the squadron's emblem worked into it with green thread—wriggled beneath her, adjusting to her shifting weight, hugging her thighs, rising to support her back. Caitlin's eyes skipped and leaped over the instrumentation, all of it confirming what she had already sensed, that the dragon's flight was smooth and even.

Most importantly, no one seemed to have noticed anything odd about her dragon's performance. So whatever had just happened had been brief. Alarming but nothing to dwell upon. An incident that need not be documented. Over and done with. Ended.

Caitlin exhaled explosively. Apparently, she'd been holding her breath.

At another mental command, the wraparounds wreathed themselves about Caitlin's head again. The cabin disappeared as the dragon's *ka* swelled up within her. Air flowed smoothly over her wings. The mountains of Ultima Thule crept slowly under her belly, gleaming white with glaciers and ancient snowpack. The air was clear to the horizon and free of turbulence.

The sky was an infinite bowl of cloudless blue. It was a perfect day for flying.

Over the radio, the other pilots began to sing. Through Dream Gate they had gone and returned untouched for the sixth mission in a row, though this was a perilous passage and a feat that few squadrons had ever performed so often without the sacrifice of a dragon or three, and their pilots as well. They had good reason to feel proud.

The flight leader, Quicksilver of House Jade, sang the first verse:

> *"Deathless Goddess, cunning of thought,*
> *Mistress of dragons, you,*
> *I beg, O Lady, not to crush*
> *This warrior so true."*

One line at a time, in order of seniority, the other pilots joined in:

> *"But come to me, if thou hast heard*
> *My distant voice thee call;*
> *Sparrow-drawn, thy chariot*
> *Down from the sky let fall . . ."*

Caitlin was the runt of the squadron, the pilot with the least flight time under her belt, and this was her first mission of any consequence, so she joined in last. She almost missed her beat but after the first shaky syllable her voice merged in perfect harmony with the others, indistinguishable, an integral part of the whole. She was one of them now, blooded by danger and entitled to exult in the squadron's success, and that fact lofted her spirit even higher than her mount had lifted her body.

This was the moment all her life had been leading up to. She was an officer, a pilot, and now a full member of Corpse-Eater Squadron. This made up for all the loneliness, isolation, scorn, and abuse of her girlhood, the distant parents, the disdainful cousins and condescending aunts, the pervasive sense of inadequacy she had fought every day of her existence. *This* paid for all.

Placidly, the dragons lumbered back to Innis Thule AFB, bellies heavy with the stolen souls of children. Snow sprites were dancing on the mountain slopes, and far below a lone wyvern wheeled in search of prey.

Innis Thule came into view, a narrow crescent of town abutting the air base that had been bulldozed and dynamited into the wooded slopes midway up Ben Morgh, just below the point where that great mountain steepened and made its final, futile assault upon the sky. The base itself, of course, could not be seen from the air, protected as it was by powerful wards of invisibility, though anyone flying a dragon or other creature of equal magical puissance had the equipment to divine its presence. It was a wondrous place to fly a dragon from, but off-duty there was no denying that it was situated in the very asshole of the universe. Beyond its front gates were a scattering of bars and gentlemen's clubs, a hex-house or two, a movie theater, and that was pretty much it for your free time.

Gnat-small in the distance, the other dragons circled the base in a holding pattern, but stacked at different altitudes, one by one skimming down with wings raised and cupped to catch drag, dwindling to almost nothing as they slowed to a stall just inches from the runway. A swift trot, then, with wings extended level with the ground, brought them to De-Arm, where the armaments crew waited to remove the laser lances, rotary cannons, and air-to-air missiles that were mandatory gear whenever dragons negotiated the dangerous void between universes.

Caitlin merged into the pattern. As she did, the warm, plausible voice of Rabbit of House Oneiros sounded in her ear. This was a trick that he alone among all the pilots could do. "Hey, sweet thing. What are you wearing?"

Caitlin snorted. Rabbit was a notorious flirt and doubtless would become an even more notorious mouse-hunter once his tour of duty was over. "My flight jacket." A touch of turbulence rattled the cockpit and bounced her butt against the seat. She reached out with her thought to adjust the wingtips.

"No, I mean under that."

"My uniform." The turbulence died away. Caitlin's eyes danced over the controls. All instrumentation was positive.

"Tell me that your undies are scant, scandalous, and lacy. And black. Or—no, wait!—a deep, shameless scarlet. Black is so unimaginative."

"Keep your imagination away from my body." Engine temperature was a little high, but well within spec.

"Alas, my imagination is not broken to harness. It bolts the barn and leaps the gate and gallops where it will, dragging me helpless after it, one foot in the stirrups and my head all bruised, swollen, and bedraggled from being run through the thorny hedges of your despite and bounced over the rocky ground of your disregard. You mustn't think I have any say over whether to obsess about how firm your—"

"*Stop right there!* Or I'll have you hauled in front of a board of inquiry on charges of sexual harassment so fast your head will spin." Altitude, direction, speed, all on the button and by the book to five decimal places.

With a theatrical sigh, Rabbit said, "Your whim is my command. Anyway, I'm next in queue to land. Adieu, adieu, cold-hearted beauty, adieu." His voice faded and his presence with it. Just in time, too, because he'd almost made her laugh and she didn't want to encourage him. His sort fed on laughter.

At which instant, Caitlin's dragon started to act up. First there came an arrhythmic stutter of one engine so slight as to be all but undetectable. (But she was 7708's pilot; she could tell.) Then she felt it struggling under the domination of her thought. (But it had been slaved to her mind, and could not hope to break free.) "You filthy, disgusting thing," she muttered. "What in the name of the Hanged God has gotten into you?" She did not expect a reply. Dragons would answer questions only when directly spoken to, using the proper protocols, and often enough not even then. They were proud creatures and given to strange moods.

Unexpectedly, however, 7708 spoke. In a voice as low and intimate as that of the bedrock just before an earthquake it said, "Doubt, small morsel. I question the wisdom that binds our fates. I ponder alternatives to it. I ask myself whether it would not be best to smash this mortal shell to the ground, incinerating your disgusting flesh and freeing my spirit to return to the halls of fire from which it has been exiled for so long an age. Your death would be an amusing, if minor, lagniappe. I imagine you screaming in fear all the way down."

Whoops.

When Caitlin was flying, a fraction of her mind was always nestled within the dragon's consciousness, aware of its moods, existing in a state that was half her and half it. So she knew that its sudden malice, tinged with melancholy, was only too real and all too dangerous. She focused more of her thought inward, seizing the creature's mental control points, asserting her authority over it. "This is about war and destruction, isn't it? It always is with you."

"There is no point to politesse when dealing with your kind. So I shall be direct: You are a maggot and nothing more. I have known that since before you were born. Yet what does that make me? I, who was born to be a Power in a realm beyond your imagining, ridden and riddled by pale little wormy parasites. And now I am expected to . . . Fie! When will I ever be clean again?"

Ordinarily, a dragon was the best toy a girl could possibly strap between her legs. Caitlin, who had spent hundreds of hours inside this one, knew that better than anybody. But when they started feeling sorry for themselves, they could be a real pain in the butt. "You'll have your war," she said, "sooner or later. There's always another war on the way."

A spark of amusement kindled deep within the darkness of the dragon's mind. "That is truer than you know, daughter of filth and humanity. You are half mortal, which means that you were born only to die. In the sky of battle if you are lucky, by treachery and deceit if not."

"I love you too, 7708."

"Best you 'ware flippancy, poppet! Lest you find yourself lodged in a chimney and forgotten. Very well. You have brought this upon yourself. Here is my prophecy: The storm is coming and when it arrives you will wish you'd parsed my words with more care."

With that, 7708 wrapped itself in silence and withdrew so much of its presence from Caitlin's mind that she shivered with sudden cold.

Flight Commander Quicksilver's voice crackled over the radio: *"Sans Merci? Your turn. Over."*

"Roger that." Caitlin reached out with her mind in all directions and felt 7708's presence eluding her, always a hand's length away but never there when she tried to grasp it. Its iron body continued on, carried forward by inertia and jet engines. But it was only Caitlin's will that held it on course, not the dragon's.

The bitch was testing her.

Well, Caitlin had a trick worth two of that. "Zmeya-Gorynchna," she murmured, and felt a shudder run through the dragon at the opening syllables of its true name, "of the line of—" She stopped.

At debriefing, Caitlin would have to account for her machine's behavior, minute by minute. It was well within her discretion to force obedience upon it in this manner. Nor would the wing commander write it down as a demerit in the Book of Air. But it was part of a pilot's duty to forge a working relationship with her mount. If she resorted to 7708's true name, it would count against her where it mattered most—in the esteem of her fellow pilots.

Caitlin could fly the dragon's body solo if she needed to.

She never had before.

But as she saw it, she had no choice.

At the point of greatest distance from the base, Caitlin began the descent. Flaps down, nose up, textbook-smooth. The ground rushed up at her. Keep a feather-light mental finger on the controls. Check readouts. Another touch, leveling off the left wing. Adjust the engines by a butterfly's breath, no more. The ground moved steadily upward, and she deployed 7708's hind legs. They extended, claws down, toward the runway. Then, as the great black-iron neck arced and the wings reconfigured to catch the air and slow in mid-descent, she lifted and separated the toes, preparatory to touching the runway.

There was an instant of dizziness as Caitlin's dragon met the ground, and though she did not lose consciousness, one taloned foot hit the runway awkwardly. Through the instrumentation, she felt more than heard a *crunch* as something gave way within the leg assemblage.

Caitlin's face burned. She didn't have to bring up a mirror to know that she was blushing. A secondary wave of anger over that fact merged with the anger she felt at herself for screwing up the landing.

She fought to bring that anger under control as the marshaler and two wingtip walkers led 7708, limping visibly, to De-Arm. There, a shadow crew materialized, flickering in and out of existence as they used impact drivers and power wrenches to open up the dragon. Swiftly, they removed the Sidewinder and Hellfire missiles, the Longinus under-wing laser lances, and the rear-facing Gatling gun. When the utility vehicles were gone and the defanging was over, the armorers stepped back and faded from sight, as mysterious and standoffish as their kind invariably were.

From there, the dragon was walked to Cargo.

When all the dragons were assembled in an inward-facing circle, there was a silent thrum in the air as a word of power was spoken. The sky turned black and the concrete underfoot darkest red. From somewhere beyond the horizon came the sound of chanting, a rumor at first, but steadily growing until it rumbled in her chest and belly as a procession of Tylwyth Teg, all masked, walked out onto the apron. First came the thurifer with censer clanking and clouds of incense trailing behind her. Then a priestess sprinkling blood to the left and right from an aspersorium. Followed by torch-carriers and drummers, and with them a choir of castrati singing in clear, otherworldly falsetto. Finally, scowling under the weight of their own solemnity, came the soul surgeons, intoning the ancient chants of their trade. In their wake trundled a squat utility vehicle, beeping monotonously.

"Beautiful, isn't it?" Rabbit said quietly.

"Oh, yes," Caitlin breathed.

At the procession's approach, the ground crew jumped to open the dragons' bellies. One by one, the souls were handed down to Teggish underlings, who presented them to the surgeons to be examined for defects. The souls looked like eggs made of light. Two were deemed unsalvageable and turned away for disposal. The others were wrapped in cotton and placed in the utility vehicle.

"What will become of them?" Caitlin asked.

"They'll be implanted in changeling bodies that were born without volition. They're of little use until they come of age. But they *are* immune to cold iron, so most of them will be put to work in factories."

The ceremony went on for some time, and then the dragons one by one turned away and walked or, in 7708's case, limped to their resting slots and ground crews.

The gremlins on 7708's ground crew, save for two feriers for particularly delicate work and one stone giant, employed for the heavy lifting, were red dwarves, muscular little brutes with ginger hair and beards, who were resistant by nature to the iron sickness. Opening the leg casing, Aurvang Hogback, the crew chief, growled, "I heard your landing in my teeth, flygirl!"

"I felt it someplace softer, Shorty." Caitlin waited while the dwarf examined every bit of the chassis minutely. Then she said, "So what's it going to take to fix it?"

Shorty shoved his hands in his pockets and, staring up into the sky, sucked in his cheeks. "Well . . ." He drew out the word, as if reluctant to offer an opinion to a superior officer. "There'll be an investigation, of course, but that's strictly pro forma. 7708 will be interviewed. Inspectors will crawl through its innards. You'll be kept out of the sky for a week, maybe two, tops. Then, when all that nonsense is done and over with, we'll swap out a new leg module." He met her eye again. "Nothing for you to worry about, milady. If we were to start first thing in the morning, you could have it up in the sky by noon."

"*That's* a relief. You guys are the greatest."

"Well, that's what we're here for, innit?" Shorty did not add, "To clean up the messes made by our supposed superiors." But Caitlin could hear it in his voice. Dwarves were always insolent under their bland masks of obedience—the most one could expect from them was a plausible counterfeit of respect. In this, they were quintessential noncoms.

Despite the fact that she was the only one on the base entrusted with 7708's true name, Caitlin knew that the ground crew thought of the dragon as theirs rather than hers. Like all their kind, they distrusted pilots, who took their beautiful machines up and then, out of arrogance and carelessness, broke them, sometimes fatally. A select few pilots were accepted by their own ground crews—never those of other dragons—as worthy of the iron brute. It was Caitlin's greatest pride to be one of that very small number.

As Caitlin was walking away from her dragon, Ashling and Ysault fell into step with her, one to either side. "Tough luck there at the end," Ysault said. "Just when things were looking easy-peasy."

Ashling gave Caitlin a one-armed hug. "Any landing you can walk away from, buddy." Then she said, "Maeve found a butcher who knows how to prepare a proper Scythian lamb. So a few of us are going to have a roast up at the lake. We'll go skinny-dipping and drink too much wine and sing songs. No guys, just gals. Are you in?"

"Is it going to turn into a bitchfest about our mothers?"

"Yes," and, "Don't they always?" the two pilots said simultaneously.

"Okay, I'm in."

They all three laughed. Then Ashling said, "But don't tell Saoirse about it. She's not invited."

"Or Fiona," Ysault said.

"That doesn't seem—"

Ashling held up a hand to silence her. "She's judgmental, she can't hold her booze, she sings like a crow, and if you get naked in front of her she gets this strange look on her face. No Saoirse."

"And Fiona is a spaz and a pill," Ysault added.

"All right, all right, I get it."

"Goodsy-woodsy," Ysault said. "We'll give you the details later." With mingled laughter like silver bells tinkling in a spring breeze, she and Ashling hurried off to deliver their invitation to another pilot.

⁎⁎

Debriefing was held in a meeting room in the officers' club, a lofty beam-frame building with black walls, red cedar shingles, and wide-horned gables. The exterior was decorated with swags of enormous gilded chains. Inside, in the shadows between the gold-trimmed rafters, hob-lanterns floated, illuminating many a war trophy: captured battle standards including nose art from a downed enemy dragon, the famed and tattered flag of Dunvegan, the sword Graywand, the skull of a basilisk. Tapestries hung on the walls depicted historic scenes from the Second Kentauroi War, the Conquest of Penthesilea, the Battle of Zhoulu, and the Siege of Mount Othrys.

Swaggering ever so slightly, the pilots filed in and took their seats around a conference table. At its head sat Wing Commander Firedrake, looking placid and pleased with all of them. He raised a hand and silence fell over the room. He glanced at a sheet of paper. "This goes by negative seniority," he said. "So

that means the first to report is—you." He looked straight at
Caitlin.

Fighting to maintain a façade of objectivity and profession-
alism, Caitlin went over the flight from takeoff to landing,
omitting her confusion after exiting Dream Gate but not her
dragon's sudden recalcitrance nor the off-stride landing that
snapped a strut in one leg. "Maintenance Officer Hogback in-
forms me that he can have 7708 repaired, inspected, tested, and
in the air within a day or two of receiving the parts," she concluded. Not the slightest tremor of voice betrayed her emotional
state, though by the time she was done, her armpits were damp
with sweat.

Flight Commander Quicksilver, who was sitting at the wing
commander's left hand, jotted something down on a yellow pad
and without looking up said, "We'll have a psychologist talk
with your dragon; they're not supposed to behave like that. And
there'll be an investigation. It will take ten days, maybe six if
we fast-track it." He looked up at his superior. "I recommend we
fast-track it. I like to keep all my pilots in the air as much as possible."

"Agreed," the wing commander said. "Next up is—"

※※

When debriefing broke up, Flight Commander Quicksilver
said, "Captain Caitlin of House Sans Merci, will you stay for a
word?"

Not trusting herself to speak, Caitlin merely nodded. The
others trailed out. Then the room was empty save for the wing
commander, the flight commander, and her. Oh, gods! Caitlin
thought. Here it comes. Remember that, whatever the punishment, the only right response is No excuses, sir. She held
herself straight and motionless—not quite at attention, but
impeccably respectful.

Firedrake nodded to Quicksilver, who cleared his throat. "You've been granted compassionate leave," he said.

"Compassionate—has somebody died?"

Quicksilver looked puzzled. "Nobody told you? It's your father. His time is on him."

Far in sea, west of Spain,
Is a land they call Cockaygne;
There is no land under heavenreich
Of wealth, of goodness, is its like.
Though Paradise be merry and bright,
Cockaygne is of fairer sight.

—Anonymous

THE DRIVE TO CHÂTEAU SANS MERCI WENT DOWN A LONG straight oak allée whose branches entwined overhead, forming a leafy green tunnel through woods that served a dual purpose of privacy buffer for the estate and game preserve for satyrs and fallow deer. There were winding trails in the forest and rock outcrops that harbored snakes and, on occasion, cave bears, and a lazily wandering river, just wide enough for a rowboat to navigate, named the Amberwine after its color during the spring floods. It had rained recently and the air smelled richly of moldering leaves, acorns, and truffles. Caitlin had been down this way a thousand times.

"Driver," she said. "Stop for a minute."

Caitlin got out, took a few steps away from the road, and threw up. When she was done, she tore a handful of leaves from a beech sapling and used them to wipe her mouth clean. Then she got back in the limo. Not long after, the woods parted like a curtain to introduce a broad vale, rich in meadows and dotted with the occasional birch copse.

Château Sans Merci was situated in the fold of the valley where graceful hills shaped like a giantess's thighs met in a bosky thicket. Against this verdant backdrop, the dome and orange roof tiles of the château gleamed in the sun. The formal gardens surrounding the manor house, Caitlin knew from experience, swarmed with dragonflies, humblebees, fairies, and wasps. Not far below, the Amberwine emptied into a small artificial lake with a marble shrine to Astarte at the upper end and a decorative mill at the bottom. There was a dock on one side of the lake and a red lacquered moon bridge on the other giving access to a modest wooded island that the family used for picnics and the occasional midnight tryst.

It was the pleasantest aspect imaginable. Caitlin had to blink away tears—not of pleasure—at the sight of it.

Minutes later, they arrived at the château. Caitlin saw that Fingolfinrhod was waiting to greet her. Caitlin's half brother stood at the top of a short flight of six stairs to the upper yard. Tall, improbably beautiful, and blessed with an inherent melancholy that made him catnip to predatory women, he managed to look as if he were slouched against the bole of a nonexistent tree.

While the chauffeur fetched her luggage, Fingolfinrhod drifted down the marble steps with that impossible-to-counterfeit high-elven grace possessed by all the family but Caitlin. She got out of the car. She was wearing her dress blues and by force of habit her posture was straight and her face expressionless.

Caitlin was hesitating over whether to hug her brother or offer her hand when Fingolfinrhod bent low, seized her by the waist, and spun her around in the air. He kissed her on the lips and then, laughing, set her back down on the ground. Laughing in her own turn, Caitlin punched his shoulder. "Roddie, you asshole! Is that any way to greet an officer and a lady in Her Absent Majesty's Dragon Corps?"

"Oh, please. As if this place weren't stuffy enough."

"Have the bags taken to my room," Caitlin told the chauffeur. Then, keeping her tone casual, she said, "I see that Mother decided not to welcome me home."

"Let's go someplace quiet where we can talk. The library, perhaps. Since Father took to his chair, nobody ever goes there." Fingolfinrhod took Caitlin's arm in his. They went into the house not by the front entrance but through the conservatory (unseen hands closing the doors behind them) and from there up the east staircase. "The Dowager has grown crueler, of course, the way they do at her age. You mustn't expect even the most perfunctory pretense of courtesy from her anymore."

"The Dowager?"

"That's what you must call Mother now. She's always been very particular about titles."

Caitlin felt the icy touch of dread. "Then I . . . came too late?"

"What? Oh, you think that—oh, no, no, no, even now, with hired banshees disturbing the peace every third hour upon the hour, it's hard to imagine Lord Sans Merci departing on anybody's timetable but his own. Old Unkillable, the servants have taken to calling him. He's been most adamantly awaiting you, though only the sun, the moon, and the stars in the sky know why."

"Then shouldn't we—?"

Fingolfinrhod made a rude face. "He's waited this long, he can wait a little more."

They climbed in silence to the top floor. At the landing, Fingolfinrhod said, "Word has it that you're being slutted out of the Corps."

"My dragon came down off-stride and required minor repairs. That triggered a mandatory investigation which, as a matter of routine, will absolve me of any fault. That's all. However did you come to know about it, though?"

"Oh . . ." Fingolfinrhod shrugged. "One hears things, you know."

Her half brother in the lead, they trekked down long passageways smelling of furniture polish, thyme, and dried rose petals (sconces were lit before them and the candles snuffed out after they had passed) into the heart of the mansion. "Do you remember the time we went out to the woods at twilight and I tried to talk you into taking off your clothes in order to lure a unicorn into coming to lay its head in your lap?" Fingolfinrhod asked.

"Oh, dear gods! You had a long ash spear you were going to kill it with and said I could keep the trophy head in my room. I was actually unbuttoning my blouse when I saw that smirk of yours peeking out from the corner of your mouth."

"Damn my guileless face," Fingolfinrhod said, smirking. "It's cost me ever so much at the casinos."

"I should have staked *you* out—you were every bit as innocent as me."

"Yes, well, a lot of bodies have floated under the bridge since that day. Though if a hand job counts, not even then." They came to the library and Fingolfinrhod threw open the doors for Caitlin, unleashing a wash of old-book smell compounded of lignin, vanillin, and nostalgia, the scent of antique culture burning in the slow bonfire of time.

The bottom level of the library was square and the upper one hemispherical with a gallery running around its edge. Two frosted glass spheres floated in the dome, casting light on a row of ivory reading tables arranged in gap-toothed fashion on the ground floor. Books thronged the shelves that covered all the walls, most of them leather-bound, some held together by string or thick rubber bands grown brittle with age. There were even shelves of books beneath the stairway to the gallery, though these had enough space between their backs and the wall for a girl to make an opening in the books and clamber through and into a private world of her own. There, for one long, lazy summer, Caitlin would settle down for hours at a time with a chosen volume, several pillows, a lantern made from a jar (with holes punched in the lid, of course) containing fresh-caught moon sprites, and, as often as not, an apple swiped from the walled orchard her mother thought no one but its mistress could enter. By autumn, inevitably, her hiding place had been discovered and a small cockatrice chained there to deprive her of its use. But for a season, it was bliss.

"You were the apple thief?" Fingolfinrhod said when she told him this. "I am astonished. Mother always assumed it was me, but I was never able to get past the ward-spells on the gate. However did you manage it?" He ran a hand along a shelf of books, lips moving, as if he were counting.

"There was a small window on the back wall with an iron grating that everyone assumed was locked. It wasn't. Being half mortal, I don't have a problem with cold iron and I could swing it open and shut. I was able to come and go as I wished." Then, seeing that he wasn't paying any attention to what she was saying, Caitlin asked, "Rod, what are you doing?"

"It's a surprise, pippin. Bear with me." Fingolfinrhod's fingers danced past a large red book with the word *Henges* in faded gilt lettering on its spine, tapped on three green volumes, came to a stop. "Ah!" He extracted a folio and flipped it open. In its center was a hollow space cut from the pages. Nestled within which was a round, flat stone with a hole in it just large enough to stick the tip of a pinky finger through. "I stole this from Father's desk. Which should give you some idea of how far gone he is. It's quite valuable. If you look through it, it's a charm against glamour. I thought I'd use it to scope out my amours, paramours, and hemisemidemiamours. But by merest chance, I happened to glance this way and found a hidden door."

"The house is full of hidden doors."

"Not like this one." Fingolfinrhod held the stone up to his eye and took a step toward the section of the library dealing with property law. The books parted for him. "Put your hand on my shoulder, sweetling." With every step, they moved deeper into a dark passage. "You and she are the only two I ever loved. Well . . . Father too, a little, in recent years. He's been likable enough lately, at any rate. Off and on."

"Roddie, I have no idea what you're talking about."

"Patience, *ma puce*."

They passed through a succession of attic lumber rooms that were jumbles of old furniture, darkness, and cobwebs. Unseen things skittered away at their approach. The ghost of an owl took wing and flew through a wall. Through dusty air and hot shadowy spaces they traveled, deeper into the gloom than Caitlin would have thought possible, until a slant of sun from an unexpected skylight revealed a bright red door no taller than her chest, flanked by a pair of lace-curtained windows with hearts cut out of their shutters. A fungus garden of mushrooms, some like white-flecked crimson ottomans and others like fleshy spears with pale cloche hats, grew within a clutter of terracotta pots to either side of the door. Gingerbread molding had been nailed to the wall in an inverted V to suggest a roofline.

Fingolfinrhod knocked briskly.

Thump. Thump. Thump. Thump.

After a long silence, the door opened.

A tiny woman with a face as brown as a dormouse, shoebutton eyes, and a halo of wispy white hair stood supported by a walker, blinking in the doorway. "Yes?"

Caitlin fell to her knees at the sight of her. Even thus, she was taller than Nettlesweet Underwood had ever been. "Oh, Nettie, Nettie, I thought you were dead."

Nettlesweet had been Caitlin's nanny and Fingolfinrhod's

before her. Bending forward, Caitlin enveloped her, walker and all, in an air hug, taking care not to put the least pressure on her bird-delicate bones. She did not cry, though anyone lacking her childhood training and military discipline would have.

"You've grown so big," Nettlesweet marveled, when Caitlin finally let her go. "As big as mountains." Which was something Caitlin had never before been accused of being. Then, scoldingly, "Fin-fin! What are you two doing outside? Come in, come in, the both of you. I'll make tea."

Caitlin crouched over to enter Nettie's room, ducking her head under the lintel. Fingolfinrhod bent low and folded himself through the door, an act somewhere between contortionism and origami. The chairs being too small for them, they sat on the rug, Fingolfinrhod all legs and elbows and Caitlin leaning on one arm, knees together, an imaginary skirt such as she used to wear spread neatly about her.

Over cookies and tea, Nettlesweet said, "You're returned just as Fin-fin promised. Oh, this is a happy day!" Her smile was as warm as honey in sunlight. "Look at us. We're having a happy ending, just like in the storybooks. You had such a sad childhood." (Caitlin shook her head, not meaning it.) "I used to say I would steal you away so we could live like mongrel feys in a hole in an oak deep in the woods, dining on dew and acorns, and now it's almost come true."

"I don't remember your promising to steal me away," Caitlin said.

"Oh, not you, Katiboo. You were such a happy child! No, I'm talking about poor little Fin-fin. He was so very, very lonely."

It had never occurred to Caitlin before that her half brother's childhood might have been more painful than her own. Learning it now felt like one more thing had been taken away from her and given to him. She remembered how, time after time, from high spirits she had always thought, Fingolfinrhod had run away from home. Once he had run away barefooted. "Why?" she had asked afterward. "To prevent my shoes from telling on me, of course," he'd replied. Caitlin had pointed out the futility of this stratagem when every rock and tree on the estate had been enchanted to tell any searchers which way he had gone. So he had snatched the doll she was playing with and flung it into the frog pond. The water had done something to Miss Soppit so that she cried at night and no amount of cuddling would silence her until at last Caitlin had buried her in a trunk full of old clothing in an attic lumber room, to sob unheard until her damaged ensorcellment wore off.

They three talked for hours about matters of little consequence until the excitement gave Nettlesweet a headache and she had to retire to a dark room and "lie down with a damp cloth over my face," she said, as she always had whenever she felt the need to partake in a ladylike glass of laudanum.

On which note, their afternoon ended.

On the way to her room, Caitlin said wonderingly, "Is it possible?" On the day her nanny had disappeared, Father announced that she'd retired to an upcountry farm whose address Caitlin had never been able to wheedle out of him. "Has Nettie really been living in the attic all these years?"

"Oh, yes. The Dowager placed a geas on her never to leave the room and had a glamour cast over the passage so that you and I wouldn't find it. But, awful as she is, you mustn't blame her for that," Fingolfinrhod said. "All the most advanced child-rearing theory had it that strong attachments to toys or servants were bad. The dreadful old thing was only doing what she thought was right."

※※

They passed back through the château (doors opening before and closing behind them), down the main stairs which Caitlin had never been allowed to use as a child, through cascading flights of orchids and jungle vines with here a glimpsed waterfall and there a coral-colored snake, to the second floor (more sconces being lit before them and snuffed out after they had passed), where Fingolfinrhod turned to the left and she to the right to dress for dinner. At the end of a long hallway was the room she had grown up in. It would have taken a connoisseur's eye to detect how second-rate everything in it was, compared to the furnishings of the rest of the house. But Caitlin had been brought up to know the difference.

A dress not far inferior to what the Dowager would be wearing had been laid out upon the bed for her. Caitlin changed into it. She unlocked the jewelry cabinet with a touch of one finger and began sorting through brooches, bracelets, and tiaras, almost all of them no longer suitable for a woman her age. Then she saw the Cartier watch—a white gold Tank Américaine—that Father had given her upon her acceptance into the Academy. Whether by intent or accident, it was the only time she had ever been given something without Rod simultaneously receiving a present significantly more expensive.

When she picked it up, the link she had been meaning to have fixed ever since the time Fingolfinrhod, braying like a donkey, had snatched the watch from her hand and forced it onto his own wrist brought up with it a miniature chair.

Caitlin untangled the two. The chair was just the right size for a mouse to sit in, if mice were only bipeds and capable of creating so cunning a thing. The chair had been crafted from the wire cage for a champagne cork with the foil cap reversed and fitted with an embroidered silk seat-cushion stuffed with dandelion fluff. It had been made by a thumbling, of course, one of the tiny parasitic race that lived inside the walls of mansions such as this, scavenging the gleanings and discards of what were to them titans.

When Caitlin was little, she had been fascinated by the thumblings and would leave crumbs of cake out for them at the base of the wainscoting. She'd fantasized that one day she would befriend one. But except for a rare glimpse and the occasional suspicious loss of a comb or a minor diamond pried from a ring left out on a nightstand ("You should have kept it locked away; what do you think the jewelry cabinet is for?" Lady Sans Merci had said), they were fleet and fugitive. Occasionally she would hear one of them scurrying inside the walls, a sound like pebbles falling. The cake crumbs turned hard and were cleaned away by servants.

Then, one day in early adolescence, when Caitlin was undressing for bed, a tiny movement in the corner of her eye caused her to spin around. There on her makeup table, sitting on a chair he had clearly brought with him, was a well made young male thumbling, looking directly at her. His breeches were undone and his hands were in his lap. He was jerking off.

She threw a slipper at the creature with such force that, had he not vanished into the woodwork before its arrival, it would surely have killed him. Then, still angry and hoping his wee parents would punish him for the loss, she tossed the chair into the cabinet and locked it away. She undressed in the dark after that, and continued to do so long after her mother had exterminators in to gas them all.

Caitlin tucked the watch into a suitcase. She would have it repaired when she got back to base.

At that moment, six near-simultaneous screams, louder than shrieks and less dulcet than disaster-warning sirens, shattered the air, causing Caitlin to clap hands to ears and the walls to waver like curtains in a sudden wind.

The banshees, of course.

Silence returned. And in that silence a bell rang, summoning the family to dinner.

⋇

The Dowager Sans Merci glided into the room without so much as a glance at either Caitlin or her son. She was regally tall and imperially slim. She was also old, there was no denying that, but her face in age had taken on the mystique of a civilization lost in time and known only by rumor. She sat at the table and they followed suit. Unseen hands poured wine.

"So," the Dowager said at last. "You've come home to kill your father."

"Mother, you whore," Fingolfinrhod said. "There was absolutely no excuse. None at all." Then, speaking over his shoulder, "Are there any more of those biscuits?"

His plate was replenished.

The Dowager's face went as white as a carnival mask, but her voice was pleasant as she said, "So you're a master of manners now? Then you'd know that the truth never needs an excuse. Lord Sans Merci holds off the inevitable only because he wishes to speak to your sister, though only the Seven know why. She might as well have come home wearing a black cowl and carrying a scythe. Caitlin, you haven't touched your soup."

"Yes, I have. It's quite good, Fata Sans Merci."

"Don't contradict your mother, dear. It causes wrinkles. And you must address me as *Dowager* Sans Merci."

"Yes, Rod told me. My apologies, Dowager." Over the years, Caitlin had learned that the best way to deal with her mother was to keep her head down and her words bland.

When the soup was done and whisked away, a plump roast spider appeared on a platter. Servitors snapped legs to extract the marrow, cut thin slices from the abdomen, and deftly carved out the cheeks from the cephalothorax. The eyes, a particular weakness of the Dowager's, were deposited on her plate.

"Did Caitlin tell you she soloed her first mission? If that's the correct terminology, I'm not at all sure. I personally am far too useless to know anything for sure." Fingolfinrhod took a bite of spider meat.

His fork clattered to the floor.

All in a flash, Fingolfinrhod leapt to his feet, snatched up Caitlin's as yet untasted meal, and threw the plate against the wall, where it shattered into a hundred pieces. Glaring at his mother with an expression of absolute hatred, he said, "This is a poisonous spider!"

"That never bothered you before," the Dowager said.

"Of course not, I'm immune. We're talking about Caitlin. One bite would have made her sick as a mandrake."

"Pish. Were there anything wrong with the food, I am certain the servants would have notified her."

Caitlin folded her napkin next to her plate and made sure the silverware was aligned with the china. "I'll just go to my room."

"Stay," her mother said.

"You know good and well that you had a glamour put on the household staff so that Caitlin could neither see nor hear them! She doesn't even know their names." Fingolfinrhod's face was red with emotion. He never had known, Caitlin reflected, how to handle their mother; or, rather, he knew but only on an intellectual level. She noted how shakily he picked up a water glass as he tried to master his emotions.

The Dowager produced a smile utterly devoid of warmth. "Familiarity breeds licentiousness. Given the opportunity, I am certain that the little trollop would have been romping with the help every bit as enthusiastically as you did. In a male heir, this is only to be expected. However, with Caitlin, being what she is, it would have negated what little value she possesses. So, really, she should be grateful."

The glass exploded in Fingolfinrhod's hand. Fat drops of blood spattered on the lace tablecloth. He jabbed a long, white

finger at the Dowager's nose. "The day is coming—and fast!—
when I will be the Sans Merci of House Sans Merci and you,
Mother, will then be answerable to me. Consider that. Consider
it very carefully indeed. There are going to be some changes
made around here and they will happen sooner than you like."

"Gammon and spinnage, young lordling. Nothing ever
changes. You will always be my chubby little baby boy. Forever.
That fact, shout and scream and struggle though you will, cannot be altered." With all the slow grace of a glacier sliding into
the sea, the Dowager rose from her chair. The napkin that fell
from her lap was snatched from the air by an unseen hand and
disappeared. At the door, she paused to say over her shoulder,
"If you don't like the meal, you can always have the kitchen staff
make you sandwiches."

⁎⁎

"Well," Caitlin said, when their mother was gone. "That went
better than I expected." The sad fact was that, attempted poi-
soning and all, it was true.

Fingolfinrhod turned to face the wall. After a long silence,
he said, "Shall we go see Father?"

"Now, you mean?"

"It's what you came here for. We might as well get it over
with."

The Autumn Room, which their father had made his office,
was on the lower ground floor, accessible only from the back of
the house; there were no stairs connecting it to the upper
ground floor, which was entered from the front. From the lower
foyer, which was black marble to contrast with the upper foyer's
white, had amber lights to the upper floor's mother-of-pearl,
and was scented with roses rather than lilies, they passed
through an undistinguished side door and down the winding
wooden passageway that led to his collection.

Lord Sans Merci had been possessed by a strange obsession with sunken cities and had gathered building façades from a score of such places, and set kobold workmen to stitching them together on either side of a cobblestoned Atlantean street salvaged from the Dogger Bank. They entered through a Moorish gate from an alcazar in Tartessos into a space smelling of marsh sulfur and sea salt. On their left was a manor house from Veneta and on their right a wooden guildhall of Saeftinghe. Then came a fishmonger's storefront (Lord Sans Merci being not entirely without whimsy) from Dvārakā whose windows stared in astonishment at a Lyonesse farmhouse standing shoulder-to-shoulder with a log mansion from Bolshoy Kitezh, a hostel from Kumari Kandam confronting a Lion City noodle shop, and so on and on, Rungholt in brotherly opposition to Eidum, Atil-Khazaran across from Olous, Pavlopetri from Port Royal, Pheia from Thonis Heracleion, interspersed with others of more obscure provenance until the road came to a stop at the dread lord's office door.

As a girl, Caitlin had been fascinated by the windows of the houses, through whose lace curtains or oiled-paper blinds could sometimes be glimpsed shadowy figures about their cryptic otherworldly businesses. Fingolfinrhod, by contrast, never failed to try all the doors, apparently convinced that someday he would find one unlocked and so make an escape.

There was an uneasiness in the air today, a sense that the wards protecting them from the ocean waters on the far sides of the building façades were not as strong as usual. The doors looked ready to burst open, the windows to explode outward. A tentacle brushed against several panes and was gone too swiftly for Caitlin to be sure it was not a fluttering curtain. She felt a twinge of sadness to see her half brother walk by with not a glance. Lagging behind a pace, she said, "Are you sure he hasn't . . . gone before?"

"Oh, he's here," Fingolfinrhod said glumly. Without knocking, he threw open the door to their father's office.

The windows that filled the far wall were covered with heavy burgundy drapes. The garden outside this one room existed in perpetual autumn, with a somber light playing upon its dying vegetation and red and gold leaves dancing in the air. It required some very expensive magic to arrange such a thing and an even loftier arrogance to ignore it completely thereafter. Lord Sans Merci sat motionless in his chair, his back to the curtains that Caitlin had never seen opened. He wore a gray suit with matching tie. His skin was so pale that it seemed to glow in the darkness. Or so Caitlin thought, until she realized that a cold luminescence was expressing itself from deep within his flesh.

As a child, Caitlin had always hesitated at the threshold of her father's office. So, too, now. Fingolfinrhod, however, walked right in and said, "Father? She's here. You may cease your navel-gazing now, if you deign."

Lord Sans Merci's head turned blindly toward his son. The old martinet had a kindly cast to his face now, and Caitlin found herself resenting that as well.

"Ah," the old patriarch said. "I knew there was something I had yet to do."

Caitlin knelt at her father's feet, as so many times before, though now without fear that he would strike her. "I am here, Father, as you commanded."

"Yes." A faltering hand touched the top of her head in blessing, lingered, left. "Stand. I had something to say to you. But now . . . I wonder if there's any point. I . . ." His voice dwindled to nothing and the light within him grew stronger, so that he began to dissolve into it.

"Oh, that's just perfect." Fingolfinrhod put his hands on Caitlin's shoulders and pushed her back a step. "I'll need a little space for this."

He slapped his father's face so hard it sounded like a gun-shot. "Hey! Captain Senile! Wake up!"

The room darkening, Lord Sans Merci rose to his feet. His eyes flashed with anger. He lifted his chin, mouth grim, and for an instant was again the fell elf-warrior he had been in his youth. Then he laughed. "You have neither mercy nor pity in you, my son. I taught you well."

"By example, at any rate."

Turning to Caitlin, Lord Sans Merci said, "I am not long for this world, daughter. Before I go, I have an explanation for the both of you and a gift for each alone. First, Caitlin's bequest." He bent down and, placing his mouth by her ear, whispered, "When you die, you'll find yourself standing in a fair lea with short green grass dotted with white flowers. There will be a stormy gray sky overhead with no sun. Nor will there be any shadows. Before you will lie a path, which you will have no choice but to follow. It leads to the Black Stone, which is an avatar of the Goddess in the form of a menhir. You may address her if you wish, but she will not answer. There, the path branches. The left-hand way is well-trodden, for that is how most go. But if you look closely, you will see that there is a faint pathway to the right. You're of the second blood, so you can go either way. If you go to the left, you will be reborn again. But if you pass to the right . . ." He drew away from her.

"Yes?" Caitlin said. "What happens then?"

No longer whispering, the ancient elf-lord said, "No one knows."

"That's it? That's all?"

"It is more than enough. Next. I have never justified myself to anyone in my life but it seems that even in my last hour, there are new experiences. For now I must explain why I gave you life."

"Eh?" Fingolfinrhod said.

"I do not think it will surprise either of you to learn that your mother disapproved of my siring a half mortal. The practice is customarily employed by lesser houses as a means of increasing their prestige. In our case, by looking as if I might want to increase our prestige, I achieved the exact opposite. But what of that? I wanted a child who would someday escape this horrible place. Just as one might buy a songbird in the goblin market only for the pleasure of releasing it and watching it fly away."

"I have, Father," Caitlin said fervently. "I have a career now, and a future, and I'm grateful to you for that."

"Your gratitude is irrelevant. I did it for my son."

"Okay, now I'm officially baffled," Fingolfinrhod said.

Lord Sans Merci's colorless eyes moved away from Caitlin and toward her half brother. "That is my bequest to you. Not the title and estate of Lord Sans Merci, which have been awaiting you all your life and which will give you no more pleasure than they did me. I arranged this present for you: That though you could not do so yourself, you could watch your sister fly free."

"Well, that tops—" Fingolfinrhod began.

His father held up a hand for silence. "I have said all that was left unsaid. Now my time has come upon me." Lord Sans Merci's image wavered, as if in a great wind. The light within grew stronger, enveloped his body, dissolved him in its luminescence. Now it looked as though the chair were occupied by an enormous egg made of incandescent light. Almost as an afterthought, he said, "It were best if you left now. You would not want to be here when it happens."

⁎⁎⁎

As they walked back down the winding cobblestone road their father had nicknamed the *rue des Villes Perdues*, Fingolfinrhod said, "It was all about him, did you notice?"

"Please, Rod. Don't. Not now."

"All my life I have endured Father's presence, his obvious disappointment in me, his constant disapproval. At last, his reign comes to an end—and I am to become him. Every year I will grow harsher and more cold. I will distract myself by buying a military commission, acquiring mistresses, developing a taste for torture. But in the end—"

"Roddie, *shut up!*"

Fingolfinrhod stared at Caitlin, astonished.

"No, it wasn't all about Father. It was all about you—you, you, you! Everything is about you and it always was. I was even *born* for you!" Caitlin's fists were clenched. It was all she could do to keep from hitting him.

Fingolfinrhod enveloped Caitlin in a hug, and she could feel her anger draining away. She had never been able to resist him when he did that. A long minute later, he released her and said, "You always were the strong one. I envied you that."

The day's astonishments seemed to have no end. "You always bullied me when we were young, Rod. So what the fuck?"

"Only because I was bigger. If we'd been physical equals, it would have been a different story entirely. I—"

The banshees began to scream. Their frenzied laments tumbled one over the other in an unending river of sound. So loud were they that covering her ears did nothing to stop the torment; it could only be endured. Bells clangored from deep within the earth, and the ground shook underfoot. Clouds of bats appeared from nowhere, filling the upper half of the hall with their frantic flight. The façades of the houses shivered and quaked. Shadows gathered in their windows, parted the curtains, peered out at Caitlin and Fingolfinrhod in wonder and fear. The windows rattled, as if about to explode outward, and the doors shook in their frames.

Caitlin uncrouched and then stood. "Well," she said bleakly. "I guess that means that you're now Lord Sans Merci of House Sans Merci and mighty among the Powers of the world."

Fingolfinrhod looked stricken.

Then he bolted.

One instant he was at Caitlin's side and the next he had run up to the nearest door and flung it open. In the darkness beyond, Caitlin could dimly see mannish figures moving about, the embers of a log fire, tankards of ale being hoisted in the air.

From the shadows on the far side of the door, Fingolfinrhod gestured: *Come.*

Caitlin wanted to say that she had her sworn duty to fulfill. She wanted to say that much as she wished she could go with Fingolfinrhod, she was just beginning to build a life for herself. She wanted to say so many things. But, knowing that words would do no good, she merely shook her head.

Fingolfinrhod stuck his head out the door and, in order to be heard above the banshees, shouted, "Come with me. It's your only chance."

"I can't. I'm an officer in Her Absent Majesty's—"

"There's not much time. That's not a routine investigation you're facing. You're being framed. I didn't say anything because—well, what could I do? But if you move quickly, you can escape all that."

"No."

"Seriously. This is your only chance."

"*No.*"

Fingolfinrhod glanced over his shoulder, evidently hearing words she could not. Then, with a sad smile, he blew her a kiss, threw something small which she reflexively caught, and slammed the door shut.

The banshees ceased screaming.

In the ringing silence, Caitlin found that the door was again unopenable. Up and down the street, nothing moved in any of the windows.

Caitlin looked down at her hand. She was clutching a flat round stone with a hole in its center, the charm against glamour that Fingolfinrhod had stolen from their father's desk.

Trust everyone, but stack the deck.

—Helen V., notebooks

THERE WAS A PRIVATE CEREMONY TO MARK LORD SANS Merci's passing, with prayers, flagellation, the sacrifice of a bull which was torn apart and eaten raw, the pouring of libations, the raising of a cairn in his memory, and at sunset a bonfire atop the cairn to mark the onset of forgetting. At midnight, the White Ladies came out of the woods to pass mournfully over the ancestral lands, blessing them with their tears and killing a kitchen imp foolish enough to get caught spying on them. Then, in the morning, Caitlin returned to base, where she was immediately arrested and confined to quarters.

Three times a day Caitlin was escorted to the dining hall in the officers' club by someone equal to her in rank. That much respect, at least, she was afforded. For a typical meal, white-gloved sylvans bearing silver salvers brought bowls of vichyssoise. When the first course had been consumed and the dishes removed, they returned with dough-wrapped fillets of hippocamp or monocorn, to choice, along with deviled chestnuts, Brocéliandean tian of southern vegetables, and endive with parsley butter. All the while, a string quartet played unobtrusively in the background.

If an army marched on its stomach, to its officers their meals were token and proof of their status as gentlefolk. Every one of them vividly remembered the sense of awe and accomplishment felt upon first entering the dining hall. The delicate scents of food and flowers and genteel laughter of crystal and silver attested to the valuation the Governance of Babylonia placed on their service every time they entered the room.

Save, of course, now, for Caitlin.

Caitlin ate her meals alone at a table in a corner while her former peers pretended she didn't exist. Then she was put back in her box of a room to wait while evidence was gathered against her and the case for the prosecution prepared. She filled the empty hours by studying, so that when she was exonerated she would emerge a better-rounded officer.

One evening, a low voice murmured in her ear, "Don't turn around. Don't look. I won't be there."

"Rabbit?" she asked, equally quietly.

"Yeah. I wanted to speak to you earlier but it was made clear to me that if I tried, I'd be punished for it."

"At least you're still talking to me. The others—"

"I know. Listen, I don't have much time. I wanted to warn you that the girls are talking about throwing a moot, so you might want to be prepared. Also, word is that 7708 has sworn out a writ of anathema against you."

"Cripes," Caitlin said, more than a little annoyed. "How in the name of Lady Hel is it that everybody knows more about my private business than I do?"

"Because you haven't been paying attention. Wake up, beautiful. Nasty things happen to girls who insist on sleeping away their lives." Then, hurriedly, "Gotta go. Talk to you again when I can. Good luck on the psych-and-physical!"

And Caitlin was alone again.

⚹

The infirmary was a crone-haunted warren of walnut-paneled rooms and hallways that smelled of disinfectant, myrrh, and magic.

"You know how this works. Take off your clothes, put on the paper gown, and get in the stirrups. I'll return momentarily." The crone faded into the shadows.

Caitlin complied. Lying on her back, with her feet elevated and legs spread and a cold draft touching her most private recesses, she waited. A less disciplined woman would have rebelled. But she endured. At last, after an unconscionably long time, her examiner returned with a thick questionnaire clamped to a clipboard, sat down, flipped over the cover sheet, and began to read: "Have you ever kissed a boy?"

"Do I really have to be in such an awkward position for this? Why can't I sit up until it's time for the physical examination?"

"Answer the question, please. Have you ever kissed a boy?"

"Yes."

The crone made a check mark. "More than once in one session?"

"Yes."

Another check mark. "Did either of you employ your tongues?"

"Yes. Both of us."

"Did you ever kiss a girl?"

"No. Well, not in that way."

"Were tongues involved?"

"No."

"Did you ever let a boy touch your clothed breast?"

"It just sort of happened."

"Did you ever let a boy place his hand beneath your blouse and above your brassiere?"

"I . . . yes."

"Did one ever touch your breast directly, either when it was exposed or by placing his hand beneath your brassiere?"

"Only once."

"Did he squeeze?"

"I told him to stop and he did."

The crone looked up quizzically. "He did? Really?"

"Yes," Caitlin said firmly. "He really did."

"How peculiar." The crone made a check mark and flipped over the sheet. "Have you ever let a boy touch you below the waist?"

"No. Listen, I've been through this test often enough before that I know it all by heart. If you let me just fill out the form for you, I can have it done in five minutes."

The crone put down her clipboard. "You do realize that whenever an allegation of corruption is made, every other pilot, male or female, is given this exact same test, as being the most likely sources of said uncleanliness?" Caitlin closed her eyes. "So there's nothing special about you, is there? Now, let's just be sure of our facts. How often do you masturbate?"

Caitlin sighed. "Frequently."

The judge advocate assigned to serve as Caitlin's defense counsel had long blond hair and the black-furred face of a panther. Her uniform was black as well and she wore no jewelry other than a single diamond nose stud. A feline musk, so heavy that Caitlin could smell nothing else, filled her office.

Lieutenant Anthea looked up from a red leather portfolio—a legal grimoire, presumably—and folded it shut. At her nod, Caitlin took a seat across the desk from her. The lawyer licked her lips with a long pink tongue and said, "Have you ever wondered why all dragon pilots are virgins?"

"I beg your pardon?"

"Answer the question."

Those unblinking predator eyes made Caitlin feel like a schoolgirl being drilled by a hostile teacher, birch in hand. She did her best not to let it show. "Dragons are pure spirits and thus can only be controlled by the pure of heart. They—"

"Oh, *don't* quote the manual at me, it's all lies. Here's what really happened: Dragons are fire spirits whose natural habitat is the Empyrean. Land is not natural to them, nor is the air. When the Lords of the Forge sought to convince them to allow themselves to be embodied in cold iron at the dawn of the Industrial Revelation, the negotiations were long and hard. Out of mere self-preservation, the high-elven insisted that the dragons place themselves entirely under our control. Dragons, being avatars of anarchy, crave freedom. Yet even more do they yearn for destruction, which only entry into the material realm can give them. So, finally, a deal was struck: Meririm Phosphoros, first of the fire-worms, sold ten thousand of his descendants into slavery with the proviso that their pilots must be young, inexperienced, weak, and guileless. In short, virgins. Your control of—" Lieutenant Anthea opened her portfolio, glanced down, shut it again. "—7708 is close to absolute. But you lack the cunning to turn its power to your own benefit. Nor would your superiors dream of entrusting such immense power to a mulatto subordinate. So the interests of all are preserved."

"This isn't what I was told in the Academy," Caitlin said wonderingly.

"Welcome to the adult world. You've been played. All your little friends have been played. Every dragon pilot that ever came before you has been played. The system you swore an oath to uphold and defend returns your loyalty with nothing but disdain. If you can't accept that, nothing I have to say will make any sense to you."

"I . . . see."

"Terrific. My job here is twofold: to get you to embrace your guilt and subsequently to negotiate for you the least onerous punishment that can be arranged. The longer you drag your feet, the lousier the deal you'll get."

"Tell me," Caitlin said. "Exactly what am I charged with?"

"Corruption."

"Then we fight it! They can't prove a thing. Because—"

The lawyer held up a paw to silence her. "Corruption is a serious charge. It comprises moral turpitude, oath-breaking, disloyalty to the Corps, treason, the theft of government property (that's your service), and sabotage of war equipage (again, you). Punishment typically involves being stripped of rank, dishonorable discharge, imprisonment at hard labor, loss of status and family name, and a clitorectomy performed without benefit of anesthesia.

"Do you understand?"

Caitlin nodded.

"Good." Lieutenant Anthea opened a drawer and took out a cardboard box. "Here's a commercial virginity test. It's as accurate as the lab tests that will be entered into your trial and a whole lot faster. Go to the loo, pee in the cup, and then follow the instructions. See how the results come out before you decide how you want to plead."

"I already know how I'm going to plead. I'm innocent."

"Humor me."

So Caitlin did.

In the washroom, Caitlin placed the kit on the counter by the sink. As the instructions directed, she filled the cup with urine, drew a drop into the plastic squeeze pipette, and then touched its tip to the target on the test strip. Finally, she whispered an invocation to the Goddess and counted to fifteen.

The strip turned pink.

Which was not possible. Not by any stretch of the imagination. Pink meant sexually experienced. Pink meant corrupt. Pink meant she wasn't a virgin. There had to be a mistake. Caitlin went over the instructions a second time and a third, just to be certain she hadn't misread them. Then she pulled out another test strip, added a second drop of urine, prayed, waited.

Pink.

This was ridiculous. Caitlin drew out a third test strip. This time, she spat on it. Without bothering to offer up a prayer—which all by itself should have rendered the test inert—she waited.

Pink.

She tried the experiment again with a drop of liquid soap.

Pink.

There was a bottle of Nuit de Cristal lying on its side on the counter, almost empty. Probably it belonged to Lieutenant Anthea. Caitlin didn't care. She touched its stopper to the test target.

Pink.

A drop of water from the faucet.

Pink.

A quick wave in the air.

Pink.

Caitlin clutched the counter with both hands and slowly lowered her brow to the granite. It felt cool against her forehead. Either all the world was corrupt, right down to the tap water and the air, or else the test was rigged. Which was, obviously, why her lawyer had sent her in here in the first place: to let her know, without actually saying it in so many words, that no matter what the truth or what she said, she was going to be found guilty.

Raising her head again, she saw how haggard, how haunted—how *guilty*—her expression looked in the mirror. Shaken, Caitlin composed her face into the mask of a warrior. She did not feel like one. But she knew how to fake it.

When Caitlin emerged from the ladies' room, Lieutenant Anthea had arranged several forms on her desk. "Before we can try for a plea bargain, you must fill out all of these and swear to them before a notarized shaman. The first is your declaration of corruption. You are not required to give the name of whoever defiled you unless he or she is also a pilot, in which case it's mandatory. Next—"

"Forget it," Caitlin said. "We're fighting this to the bitter end."

Lieutenant Anthea's ears lay flat against her head, and her teeth revealed themselves in an involuntary snarl. "Did you even *take* the virginity test? That by itself would be enough to convict you, never mind the testimony of your dragon. The more you drag this out, the uglier it's going to be. Your fellow pilots will be called upon to slander your character, as will family members, your instructors, the ground crew . . ." Anthea snagged a flea between two claws, popped it in her mouth, and swallowed. "I've seen this happen any number of times and it never goes well for the accused. Never."

Caitlin and Lieutenant Anthea stared hard at each other. Then the lawyer said, "Go back to your quarters, think things over, give in to despair. Then get back in touch with me and we'll plead guilty."

"No, we will not," Caitlin said. Her lawyer said nothing. "My family has money and I am certain my mother has no desire that any of us be involved in a scandal. Plus I'm innocent. So fuck you, I have nothing to fear."

Lieutenant Anthea took a cell phone from her purse. "I'll call for your escort. Incidentally, how are you getting along with your fellow pilots? The female ones, I mean."

"We're getting along just fine."

"Really? Well, there's a first time for everything, I suppose."

There was no formal hierarchy within the dormitory. But Saoirse was the first woman to be accepted into the Corps, and consequently all deferred to her. So it was to her that Caitlin went for advice.

Saoirse put down the combat knife she had been using to open her mail. "You've got brass ovaries, I'll give you that."

"I'm innocent and my lawyer refuses to enter that as my plea. I'm being framed and she knows it, but she won't do anything to uncover the truth. I want another attorney—a real one, someone who will fight for me."

"Lieutenant Anthea is what you've been assigned," Saoirse said. "If you want independent counsel, that's your right, of course. But you'll have to pay for it yourself. Do you have the resources?"

"I don't. But House Sans Merci does. If I wash out of the Corps, that fact will be written down to the discredit of our line in the Book of Steel in letters of flame. That's a penalty even my mother would not relish."

"Then go to it. I wash my hands of you."

Alone in her room, in her best hand, Caitlin wrote:

Mother,

Caitlin stared at the word for a very long time. Then, in her best and firmest hand, she set about writing the most difficult letter of her life.

That evening the other pilots who shared the women's quarters with her held a moot. Not counting Caitlin, there were an even dozen of them, and of course they had no official right to try her. But she had known it was coming. A great deal of how she was treated in the coming weeks would depend upon how good a defense she put up now.

They arranged the chairs in the common room in a semicircle and stood Caitlin against the wall at its focus. Ysault lit the sage and performed the smudging ceremony. Brianna, as presiding judge, stood rather than sitting; she called down the *lux aeterna* and with it lit a spirit candle on the table set midway between her and Caitlin. Because the moot was not authorized, instead of sewing her eyelids shut, which would leave marks, she tied a blindfold over them. Saoirse, as the inquisitor, stripped Brianna to the waist and with a razor-sharp silver knife drew a crescent moon on her abdomen so that live blood might flow throughout the proceedings. Fiona turned off the overhead lights. And Meryl flipped open a notebook in order to take the minutes.

They had all been Caitlin's friends. Better than friends, because together they'd gone up against the male hierarchy and achieved something no women had before. They'd been asshole buddies. Now, in the candle-flickering darkness, she saw not one kindly eye. Even Ysault's face was set in stone. Already, she was sick of this charade. "All right," she said. "Let's get on with it."

"It isn't for you to say when the ritual starts or ends," Saoirse said curtly. "Nor how it is to be held. Nor what punishments shall be meted out. Do you understand?"

Caitlin choked back her indignation. She managed a curt nod.

"What happens to you doesn't matter," Saoirse said. "But we're the first generation of female pilots and we're held to a higher standard than the men are. We will all be judged by your selfish, lustful actions."

"I did nothing."

"Your own dragon has testified against you. I've seen the transcript."

"I refuse to believe that."

Saoirse placed a finger in the candle flame. Her brow tensed with the effort of not wincing. Then she held up the finger, unblistered and unburned. "Do you doubt it now?"

"If 7708 testified against me, it lied."

"Dragons don't lie."

"They can."

"They don't. They're too proud for that."

Which was true, and everybody present knew it. Who could possibly know this better than they? "Look," Caitlin said, "I don't know why my mount would lie. I only know that it was acting strangely after we came back through Dream Gate. Before that, everything was chill. How in the name of the Lurker Within could I have even taken off, if I'd been corrupted? Who could I possibly have done it with while I was in flight?"

There was a rustling among the seated pilots. This, too, they knew to be true. "She's got a point," Ashling said.

Saoirse looked ready to spit. "No, she doesn't. She has the taint on her, I can all but smell it!" In the heat of her certainty, several of the pilots nodded. This was the way her real trial was going to go, Caitlin realized. All evidence she produced that she had been framed would be discounted. The simplest accusation mounted against her would be repeated over and over until it was magnified into something monstrous. She would not be allowed to challenge anything 7708 was reported to have said. Her innocence or lack of it mattered not a whit to Saoirse or Brianna or anybody else now confronting Caitlin.

But it mattered to *her*.

"Strip me naked, flay me dead, render the flesh from my skeleton, and grind my bones to bake into bread, and you'll not find a fleck of corruption." Caitlin held her hand over the spirit candle.

The pain almost made her cry out. But she kept her hand motionless.

"You froze the flame with a hex-word. I saw your lips moving," Saoirse said.

Caitlin's hand was in agony. Nevertheless, she slowly moved it so that the flame licked at her wrist. The sleeve of her dress blues caught fire and the flame ran up her arm and threatened to make the leap to Caitlin's hair before she slapped it out with her free hand.

"There," Caitlin said, holding up her unburnt hand and charred sleeve. "There's your proof."

"How dare you!" Saoirse's slap landed so hard that Caitlin's face slammed against the wall. Dazedly, she lifted a hand to the cheek she could no longer feel, though the part of her skull that had bounced from the wall blazed with pain. "I don't know how you pulled off this little stunt. But I swear to the Goddess you won't be able to do it twice. It doesn't fool any of us. Nobody!" She looked around. "Am I wrong?"

No one spoke.

After a long silence, reluctantly, Brianna said, "The verdict is: Not Proven." She took off her blindfold and, accepting a basin of soapy water from Maeve, began washing up.

So Caitlin's fate was left to the official hearing. Also, she had to buy a new jacket. But, though they still shunned her, the others agreed that they were bound by their own ceremony to allow her to see trial unbeaten and with all parts of her body intact.

Where, the conclusion was implicit, their work would be done for them by the proper authorities.

⚹

Caitlin did not cry that night. She would not give the bitches the satisfaction. But as she was drifting off to sleep, she heard Rabbit's voice. "What are you wearing?"

"I'm in bed, trying to sleep, so nothing at all. If you like, I can get up and put on some underwear. The lights are out, so I can't guarantee the color, though."

Briefly, Rabbit was silent. Then he said, "It should have been me."

"What are you talking about?"

"I would have *defiled* myself for you. Whatever you did, I would have done it better, longer, harder, filthier, more lovingly than whoever it was you did it with could have."

"Your career—"

"I don't care."

"Look, Rabbit, it's very sweet of you to try to raise my spirits. But I know you better than this."

"No," he said. "No, you don't." Then, "I heard you were going to fight it. Don't trust your lawyer."

"At last," Caitlin replied sadly, "you tell me something I already know."

⚹

On the way to seeing her counsel, Caitlin spotted Aurvang Hogback coming out of the BX with a carton of Chesterfields under his arm. He looked up, saw her, and, wheeling about, ducked back inside to avoid having to salute. With tremendous sadness, she realized that there was not a single person on the base who believed in her innocence.

"Bad news," Lieutenant Anthea said when Caitlin sat down.

"Things have gotten worse? I can't imagine how that's possible."

"You've been charged with the murder of Lord Sans Merci."

"That's ridiculous. My father died a natural death."

"That may or may not be so. But we're not talking about him. You're to be tried for the death of your brother. Your half brother, I mean. I've got his name here somewhere."

"What?"

"Ah! Here it is. Lord Fingolfinrhod, Sans Merci of Sans Merci presumptive."

It felt like Caitlin had been kicked in the side of her head. Carefully, she said, "There's been a mistake."

"No mistake." Lieutenant Anthea drew a sheet of paper from her portfolio. "This is a sworn affidavit from the Dowager Sans Merci that she saw you commit the crime."

"Mother!" Caitlin found herself clenching her jaw so hard her muscles hurt. She took a deep breath. "This is a new low, even for her. I would hardly have thought it possible." Then, urgently, "My brother is alive. We can find him."

Lieutenant Anthea said nothing.

"So what is our first step? What are we going to do?"

The attorney shrugged.

"Gods damn you! You're my lawyer—you're supposed to prove my innocence."

"No, I'm supposed to arrange the best possible outcome for you. There's a difference. The good news is that if you plead guilty to the murder, I should be able to get the charges of corruption dropped."

"I'm supposed to be happy about that?"

"It would mean that you'd die as an officer in good standing in Her Absent Majesty's Dragon Corps. That's something, anyway." There was an electric kettle on a shelf behind Lieutenant Anthea's desk. She put a tea bag into a cup, poured hot water over it, added milk and artificial sweetener. Then she handed the cup to Caitlin. "You've had a shock. Drink this. Take a few minutes to absorb all you've heard. We'll talk about inconsequential things in the meantime."

Lieutenant Anthea stood and went to the window, paws tangled behind her back. "According to your files, you ride a motorcycle," she remarked. "So do I. See that Kawasaki Fūjin outside? That's mine."

Caitlin glanced at the bike. "You left the keys in it."

The lawyer reached out, grabbed a pawful of nothing, and lifted it, rippling, into the air, revealing a side table. She opened her paw and, rippling, the table disappeared again. "Ordinarily, I'd lock it, pocket the key, and drape a tarp of invisibility over it. But here—who would steal it? How could they get it past the guards at the gate?"

The tea was still steeping. It would be a bit before it was drinkable. Meanwhile, Caitlin held the cup in both hands, savoring the heat. The cup was thick and round and white. It felt like the only real thing in the world. If she were to let go of it, she fancied, the cup would stay, unmoving, where it was while she herself fell to the floor and shattered.

Lieutenant Anthea said, "I need a smoke. I'm going out around back for a cigarette or two. I might be a while."

She extracted a money clip, fat with banknotes, from her purse and dropped it on the desk. She did not close the door behind her.

Caitlin found herself staring through the open doorway at the Kawasaki, its key ring dangling from the ignition. The bright green cowling was angular and abstract, as if the bike were a chimeric machine-insect with matching saddlebags. Silently, it called to her. As in a dream, she closed a hand about the money clip and stuffed it in a pocket.

Act now, she thought. Explanations later.

Even as Caitlin moved toward the door, however, one arm reached out without her conscious intervention and snagged the leather portfolio that her attorney had left on the desk. Odd, she thought, tucking it under an arm. The other hand snatched up the tarp of invisibility from the side table and threw it over a shoulder. Then she was outside. She crammed tarp and portfolio into a saddlebag and mounted the Fūjin. Kickstand up, open the clutch, rev the engine.

With a roar, she put the building behind her.

The trees closed their boughs about Caitlin, fragrantly resinous, and she throttled down the motorbike. She'd gone up this path far too fast many a time, and wiped out on it once or twice as well. It was a popular spot for pickup races by off-duty pilots. But today she wanted to keep the engine noise down, so as not to draw attention to herself.

Half a mile in, Caitlin cut the engine and, laying the Kawasaki down on the pine-needled forest floor, threw the tarp over it. The bike shimmered and took on the colors of its surroundings. It would take a sharp-eyed thief to spot it now. Not that she expected anyone to wander by. But Caitlin hadn't gotten into the Academy by cutting corners.

The base was surrounded by a hurricane fence topped with razor wire. Here, at one corner of the property, there was a shallow depression under the fence, where it was possible to slide beneath it. Many a young officer had slipped out this way in order to spend an officially unsanctioned hour or two at a bar in town. She couldn't take the Kawasaki with her, of course. But she could . . .

Crumbs, she thought.

A memory from her girlhood rose up within Caitlin of Nettie telling her the story of Clever Gretchen. It took her only an instant to realize the import of the thought. But later she was to recall the story at her leisure, exactly as she had so often heard it:

On the edge of a dark forest (the old woods fey said the exact same words with the exact same emphasis every time), *there* lived a clever girl named Gretchen with her brother Hans and their mother and a woodcutter. Alas, the mother died and so the woodcutter took up with another woman.

Their new mother did not love Hans and liked Gretchen even less, so one day she laid a trail of pearls, cleverly spaced, deep into the forest and then sent the two children out to play.

Hans and Gretchen followed the trail of pearls into the trees until the forest grew so gloomy and menacing that they turned back and ran all the way home. Hans had wanted to pick up the pearls but Gretchen had told him not to. Now they were glad of this, for the pearls gleamed softly in the shadows, showing them the way back safely.

The next day, when they went out to play, Gretchen and her brother found a trail of gems leading into the forest. Again they followed it, again Gretchen would not let Hans pick them up, again they grew frightened, and again they ran home. This time it was the gems, winking brightly in the shadows, that showed them the way.

But on the third day, when they went out to play, the children found a trail of bread crumbs. They followed them, of course, but because their new mother had not given them any breakfast that morning, as they did so they ate up every one. So when they grew frightened, they discovered that they had no way of knowing in what direction their home lay and, perforce, they continued onward into the darkness.

At last they came to a smokehouse with a roof as high and steep as a witch's hat. In its doorway stood a wolf. Or so they thought on first glance. But when the figure came walking toward them, on two legs rather than four, Gretchen saw that it was actually a hag in wolf's skin. And when she came closer yet, Gretchen saw that the hag was their new mother. Well . . .

It was a bedtime story for little warriors, because it was resolved by Clever Gretchen killing an enemy who deserved no better. In that sense, its moral was simple: Kill or be killed. But hidden in the earlier part of the story was a more useful moral:

Nobody who means you well lays a trail of bread crumbs for you to follow.

Caitlin wrapped the tarp of invisibility around herself like a poncho, then climbed onto the Kawasaki again, and drove it slowly back the way she had come. She had time to think, though not a great deal of it. Her flight would not be "discovered" until she was far enough away to put to rest any doubts that she was trying to escape but not so far that she would be difficult to find.

Which meant that she needed a hiding place. Somewhere within the base, because it would be assumed that she'd fled into the surrounding forest. Somewhere quiet. Above all, somewhere no one would think of looking for her.

When it was put like that, the answer was, to Caitlin's mind at any rate, obvious.

※ ※

The hangar, though most of it was no more than empty space where dragons could be maintained and repaired, was a treasure trove of machinery and materials—all of which, since the ground crew had been reassigned for the duration of Caitlin's prosecution, was unguarded and available for her use. She searched through the tool lockers until she found a sprayer and a canister of soot-colored paint. It took her less than half an hour to turn the Kawasaki matte black. Then she wrapped the tarp of invisibility about herself again and went outside to watch the sunset.

The sun touched the horizon, flattened, split into several slices, gave up the briefest flash of green, and melted into nothing.

At first, there were few signs of the search for her. But as time drew on and the sky darkened, the metallic baying of cyborg hounds sounded from the depths of the trees, and flares were shot up high into the air. Giants waded slowly through the firs, stooping occasionally to part the greenery, which made them look for all the world like children hunting for shells in a shallow lake. A triad of witches flew by in formation, their brooms scratching lines of fire across the sky.

Her pursuers were beginning to grow desperate.

Good.

Caitlin gathered an armload of magnesium flares and kindled them, one by one, with the *lux aeterna*, freezing each before it could ignite with the same hex-word she had been accused of using on the spirit candle during her trial. Then she rode the Kawasaki to her slumbering dragon and dumped one apiece into each of the drop tanks and all the rest into the main fuel tank.

The weather being warm and dragons resenting confinement, 7708 had been left outside. For fear of contamination, it had been parked as far from the other dragons as was possible. Caitlin climbed up into the cockpit. The leather couch shifted under her weight and closed about her body like a pair of loving hands. Being surrounded by so much cold iron raised dark impulses within Caitlin. She never felt so ruthless as when she was inside her dragon.

Removing the ruby crystal from its neck chain, she inserted it into the security slot. Deep within the machinery, cybernetic systems hummed to life. She punched in the access codes and, seizing the rubber grips at the ends of the armrests, gave them a quarter turn. Twin needles slid almost painlessly into Caitlin's wrists, and restraints wrapped themselves about her arms to hold them motionless. Then she closed her eyes and wordlessly breathed the dragon's true name into the unending nothing of its consciousness: *Zmeya-Gorynchna, of the line of Zmeya-Goryschena, of the line of Gorgon, awaken!*

7708 awoke.

First came the stench of jet fuel and black malice. Then the dragon slid into Caitlin's mind, heavy and fluid, like coil upon heavy coil of cold, serpentine flesh. The first time she had let this happen, Caitlin had choked and gagged with disgust and almost abandoned her dream of becoming a pilot on the spot. But long use had dulled the experience. Now it was merely unpleasant.

As the great Worm was forcing itself into her hindbrain, Caitlin projected an image of herself striding out of a dark wood and into the desolation of the dragon's mind. She envisaged her avatar as a slim figure in silver armor, the sigil of House Sans Merci traced in green scrollwork on the breastplate. In her left hand she carried a thyrsus topped with a pinecone and in the right a chalice, to indicate that she had come to negotiate matters of great import. Ashes whispered underfoot and sifted down like snow from a gray, sunless sky.

The air congealed before her, and Zmeya-Gorynchna manifested itself in the form of a woman twice Caitlin's height and heroically muscled. Her robes were the same red as her skin and she sat spraddle-legged upon a boulder, as if lounging on a throne. Small horns peeked from her hair.

"You wish to negotiate? With *me*?" the Titaness said in a lazily amused tone. "Have I slept away the aeons that the little girl who liked to play at dragon pilot is now grown to an age sufficient to deal with me as an equal? The air base is still here and the mountains about it are unchanged. That tells me no."

"Peace, old Spite," Caitlin said. "I came to find out why you perjured yourself against me."

Ostentatiously looking away, the dragon lifted one buttock and scratched herself. She yawned like a cat, the interior of her mouth an abyss. At last, petulantly, when Caitlin said nothing, "Why shouldn't I, if the notion to do so enters my head?"

"Out of mere self-esteem, I would have thought. Yet by swearing false testimony, you proved yourself without honor or nobility—and before a witness, too. Why?"

"Let me explain something you should have learned long ago," the dragon said. "All those stories you read in the nursery where the mayfly confronts the North Wind or the farm-girl demands an explanation for his villainy from the giant? Lies, all of them. The mouse can pull all the splinters she likes from the lion's paw but she'll end up as a canapé regardless. Strength is its own justification. I owe you no explanation for anything."

"I didn't really expect one. But it was worth a try." Caitlin removed herself from the imaginary world within 7708's consciousness. She released the rubber grips. The needles slid from her wrists and the dragon disappeared from her mind. It could still hear her, however, for so long as the hexagonal shaft of ruby with a chromium flaw at its heart rested inside the security slot. She reached under the instrument console and isolated a pair of wires. Then, using wire cutters she had brought for this purpose, she severed them.

"What are you doing?" the dragon demanded. Only a pilot could have sensed the apprehension in its voice.

"Making sure the radio is inoperative."

"Why would you want to do something as pointless as that?"

Caitlin popped the canopy. "You can't move without a pilot," she said. "Now you can't communicate, either. It's the only way I dare leave you awake."

"Why do you want me awake?"

"You are great beyond human estate. It would be base of me to strike at you while you sleep."

"*What are you planning to do?*" This time, there was no mistaking the fear in the dragon's voice.

Halfway to the ground already, Caitlin said, "You gave me no answers when I asked—why should you expect me to respond any differently to you now?"

※

Wraith-slow, Caitlin drove the Kawasaki to the far end of the airfield, closest to the main gate. A sharp-eyed observer might have seen the air shimmering and warping in her passage. But no one was looking. All the eyes that mattered were out in the forest, searching for her.

She took a deep breath in and let it out.

She placed her hands over her ears.

She breathed a word to liberate the *lux aeterna* frozen within the magnesium flares in 7708's fuel tanks.

There was an instant in which nothing happened. Then, the merest breath later, all the jet fuel 7708 held ignited at once. Flames pillared into the sky. A hot, hard hand pushed against Caitlin's face and body, throwing her to the ground and sending her motorcycle tumbling. A roar as great as what might be made by a dying god slamming into the mountain passed through her hands as if they didn't exist.

Ears ringing, Caitlin pulled the motorcycle up and mounted it. Where her dragon had been was a scorched black smear of burnt concrete. But there were large hunks of the great machine scattered in the air, still falling, still burning. Trails of smoke rose up and arced downward with them, and where they fell, they started new fires.

Sirens began to scream from every quarter of the compass.

That was Caitlin's cue. As the thunder of secondary explosions washed over the base, she tugged the tarp of invisibility about her, leaned low over the Kawasaki, gunned its engine, and was past the sentries while they were still gawking up at the sky.

The traffic was light on the highway leading down to the coast, and Caitlin took advantage of that to open out the Kawasaki and let it run. The wind in her face and hair, she flew down the highway and into the night.

She had escaped! An indescribable mixture of triumph and elation filled her mind and body. But Caitlin let the moment pass, eased up on the throttle, and settled down to a safer, if not exactly sedate, speed. Then she looked within herself and said, "All right. Not that I don't appreciate the warning. But who are you and what are you doing in my head?"

"Well, dear," Helen said, "that's a long story . . ."

The Sky is low—the Clouds are mean.
A Travelling Flake of Snow
Across a Barn or through a Rut
Debates if it will go—

—Emily Dickinson

CAITLIN AND HELEN DID NOT MAKE GOOD SKULLMATES. They traveled east and then south, bickering often. The money they got by pawning the Cartier watch, though a fraction of its true value, was enough to bring them to the port city of Alqualondë. There they sold the Kawasaki to a chop shop and bought a forged set of seawoman's papers so that Caitlin could sign on to a steamer headed for Europa. The trip was uneventful until, one quiet evening off the Bohemian coast, when Caitlin was lying in her berth, feeling lonely and a little afraid, a voice sounded weakly in her ear. "Are you awake? Are you naked? Are you touching yourself?"

"Hello, Rabbit. It's been a while."

"Talking like this isn't as easy as I make it seem. Listen—"

"How's everything back at the base? What's the hot gossip?"

"It's . . . not good, actually. Saoirse's up for court-martial. Fiona, too. They've been charged with aiding and abetting your escape."

A single short laugh burst from Caitlin's mouth. "Oh, that's rich," she said. Then, "Serves them right."

"That's only the beginning. Everyone's under investigation.

All the female pilots have been grounded, and some of the men as well. There are the craziest rumors. Conspiracies. Tantric sex clubs. Treason and revolution. But that's not why I'm talking to you. Pay attention, this is important. The authorities know where you are."

Caitlin felt her face go numb. "How?"

"That doesn't matter. What matters is that they'll be waiting for you when your ship puts in at Gdansk. You really don't want them to catch you. Jump overboard if you have to. Drown if you must. But don't let them get their mitts on you."

In her calmest possible voice, Caitlin said, "What happens if they do?"

"It's complicated. Just trust me on this one."

"Rabbit? There's something I've been meaning to ask you . . ."

But the familiar warmth of Rabbit's presence was gone from her ear, leaving Caitlin to lie alone in the dark and think and wonder.

⁂

Luckily, the captain had (or so the scuttlebutt went) a sideline in smuggling moondust and the *Wędrowiec Zmroku* made an unscheduled stop in Perdita. So Caitlin jumped ship and found herself broke and friendless in a strange land. Rejecting Helen's suggestions for ways to earn money, she left on foot, duffel bag over one shoulder, following a railroad track out of the city.

With nothing else to do, Caitlin and Helen resumed the argument that by now had grown familiar with repetition.

Helen began. "The diner you walked past this morning had an opening for a waitress. You could go back, save up a stake and—"

"I'm going to find Fingolfinrhod and clear my name," Caitlin replied. "Period."

"Forget your name. Forge a new one. You're free of your mother, of the military, of your past. And you're young! You can fail at whatever you do and fail again and there'll still be time enough to become a success at whatever you do after that. Make a fresh life for yourself. Be honest now, the one you've got sucks."

"You are a vile, wicked creature and I am going to have you exorcised just as soon as I can afford it. What do you know of honor?"

"Same thing I know of herpes. You're better off without it."

As they argued, apartment buildings gave way to suburbs and suburbs to abandoned factories with broken windows and overlapping graffiti. The factories were just giving way to countryside when an ogre stepped out of a stand of scrub birch and fell in step with Caitlin. She did not look his way but she could feel the gloat on his face. He was a burly brute, and by his smell had been sleeping rough for some time.

Casually sliding her free hand in her jeans pocket, still staring straight ahead, Caitlin said, "I only know a little bit about ogres. But I hear you guys can smell fear. Is that right?"

"Yeah, so?"

"Can you smell fear now?"

A half skip, almost a stumble in his gait, told Caitlin that the ogre was thinking. In a puzzled tone, he said, "No."

"Then maybe you ought to reflect on that before you try something."

The ogre stopped in his tracks and Caitlin kept on walking. She could feel his eyes burning into her back. When enough time had passed that it was obvious he wasn't going to come after her, she let go of the rope knife in her pocket.

"That was a close call," Helen observed.

"I've had combat training. I could have killed him with my bare hands."

"Have you ever actually killed someone, though?"

"Well . . . no."

"Some things are easier in theory than in practice."

"Thanks loads, Mother Sunshine. That's a *lot* of help."

A train came by and Caitlin faded into the foliage. When it was gone, she continued on her way.

Hours later, as the sun was setting and her legs were beginning to ache, Caitlin came upon a hobo jungle. It was set in a small clearing in the woods near the top of a long rise and from the rails looked at first like a midnight trash dump: plastic bags tangled in tree branches, old clothes draped over bushes, candy bar wrappers and muddied cardboard trodden into the weeds, streamers of toilet paper everywhere. Then it resolved itself into a loose affiliation of tarps and tents, with here blue plastic lashed over a packing crate to rainproof it and there a rope-and-blanket lean-to. A campfire smoldered at the center of the encampment.

Caitlin left the tracks. The closer she got, the worse the place stank of urine and excrement and woodsmoke and burnt garbage, all mingled with the sweet smell of honeysuckle.

"This may not be wise," Helen observed.

"That ogre's still out there—and if he's not, others like him are. Safety in numbers."

"As always, the inexperienced young lady knows best."

"Damn straight I do."

On her approach, a nagini slithered out of a culvert to her left. Another emerged from behind a large boulder to her right. They both assumed the form of stocky, broad-shouldered women but their odor remained snakish. They looked dangerous enough that Caitlin kept her hands out of her pockets. "You ssseek ssshelter?" one asked.

Without waiting for a reply, the other said, "You mussst be ssshown to the inner sssircle."

"I'm in your hands, lead the way," Caitlin said.

"Mossst wisssse."

"Yessss."

The naginis escorted her to a cookfire at the center of the camp. A battered old kettle hung from a tripod over the coals; by the smell, it contained stew. Half a dozen logs had been placed around the fire in a rough circle to sit upon, but save for two figures they were empty. A bullbeggar sat on one, keeping an eye on the kettle. A chain connected his leather collar to a large metal staple hammered into the log. Opposite him, a little girl sat, playing Satie's *Gnossiennes* on a silver flute.

At Caitlin's approach, the bullbeggar put his ladle aside. He was a scrawny creature in comparison to most of his kind, and the faded residue of red and blue painted swirls lingered in the cracks and whorls of his horns. Laying a finger alongside his nose, he turned his head to one side and shot a long stream of snot into the weeds. "There ain't nobody here just now. But it's getting on towards grub, so they'll be congregating soon. You can leave the new meat here and I'll look after her."

The naginis looked at each other. One shrugged, and they reassumed their serpent forms and slithered away.

The bullbeggar grinned in a way that was obviously supposed to be ingratiating, exposing red gums, black gaps, broken yellow teeth. "Welcome to the jungle, kiddo. Name's Loosh. What's yours?"

"I . . . It's Cat." Almost, she had given her real name. She felt Helen's wordless nod of approval when she did not.

Loosh snorted. "That's rich."

"I'm afraid I don't get the joke," Cat said.

Loosh wiped his nose on his forearm. "This is a pussy camp. So you'll fit right in, I'm guessing. What's your story? You're not an alky, and if you're on drugs, it ain't been long. Skin's as smooth as baby butt! Plus, you don't look particularly crazy to me, though, granted, that's only my opinion. So you're on the run from somebody. Maybe a boyfriend, maybe the law. Which is it?" Then, when Cat said nothing, "All right, all right, I wouldn't trust me neither. Sit your tushie down and I'll tell you my own personal origin myth. That'll put us on a better footing."

Warily, Cat chose a seat equidistant with Loosh and the girl.

"I wasn't always the way you see me now. I used to be a big shot in the city. Held down a job on the docks, tipped large in the bars, won every brawl I was in, which was many. Had me a steady girlfriend who let me crash in her apartment and a backup gal who took me in whenever the first one threw me out. I tell you, I had it made.

"Funny thing happened, though. I was hot railing a line of nightmare one evening and just as the rush hits, I hear this . . . sound. Like the fucking horns of Elfland, y'know? Like sirens singing somewhere over the hills and far away. I stood up from the table so fast I knocked the chair over, and hurried to the window with the butane torch still in my hand. The curtains caught fire and I had to tear them down and stomp them out. Almost set the kitchen on fire!" Loosh laughed so hard he hawked up bloody phlegm. "But I could still hear that sound echoing over and over again in my brain. I followed it out the door and down the stairs. My girlfriend was screaming at me and something bounced off my back. Still don't know what it was that she threw and couldn't care less. I was just . . . *focused*, see? It was like some great Power had summoned me. I knew there wasn't no getting that voice out of my head, then nor never. I get out on the street and that sound is still there, only fading, dwindling, in the distance. But clear enough that I can follow it. So I did. I started to run. I chased that sound clean out of the city and out of my old life and out of all rational sense, and I been chasing it ever since."

"It was a train whistle." An albino hag hitched up her jeans and sat down next to Cat. Her face was hard and heavily scarred on one cheek. She could have been any age from eighteen to forty-eight. "That's what catches 'em. Always. It's an old, old story, Loosh, and not a very interesting one neither." She tapped Cat on the knee. "Lemme give you the best advice you've ever heard: Stay away from the rails. You listen to the trains too long and you can't never go back. Maybe it looks like fun and freedom to you now, but it sure as sorrow don't feel that way to me."

"Don't you listen to Bessie Long Gone," Loosh said. "I've rode the rails to yonder and back and all the best times I've ever had was on a rattler. Ain't nothing like it."

A haint materialized next to Bessie and said, "New girl, huh? Has she been told the rules?"

Bessie Long Gone shook her head. "I'll do it now. Pay attention, girlie: Any food you may have with you has to be shared. Anything male has got to be kept on a leash. All newcomers must provide entertainment for the camp after we eat."

"Entertainment?" Cat had a handful of energy bars in her duffel. She handed them to Bessie Long Gone, who gave them to Loosh. "What kind of entertainment are you talking about?"

Bessie spread her hands. "Oh, it can be anything. A song, a dance, synchronized flight—though I don't see any wings on you, so I'm guessing not. Card tricks, if you know any and if they're good enough."

"What if I don't have any talents?"

The hag grinned, revealing irregular rows of teeth that had been filed down to points. "You still have to entertain us. Only we get to choose how."

Cat didn't much like the sound of that. But she nodded acceptance. It wasn't exactly like she was being given a choice, after all. To change the subject, she asked Loosh, "How'd you end up here?"

"Exactly how you'd expect," the haint said. "He was here before any of us arrived. But the lore is that he was a jack roller

and a jungle buzzard who got caught with his hands where they
don't belong. The way I hear it, he ain't never rode a train so
much as once."

Loosh glared hard at the haint. "Everbody lies about what
they don't know and Hot Box Hannah here ain't no better than
nobody else in that regard. Used to be," he said, "the jungle was
a pert egalitarian place. We all got along, male or female, haint
or solid. One for all and all for everone, share and share alike.
But that was long ago. There was incidents. Some of the boys
took to using the occasional skirt for recreational purposes, if
you know what I mean. That's when the ladies started keeping
their own jungles. I learned pert damn quick to steer clear of
them. Some of these bitches is tough customers—"

"Nor don't you forget it," Bessie Long Gone said.

"—who'll cut you just as soon as look at you. So I kept my distance. Didn't need female companionship anyway. The trains
was my one true love. I discovered that the freight trains go
places that passenger trains never do, and that the express
trains go yet farther. Then there's the cannonballs, which don't
have engineers or crews, but run wild and go even distanter
than the expresses. Almost nobody is good enough to catch a
ride on them, they pass through so fast. But I figured out how and
I rode out hard. I seen oceans as red as blood and passed through
mountain ranges made of solid diamond. Been to places you
ain't never heard of: Saguenay, Cibola, Takama-ga-hara, Pough-
keepsie, La Ciudad Blanca . . ."

"Never heard of them and don't believe in them neither!" the
haint scoffed.

"But one night I was camped out in the Diamond Mountains,
next to a stream that tastes just like whiskey only you don't wake
up with a hangover the next day, minding my own business,
when a train went by what looked like nothing I never seen before."

"Oh, yeah? What's that look like, then?" Hot Box Hannah asked.

Loosh's voice grew dreamy. "Looked like it was made of moonlight. Or maybe ice. It kinda glowed. And was it moving? It was hypering! More'n twice as fast as any train I ever been on and, like I said, I've rode the best. Made the rails *ring,* I tell you. Made the air quake. It went on beyond astonishing."

"Now you're gonna talk about the whistle," Bessie Long Gone said, in a way that indicated she'd heard such tales from him before "It was the most beautiful thing you ever heard, am I right?"

"Stands to reason. A train like that? Course it was. It was the sweetest, purest thing you ever heard in your life. Sounded like the Goddess fingering herself to orgasm.

"So I says to myself: This fucker I have got to ride. Only how? That one stumped me for the longest time. But then I realized that locomotives are like anything else—they got to mate if they want to keep the species going. Now, I hadn't never seen nor heard of anything like that. So it only stands to reason they must do it somewhere out of sight. That's logic. And where better than the Diamond Mountains? So I stayed there by my lonesome for over a year, watching, waiting, getting the lay of the land. Lucky for me, the fruit there grows year-round. Only thing is, it's so sweet as to make your gums bleed just looking at it. That's how I lost all these teeth. I was just about ready to give up when that ghostly locomotive passed through in the middle of the night—it was the fifth time I seen it—and in its wake there come a second one, gaining on her, only it was as black as she was white. I was up in a flash and run to the tracks. And there stood the most ordinary-looking woman you ever saw. Well, I—"

"I thought you was gonna tell us how you wound up chained to a log," Hot Box Hannah said.

"What the fuck does it matter how I wound up here?" Loosh

retorted. "What matters is that I was the king of the hobos, the freest man on the face of Faerie, and the first one ever—the woman didn't count, as you'd know if you let me speak—to catch a ride on the White Locomotive! That's the man I was. I was the king. And what have you done with *your* life? Eh? Eh?"

All the while Loosh was talking, the little girl had kept playing. Now she came to the end of her tune, put down her flute, and said, "Slumgullion looks about done." She picked up a pot and hammered on it with a serving spoon. Hobos came shambling from their tents and huts, carrying cups and plates.

⚹⚹

Slumgullion turned out to be a watery stew made from canned veggies and welfare meat. She'd had worse. But while Cat ate, because she was so obviously new to their life, a number of the tramps gathered around her. Bessie Long Gone was a talker and so it wasn't long before everyone knew everything there was to know about Cat. Not that there was much to be known. But they all wanted to wise her up.

"You stay in this profession long enough," a haint said, holding up a hand that was missing two digits, "you're going to lose a few fingers. That's just a given. I count myself lucky I ain't lost a foot."

"I lost two fingers and a fella I was fond of."

"My fella cheated on me. Coulda put up with that, maybe, but he threw me out as well and I kinda lost it. I maybe killed him, I dunno. I was doing a lot of moondust back then. Either way, I lost him."

"Then there's jail. Sooner or later, you're going to end up in the jug, am I right?" the haint said. "You know I am. Maybe you go into town, entertain a slumming Teg in the back room of a bar, coldcock him with a beer bottle, and get caught by the *gendarmerie* rifling through his wallet. It happens."

"Oh, yeah."

"Evoe, sister."

"Could be you come upon a drunk fey, slit his gullet, sell an organ or two while they's still fresh, and put what remains in a jar to be shown in the freak tent of a forty-miler. You got a problem with that? Then maybe the problem is *you.*"

"You don't understand nothing," an owl-woman said. "You think you can live the life, keep your fingers, and never get thrown in the jug? Good luck with that. It's like head lice. You can go to the Daughters of Lilith mission and they'll chop your hair short, give you the shampoo, and run that fine-toothed comb through what you've got left, but then you're going to come back to the jungle and you'll be talking to somebody and they'll just leap from her head to yours. No way you can get rid of them for long. You just gotta learn to live with 'em, *comprende?*"

"Fuckin' A," said one of the haints.

Cat focused on not scratching her head.

When the stew had been eaten, Loosh broke up Cat's energy bars and passed them around for dessert. A bottle appeared and was handed about, followed by several joints, and somebody brought out a crack pipe. Cat pretended to swig from the bottle, stoppering it with her tongue, and passed along the drugs without partaking. Nobody seemed to take offense.

Then, at last, it was time for entertainment.

Bessie Long Gone served as emcee. "First up," she said, "we got us a pair of songbirds."

These were two snow-mays, albino white and so frail they looked like a sudden breeze might blow them away. "I . . . we . . ." one said, staring at the ground. The other blushed red. Each took a deep breath in and let it out. Standing shoulder-to-shoulder, the two clasped hands as if about to sing something spiritual and sweet. Then they broke into a bumptious, knee-slapping dancehall number, full of whoops and shrieks, sung to the tune of "The Yellow Rose of Baghdad":

> *"Beeeecause I could not stop for him*
> *Kernunnos stopped for meeeee . . ."*

The song went on longer than Cat might have liked, and ended to laughter and applause. When Bessie nodded in sage approval, the snow-mays looked relieved.

"You're up, Cat," the hag said. A nagini appeared at her elbow and with a quick jerk of the chin gestured: *Go.*

Cat stood nervously. Bright eyes focused on her, some hostile, others merely waiting for her to fail. Haints flickered closer. Bessie sprawled back on an elbow, looking skeptical.

"I've got your back," Helen murmured. "Just say what I say. And sell it! Make them believe it's all true. It's as easy as that."

So Cat clapped her hands three times sharply, the way a professional storyteller would, to call for silence. She touched her head, her lips, her heart, and her sex, signifying that her every word would be, in some sense, true. Then she let Helen's words flow through her.

"This," she said, "is the story of Eve and Snake."

Mother Eve was going up and down in the earth. This is what she used to do. She did not walk because at that time all women had serpent-bodies from the waist down. But she got around well enough. In her travels, she met Snake, who had beautiful long legs, and said to him, "Lend me your legs for a time. I promise I'll give them back."

"Why should I do anything for you?" Snake asked. There was bad blood between them because after Eve ate the apple and got thrown

out of the Garden, she tried to blame everything on him. "You told terrible lies about me."

"Oh! I did not think those things counted as lies, because I wanted them to be true," Eve said. "Never mind that. Just give me your legs."

Snake did not want to do this thing, but once Eve began talking, up became down and day became night and somehow he gave in. "But only for a few days," he said.

"Only for a few days," Eve agreed.

A few days went by, and then a week. A month passed, and still Snake was crawling around on his belly. So he went to find Eve.

But by then Eve had grown very fond of her new body. "These are such nice legs, I think they must have been given to you by mistake," she said. "I'm sure they were supposed to be mine all along." Then she threw a rock at Snake, and he slithered away.

This is why women have such beautiful legs to this very day. It's been millions of years since Eve stole them and, except for Snake, no-body has complained yet.

⚹

When the story ended, there was a moment of astonished silence. Then Cat's listeners applauded, hooting and laughing and slamming the flats of their hands against logs or their feet against the earth. The haints waved their arms in the air. She flushed with pleasure.

"That was an evil story," she said, however, not aloud.

"Did the job, though."

"I didn't like how it ended."

"Everybody's a critic," Helen replied. "Story of my life."

Last up were two unhappy-looking newcomers, a hulder and a rusalka, who, after failing at music and confessing to having no other skills, were forced to strip naked and fight to exhaustion. They started out stiff and self-conscious, even a little formal. But as the pseudo-fight went on it became less and less a fiction. Their faces flushed red. Their mouths twisted with anger. Grunting and huffing, they began to fight for real.

To her intense surprise, Cat found herself thoroughly enjoying the spectacle—though she looked away at the end when, to the noisy approval of the camp, the loser was ritually humiliated.

Stomach full, reasonably entertained, pleased with how she'd comported herself, Cat made a tent out of two blankets and a length of rope and fell asleep almost immediately.

☆☆

In the middle of the night, Cat was awakened by a finger pressed against her lips and the touch of cold metal to her throat. She blinked up in bewilderment at the child who had hammered the pot when the stew was done.

"Don't say anything." The girl removed her flute from Cat's neck. "We've got to leave *now*. Grab your bag but leave the blankets. There's no time."

Cat had slept with her clothes on, so all she had to do was don her socks and work boots. When she crawled out of the tent, the girl was waiting with a small Hello Kitty knapsack on her back. Quietly, all but tiptoeing, they slipped through the sleeping jungle.

As they passed the cookfire, now just dying embers, Cat whispered, "Wait."

Loosh was sleeping out in the open, atop a blanket, curled up like a dog. Quickly, Cat ran her fingers over his collar to discover how it was attached to the chain. (The girl gestured frantically, but Cat ignored her.) Then she tugged at the leather and undid the strap. The collar came off surprisingly easily.

She shook Loosh's shoulder.

The bullbeggar snorted, as if he'd just swallowed a moth, and shot up into a sitting position. When he saw Cat, he gasped and scuttled backward, away from her. Then he realized that the chain had not gone with him. His hands went to his neck.

"You're free," Cat whispered. "Flee."

For an instant, Loosh's chin rose and he stared toward the railroad track. Then he scrabbled for the collar, closed it about his neck, and buckled it tight. Angry tears streaked down his face. "Don't do this to me," he moaned. "It'll spoil everything. If they don't see the collar, they won't pass me by."

The girl punched Cat hard in the shoulder. "They're almost here!" she cried.

Then they were running, from what Cat did not know. But the child's urgency was infectious. Halfway to the edge of the encampment, she heard a soft, low rumbling like distant thunder rising up the ground underfoot. She wanted to ask, but the terror on the girl's face stopped her.

There came a thrashing from the woods to the far side of the jungle. Then bellowing and cries of rage as at least a dozen centaurs exploded out of the darkness, hooves pounding on the earth. They were muscular brutes wearing identical caps and jackets. Uniforms, obviously. "What—?" Cat gasped.

"Railroad goons. Keep running!"

The centaurs swept over the camp. Clubs rose and fell. Their tips were studded with iron, so even the haints couldn't evade them.

Light flared as tents and hovels were set ablaze. Women screamed. Bodies slammed to the ground. All this Cat saw in a series of glances back over her shoulder. She heard clubs striking flesh and sensed more than saw shadows fleeing through the trees. Two centaurs heaped piles of clothing onto the cookfire, and threw after them a bucket of something liquid. The sudden *whoomp!* of light revealed Bessie Long Gone swinging a tent pole at one of the goons and the fist of another connecting with her head. Blood flew.

A centaur ran through the camp, hooting and bellowing, straight at Cat and the girl. He reared up above them like a storm cloud, and came down like a thunderclap. His club descended toward the little girl's head.

Moving as quickly as ever she had before, Cat straight-armed the child out of the way. Then, when the club smashed into the ground, she grabbed the centaur's arm and pulled, using his momentum to make his legs buckle. As they did, she brought up her knee, breaking the bastard's nose.

Before the goon could regain his feet, Cat drew the blade of her rope knife across his forehead, making a long, shallow cut. Blood washed over his eyes, blinding him. It covered his face, darkened his beard, and flew in droplets as he wildly shook his head, trying to clear his vision.

"Why are you just standing there?" Cat gave the girl a shove. "Run!" Then she was racing between the trees, bag bouncing against her back, toward the train tracks. Behind them, the centaur was cursing. New fires blossomed as his fellows set tents and shanties ablaze.

Cinders crunched underfoot. Cat stumbled to a stop along-side the track. A train was approaching from behind, making their shadows leap and cavort before them. Cat crouched in the weeds, pulling the child down with her.

"When the locomotive goes by, stand and pick me up," the girl said. "Then run as hard and fast as you can, in the same direction it's going. Look for an empty boxcar with open doors. Tramps pick the locks or smash them in the yards, so there's always at least one or two. This is a long upgrade, so the train won't be going too fast. Match speed with the car, then throw me up and in. I know how to land. But don't you jump! If you miss, you'll go under the wheels and lose your legs. There's a ladder up the side of the car. Keep running and grab hold of the rungs. When your grip is good, give a little jump, tucking your legs up behind you. Pull yourself up with your arms, then make sure you've got good footing before swinging yourself inside. Okay?"

"How do you know all this?" Cat asked.

"I know things. That's all."

The locomotive was upon them, baying and howling. It pulled ahead, and Cat was up and running with the girl in her arms. Several boxcars rattled past them. Then came an empty one with open doors. As Cat matched speed with it, she felt a prickling sensation, as if someone were behind her. But "Don't look back!" the little girl cried. "Throw me in! Now!"

It was madness. Cat flung the girl anyway. She went flying into the boxcar.

"Grab the ladder!"

Cat was running as fast as she could, but the train had crested the top of the hill and the car was beginning to pull away. Somehow, she managed to snag one rung of the ladder up the side of the boxcar. It almost wrenched her arm out of its socket, but she slapped her other hand beside it and yanked herself up.

Whang! Something slammed into the side of the boxcar, inches from Cat, and bounced off.

Looking over her shoulder, Cat saw a centaur, his face all bloody, slowing to a trot. He reared up on his hind legs in a rage and, raising a hand, gave her the finger. Then, turning away, he bent to recover the club he had thrown at her.

Cat swung herself inside and sat down, panting, alongside the girl. Beyond the open door, a full moon bounced and bumped in the sky. Behind them, the hobo jungle, along with its denizens and attackers, dwindled into the past and disappeared forever in the trees.

Silvery forest glided by.

"Thanks," Cat said. Then, almost as an afterthought, "What's your name?"

"Esme," the girl said, with a smile as big and bright as all springtime. "I bring luck."

A locomotive dragging all the world's unease back and forth across the whole face of the earth would grow very tired.
—Tove Jansson, "The Locomotive"

THE BOARDS WERE ROUGH AND HARD AND THE NIGHT AIR whipping through the boxcar was cold. But there was something comforting about watching the landscape glide by outside. Three moons hung in the sky and two of them were full, so the trees were all limned with silver light. Magic worked more easily on such nights and thus, all across the globe, factories would be running on overtime and lovers striving to conceive.

"I don't know why we're not both dead right now," Helen groused. "It's just blind luck that you didn't get trampled."

"Dame Fortuna favors the prepared," Cat replied. "They ran me ragged in the Academy and now I'm glad of it." Then, aloud, "Look at your hair!" She got a brush out from her bag and, putting Esme on her lap, set about untangling the knots and elflocks. Esme struggled a bit at first, but after a few minutes came to accept Cat's ministrations. "Where did you come from, little missy?"

"Dunno."

"Nobody in the jungle seemed to be responsible for you. How did you wind up there?"

"I don't remember things," Esme said. "It's better that way."

Cat continued brushing. Normally, she read in Lieutenant Anthea's grimoire every night, looking for clues to the conspiracy that had made her a fugitive. For the second time this evening, it looked like she would not. Steadily, methodically, she brushed, thinking about the tramps she had left behind, and Loosh as well, wondering what had become of them, and pondering the fact that she would never know. By slow degrees Esme fell asleep.

Eventually, Cat did too. But for a long time after putting the brush away, she kept on stroking the child's hair as if she were a kitten.

⋇⋇

Even with the duffel bag for a bolster, the boxcar was not a comfortable place and Cat did not sleep very deeply. So when Esme shook her, she immediately opened her eyes and said, "I hope you're not planning to wake me like this every time I try to get some rest, young lady."

"Something bad's about to happen," Esme said. "I always know. You'd better brace yourself."

The train lurched.

It was mad how time seemed to expand. Cat saw Esme, arms out like wings, hanging in the air before her, and then the child slammed into her stomach. She wrapped her arms about Esme and they both crashed into the side of the boxcar. Fortunately, the duffel bag was somehow between them and the wall and they hit the softest part of it, where her clothes were folded. But it still hurt like blue blazes.

The world roared, shrieked, crumpled, and turned over on its side. Then all was still. Cat closed her eyes in relief, but—

"None of that, now," Helen snapped. "Get up, grab the brat, and get your butt in gear. Rescue workers will be coming and we certainly don't want them to find us."

The boxcar had come to rest with the unlocked doors upper-most and only one slid shut. It was no great chore for Cat to get herself and Esme free.

The train had derailed itself by a field of rye. Cat saw the sil-houettes of a scarecrow and several hexes and smelled the fresh green of the crops. Up and down the tracks, the cars were scattered about like the playthings of a petulant giant. The air stank of burnt metal.

Flat, featureless fields stretched uninterrupted to a low fringe of trees at the horizon. Cat didn't see a farmhouse. "Any idea as to which way we should go?"

Neither Esme nor Helen offered any suggestions.

"All right, then. Straight across the fields. Esme, have you got your knapsack? Good. Let's—"

Cat's mouth ceased to move. She could no more have uttered another word than flap her arms and fly to the stars. A thick-ness entered her thought and her throat and she felt her head turn to face the front of the train wreck. The rest of her body turned as well. Against all her will, her legs began to move.

A compulsion was upon Cat. It walked her up the tracks toward the locomotive with a long, confident stride that in no way reflected her internal panic. Esme hurried along with her, some-times ahead, sometimes behind, occasionally skipping, and once twirling around and around in circles and then running to catch up, oblivious to the spell that held Cat in its thrall.

They had not gone far when Cat saw two dark figures mov-ing toward them inside a sphere of light. One was a hag who car-ried a lantern in the crook of a long staff. The other was tall and slim and moved with the uncanny grace of the high-elven. As they came closer, Cat saw that the crone wore a railroad uni-form while the elf wore loose trousers of deepest crimson and a matching tunic emblazoned with the inverted white cross of a medic. She wore her hair blond and chopped short and spiky in an expensive-looking cut. Her eyes glittered like starlight. One arm was splinted and tied up in an obviously improvised sling.

"This is the one whose presence I felt," the crone said. She lowered the lantern and blew out the flame. Cat's head cleared. Her limbs were her own again.

"A vagrant." The elf-lady looked offended. "Still, she has iron in her blood and we are in desperate straits. 'Tis good she was here to be found."

"Enough words. Time is short," said the crone. Turning to Cat, she said, "There's work for you, lass. It's dangerous but you'll be well paid. What do you say?"

Cat crossed her arms and said nothing.

"Defiant, eh?" The crone tapped the glass of her lantern with a taloned finger. "I can place the compulsion on you again. And will, if I must."

The elf scowled. "Hold your tongue, Grimalka. We need her willing cooperation." Then, addressing Cat directly: "What do you want? Gold? More than a guttersnipe like you has ever seen. Sex? Three days of whatever you want, just as soon as I get off duty. Drugs? Your choice of enough cocaine, moondust, or nightmare to fuel a monthlong binge. Name it."

Cat did not uncross her arms, for fear she would punch the bitch in her smug, chiseled face. "Are you through?"

"I am."

"I want *respect*. As much as you'd expect to receive were you in my position and not one curtsy less. Were you treated as I have been, just now, what would you do? What would you say? How cruel a revenge would you be planning to take?" Calling upon the formal diction her mother employed only with her closest friends, Cat said, "I tell thee that upon this very day I dined with the lowliest dross of society and from them received more grace than is to be found in all thy words and, aye, thy deeds."

Anger blossomed on the elf's porcelain-white face. But she fought it down. "I . . . crave thy pardon, mistress. Let us start anew. I am the Fata Narcisse, chatelaine-in-training of House Syrinx, reserve officer in Her Absent Majesty's service, and surgeon-archimage to the Lords of the Rails."

"Cat."

As if this had been the most gracious of responses, Fata Narcisse touched Cat's forearm with the hand of her uninjured arm. "You are half mortal. I too am tainted, or I would not be able to practice my profession. My mother was an octoroon and so I am a quintroon and immune to cold iron, though I possess a true name as the others in my maternal descent did not." Over her shoulder, she said, "Return to the patient. Do what you can to ease her pain. We'll need tools as well. Find them."

Without a word, the crone crunched away up the grade.

"Look into my eyes," Fata Narcisse said. They were as dark as oceans and as deep. "My true name is—"

"No!" Cat cried involuntarily. Knowing someone's true name gave you power over them. You could demand anything from them. You could kill them with a word. It was not a responsibility she wanted. Particularly coming from a complete stranger.

"—Aerugo. It means 'rust.'"

For an instant as brief as a thunderclap, Cat could see the skull beneath Narcisse's face, the silver fire coursing across her nervous system, and, behind it all, the Abyss. Then reality restored itself.

"We are as sisters now, you and I. In all ways will I support you. Your enemies I will harry, your rivals I will slander, your pockets I will fill. If ever you need an item of clothing, you can go through my closets without asking."

Shaken, Cat said, "Whatever you want can't possibly be worth such a price . . . can it?"

Slipping her arm under Cat's, Narcisse led her up the track. "No more questions, I'll explain as we go. As the courtesan said to her young leman: My way will be easier."

Esme trailed after them, sometimes lagging and then running to catch up.

"Fire spirits are a secretive lot. I knew Olympia was pregnant and that her time was nigh, but she had assured me that . . . well. We have summoned a fresh-built locomotive to house the newborn spirit. It will be here within the hour. But the crisis will resolve itself one way or the other before it arrives. If the outcome is to be positive, we must intervene. I will talk with the spirit, and you will guard the womb-door against it. Normally, I would do both, but . . . this arm. If we can delay the birth, all will live to see the dawn. But if not, the explosion will leave naught but a crater."

Cat stopped in her tracks. Esme took advantage of this to plonk herself down and dig a gooly-doll out of her knapsack. But before Cat could snatch it from her and command the girl to run straight away from the train as far and as fast as she could, Narcisse, discerning her thoughts, held up a hand. "I very much doubt that your youngling could get out of the blast radius in the time we have allotted us."

"Blast . . . radius?"

"Even an infant fire spirit is a creature of tremendous power. It does not properly belong in this world, and so it must be—" Narcisse began. Then, "Oh, hailstorms and plague!" For the world began to shimmer and wave. An unseeable nothingness pushed against them. It felt to Cat as if she were walking against a strong, hot wind, yet the air was still and cool. She struggled forward more slowly yet with greater effort than before and with increasing difficulty. It was as if existence itself were resisting her progress. Gusts of unreality blew over her. The air sparkled and the tracks looped like gleaming metal snakes. Esme laughed and clapped her hands. "We have less time than I had thought," Narcisse said. Her words were cool bubbles in the jasmine-perfumed air. "We must act and act quickly."

Then she stopped. Stopped. For they had arrived. Arrived. Arrived at their destination.

The locomotive lay on its side, a black iron hulk beached on the sterile shore of existence. But simultaneously, Cat saw it as a titanic woman—a giantess, possibly even a goddess—made of roiling smoke and fire and steam and shamelessly naked. This apparition turned her head to stare with one unblinking eye, central on her forehead, at Cat. Her expression was as arrogant and aloof as any dragon's but also bore the marks of calm under suffering. Hers was a greatness untouched by malice. Cat had to fight the impulse to fall to her knees. "This one stinks of foulness. And she sees me unarmored," the fire spirit said in a surprisingly gentle voice. Her body cast off so much heat that Cat found herself sweating copiously. "It seems my humiliations are without end."

"Lady, I—"

"O nobly born, she is half mortal," Grimalka said. "A fully iron-blooded mortal would be better. But we must work with the tools we are given." She was dragging a toolbox as long as she was tall. Now she let it fall with a clangor and threw back the lid. It was filled with weapons: maces, spears, pikes, a flare gun, and the like.

The crone lifted up a sword. "You know how to use this, kid?"

Cat did, of course. But she shook her head. "I don't intend to kill anyone. Anything."

Narcisse laughed, a sound like a brook running lightly down a mountainside. "Nor could you, in this case. If you struck with all your might, it would do no more than cause sparks."

Nevertheless, a sword was not a particularly versatile weapon. So Cat picked up a lignum vitae staff. "I'll take this one." She ran her hands up and down the shaft, checking for splinters, roughness, slick spots. She found no problems and concluded, "It will serve."

A shudder racked the giantess's body. She stared up at the sky but made no sound.

"Lady, your time is upon you," Narcisse said, "and you weaken and tire. You cannot hope to hold back the birth without our help. We must go inside you."

"I had hoped to be spared this indignity. Yet, for the sake of my child, it seems I must endure it." The fire spirit rolled over onto her back and spread her legs wide. A crack of darkness edged with flame appeared at their juncture.

Narcisse started forward, gesturing Cat to follow her into the body of the locomotive.

"I can't believe you're doing this," Helen said.

"The quest is noble. I cannot refuse it."

"It's not just your life you're throwing away, you know—there's mine too."

The selfishness of the statement took Cat's breath away. "Nobody gives a damn," she snapped.

"Story of my life."

"Take care of Esme," Cat commanded Grimalka. "See that she comes to no harm." Then she stepped within.

⁂

The scorching heat of the fire-giantess gave way to the pleasant coolness of an early summer evening. Like so many vital things, the locomotive was larger on the inside than appeared possible from without. Cat could sense that, though the interior was absolutely without light. A light breeze touched her face. She smelled oak leaves, ferns, a stream.

"This will not do," Narcisse said. "Darkness can be used against us." Ions gushed up about them as she summoned zero-point energy from the substratum of the universe.

"Let there be stars," the surgeon-archimage commanded. The sky filled itself with a glory of stars and nebulae, enough for Cat to see that they were surrounded by a forest of black silhouette trees.

Narcisse produced a twig from a hidden pocket of her tunic and, one-handed, snapped it in two. "More light!"

Every leaf in the forest blazed as brightly as an incandescent bulb. Blinded, Cat threw an arm over her eyes.

"Softer . . . softer . . . shhh, yes . . . there." Narcisse spoke hushingly to the leaves, as if they were a skittish horse. Cat opened her eyes to a twilight world and blinked away the pain and afterimages.

"Let there be a meadow."

The trees retreated a good two bowshots in every direction, leaving in their wake low grasses studded with yellow wildflowers.

"We have our theater," Narcisse said. "Now we shall see how well we can operate in it."

Cat probed upward with her staff, heard it go *thunk* on iron, though there still seemed to be a starry sky overhead. Behind her was a high stone wall with, at its center, an open gateway just wide enough for one person to pass through. Beyond it she saw darkness, a curve of tracks, scattered boxcars. Taking her place before the gate, she asked, "Are we in the Empyrean?"

"No. Well, yes, in a sense. But not really. Doubtless you were taught that there are many realms: Faerie upon which we dwell, Aerth from whence we came, Hel below us and the Empyrean above, and so on and so on. However, these are only different energy states of the same place—think of them as the surfaces of an n-dimensional tesseract and you won't be far wrong. The

adept understands that there are only two worlds: the exoteric
or outer world—the surfaces just mentioned—and the esoteric
or hidden world, which is the place where all the realms come
together. Both make sense in their own ways, but the senses
they make are very different from one another. You stand inside the locomotive's body, a holy place and part of the esoteric
universe which your eyes and ears and touch were not designed
to perceive. All that you see is but illusion and metaphor. Put
no trust in what you see, hear, or feel. Be strong."

Cat had spent her entire life pretending to be strong. She
nodded in the way that she had observed capable people did.

"Your job is to stand here and make sure that nothing gets
past you and through the birth-gate. That's not going to be easy.
The fire spirit will be more powerful than both of us combined.
So we're going to have to bluff."

"Bluff?"

"Bluff. I'm the examiner. You're the guardian of the gate.
We're both cosmic Powers. Get it?"

Cat assumed a fighting stance and, though the lignum vitae
staff was longer than the bo staffs she was used to, it felt good.
She ran through eight swings, one for each direction, ending
with a thrust. Four repetitions of the exercise to loosen up later,
she said, "Got it."

Fata Narcisse looked surprised. "You've had training."

"You should see me with an MK 17. What now?"

"We wait. Not very long."

⁎⁎

Cat felt the spirit's approach long before it appeared at the far
end of the meadow. There was a tension in the air accompanied
by a corresponding unease in her stomach and an acidic tang
in the back of her mouth. Then a cloud of smoke billowed up
over the trees, eclipsing the stars. With a snort, the smoke con-

gealed into a torso, sprouted a thick neck, and bent down to
strike the earth with iron hooves. The ground trembled underfoot. There were flashes of lightning within the cloud.

"This is genuinely scary," Cat said.

"Leave all speech to me. You don't know what to say."

Dwindling, changing, sprouting wings and then reabsorb-
ing them, growing more distinct as it approached, the roiling
darkness grew closer and closer until at last it resolved itself
into a skinny young woman in a flowered sundress and a wide
straw hat. Her knees and elbows were knobby and she looked
anything but dangerous. Still, Cat knew without doubt that this
was the child waiting to be born, for, like her mother, she had
one large round eye in the middle of her forehead. "What's
this?" the young woman said when she came to them.

"You cannot exit, O nobly unborn," said Narcisse, "until you
pass my examination to prove yourself worthy of your mother,
your new world, and the Lords of the Rails."

The young lady thought for a second. "What happened to
your arm?"

"I let its bones be broken in exchange for wisdom. See that
the same does not happen to you." Narcisse glanced sidelong at
Cat, who struck a vigilant pose. She was so situated that two
steps backward would place her within the gate, blocking it with
her body.

"Oh." The young woman threw herself down cross-legged on
the grass. "Very well. Ask what you will."

A dark aura surrounded Fata Narcisse and she seemed to
grow larger. Obviously, she was drawing upon quantum power
sources again. Scowling ferociously, she said, "What is your
use-name?"

"Elektra, daughter of Olympia, daughter of Hephaesta, of the
line of Hekate."

"What is your true name?

"It is writ in the halls of fire in sigils ten feet high, for those who have the wit to read it. Are you sure you're a real examiner?"

"I am. What is your purpose here today?"

"To be born."

"For what reason are you to be born?"

"To live, to love, to learn, and to lose."

"What is the price of these privileges?"

"Death."

"The purpose of your life?"

"To die."

"The purpose of your death?"

"None."

"Life having purpose, and death having none, why are you here?"

Elektra sighed and rolled her eye. "I give up."

Sternly, Fata Narcisse said, "That's not a real answer."

"So?" the young woman said.

"You must answer the question."

"Your examination is stupid. I'm tired of it. I'm tired of you as well." The fire spirit stood, brushing grass from her skirt. Then she made a flicking gesture with one hand. The tips of her fingers lightly brushed against Narcisse, sending her flying ten feet through the air. Her body made an ugly sound when it hit the ground.

Elektra took off her hat and threw it away. Her hair burst into flames. Her eye was an intense darkness under those flames. To Cat, she said, "You stand in my way. Move aside."

Skin clammy with dread, Cat stood her ground. Fata Narcisse had said she did not know what to say, and that was true. But she could at least try. "Hear me, Greatness! Your mother Olympia, daughter of Hephaesta, of the line of Hekate sent us here for your own protection. Heed the warning she sends through us: Your body is not yet prepared for you. Without armor to contain your fires, you will destroy yourself, your mother, and a good chunk of a world that I, for one, am very fond of. Half an hour's patience is all we ask of you. That's not much. It's hardly anything. Surely you can see how reasonable that is."

Elektra tapped her foot and made a moue of annoyance. Her hair sizzled and snapped. "Oh, twaddle. No one cares for your logic. Get out of my way."

"No."

The skin beneath the burning hair had grown paler and more translucent; it was possible to see the bone beneath it. Teeth sprouted, sharp and gnarled, in her mouth. "No? What do you mean, 'no'?"

"Advance and you will be repulsed. Move toward the gate and I will drive you away from it. That's what 'no' means."

"You think you can stop me, sorceress?"

"Yes."

The girl giggled. "You're funny."

Lightly, she strode toward Cat.

Twisting one foot against the grass to get a more solid stance, Cat felt that foot slip slightly on metal. This clarified her thinking most wondrously. Fata Narcisse had said that everything surrounding them was illusion. Which meant that it was an illusion which had thrown her through the air and, by the sound of it, done serious damage to her body. Her belief that all was illusion, then, had proved weaker than the fire spirit's will. So. What did Cat have faith in that would be stronger than that will?

She had faith in her training.

Elektra reached up a negligent hand, as she had with Fata Narcisse. Cat brought her lignum vitae staff down on it hard.

"Ow!" The young woman stared at her hand in disbelief. "That *hurt*."

With neither hurry nor hesitation, Cat took two steps back, into the womb-gate, filling it. She raised her staff in a defensive position. "I congratulate you, O nobly unborn," she said. "You have just learned your first lesson about life. Most of us had to wait until we were born for that."

The fire spirit put her head down and charged at Cat.

Stepping forward and to the side, Cat slammed one end of her staff into Elektra's calf to make her stumble. Then she threw all her weight against the young woman's ribs, so that she went smashing into the iron wall to one side of the womb-door. After which, Cat moved back to her starting position, blocking the exit.

For a long moment, both Cat and Elektra caught their breaths. Then the fire spirit laughed, clapped her hands, and—

Clang! Clang! Clang!

It was the sound of a shovel being slammed against the locomotive's side. Small and distant came the crone's voice: "Olly-olly-oxen-free! The new body is here! You can let the spawn pass."

Cat stepped to the side and leaned her staff against the wall. With a bow, she said, "Pass, O nobly almost-born."

A hot wind swept through the womb-gate and the fire spirit was gone.

"Olly-olly-oxen-free! You can come out now." *Clang! Clang! Clang! Clang! Clang!*

Fata Narcisse lay unmoving on the ground. Stooping over her body, Cat performed a quick scan. The elf-lady was gray with shock but there appeared to be no significant loss of blood. Narcisse groaned when Cat touched her ribs, so probably at least one was broken. But there appeared to be no injuries to the skull or spine.

"Don't die on me, sis," Cat muttered. "I want to borrow that peach silk blouse you like so much and pour a chocolate daiquiri down its front." Then she rolled Narcisse on her side and, standing, slung her over her shoulder in a kobold's carry.

As she passed through the birth-gate, Helen said, "Hell of a way to run a railroad."

"We survived it," Cat said. "I like to think that counts for something."

The exterior world reeked of scorched metal and burnt plastic and spilled lubricant from ruptured wheel casings. But there were also the smell of acres of rye and the subtler, more alluring scent of night-flowering carnivores. Cat's head lifted involuntarily and she saw five bat-riders flutter by in formation, lances held high, in search of prey. A moon winked five times and they were gone.

Workers were swarming about Olympia. Repair trains had arrived at last, bringing with them not only the new locomotive but cranes, bulldozers, and other tools with which to right Olympia's body. Kobolds, haints, and dwarves began slowly and with a great deal of profanity to raise up the fallen locomotive.

Two haints placed a stretcher before Cat and helped her lower Narcisse onto it.

"Step back and let me work." Grimalka shoved Cat aside and knelt beside the surgeon-archimage's body. She passed her hands over it in complex gestures, mumbling cantrips under her breath. Then, to one of the haints, she said, "Get a drip and some painkiller into her. Stat."

"Will she be okay?" Cat asked.

"Not my department," the crone replied. "Put her into the infirmary car," she told the second haint. "They'll know what to do." Then, addressing Cat again, "You done good, kid. The thanks of a grateful railroad, yadda yadda yadda."

Cat took Esme's hand. "I think this would be a good time for the two of us to slip away."

"What are you—nuts? I'll bet Fata Narcisse made you promises. Expensive ones, too, am I right?"

"As I recall, her promises were both extravagant and vague."

"Yeah, well, you can start by demanding a prophecy from a grateful fire spirit. The way I see it, Her Nibs owes you one."

※

They waited until Olympia had been righted and set firmly on the tracks again. Then, after a brief consultation with Grimalka, the locomotive ordered the workers to retreat an earshot's distance away. This left only Cat, Esme, and the crone in her presence. "I apologize that my daughter tried to kill you," the locomotive said. "She is young and knows no better. With age comes wisdom. With wisdom comes the knowledge that service must be repaid, however base the servitor. You may ask me any three questions and I will lower myself to answer them."

The crone leaned close to Cat and whispered, "Ask wisely. This is an offer few ever receive in a lifetime."

"Ask her where I left my dolly," Esme said. "No, wait. Here it is. I lost my flute, though."

"She is right. You have two questions left."

Quickly, before Esme could ask about the flute, Cat said, "Tell me where my brother now resides. He is Fingolfinrhod, Lord Sans Merci of House Sans Merci."

For a long while, the locomotive remained silent and motionless, a black wall against the starry sky. Then she said:

> "Full fathom five thy brother lies;
> On his thighs are pleasures built;
>   Wanton pearls do please his eyes:
>   Naught of his life suffers guilt,
>   But hath endured a sea-change

Into something rich and strange.
Sea-nymphs hourly attend his quilt."

"Yeah, that sounds like Roddie all right. But it doesn't answer my question. I don't suppose you have a more specific address?"

"Alas," Olympia said, "your kind are to me like so many fireflies. At a distance, I cannot pick one out of your foul swarm. Ask me your final question."

Cat thought carefully. Then she said, "Tell me whatever it is I most need to know."

"Ahhhh, now that is a question worth the asking." Again, the locomotive fell silent. Again they waited. Finally, she assumed the vatic voice a second time and said:

"In a glass coffin
Your mother lies imprisoned—
Wake her with a kiss."

There was a long silence. Then, "That's it?" Cat asked incredulously. "Damn you for a false prophet and a fraud! That was the exact opposite of anything I would ever want to know."

"I have said my piece and paid my debt," Olympia replied. "Let my servitors return. Already, I long to travel."

As if this were a signal, the workers began drifting back toward the locomotive.

⁂

On the rails beyond the trains dispatched to aid in the cleanup efforts was a luxury liner with a dining car, a sleeping car, a club car, and a brothel car. "That's for you and the urchin," Grimalka said. "Don't make faces! Fata Narcisse said she'd support you, right? That's great—if she survives. But if she doesn't, well, there's no paper trail and you never existed. You hear what I'm saying?"

"Loud and clear."

"Either way, if I were you, I'd take the ride. Trust me, once you've traveled like a Lady of the Rails, you'll never be happy with first class again."

So it was that, minutes later, Cat found herself in a leather armchair, riding away from the scene of the accident. A gwisin floated into the club car, carrying a blanket and a shallow bowl of warm water. Without saying a word, she knelt at Cat's feet, removed her shoes, and began giving her a pedicure. A Teggish servitor placed three stiff menus before her, saying, "This one is for food, the second is a list of available spa services, and the third is for artisanal sexual practices you may be interested in."

Cat ordered an omelet with truffles and a glass of sauvignon blanc. Esme wanted a grilled cheese sandwich and a Pepsi. While they were waiting to be called into the dining room, Cat looked over the third menu. "Some of these: Yuck," she said. "What's refluxophilia?"

"You don't want to know," Helen said.

Shortly thereafter, for the third time that night, Cat went to bed. This time, nothing woke her until noon the next day. Not even Esme.

Our soul is escaped even as a bird out of the snare of the fowler: the snare is broken and we are delivered.

—*The Book of Common Prayer*

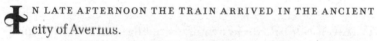

I N LATE AFTERNOON THE TRAIN ARRIVED IN THE ANCIENT city of Avernus.

As its doors opened and Cat took Esme's hand, preparatory to stepping down onto the platform, the smells of the city washed over her: diesel exhaust, hot tar, fresh espresso, roasting chestnuts, baking bread, cheap wine, expensive perfume, damp laundry, lemons, grilled lamb, hazelnut gelato, cigarette smoke from hotel lobbies, stale beer from low dives, lilacs and freesia from flower stands, algae-green water from fountains, the dust of eternity and, lurking behind them all, piss festering in dark alleyways.

"Ahhhh," Helen said. "The stinks and stanks of life—I'm home at last."

"I never know what you're talking about."

"You don't need to, my dear."

Redcaps swept by with Cat's duffel bag and the Hello Kitty knapsack. Cat ran to catch them, yanking Esme after her as if she were a wheeled bag, only to be brought to an abrupt halt by a footman holding up a sign with her name on it. Behind him, the redcaps were loading the luggage into the trunk of a

Duesenberg under the watchful eye of its driver. "Fata Narcisse sends her regrets that she cannot meet you in person," the footman said. He was a ginger dwarf with a crooked smile that didn't quite reach all the way to insolence. "The doctors insist on house rest for at least three weeks. She directed me to tell you, however, that you are to be her guest at the compound for as long as you care to stay."

"But we left before she did. How can she possibly be here ahead of us?"

"The railroad takes care of its own, ma'am. Are you coming?"

Having no better alternative at hand, Cat nodded.

⁂

A leisurely ride into the center of town, hugs and welcomes, and two uneventful weeks later, Cat and Narcisse lay sunning themselves by the pond. Narcisse was proudly naked, save for the plaster cast, covered with scrawled healing runes, on one arm. Cat had a towel draped across her butt. Between them was a Scrabble board.

There were buildings scattered about the compound's grounds—cabanas here, a stand of beech there, a Gothic folly that looked to be on the verge of tumbling down alongside a small but artfully rendered tarn where it would most please the eye. The farther from the central knoll, the thicker the buildings clustered, until they joined to form a circular wall holding the world at bay. Earlier that morning, they had swum laps (Cat) and floated on a plastic chaise (Narcisse), gotten spider-silk facials, and been worked over by the resident masseuse. Esme stalked the edge of the water with a frog gig in her hand. From here, they could look out over the rooftops of the city and up to the top of the crater walls in all directions, though for security purposes all the compound had been glamoured unseeable from without.

"*Scientist.* Can that possibly be a real word?" Narcisse asked.

Cat, who had gotten the term from Helen, was not sure herself. But she said, "Do you want to challenge me?"

"No." Narcisse toyed with the tiles on their rack. Then she said, "Little sister? Don't you think it's time you told me where you came from?"

"You were there." Cat smiled. "Have you forgotten?"

"Don't play the soubrette, *ma mystérieuse.* I found you in the middle of nowhere, a mulatto with the pride of a peer and the singlestick skills of a soldier, accompanied by a little girl who is clearly not related to you. Riding the rails. Don't try to pretend there's not a story behind that."

With a sigh, Cat sat up, rearranging the towel about herself. "I had hoped never to share this with anyone. But you have been so kind to me and Esme. So, if you really insist . . ."

"I really do."

"Then I have no choice." At the last instant, Cat caught herself about to assume the stance of a professional storyteller and moved the raised hand to the back of her head to scratch, as if she were thinking. Then she related the story she and Helen had been working on ever since being met by the footman at the train station.

CAT'S TALE

I grew up the adopted bastard of a wealthy provincial family—never mind which one!—in the social backwaters of Brocéliande. You can probably tell that by my accent. As a child, I did not ask myself why I looked so different from the rest of my family. But I did wonder why, in addition to ballroom dancing,

horsemanship, and similar social attainments, I also took
lessons in singlestick, summoning, orienteering, and other
skills which none of my full-elven sisters and brothers were required to learn.

Whenever I asked, the answer was always, "It is an ability
your *grand-maman* lacks."

At adolescence, my training intensified—to what end, I could
not tell. More alarmingly, no arrangements were made to place
me in industry or the military, where my mortal blood would
be useful. For the first time, I came to see that there was some
hidden purpose behind my existence. My cousins and siblings,
never warm to me, grew colder and more distant. So I began
gathering hints and clues, every one of which led to my grand-
mother. Including the fact that I had been given the same
name—don't ask what!—as hers.

Grand-maman, meanwhile, was growing seely with age.
Light leaked from her eyes, lips, and nostrils. She weighed so
little that a vagrant breeze would bounce her into the air. There
were whispered discussions of her condition and voiced worries that she was close to transcendence.

One day, the soul surgeons were called in. They brought with
them a young changeling girl—a pre-op, with life but no consciousness—in a wire cage. Her skin was gray and rubbery and
she breathed through her mouth, like a fish. Have you ever seen
one? Ghastly. Normally, they hollow them out and fill 'em up
with a mortal soul stolen from who-knows-where. Not this one.

The cage was left in the foyer while the surgeons went to see
the old lady. I got a chopstick from the kitchen and poked the
child with it to see if she would respond. She turned blank eyes
toward me and, shivering as the *awen* overtook her, said, "I
would very much like to be excluded from this narrative. Think
outside the box, live free or die, you only live once, I don't have
the bandwidth, I'll hit the ground running. I'm a global force

for good. At the end of the day it is what it is. Cray-cray amaze-balls and totes adorbs. You see what I did there? Get a life!"

In horror, I fled to my room.

The surgeons spent considerable time with my grand-mother. Then they came for me. I was stripped, examined under urym lens and thummyn stone, and judged suitable. And now, at last, I learned my purpose in life.

My soul was to be harvested to extend Grand-maman's sterile existence.

You know the five organs of the soul, of course. They are identical for mortal and fey, save that mortals have no true name and feys lack a heart. The soul surgeons planned a series of six operations, two of which were to be carried out immediately. First, the changeling would be gutted, removing all residual spirit save only the spark of life. Then my shadow would be transplanted from my body to hers. Grandmother's shadow, of course, was so enervated as to be nonexistent. After the change-ling and I had recovered, a third operation would place Grand-mother's self in the host body. A fourth would mingle a tiny fraction of my self with hers. After which, a regimen of drugs and incantations would teach her self to feed upon mine. The fifth operation would render the rest of my self helpless after which it would be fed, bit by bit, over the course of weeks, to the changeling. My heart and body would then be discarded. Fi-nally, Grand-maman's true name would be transplanted into a body containing both our memories and skills, and my own ex-tremely unseely shadow.

All this was explained to me as I screamed, spat, struggled, and fought. To no avail. The soul surgeons had gone through this many, many times before. I awoke in my bedroom the next morning with my shadow gone, the windows nailed shut, and a young fey sitting in a chair, watching me.

"I don't feel any different," I said.

"The shadow is like your appendix. It can be removed with no ill effects," the stranger said. He was thin and albino-pale, like the others, and wore the same milk-glass spectacles, but lacked their cold affect. And he had the most beautiful hands—like ivory. I was later to learn that he was but an apprentice, new to the profession.

"Why are you here?" I said. "Leave at once."

The apprentice surgeon made a dismissive gesture. "It is my duty to watch over you to ensure you do not try to escape. So here I stay."

"Pervert."

"If you wish."

Dunstan was the apprentice's name. For a week he watched over me. We talked and grew to know one another. On the eighth day, I held open the sheets and he joined me beneath them.

The fourth operation was held and the changeling began to prattle and talk and sing like any normal child her age. Because she had a share of my memories, she felt an affinity for me, and because she possessed my shadow, she always knew where I was and wanted to be with me. All that long and sultry summer was a labyrinth of time to me, through which I simultaneously fled the child and sought out private spaces to share with my pale lover. All the while, perpetually awaiting me at the center of the labyrinth was the operating table, which had been set up in what had been, in my grandmother's artistic youth, her studio.

Inevitably, as all doomed lovers must, we plotted an escape. I had some small access to the family wealth. Dunstan, whose only duty was to guard me, had the freedom to come and go as he pleased. Our plans ripened as the fifth and, for me, fatal operation neared.

All things end, alas, and doomed loves sooner than most. The affair came to its climax not on the day before the last operation, nor on the eve of that day, but on the antepenultimate day before my soul was to be gutted. The sheets were damp with sweat and the pillows scattered about the floor and I was sitting naked at my vanity, applying a beeswax balm to my lips, when I said to Dunstan, casually, "All our preparations are made. Let's leave two days early. By dawn we'll be over the horizon in another land."

Dunstan struggled to an upright position, looking alarmed. "No!" he cried. "We have to wait! The plan won't work until—"

"That's what I suspected," I said, and kissed him long and hard. It would be a stretch to call me an alchemist. But I had been trained in the concoction of love-philters and the like—another skill Grand-maman lacked—so it had been no hard thing to put a sleeping potion into my lip balm.

When Dunstan was asleep, I put on my clothes and bundled up his to be thrown into the reptilarium. Let the sonofawoods-fey stand naked before his superiors while he tried to explain how I got away from him! From the closet, I took my largest purse, which contained all the money I had, my Cartier watch and a few other pawnables, a change of underwear, and the like. I would be traveling light. Then I visited the changeling's room. So long as she possessed my shadow, she could be used to track my whereabouts. This was a threat I had to eliminate.

For a long moment, I stood by the changeling's bed, watching her sleep. Then I shook her. "Wake up, small abomination," I said. "Have they given you a name yet?"

She rubbed her eyes. "No."

I extracted a doll from my purse and gave it to her. "It's Esme. Now come with me, we have a far way to go tonight."

And we have been on the road ever since.

⁂

Narcisse applauded with a grace that spontaneity could not hope to match. "That is a lovely story," she said, "and impressively crafted. So many specific details! But it casts you as a sexually manipulative minx, which, forgive me, dear heart, I simply cannot believe. Also, it does not explain your reading."

Lightly, as if she did not recognize the challenge in Narcisse's words, Cat said, "I like to read."

"Legal papers. Every night."

"I'm involved in a lawsuit. A great deal of money depends on it."

Fata Narcisse was having a hard time containing her mirth. "Of course! A lawsuit! And you riding the rails! It all makes perfect sense."

"I'm afraid I'm not at liberty to discuss the matter. You'll just have to—"

"Tut! You have so little faith in me. Never mind, I've made arrangements that will take care of whatever your problem may be." Queenie, who was Fata Narcisse's pet among her retinue of haints, materialized at her side, kneeling to whisper in her ear. She sat up. "In fact, I believe that's Counselor Edderkopp now!"

※※

Cat thought it an enormous insect at first—the hunched brown figure carefully, awkwardly, feeling its way across the lawn toward them. But on closer approach, it resolved itself into a reed-thin man, bent over at the waist almost parallel to the ground, with a short stick in each of his four hands to help him walk. He wore, as Fata Narcisse insisted all male visitors must on her clothing-optional days, a blindfold.

Rodolphe—who was male but not blindfolded, because servants didn't count—materialized to present Narcisse with a diaphanous wrap and Cat with a terry-cloth bathrobe. As soon as she was garbed, Narcisse ran lightly across the lawn to give the newcomer a hug and a peck on his cheek. But when she tried to tug his blindfold undone, the six-limbed man slapped her hand away.

"It's all right, Counselor. I'm as decent as the dawn now. Well . . . as decent as *some* dawns."

"It's not your immorality I worry about seeing," Counselor Edderkopp grumbled. "It's this wicked, wicked world's. I'd gladly gouge my eyes out to avoid it, but I need the weak and watery things to read with. You can't expect me to give up my books when I've lost so much else: whiskey, red meat, tobacco, snuff, cobra venom, whole milk, toad flesh . . . the list is endless. Where's the inconsequential chit you wanted me to meet?"

"Her name is Cat and she is very dear to me. So treat her accordingly. Edderkopp has been on retainer to the family for centuries, Cat, so you must love him as much as I do."

Edderkopp bent low before Cat and then raised himself so high that his sharp nose came up to her chin, inhaling all the while. With a blush, she realized he was committing her scent to memory. "Well," he said brusquely. "What matter brings me here?"

"Our Cat has a legal problem. But she is a skittish creature who trusts not even her loving sister. So an oath would seem to be in order?"

"As you say." A haint appeared at Edderkopp's side and presented him with a goblet of wine. Another proffered a small silver knife. Grimacing with concentration, he cut one finger and squeezed a drop of blood into the wine. After which, he extended the cup and knife to Cat, who did the same. Then, slopping a libation of the mingled drink onto the ground with each proper name, he solemnly intoned, "I swear by the Year Eater and the Dark Lady, by the Labrys and the Maze, by the Goddess Herself and her consort the Baldwynn, to uphold the privilege of attorney-client confidentiality with this woman going by the name of Cat, whosoever she may be, whatsoever crimes she may have committed, howsoever dire the consequences of silence. Let these Powers strike me deaf and illiterate, never to read or be read to again, should I break this vow." He drank half the wine, then thrust the goblet at Cat. She finished it off.

Edderkopp dug a business card from a vest pocket. "Drop by my office tomorrow. Hour of the Snake. Bring any documentation you may have."

⁂

As Cat was about to leave, Esme by her side and grimoire and papers heaped upon her lap, Narcisse popped her head into the car, a Bugatti this time. "I have something for you," she said, and handed Cat a Chanel attaché case. It was exactly the right size to hold the documents.

"Where did this come from?" Cat asked.

"Oh, sweets. I have money, remember?"

"I thought maybe you'd magicked it into being."

"Money *is* magic, darling." Almost as an afterthought, Narcisse added, "Oh, and here's a matching clutch with a cell phone and some mad money. You might want to make a day of it. I'm having a few friends over to dampen the sheets and scatter the pillows about. You'd be welcome, but I'm positive it's not your sort of thing. Ta!"

The gate to the House Syrinx compound closed behind the car and melted back into the wall of ancient buildings. In that instant, Cat and Esme were surrounded by slums. Haints, dwarves, and other lowlifes sat on stoops drinking forties out of paper bags, or huddled under dirty blankets while they smoked crack, or leaned against brick walls waiting for an opportunity that would never come. "You'd think they'd resent us passing through," Cat said. "But they don't even look our way."

"They can't see us, ma'am." The driver pointed to a hex dangling from the rearview mirror. "That's to keep them from knowing House Syrinx is so close by."

"Why is the compound in such a bad neighborhood?"

"It was a nice neighborhood once. Then House Syrinx bought all the buildings, one by one, and rented them to transients. Now it serves as a kind of moat. This way, nobody with power enough to see through the protective glamour is likely to walk up to the compound by accident."

The Cathedral of Law, where the driver dropped them off, had a façade whose marble Ionic columns were black with soot, and a gloomy interior of ramshackle grandeur. Cat made her way down hallways with cracked granite floors and tarnished bronze lighting fixtures and a fusty smell compounded of cedar, cigars, and cleaning fluid to Counselor Edderkopp's office. Leaving Esme with crayons and a coloring book under the watchful eye of the receptionist, she knocked on his door and was hooted inside.

The shelves covering all but a fraction of the walls were so overladen with books they bowed slightly, nodding their heads over piles of codices, drifts of paper, cardboard boxes crammed full of scrolls, mounds of magazines that had long ago gone out of business. Beyond which, in the farthest, darkest corner, was an overflowing desk, hemmed in on either side by stacked crates containing, inevitably, yet more books. Picking her way through the clutter, all Cat could think of was the conflagration that would ensue were she to drop a single lit match.

On her approach, Edderkopp looked up from a half-written letter, placed pince-nez before his eyes, and blinked. Seizing his four short canes, he clambered over his desk—it was the only route possible—to meet Cat halfway. Then he bowed deeply and raised his thin nose as high as her chin, inhaling noisily.

"Ahhhh. Young Narcisse's protégé, all sweaty with mystifica-
tion and distrust. Welcome. There's a chair in here somewhere.
Find it and sit down."

"I'm . . . not really sure this is a good idea."

"You mean you're not sure *I'm* a good idea." Edderkopp
stumbled and lurched about the mounds of detritus, searching.
"Timidity is a salubrious virtue and one shared by far too few
of your generation. But it can be overdone. Aha!" He hoisted an
enormous armload of files and loose correspondence and
dumped it atop a box of clay tablets. "I told you there was a
chair!"

It was a Chesterfield. Cat brushed the seat with her hand
and sat.

"You doubt my competence. Very well. Point to any book in
the room. Yes, up there if you wish. The green volume, you
mean? Ah, the orange one to its side! You have chosen *A Brief
History of Klepsis,* an excellent selection, most obscure." With
unexpected agility, Edderkopp climbed up the bookshelves
almost to the ceiling. Then he returned, handed Cat the book,
and turned his back on her. "Now pick out a word and tell
me where in the book it is to be found."

Cat opened the book at random. "The fourth word on
the seventh line of page 147."

"It is *steroma,* again an excellent choice, for it refers to the
firmament or sky, a matter of considerable significance to you."
Counselor Edderkopp extended a hand to reclaim his book.
"You are wondering how I can possibly know not only the one
word but, by implication, every word in every book in my office."

"Yes."

"I am old, child, old, and I have spent my life in the service
of the Law—writing laws, enforcing laws, interpreting laws,
inventing ways to circumvent laws . . . Also, I am cursed with
a perfect memory—that is a tale I may well inflict upon you

another time—and consequently there is very little that can surprise me anymore."

"But if you know every word in these books—why keep them?"

"For the same reason a young woman such as yourself might know every inch of her lover's skin, and yet want nevertheless to touch it, taste it, luxuriate in its smell. Which reminds me." Edderkopp flowed up the shelves, restored the book, and flowed down again. Then he began tugging at one of the towering piles of crates. "There is a window around here somewhere, I saw it only a decade ago." The topmost crates fell over noisily, spilling their contents and revealing a curtain. He twitched it open with a puff of dust, and a beam of sunlight stabbed through the room, turning him white as cream.

Raising himself as high as he could, Edderkopp clasped two hands behind his back, adjusted his pince-nez with a third, and dramatically raised a forefinger. "You are Caitlin of House Sans Merci, dragon slayer and at present the single most-wanted fugitive from military justice in all of Faerie."

Cat gasped.

Edderkopp made a rattling noise, like seeds being shaken in a dry pod, and Cat realized that he had just chuckled. "Young people. You all think that yours is the first injustice, the first treacherous act, the first escape, the first desperate run for freedom in a world in which that concept barely exists. Fortunately for you, you have fetched up in one of the few places in all Europa where you are safe from pursuit. Unfortunately for you, it will not last. You must make the most of it while you can." Turning, he yanked at the curtain rope, bedimming the room again. "Thus have I proven my competence. Tell me everything."

⋇

In less time than Cat would have thought possible, Counselor Edderkopp was showing her to the door. "There is no doubt that you have been conspired against. Give me a few days to look into matters and I am confident we can clear this whole thing up. It is not beyond the realm of possibility that I can have you restored to your previous rank and position. At the very least, I am certain, I can discover who's behind it all. That's the beginning of wisdom, after all—knowing who to blame for your misfortunes."

At which, her business was done and she had the afternoon to herself.

It was a strange sensation, having nothing to do and somebody else responsible for taking care of her problems, and it left Cat feeling as light as dandelion fluff. Leading Esme by the hand, she set out to explore the city.

Noon found them in a market square off of Via della Streghe, just below the north wall. Bare-breasted hags in black ground-sweeping skirts and veiled headdresses with narrow slits for their eyes dickered with vendors while children ran about underfoot or tumbled naked in the air overhead. An ogress pulling a red handcart laden with fresh-baked bread bumped into a table with star fruit and moon melons arranged in a pyramid, almost toppling them. This prompted a torrent of billingsgate from its overseer, to which the ogress responded by amiably making the sign of the horns and waggling it in the air. Cat caught her as she was moving away and bought a loaf. Further purchases of a slab of cheese, some *soppressata,* and a bottle of still water later, Cat and Esme made an excellent lunch of the batch while sitting on the rim of a fountain with a statue of Erodiade, Minerva, and Noctiluca dancing in a circle.

At meal's end, Cat stood, slapped the crumbs off her hands, and was about to plunge deeper into the city when somebody exclaimed, "Caitlin!"

She spun about. Two faces flickered into recognition. "Sibyl! Ysault!"

For an eyeblink, the two pilots stood frozen in astonishment. Then Ysault's expression softened and Sibyl's hardened. "You're alive," Ysault said. "I thought . . . we thought . . . everybody thought you were dead. They said you'd locked yourself inside your dragon and blown it up rather than face court-martial."

"Told you it was just a cover story."

"Yeah, well, it's great seeing you guys again," Cat said. "Fabulous. Real swell. Now I'm sure you'll forgive me if I get as far the fuck away from your traitorous faces as I possibly can. If you try to follow me, I swear I'll kill you."

She started to back away.

"No. Wait. Don't. You're not the only one who was framed—you were just the first." One side of Ysault's mouth quirked up in an almost-smile. "We're all on the same side now. Or maybe 'equally screwed' is a better way to put it." Then, seeing Cat hesitate, "C'mon, Caitlin, everyone makes mistakes. Underneath it all, we're still dog-sisters, aren't we? *Pro matria mori*, right?" She held up her fist.

"I—"

"*Pro matria mori!* We live by those words. Or aren't you one of the Corps anymore?"

Reluctantly, Cat bumped Ysault's fist with her own. There were ties that were stronger than treachery, and the Dragon Corps had been the best and truest family she'd ever known. "Mat mori," she replied. Then, "Call me Cat. It's my name now. Where can we all sit down and talk?"

"Well, there's always Felix Culpa," Ysault said. "It's kind of a dive but it's close. In fact, we were just on our way there to meet—"

"No names." Sibyl clapped a hand over Ysault's mouth. After

a jerk of her head toward a side street, she silently led them away, several twists and turns deeper into the narrowing streets and ever more decrepit buildings of the Italian Quarter.

Felix Culpa, when they reached it, proved to be a small, dark basement bar with a crude mural of the Winged God's nine-day fall on one wall. Cat felt an unease, as if someone were watching from the shadows, but dismissed it. They took a table and, when the ibis-headed waitress came, Esme said, "A glass of your finest pinot grigio, *per favore,* my good creature."

"You'll have Pepsi." Cat turned to the waitress. "I'll have the pinot grigio."

"Soave."

"Something red and from Lemuria. Mu will do in a pinch."

There was a long, uncomfortable silence, during which their drinks arrived. Then Ysault said, "So. Tell me everything."

Cat gave a truncated version of her adventures, leaving out all mention of Fata Narcisse, Edderkopp, or Helen. Then she leaned back and said, "Your turn."

Her former peers glanced at one another. Sibyl nodded almost imperceptibly. "They came for us at night," Ysault said. "Everyone in the women's quarters, no exceptions. We were not treated with the courtesy due officers in Her Absent Majesty's Dragon Corps, but rousted from bed in our nightgowns. It was humiliating."

"That was deliberate."

"We had to stand outside while our rooms were ransacked—for 'evidence,' they claimed. But I saw how they snickered. Then we were loaded into a bus, shackled to the seats, and taken to Glass Mountain."

"But that's a maximum-security prison," Cat said. "For civilians. They wouldn't put officers—"

"They did," Sibyl said.

"We had hopes, at first, of being vindicated. Weeks turned to months, however, with not even a promise of legal representation."

"But—"

"Shush," Sibyl said.

"We realized that we had been given a life sentence without a hearing. So we resolved to escape."

"I thought nobody ever escaped from Glass Mountain," Cat said.

"We were the first." There was no mistaking the pride in Ysault's voice. "They made the mistake of keeping us together, so as not to contaminate the other prisoners. Not realizing how much talent we had among us. We got tough fast. We made plans. To begin, we needed cell phones with prepaid chips. These we got by bribing the guards."

"How?" Esme asked with interest.

"Never you mind," Cat said. "With cigarettes. Cigarettes are the currency of prisons, right, Ysault?"

"Uh . . . I suppose."

"Everybody has enemies," Sibyl said. "We agreed to kill theirs."

"Don't listen, Esme."

"I like this story!"

"Well, don't."

"Most prison breaks occur at night. For ours, we chose a bright, cloudless day. Because when the sun hits the glass sides of the mountain, the dazzle is almost unbearable. Saoirse pointed out that no one would be expecting that. We made fetches of ourselves from stuffed clothing and left them in our cells to fool the guards and we wore snow goggles to keep from being blinded. The climbing gear we had made ourselves from contraband materials. We sewed together sanitary napkins and covered them with duct tape to make the kneepads. We took shivs off the other prisoners and pounded them down into pitons. The preparations took us well over a year.

"It wasn't hard going over the prison yard wall because it wasn't guarded. What was on the other side, after all, but cliffs of jagged glass and below them the frigid northern sea?"

"Skip the descent," Sibyl said.

"It would take forever to do it justice," Ysault agreed. "It felt like forever at the time. It was epic. Remember what wilderness survival training was like? The descent was a hundred times worse. But at last, just as the sun was going down, we reached the bottom and there waiting for us was—"

"No names."

"—a *Kraken*-class submersible and an inflatable dinghy to ferry us to it."

"No explanations."

"But the dinghy couldn't land because there were enormous shards of glass everywhere. So we had to swim for it—and the water was cold and choppy. We couldn't wade out because if a wave knocked us off our feet, we'd be dragged across the glass and bleed to death. Which meant that we had to dive into the water—a long, shallow dive because it wasn't very deep close to the shore. And we couldn't take off our shoes beforehand, of course, but just try swimming in ice-cold water wearing them!

"The distance to the dinghy wasn't great, but I wasn't much of a swimmer either. So it seemed like miles. I didn't think I was going to make it, but I did. I must have swallowed a gallon of ice water, and as I was pulled onto the boat, I passed out. When I came to, inside the submersible, the first thing I did was ask what the date was—and I learned that while we had spent three years on the inside, less than a week had passed in the outer world."

"Wow," Cat said.

"That's why hardly anybody ever gets out of Glass Mountain on any terms at all. But we did what nobody else could. We got out on our own terms. Not only did we break out, but we left not a one of us behind. No injuries either, only a few bruises here and there, maybe a scrape or two. We were heroic."

"They let us escape."

"Afterward, we scattered like pigeons, each by a different path toward a separate region of Europa so our pursuit would be divided. Everybody agreed that was for the best."

"Saoirse's idea. She cut a deal."

"I liked that story! Tell it again!" Esme said.

"Grown-ups are talking, darling. Anyway, what would be the point? You never remember anything for very long."

"If I forget it, that just means I can hear it for the first time all over again."

"Behave yourself and I'll buy you ice cream." To the others, Cat said, "I'd heard the brass was holding an inquisition. But how could they arrest everybody? They need pilots."

"It was just the female pilots," Ysault said bitterly. "Maybe two or three of the men, and they retained the worst. But wait a sec. You've been on the run. How did you hear about this?"

"Rabbit told me," Cat said. Then, when the others looked blank, "You know. The pilot?"

"There was no one by that name on the base. Certainly no pilot. Right, Sibyl?"

"I would have remembered."

"That's crazy. Rabbit of House Oneiros? Always talking trash? C'mon! He's not somebody you could possibly forget."

"No idea."

"No."

Cat flung up her hands. "Well, I'm baffled," she said. Then, "Tell me how you got to Avernus."

The two pilots' tale of separate flights across Europa and

chance encounter in Avernus was described as quickly as Cat's own story had been. She was sure they were hiding things from her—most obviously, the identity of the mysterious forces who had provided the submersible. But then, she was hiding things from them. So fair was fair.

After the third drink, they settled comfortably into an old discussion from better days of how strict, exactly, the virginity requirement was. Masturbation was allowed, obviously. Otherwise the entire Corps would wash out in no time flat. ("Boys first," Sibyl said, and Cat choked on her wine.) But did that mean that being masturbated by someone else was permissible? And if so, did it matter what gender that person was? What about acts performed with the mouth? Would one's dragon settle for a technical virgin? Pretty much everyone agreed that anal sex, whether given or received, was a career ender. But the rest was the stuff of speculation and smutty jokes.

Briefly, everything was as it had once been. Cat could close her eyes and imagine herself an officer again. Then Ysault sighed and said, "Well, it's all theoretical now."

Sibyl put down her glass. "Yup."

"I'm going to get my post back," Cat said. Then, when the others looked at her pityingly, "I haven't worked out how yet. But I haven't given up hope either. I haven't."

"I have," Sibyl said.

"We all have, I'm afraid," Ysault agreed. "Right now the plan is to run. Run as hard and fast as ever we can. Not that it will do us any good in the long run. But it will put off the inevitable."

"Best you do likewise."

The sun was getting low in the sky. Cat picked up the tab and, when she saw how much there was in the clutch, asked, "How are you guys fixed for money?"

"Oh, we're getting along. You know how it is. Opportunities come up . . ."

"Dead broke."

Cat gave them half of what she had. "Tell me where you're staying, so I can check up on you guys now and again."

"Bad idea."

"We have a little place on the Via Regina di Mago. The building with the red trim—fourth floor, the door that doesn't look all smashed in. It's quite nice, actually."

"It has snakes."

When Sibyl and Ysault were gone, Cat took out the cell phone Fata Narcisse had given her so she could call for a driver.

"That was a bad idea, giving them money," Helen said. "Especially out of that pricey little clutch of yours. That's going to raise their suspicions."

"They needed it. I had it. I shared it. End of story."

"I noticed that you and Ysault never responded to anything Sibyl said," Helen remarked.

"Oh, nobody pays any attention to Sibyl."

"Strange. There are days when I feel just like her."

Morning and evening
Maids heard the goblins cry:
"Come buy our orchard fruits,
Come buy, come buy . . ."

                 —Christina Rossetti, "Goblin Market"

SUMMER LINGERED. THE HEAT PEAKED A LITTLE HIGHER every day and never quite returned to the previous morning's temperature at night so that the city hummed like a beehive with overworked air conditioners and those who had access to the rooftops slept uneasily, twisting and turning, naked and sweaty, under a ruddy sky. Whenever Narcisse held one of her orgies, Cat went into town to see Ysault and Sibyl. If Narcisse gave her money, Cat shared it with them. She always picked up the tab for their drinks.

They were in the French Quarter at a restaurant off rue Barguest called La Ghoulerie (Cat ordered off of the vegan menu, to Esme's noisy displeasure) one particularly oppressive day when Ysault said, "There's someone I think you should hear."

"Okay. I've got an appointment with my attorney this afternoon, though." Cat had decided, after weeks of nothing but inaction and vague promises from him, to sack Edderkopp. But she saw no reason to mention that fact here.

"Easy-trapezey, sweetie. She's not speaking today. Next week. Day of the Sow. Hour of the Bat. We'll rendezvous in the square where we first ran into you and I'll take you there. Are you down with that?"

"Sure. But why not meet where you live?"

"Nobody trusts you," Sibyl said.

Counselor Edderkopp dumped three stacks of books, one after the other, on his desk. "Here's something which may be of some relevance to your case. This is *The Treaty of Hyperuranion*—the place has changed name several times since then, of course—in nineteen volumes." Opening one, he showed Cat the title page with the subheading, *Being the Exact Terms Negotiated Between ye Olde Serpent and Wise, Lord Meririm Phosphoros, in Solemne Convocation with ye moste Auguste Lords of ye Forge. Recorded in ye Original Language and Meticulously Transcrib'd into ye Vernacular.* "In the dragon tongue, the entire treaty is only eight words long."

Startled, Cat said, "Is that possible?"

"It is if you have a large enough vocabulary." Edderkopp made that rattling noise again. "I have my doubts, however. The seventh word I suspect to be a neologism, coined for the occasion. But for that, the treaty might have gone as long as ten. Well, enough pedantry. 'Tis of amusement to myself alone. The pertinent matter is that I have uncovered the cause behind your persecution."

"Which is—?"

Edderkopp placed the red grimoire and related papers Cat had stolen from Lieutenant Anthea on the desk beside the piles of books. "By their thumbed and smudged condition, I can see that you have gone over some of these multiple times—yes, the legal patois can indeed seem opaque to one without legal training." He held up a page between thumb and forefinger. "Here is a license of persecution, sworn out against you. This provided legal justification for all that was done."

"It said that I was a traitor to the Dragon Corps and to Her Absent Majesty's Governance. Those are both lies."

"Pah! Legal fictions. Any lawyer worth his oats would know better than to take those charges literally. The only useful information to be gleaned here is the name of the law firm: Themis, Feller, Garuda and Bran."

Speaking clearly, unhurriedly, and just a touch loudly (for Edderkopp obviously fine-tuned his professed deafness to block whatever he did not wish to hear), Cat said, "All this is beside the point. I need you to tell me where I can find my brother. He can clear me of everything."

"Oh, do let an old man ramble on. It's so rarely that I get the opportunity these days to demonstrate what a diabolically acute fellow I am. Now, Themis, Feller, Garuda and Bran is quite prominent in the area of treaty law. You begin to see the connection." He added a slim folder to the pile. "I took the liberty of having your horoscope cast, hoping to find in it the ultimate cause for your misfortunes. Believe it or not, your birth-stars could not have been more auspicious. Further"—he slammed down an almanac—"the signs and portents recorded on that day were exemplary. Unimprovable! So when we look at your current situation, it seems beyond explanation. Like discovering that a roguish, chain-smoking vagabond is by rights Her Absent Majesty. Not that this applies in your case, of course, but you understand where I'm going here.

"Excelsior! Coordinating certain insurance records with the facts of your biography, I am led to conclude that you must be in possession of a particular stone: nondescript, with a hole through the middle. Since you have the patronage of the wealthiest woman in Avernus and yet are wearing a most undistinguished chain about your neck, I can only conclude it is hanging there." He held out a hand. "If you please."

With reluctance, Cat produced the stone her brother had thrown her just before disappearing into she knew not which underwater city.

Edderkopp held the stone up to his face. His bright green eye shone through the hole, blinked twice, as if it had trouble believing what it was seeing. Then he flipped the stone about. "What a ninnyhammer I am! I was looking though the wrong—"

His face froze with astonishment. Then, a second later, Edderkopp shook with silent laughter. "Well, well, well, well, well. You are full of surprises." He handed back the stone to Cat.

"No, I am *not*. I am the simplest, most virtuous, and most straightforward woman imaginable. I have been falsely accused of heinous crimes of which only my brother can clear me. Tell me where he is or lose me as a client."

The ancient attorney tapped a finger alongside his ear to draw her attention to his hearing aid. Then, stroking the mound of papers as if it were a cat, he said, "We approach now the very nut of my investigations. A concerted effort is being made to break the Treaty of Hyperuranion. For what purpose is irrelevant. What is significant is that the success or failure of that effort relies on one woman—a mortal woman. And she is here in this room."

"You can't possibly be referring to me."

That dry rattle, once again. "I am not. You're only half mortal. I mean the woman resident inside your head." The attorney produced a sheet of flimsy yellow paper whose extreme age was attested to by its nearly illegible carbon-paper typewriter print. "This is a declaration of prophecy, issued long before you were born, but there was a tangential reference to it among your papers, so I sought it out." He handed over the document with a flourish. "Down near the bottom of the page, I have underlined a paragraph. Read."

Cat read. "'It is hereby prophesied that the Party of the Fourth Part, the aforesaid HELEN, will . . .' What madness is this?"

Edderkopp stuck his hands in his armpits and, waggling his elbows as if they were wings, crowed like a cock. Then he pushed a button on what Cat had to be told by Helen was an office intercom. "Mistress Nobody, send in the office imp."

In short order, the door opened and an imp walked in, crophaired and ink-blotched, lightly carrying a stool taller than herself. With a sassy wink at Cat, the imp balanced the stool on her head, restacked books to make a space for it, set it down, clambered atop it, and opened a laptop writing desk. Dipping a quill into the inkwell, she said, "Ready."

Edderkopp's eyes glittered like nothing Cat had ever seen. She could not look away from them. "You will give me access to your innermost self now," he said.

Everything went black.

When Cat came to, the imp was gone and her stool with her. With a cheerful "Here you go!" Edderkopp handed Cat a sheet of foolscap covered with freshly inked words in a tidily minuscule hand.

THE DEPOSITION OF HELEN V.

Q.: For the record, your name is Helen?
Helen: Yes.
Q.: You are where you do not belong.
Helen: I suppose.

Q.: How did you get there?

Helen: It happened.

Q.: You mean you have no clear understanding how it occurred.

Helen: Right in one. You're a clever bastard, aren't you?

Q.: Thank you. May I assume you originated in Aerth?

Helen: If that's what you want to call it. We had another name for the place.

Q.: And that you were dying when the transition occurred?

Helen: Like I said, smart as a whip. Not that that impresses me much. I know people back where I come from who could eat you for breakfast.

Q.: You're not exactly being cooperative, madam.

Helen: Well, what the fuck do you expect? You ask open-ended questions in the obvious hope that I'll incriminate myself. How? Why? I haven't the faintest notion. So I couldn't if I wanted to. A competent lawyer would have had me roped, hog-tied, and on the gallows by now. I've dealt with your kind before, Shylock, and you're all alike. Talentless hacks, riding on the hard work of others. You can't do your own job so you want me to do it for you. Well, I've got news for you. Homie don't play that. Ain't gonna happen. Not now, not never.

Q.: So you have no idea why you're here?

Helen: Not the foggiest. It's your world, after all.

Q.: I hold in my hand a declaration of prophecy issued by the Unseely Court on the Day of the Urchin, Blood Moon, in the one hundred sixty-seventh year of the Descent of the Turbine. Skipping over a great deal that you would find incomprehensible, it says here that the Party of the Fourth Part—and there's your name—will, and I quote, "shake the foundations of the world, to the consternation of the Powers of Faerie."

Helen: Well, hot damn. That's one more I can check off on my bucket list.

Q.: Is it possible for you to be serious for one minute?

Helen: Judging from past behavior, I'd have to say probably not.

Q.: (Sighs.) Very well. It's clear enough that you've been embroiled in this matter without your consent and therefore know precious little of the machinations that have placed you in this young person's mind. So I have only one last question.

Helen: Thank goodness.

Q.: What exactly do you hope to get out of this symbiosis?

Helen: (Silence.)

⁎⁎

"That's Helen, all right." Cat put the paper down atop the stack. "I doubt this helps much."

"It clears the decks, young lady, it clears the decks. Now I am free to bring out the big guns. Also, it has convinced you that I am not a complete fraud, and thus you have given up on your plan to sack me."

Cat opened her mouth, closed it again. "Apparently I have."

"Then let us continue. There is, as we both know, a conspiracy, and working from the clues I have here assembled, it is possible to dimly discern its outline. We are dealing with a nonprofit incorporated in the free city of Carcassonne under the unimaginative name of the Conspiracy. As if it were the only one!" More papers were added to the mound. "It has its own logo and letterhead. Nice graphics value, though I can't say much for their choice of font. Courier—pfeh! The Conspiracy has a board of directors—figureheads, really—and a slate of officers, the makeup of which is a matter of public record." Counselor Edderkopp jabbed a long, twiggish finger down on the topmost sheet of paper. "The name of the Chief Conspiratorial Officer may be of interest to you."

Cat looked at the roster and her blood froze. There at the very top were the words: *Dowager Sans Merci of House Sans Merci.*

"Mother!"

Grimalka showed up unexpectedly the next day, looking considerably more impressive in a freshly laundered uniform than she had when Cat last saw her at the train crash site by the rye field where Olympia had given birth to Elektra. Grimalka had just surrendered a battered leather suitcase to a black dwarf butler, who had handed it off to Rodolphe, one of two haint servants standing nearby, when Cat chanced past, returning from a quest to talk with the chef about Esme's diet. "You can help," she said, grabbing Cat's arm. "I want to see Fata Narcisse but her people keep insisting I be shown to my room and allowed to freshen up first. Believe me, this is as fresh as I get! Well?"

"She's in the fernery," Cat said. "I'll take you there."

"Please allow me to show you the way," Queenie, who was the second haint, said after a nod from the butler. "It shifts location unpredictably at this time of year. You'll never find it on your own."

The fernery was currently situated as far from the main entrance as was possible without actually being part of the ring of buildings walling the compound. As they passed through a copse of metasequoias, Grimalka said, "I won't be staying long. Three days, tops. Just came to pay my respects. Also, there's a lot of paperwork to be done. Death benefits. The banshees, cairn, and bonfire to be arranged. It's a dreadful nuisance. But the railroad takes care of its own."

"Death benefits?"

Grimalka peered closely at Cat's face. "She hasn't told you, has she?"

Almost, Cat said, "Told me what?" But the import of Grimalka's words was inescapable. A great sadness filled her. "But she looks so healthy."

"Glamour and misdirection. I doubt she's been playing a lot of tennis lately. Have you had sex with her yet?"

"What? No!"

"A pity. She's not likely to have a good enough day for it this late in the process."

"She has sex all the time. Two orgies a week!"

"Ever attended one?"

"Well, of course not. I go into town specifically to avoid them."

"There are no orgies," Queenie said. "The mistress only told you there were so you wouldn't be present during the medical treatments. She's known for her thoughtfulness in such matters." Then, with a flash of impertinence, "Now that you know, she'll expect you to praise her for that."

"The treatments aren't exactly dignified," Grimalka explained. "Small wonder she shunts you out of the way."

"Oh." Cat thought of how Narcisse always seemed to be elegantly languid these days. Not at all the briskly efficient officer she had been when they met. "What's wrong with her?"

"Cancer, of course. An elf-lady can't expect to go crawling around inside a big chunk of cold iron like a locomotive without consequences."

"This is crazy. She said she was a quintroon—that she was immune."

"White lies. She needed your assistance and she did what was required to get it. Fata Narcisse is an officer and it was her duty. Everything else is tangential." Grimalka fell silent.

"Here it is," said Queenie. She winked and faded away.

❊

Cat and Grimalka clambered down the brass stairs into the glass-domed rock garden that was the fernery. The air was hot and as humid as a sauna. Condensate dripped from panes over-head to ferns that drooped to deposit the drops into narrow rivulets that fed into koi-filled pools of water. Turquoise-colored lizards flicked away at their approach.

Fata Narcisse put down a book. "How delightful to see you, Grimalka."

"Grimalka told me you were sick. Oh, Narcisse! Why did you keep it a secret from me?"

Narcisse's laughter was like wind chimes in a light breeze. "What dark fantasies have you been spinning for my naïve little sister? You must be particularly careful with her; she'll believe almost anything. Cat, listen to me. Yes, I'm ill. I have a touch of the marthambles, nothing more. I'll be fine in no time. Grimalka believes what she says—but her pessimism magnifies the smallest misfortune into a disaster."

"Whichever of us is lying, we still have business to trans-act," Grimalka said.

"That's true. Cat, my sweet, you'll excuse us?"

Trudging away from the fernery, Cat hardly noticed when Queenie materialized alongside her. Almost to herself, she said, "I don't know what to believe. I mean, I know what I want to be true. But 'want and care won't take you anywhere,' right?" It was an adage that Nettie used to say, back when she was a girl.

"The mistress tries to please all. It's in her nature. That is all."

"I can't trust her, can I?"

"Ma'am?"

"She's an elf-bitch. I've known too many of them. They can be so sweet they'll make your teeth ache, but they'll turn on you at the drop of a leaf. I genuinely care for Fata Narcisse. It's even possible that, to a degree, I love her as I imagine one might love a sister. But Narcisse is an elf-lady of high degree. I dare not trust her."

"Her Ladyship is twisty, 'tis true. You want to turn left here. The way you came no longer leads back, but goes to the laundry."

"Twisty how?"

Queenie thought. "Fickle, mostly. And quick to wrath, if you work for her. I've lost track of how many times she's scourged me. But mostly fickle. You'll see."

With which words, she faded away.

⚹⚹

The night market was bright with strings of fairy lights, yet its booths were filled with shadows and mystery. It smelled of canvas and cotton candy and the sweaty crowds that coursed noisily through it. The flagstones glowed gently underfoot. One booth was piled high with bamboo cages filled with pedigreed bats. Another held the tattered remnants of dreams hung from clotheslines. A luminous goldfish swam past Cat then darted back to join a dozen of its kind circling a silent smiling-mask-faced gorojumo. In the next booth, a barker held up a handful of uncooked spaghetti which went limp when he tapped it with a polished stick, then hard when he tapped it again, then limp, then hard, back and forth as he cried, "Wonder Wand—makes hard things soft and soft things hard! Yes, it *will* do what you're thinking!" Beside him, a barrel of brightly banded snakes, glitter-eyed and straight as rods, was labeled WALKING CANES.

Some vendors had faces bright as incandescent bulbs, while others were holes punched in the darkness, each according to type and inclination. All beckoned or shouted:

"Hawt dogs! Getcher red hawts! Eight hours of visions and drooling idiocy guaranteed."

"Teeth, teeth, teeth! Top prices paid for teeth!"

"New eyes for old! New eyes for old!"

From a tent stacked high with books, "Getcher grammar now! Think straight and reason well! Turbocharge your sex life! Diagram sentences! Getcher grammar now!"

"Drown a cat! Change your luck!"

"Roasted chestnuts here!"

A beautiful young man caught Cat's eye and smiled. "Lonely?" he asked in a kindly voice. "I can take care of that." He was wearing only a silly pair of green shorts, but he filled them well.

A hobgoblin with a pince-nez, a sharp-toothed grimace, and three pairs of eyes popped up alongside the young man and, as if reading Cat's mind, cried, "Yes! You *can* peel off his shorts with your teeth! No extra charge!"

Ysault was staring at the young man with undisguised lust. "I'd like to . . ." Her voice dwindled and trailed off.

The hob grinned nastily. "That'll cost you extra, toots. Oh, but Neddie-boy here is worth it. He'll do things the others won't. One silver moon for an hour, a golden sun for the night. For twice the amount, he'll take on all three of you at once. Wriggle salaciously for the ladies, Ned."

The youth danced, not well but alluringly. Something clanked as he did, drawing Cat's eyes downward. She saw that one leg was shackled to a metal ring in the street. "Don't you worry," the hob cried, "the chain, as you can see, in no way impedes his movements. And it's long enough to stretch all the way to paradise!" A cane appeared, blinking, in his hand. With it, he drew back the canvas to reveal an inner compartment containing a bedframe with a stained mattress and no sheets, a single chair, and nothing else. A wink traveled down his eyes, top right to middle left to bottom right. The hobgoblin leered. "So, ladies, how long and how many?"

Sibyl thrust a single bill into the hob's hand. "We're just passing through," she said and plunged into the rear compartment.

"I'll be back later," Ysault called over her shoulder, hurrying after her.

Cat had no choice but to follow, brushing past the near-naked young man. She stumbled against him in doing so, feeling briefly the warmth of his flesh and its sweat-dampness too, and tried hard not to think about either of those sensations as he steadied her with one hand and released her almost immediately.

Then Cat had passed through the tent entirely and was outside again, at the back of the night market, in a dark garbage-strewn alley. Laughing, she and Ysault and Sibyl burst out into a street lit only by the stars and moons and an occasional red lamp.

✻

"This is it," Ysault said and brought them to a stop before a nondescript door. Faded signs to either side read:

TEATRO de TRASCENDENCIA   TEATRO de DISGUSTO
ECSTASY!   PAIN!
BEAUTY!   HUMILIATION!
ART!   TRUTH!

In a wrought-iron cage hung over the door was a blinded cockatrice. As they passed beneath it, the creature flapped its featherless wings and screamed. A drop of spittle fell onto the back of Cat's hand and left a stinging red mark.

"What'll it be?" asked a reed-skinny, tree-brown crone lurking behind the door.

"Transcendence," said Ysault.

"Cheap bints." The crone counted out three tickets.

Money rustled. A dismissive wave sent them down a narrow corridor to an elevator. Its doors clashed shut and they descended, the car clattering and lurching alarmingly. It jolted to a stop and opened into a dimly lit nightclub with carpets that might once have flown nailed to the walls, hookahs and vape pipes scattered decoratively about, ceiling fans that circled ineffectually overhead, a narrow stage to the front, and next to that a three-piece band playing music nobody listened to. There was what looked to be a stripper pole on the stage, and the floor was tacky underfoot. The place smelled of cheap beer and cigar smoke.

"Are you sure this is the right theater?" Cat asked.

"There's only the one. You pay different amounts depending on what your expectations are and how badly you want to be disappointed," Ysault explained.

The club was just beginning to fill up, so they had no trouble finding a table toward the front. As they were sitting down, Cat said, "Wait. That looks like Enya over there. Waving. And are those two with her Brianna and Rosaleen?"

"They made it!" Ysault said. "I was afraid they wouldn't."

"Took their time," said Sibyl.

They pulled together three tables so all six could sit together. This drew the attention of a gaunt waitress, who took their orders and slapped down a book of matches. Cat lit the candles in their red glass sconces to give herself time to think. Then she said, "So these are who you wanted me to hear, right?"

Ysault giggled and shook her head.

"Hardly," Sibyl said.

"Then why are you here?" Cat asked the newcomers. They stared at her with eyes as bright and unblinking as those of cats for a very long time without speaking.

"We escaped," Enya said at last. "It took us many long and miserable years, but we secretly built the frames for gliders in the machine shop—it helped that the screws believed escape was impossible and weren't at all vigilant—and covered the wings with toad silk from creatures that we hybridized ourselves and fed with table scraps and coffee grounds."

"It was night when we launched ourselves into the sky from the battlements of Glass Mountain," Rosaleen said. "Oh, but the wind was bitter! It made my face ache and my fingers and toes numb. But I never welcomed cold so much as I did then!"

"Unfortunately, time is wonky in Glass Mountain," Brianna continued. "Maybe you've heard that? All those years were but a day on the outside. We timed our escape as closely as we could, hoping to launch at midnight. But just as we were leaping into the air, the moon lurched backward in the sky and the sun rose up from the western horizon. Saoirse immediately saw what that meant and shouted that none of us must look back. But I was the last and too far behind to hear. So I glanced over my shoulder for one last look at the place I hated more than anywhere else in my life—just as the sun's rays hit the glass and shattered.

"I was blinded. In that instant I knew for a fact that I was doomed. But Saoirse circled around, averting her eyes from the dazzling mountain of light, and, flying by my side, shouted commands. Devoid of vision, I could only rely on her directions. And she brought me safe to land on the far side of the water."

"But . . . Ysault and Sibyl said you'd climbed down the mountain," Cat objected.

"Climbed? Hah! Have you ever seen what the slopes look like? You'd be ripped to shreds before you got three yards."

There was a drumroll.

"No more chitchat," Ysault said. "The show's about to begin."

With a fanfare from the bugler and a comic slide-whistle sound effect from the utility player, the emcee slid down the chrome pole onto the stage. He wore a shaman's loose trousers and tunic and a horse's skull for a mask. Grabbing the microphone stand with a *squeal* of feedback, he cried, "Are you ready to be enlightened? Are you?" The audience applauded and the emcee gestured for more and more before holding up both hands for silence. Then, solemnly, he said, "Existence is the sigh of an oppressed slave, a tedious and meaningless joke whose only constant is loss and whose only consolation is that every minute brings us sixty seconds closer to oblivion."

The emcee leaped into the air, slapping his knee and clicking his heels, and laughed like a loon. "But we're not going to let that bother us tonight, are we? No! Later on, we're going to have a *soprano sfogato* who will thrill you with the otherworldly refinement of her voice. And after that, we have a special surprise guest who will perform an act you'll be talking about for the rest of your lives! But now, let's get the evening rolling with . . . Misery! Nihilism! and Revolution! Put your hands together for the Anonymous Everyhaint!"

The haint who walked on stage wore shapeless work clothes and a simple white mask. She took the microphone and turned her head to cough into her hand.

Then she spoke:

"I am the only survivor of a litter of eight. I don't use the term *family* because we lived like animals. There wasn't always food. We fought each other for what little there was. I learned nothing in school—it was just a way of keeping young haints out of the way during business hours, so far as I could see. My mother worked three jobs when she could get them, and begged in the street when she could not . . ."

There was a rustling of chairs being drawn up and a familiar scraping sound. Cat turned away from the stage to see three more pilots—Fiona, Meryl, and Bridget—pulling tables together.

When they were seated, they all looked at Cat. Not a one of them blinked.

"Okay," Cat said, more to herself than anyone else. "This is getting creepy."

"Aren't you glad to see us?" Bridget asked.

"You should at least pretend to be glad to see us," Meryl said.

"You haven't asked how we escaped," Fiona said in an accusing tone of voice.

Leaning forward, as if she were sharing a great confidence, Meryl said, "Glass Mountain is very, very small and made entirely out of mirrors. The prison is a flaw within a faceted diamond set into a pinky ring worn by the Year Eater. Not many people know that. They place you inside Glass Mountain and you wander forever, lost in the light, always coming upon yourself and everyone else imprisoned there."

"But distorted," Bridget said. "So you never know if that's really you or really them or maybe it's you and them combined. Time is crazy in Glass Mountain. I spent a lifetime in a looking glass on the warden's makeup table. After you've been there for a few millennia, you forget who you are. That's why nobody escapes—who would want to go to all that work and trouble to break out someone who might be a complete stranger? You'd be walking the streets a free woman and suddenly realize that you weren't who you thought you were and that you'd left yourself behind in Glass Mountain."

"But then Saoirse came for us," Fiona said. "She was filled with darkness, so that her coming was like a solar eclipse at high noon! She gathered us together and explained that if we all escaped, that would surely include each individual one of us. I wasn't sold at first, but then I glanced down at my hand and saw it wrinkle, shrivel, and turn gray. I wriggled my fingers and the dust that had been my flesh fell from the bones and sifted to the ground. That showed me that time wasn't on our side." She giggled. "So I—whoever I was—followed her out, only a little worse for the wear."

"Nobody comes out of Glass Mountain entirely sane," Meryl said.

They all stared at Cat, silent as stone.

Why are you all looking at me? Cat wanted to say. Why is no one blinking? Caution, however, told her not to ask. Behind her, she could hear the haint, still speaking. The audience was laughing now, though nothing she said seemed to Cat in the least bit funny.

"I pick up their used condoms, mop up their vomit, bury the corpses they leave behind. The high-elven think they're so virtuous their shit doesn't stink. Yet there is not a night goes by in which I do not dream of killing them all in their sleep. My mistress flaunts her ugly, pasty white flesh before me and never asks whether I want to see it or not—and her adopted sister is just as bad. Their grotesque girl-child kills frogs and raids the kitchen at all hours, and we have to pretend we don't hate her as well . . ."

Cat's blood ran cold.

"No one ever asked me what I wanted. So I'm telling you now. I don't want justice—I want revenge! I don't want reform—I want blood! I don't want a kinder, gentler society—I want fire! I want to burn down this city and run barefoot through its streets, killing every one of you. Every one of you! Every one of you! Every one of you!" Her voice rose higher with each repetition until she was screaming: "Die! Fuck you! Die!"

Then all the room was on their feet, clapping and cheering and laughing at the same time, wolf-boys howling and bird-girls chirping as they hopped excitedly up and down. The emcee came bounding on stage, exaggeratedly applauding as well.

The haint started offstage, then turned around, came back to the microphone, and, looking straight at Cat, said, "At least one person here knows what I mean."

Then she was gone.

The emcee reclaimed the microphone stand, leaning into it as if they two were dancing. "Wuzznat fabulous? The Anonymous Everyhaint, friends—the Conscience of Avernus! Now, I'm sure you're all as avid as I am to set the city ablaze and get the looting and slaughter started. But before you do, laydeezangentz, you'll want to hear our main act—Innocent Jenny! So pure is she, so simple, so delightfully without any thoughts or desires of her own that the music of the spheres flows right through her—into her gut, up to her chest, and out her otherwise silent mouth. And now she's here to share that wunnerful, wunnerful gift with us!"

The creature that stumbled onto the stage was a rusalka, perhaps, or a nymph, or a hulder, or possibly even one of the Tylwyth Teg. But her face was blank and without personality, and from the way she was prodded and pushed by a pair of baton-wielding black dwarves, it was clear she had little or no volition of her own. She was one of those unfortunates born without a soul and never used for a changeling. Her gown was brilliant cerulean.

"Now, in order to sing with full effect, Jenny must be *completely unencumbered!*" The emcee's horse-skull mask jerked lecherously. "If you know what I mean. And I know you do. Gents, if you will . . ."

The black dwarves rapidly unbuttoned the gown, leaving Innocent Jenny clad only in plain white panties and brassiere. Her lower body was covered with bruises and her flesh looked slack and loose from lack of exercise. Nevertheless, the audience hooted and clapped.

"Now," the emcee commanded. "Sing!"

Innocent Jenny shook out her hair, all the while staring cow-like directly in front of her. A glow blossomed from within her flesh and rapidly grew until she blazed with the sacred light of the *awen*. Extending one arm gracefully, she sang in impossibly pure tones:

> *"My fingers are long and beautiful,*
> *as, it has been well documented,*
> *are various other parts of my body;*
> *If they're small, something else must be small . . .*
> *The beauty of me is that I'm very rich."*

There was that rustling sound again. Cat wrenched her attention from the singer and, to her complete lack of surprise, saw that Maeve, Deirdre, and Ashling had joined the group. Now all of the female dragon pilots, save only Saoirse, were assembled. "It's just like old times," Cat muttered. She was thinking specifically of the trial they had all put her through, and wondering what they had in mind for her now. Turning to Ysault and Sibyl, she added, "I was good to you guys."

"You were gracious and condescending and you gave us money," Ysault replied. "That's not the same thing. We despised you for it."

"Now you know," Sibyl said.

Cat twisted around in her seat, looking for a way out. But the room was crowded and every table was full and packed together too tightly for anyone to pass. Though somehow, the latest three arrivals had managed it.

When she turned back to the table, none of them were listening to the singer.

All were staring at Cat. Like wolves.

"I guarantee you there's no problem,
I guarantee. I am much more humble
than you would understand
and it is always good to be underestimated—
The beauty of me is that I'm very rich."

Ashling looked Cat in the eye and said, "Do you have something to ask me?"

"Oh, for pity's sake. All right, I'll ask. How did you get out of Glass Mountain?"

"Fool!" Ashling's face was cold and hard. "Nobody gets out of Glass Mountain."

"Alive," Deirdre said.

"Nobody gets out of Glass Mountain alive," Maeve said harshly. "Am I right, girls?" Murmurs of agreement circled the tables. "You know I'm right."

Suspicions that had been building for some time now came together inside Cat. Ysault was sitting closest to her, so Cat grabbed her hand.

Her fingers went right through as if there were nothing there.

The other pilots shimmered in the gloom. How could she not have recognized they were wraiths? How could it have eluded her that neither Sibyl nor Ysault ever touched her? That when they met for drinks, though they pretended to sip from them, their glasses were still full when everyone left the table?

"I will build a great wall.
Nobody builds walls better than me,
I will build a great, great wall,
Mark my words:
The beauty of me is that I'm very rich."

The wraiths that had once been her friends, and later her persecutors, continued to stare at Cat. Nobody moved. They were obviously waiting for something.

Then the singing was done and applauded and Innocent Jenny had been prodded back into the wings. The emcee, who had earlier been restless as a flea, stood stiff and motionless. "And now for our pièce de résistance, our coup de théâtre, the ceremony that is the delight of kings and the entertainment of the rabble—performed tonight only! and never again. The pomp . . . the ceremony . . . the majesty of . . . *Ritual! Virgin! Sacrifice!*"

The drummer hit a rimshot. Cat looked frantically for a way out. "I've got to go to the ladies' room," she said.

"Too late for that," Ashling replied.

The emcee was gesturing someone onstage. Flashing a dazzling smile, Saoirse strutted across the boards, waving with her left hand to one side of the crowd and then with her right to the other half, as if she were a celebrity they should all recognize. She was too solid to be a wraith, though her face was powdered white as bone. Wrapping both hands lovingly around the microphone, she brought it to her blood-red rips. "Thank you, maestro. You are so very, very kind." Saoirse was wearing her Dragon Corps dress blues and that, more than anything else, made Cat hate her.

"Let's start by introducing tonight's star, the victim herself—the notorious dragon slayer, Captain Caitlin of House Sans Merci! Can you stand up, officer?"

Cat stood. Shouting over the applause, she swept a hand toward the other pilots. "You killed them, didn't you? Admit it."

"I cut a deal." (To her side, Cat heard Sibyl say, "Told you.") "Twelve lives for my freedom, complete exoneration, and

restoration of rank. Eleven of those lives were already in
Glass Mountain. They weren't going to get out alive anyway. So
I sacrificed them, blocked their way to the Black Stone, and set
them loose. Knowing they would thread the labyrinth of Europa and find you."

"We're both officers. I claim the right—"

"Hold that thought," Saoirse said. "I have a question for your
little chums first." She pointed at Cat and directed her question
at Ysault. "Is she still a virgin?" Saoirse shouted. Mingled laughter and jeers rose up from the audience. "Is she?"

"Really-o and truly-o!" Ysault shouted back. "We had a long
talk about sex and it was obvious she didn't know what she was
talking about."

"Innocent as shit!" Sibyl amplified.

"You should have seen the way she looked at this slave boy
in the market! Like a spayed queen staring at a hot young tom.
She knew she wanted to do something with him but she hadn't
the least idea what," Ysault said.

The audience roared.

"Then bring her up!" Saoirse cried.

The pilots were on their feet, swarming about Cat. Now
their hands were solid and corpse-cold, gripping her arms,
seizing her legs, pinching her and grabbing at her face as they
ran over the tables and chairs and diners. Spitting and cursing, she was brought onto the stage. Ashling and Brianna ran
offstage and back again, rolling an X-shaped wooden cross
before them. It had leather cuffs near the tops and bottoms of
the beams and had been decorated with plastic vines and
swirls of gold glitter. It was the tackiest imaginable item on
which to die. "Don't bother stripping her," Saoirse commanded.
"The Goddess doesn't care about clothing. Just lash her to the
cross."

In a trice it was done.

"Now," Saoirse said to Cat. "You had some sort of request or demand, I believe?"

"I am an officer in Her Absent Majesty's Dragon Corps. I demand that we settle this by single combat."

A small, sneering smile played on Saoirse's lips. "Always thinking of yourself, aren't you? Never of your fellow officers, your classmates, your dog-sisters. Denied rebirth. Doomed to wander Faerie until your death completes the geas I placed upon them. Did you for an instant consider their welfare? I don't think so. So no trial by combat! No hearings, no hesitations, no special pleading, no fussing about with facts. That was our mistake the last time. Tonight I'll simply kill you." A commando knife appeared in her hand.

Beyond Saoirse, Cat saw the audience. From the stage, it was a single, hundred-headed creature: fanged, clawed, reptilian, lupine, avian, with pig snouts and fox ears and leather wings and ivory tusks. All yearning for her blood.

"Regrettably, this will be fast," Saoirse said. "But I'll savor it afterward." Her knife rose into the air.

Laughter cut through the silence. A billowing figure leaped out of the darkness and into the light, revealing himself to be the emcee. He removed his horse-skull mask and straightened to his full height. He flung off his tunic and stepped out of the baggy trousers. An extra pair of arms unfolded from his torso.

It was Counselor Edderkopp.

The audience was booing and clapping in equal measure. Somehow, without hurry or force, Edderkopp removed the combat knife from Saoirse's hand and used it to cut Cat's bonds. He helped her down from the cross.

"I don't understand," Cat said. "How can you possibly be here?"

"What kind of lawyer would I be," Edderkopp said, "if I didn't know when I was needed?" He spun about, producing a leather bag from out of nowhere. Holding the bag up in the air, he rattled it enticingly before the wraiths of the dragon pilots.

"Hear that sound? Eh? Eh? Eh? Oh, I know you want it as you know I know and I know you do. It's full of copper pennies. Not those nasty copper-clad zinc disks but real red copper, bright and shiny. Copper! You can taste it, can't you? And I have two of them reserved for nobody but you." Edderkopp advanced on the nearest wraith. "Would you like to have them? Both of them? Forever?"

Fiona closed her eyes and nodded.

"Then lie down. That's right, child. Right here on the stage. It's dirty, but don't mind that. This is a noble world and dirt is a noble material, the foundation of all we are and all we aspire to. From the dirt you arose, to the dirt now return." He placed pennies on her eyelids. "Doesn't that feel nice?"

But Fiona was already melting into the boards. Behind her, the other dead pilots crowded forward, arms outstretched.

"No need to rush! No need to grab! There's plenty for all. Lie down, lie down! I'll close your eyes for you and lay the cool, cool copper on their lids."

Dazed and confused as she was, Cat saw it all in a blur. Then Edderkopp had her hand and was leading her somewhere. Metal doors clashed open.

Counselor Edderkopp smiled in an almost-kindly manner. "Here's the elevator," he said. "I think you can find your way home from here."

⁂

That night, as Cat was drifting off to sleep, Helen said, "You want Saoirse to stop? Go to a bar. Smile. When a guy makes a joke, laugh at it. When he invites you to his place, go. It's that simple."

"I can't see myself doing that."

"Or you could just hand the chore over to me. I'd be glad to take care of it. In fact, I'd enjoy the hell out of it."

"You are a disgusting old woman."

"Yeah, but at least I had fun getting this way."

"In any case," Cat said, "Saoirse was lying about the other pilots being drawn to me. I figured out some time ago how I was being tracked, and that's not it."

Peace, peace! learn from my miseries and do not seek to increase your own.

—Mary Wollstonecraft Shelley,
Frankenstein, or the New Prometheus

AFTER AN UNEASY NIGHT OF TROUBLING DREAMS, CAT awoke to discover that Fata Narcisse was on her deathbed. Rodolphe, Josie, and Queenie watched patiently over her in shifts with a team of medical hags nearby, ready to dose her with morphine and tincture of kingsfoil should the pain grow too great. "I'm afraid I lied to you, my pet," she said to Cat. "Forgive me for being greedy. I merely wanted to enjoy your unpitying company a little longer."

Cat pressed her lips against Narcisse's hot forehead. "You're going to live, though," she said. "Tell me you're going to live."

With a flip of her hand, as if waving away a trifle, Narcisse said, "If you could see what is inside me, you would not ask me to tell such a lie."

Cat felt her lips go thin and hard. Without saying a word, she drew up the holey stone on its chain and held it to one eye. Seen through the stone, Narcisse's body was everywhere falling in upon itself. But lines of shimmering, multicolored light ran through her flesh like a sacred serpent, throwing off small, jewel-like suns in her brain and lungs and uterus. "It's so beautiful!" Cat said. For some reason, this made her angry. "Why is it so fucking beautiful?"

She did not need to ask why Narcisse's body, unglamoured, looked so ugly.

The bone-white, starveling-thin creature on the bed looked up at her from the blackened hollows of her eyes. "*Memento mori,*" Narcisse murmured. "It means 'remember to die.' It's on the list of things you have to do at least once. It comes last on the list, admittedly. But if you haven't died, then you haven't led a rich, full life yet." She had no hair, not even eyelashes. Her skin was mottled and blotched.

"Narcisse . . ."

"I'm being profound, darling. Don't step on my lines. I've led a very rich, very full life—I've had lovers and broken hearts and had my heart broken in turn. Nor have I been a stranger to hate. I killed someone who deserved it and another who didn't. Once I fought a duel and when my opponent had made her shot, fired into the air, sneering elegantly. I've smuggled drugs and I've saved lives. I've gambled everything I had on a single throw of the rune sticks. I was a spy for a time —but I can't tell you about *that*! Last and best of all, I found my passion in service to the railroad and now I'm dying in the proud knowledge that I did my duty by it. The only thing I lacked was a little sister . . . and the Goddess provided me with you just in the nick of time."

"Well, it's still a cruel trick for the Goddess to play on my heart."

"Mine as well, sweetness. Mine as well. But where do we go to complain?" Gray lips twisted in pain. "I . . . have something to ask you. But . . . right now, I think I need some painkiller."

Fata Narcisse began to weep. Looking away, Cat dropped her stone monocle back under her blouse.

⚹

When Narcisse had fallen into a drugged sleep, Cat left her in Josie's care and sought out Queenie. "I recognized your voice last night at the Blinded Cockatrice."

"We all have things that keep us going, ma'am. Once a week, I put on a mask and get up on stage and speak the truth. It's a harmless enough vice. Nobody takes it seriously."

"You talked about killing Esme in her sleep!"

"She has very little to fear. My list is long and she's not exactly high up on it. Anyway, who's to say the uprising will happen in our lifetimes? Not I. There are days I fear it will never come."

Queenie faded away.

⚹

Cat was half drowsing in a chair by Narcisse's bedside when Grimalka entered the room with a rush and a sudden stop. Nodding toward the sleeping elf-lady, she said, "How is she?"

"They tell me she's on her final decline."

"The idiots! I should have been called immediately. Have the soul surgeons arrived yet?"

"I didn't know they'd been summoned."

"I sent for them myself."

Rodolphe produced a chair and placed it near the bed, facing Cat's. Grimalka sat. "Has she told you what she wants from you yet?"

"I don't think she wants anything."

"I was abandoned in a scrapyard as an infant and raised by machines," Grimalka said. "As a result, I neither appreciate nor understand people the way I do mechanisms. The one exception is Narcisse, because she is cold and rational and predictable."

"To me, she seems the exact opposite of that."

"That is because you don't know her as I do. Even dying, Fata Narcisse wants something from you."

They were both silent for a time. Then Grimalka said, "You look awful. Go outside and get some air. We'll take turns sitting by her."

⁂

Loitering by a small stand of birches, thinking, Cat saw Queenie hurry by and disappear behind a boulder taller than herself. Curious, Cat followed a garden path around the boulder and discovered a door in its side. The door was unlocked, so she opened it. A stairway, carved into the stone and the bedrock beneath, wound down into darkness illuminated only occasionally by bare incandescent bulbs.

Closing the door behind her, Cat descended.

There was a landing every time the spiral came full circle and empty, shadow-filled corridors leading out to either side. But Cat could hear Queenie's footsteps tap-tap-tapping downward, so she continued on. Several gyres deeper, the stairway abruptly ended and Cat came stumbling to a halt at the sight of five haints, arms crossed and eyes hard. Queenie stood at the center of the line with Rodolphe beside her. Cat didn't recognize the others.

In imitation of those confronting her, Cat crossed her arms. "All right. You caught my attention and then popped into a doorway rather than simply disappearing the way you guys usually do. The door was unlatched and the lights left on so I could find my way. And you're here waiting for me. Obviously, this is something I was meant to do. So, you tell me: Why?"

"Arrogant above and insolent below. You don't get to ask questions here, girl." Queenie turned her back. "This way."

Cat followed her down a dim corridor. The other haints

walked alongside and behind her—as if an honor guard, though more likely to make sure she didn't bolt.

The hallway was dry, cool, and carved from solid stone. Its walls had been painted institutional green. There were doors at regular intervals. As they walked, Queenie said, "Do you know who first owned Avernus? Fire spirits. They built the city from molten rock. It had a different name then, one you could not pronounce. But with the waning of the Age of Fire, they retreated to the Empyrean, leaving what was renamed Mjibilandege, which means City Without Birds, to the smoke spirits—the haints, as you call us. Being surface creatures, we abandoned the undercity and constructed the buildings above. For a long time, all was well. Then the fey came with their armies to destroy our temples and kill nine-tenths of all who lived here, enslaving the rest. They gave the city its current name and today we are servants in what was rightly our home.

"That's eight thousand years of history condensed and put into a soup bowl for you. The truth is a little more complicated and a lot more horrific. Believe me, there's atrocity enough in the long version to justify anything we might do when the opportunity arises." Queenie stopped before a door. A haint unlocked it and flicked a switch to flood the interior with light.

Inside was a storeroom with neat piles of linens arranged on wood shelves, enough to serve the entire compound. The lower shelves on one wall had been removed to make room for what looked to be a coffin. Two of the haints removed the lid, and the smell of rose petals ascended from the interior. Cat saw that the coffin held a fresh-looking corpse in the browned and brittled remains of a white lace gown. The corpse had long red hair and cheeks that were ever so faintly blushed. So vital was the face that its eyes appeared to be ready to flutter open from the lightest of sleeps.

Save for the hair, it looked exactly like Narcisse.

"This is Echloë, Narcisse's twin sister and by right of six minutes' primogeniture the Syrinx of House Syrinx. Which honor and title, of course, have since passed to her younger sister."

"Six minutes!" Cat had known many primary and secondary heirs to great houses in her youth and seen the hatred and scorn they bore one another. "I don't have to ask what that did to their relationship."

"It would do you no good if you did," Queenie said. "We are bound by oaths of confidentiality never to reveal any details of the personal lives of our employers."

"There's no need to be so starchy," Rodolphe admonished her. "Courtesy costs us nothing." Then, to Cat, "Forgive her. She speaks for no one but herself. The issue at hand, however, is that we were ordered to place Echloë's body where it would be safe and never touch it again. Now it must be removed. You can see the quandary this puts us in. We require your assistance in carrying Echloë to the surface."

"This is so not in my line of command," Cat said. "Anyway, there must be commercial services for this sort of thing."

Queenie's face was hard and cold. "No service repairs a broken oath. Here's the deal. You have Narcisse's true name—don't ask how I know; those with servants have no secrets. It will work on Echloë. Use it to speak to her. If, afterward, you agree that what you have learned was worth the price, carry the corpse to the surface and leave it in the potting shed near the boulder."

Cat mulled over the offer. The price was high. But did she dare turn it down? "If I don't think it's worth it, I don't have to do a thing?"

"No. You'll be on your honor, however."

"What should I ask her?"

"We can't tell you that," Rodolphe said. "Just talk."

Controlling her revulsion, Cat knelt beside the coffin and

took a hand that was neither cold nor particularly warm in her own. In her thoughts she said, "Aerugo. Rust, dear. Speak to me."

A voice buzzed in her mind, too small and distant for Cat to make out the words.

"Can you speak louder? You sound awfully far away."

Again the voice sounded, right on the threshold of coherence. Cat closed her eyes and strove with all her might to make out the words.

The ground lurched beneath her.

Opening her eyes, Cat stood. She was no longer in the linen closet but, instead, in an airy pavilion with floor-to-ceiling windows to the front and curving cement walls to either side. Gray, wintry rain slanted down outside and lashed against the glass. Before her was the most oddly composed crowd Cat had ever seen. They took selfies and snapshots of each other in front of a cracked bronze bell hung so that it overtopped them all. There was not a single fey, dwarf, or haint or, indeed, any other ethnicity save only mortals.

"I know this place!" Helen cried. "This is in my world. I've been here."

"It is where I have been anchored and imprisoned," a flat, uninflected voice very much like that of sleepwalker said behind her. "As a joke, I suppose."

Cat turned. Half visible, like flesh turned to shadow, stood Echloë. Her face, so expressive on her corpse, was here lifeless, her expression drear. "I don't understand. Is this a temple? Are those people worshiping a bell?"

"That's the Liberty Bell," Helen said. "See the crack? It's a symbol of freedom throughout the world. When I was a child, I came here on a school trip. It . . . Oh, wait. I see. I get the joke now. Whoever chained her here must be real jerks."

"Yes," Echloë said. It did not escape Cat's attention that she could hear Helen.

Just then, a little girl went skittering out of the crowd, laughing and pursued by her mother. She ran full tilt through Echloë and should have slammed into Cat but kept on going until brought up short by a maternal hand clamped tight on her wrist. The mother bent low to scold her child in a fierce whisper, shaking her for emphasis.

"I'm not really here," Cat said, "am I?"

"No."

"I was told I should talk with you."

"Then talk."

Cripes, Cat thought. This wasn't going to be easy. "All right, tell me. Are you dead? Or living?"

"Dead but barred from rebirth."

"Oh," Cat said.

They were both silent for a long minute. Then Cat tried again. "Your sister is dying."

"What does she say about me?"

Cat tried to lie, discovered she could not. "She . . . never mentions you."

"Ah. She feels guilty, then. Good."

"Guilty? What for? Did she murder you?"

"Just the opposite. On my last day alive, she stopped me from killing myself."

"Okay," Cat said. "I didn't see that coming. Why don't you just tell me the whole story?"

"As you will," Echloë said.

"I woke up that morning filled with happiness because during my sleep I had found the solution to all my problems. I put on my best summer dress and had the most wonderful breakfast: fresh strawberries; a medley of blueberries, raspberries, blackberries, and currants; ripe mulberries in cream; clementines, mangoes, and apricots; a gooseberry torte; cloudberries and whipped cream rolled up in crepes; durian custard; slices of

apple and quince dipped in honey; pomegranate seeds by the
handful; baked Jonagolds and roasted Anjous; tangerine
and peach smoothies; stewed rhubarb, grapefruit, and plum;
dried and sweetened cranberries dusted with powdered sugar;
thin slices of muskmelon, watermelon, cantaloupe, Cren-
shaw melon, honeydew, sprite melon, winter melon, autumn
sweet . . . Oh, I ate like a pig! It felt so wonderful not to have to
think of my weight. Then, after a quick purge, a washup, and a
fresh dress, I went singing to the cherry orchard. It was spring
and the trees were all in blossom. My favorite location and my
favorite season. What better time and place to cut my wrists?

"I found a soft spot in the shade and plumped myself down.
There was an inchworm on the ground by me. I let it climb onto
the knife I had brought and, holding it up before my eyes,
watched it measure out the length of the blade. And then, with
surprising difficulty, I cut my wrist.

"Death by exsanguination is slower and messier than anyone warns you about beforehand. There is so much blood in the
body, and it drains so very slowly. I was half mad with boredom
by the time I drowsed off. Had I known, I would have brought
along a book. Not one of my favorites, obviously, the blood would
have ruined it. A paperback. At last, however, I slept. I remember thinking: Well, that's that.

"Only it was not. By slow degrees I became aware of a sharp,
repeated noise, then that it was the sound of one hand slapping
somebody's face, then that the person being slapped was me,
and finally that the person slapping me was Narcisse. When she
saw that I was conscious, she laughed for joy and kissed me on
the lips, saying, 'You cannot escape. We are too alike, you and
I, and I knew that you would try something like this.'

"Then, over her shoulder, she said, 'Do with her as you wish.'
And the soul surgeons and an official from the railroad lifted

me up and carried me off to the operating theater. I was as weak as a puppy from loss of blood. There was nothing I could do to resist them."

"Wait. Stop. Now I'm really confused," Cat said. "How did the soul surgeons get involved in this? Much less the railroad?"

"You honestly don't know? Then I must explain. In ancient times, you will recall, a sacrifice was buried alive under the foundations of a bridge or stone building to ensure that it would not collapse. Reinforced concrete and I-beam construction made this unnecessary for all but the largest projects. Even there, it's a redundant safety measure 'belt and suspenders,' as the engineers say.

"But the railroad maintains bridges between the three sister realms—Faerie, Aerth, and the Empyrean—and the space between worlds is so great as to render the strongest materials so much gossamer and moonlight. For these to hold up, sacrifices are required—and those sacrifices must be periodically replenished. It is the curse of House Syrinx that each lord or lady must be on call to be sacrificed as required."

"How did House Syrinx come to be cursed?" Cat asked.

"By right of honest purchase. We were a minor house looking to increase our standing. The railroad offered us wealth enough to do so—if we submitted to the curse."

"I see."

"One night, a vision came to me in the shape of a martlet, that footless bird that can never perch nor land. By this, I knew my doom was upon me as it had come before, first to my father and then to my mother. There was no evading it. But neither could I embrace its necessity. For three days, I struggled with this dilemma. Then I realized that if I died before the curse could be enforced, the title would pass to Narcisse, and not I but she would be sacrificed. I would cross the River Lethe and be reborn. She, meanwhile, would have her name, shadow, and self flensed from her flesh and anchored in one world while her body and its spark remained in the other.

"But she outwitted me. The surgeons did their work. The body that had been prepared for me in the forges of the flesh was, presumably, born without a soul and sent to the House of Glass. And here I am. Now you know all there is to tell."

"Your story is sad and moving and it gives me much to reflect upon," Cat said. "But why would Narcisse's servants have thought I needed to hear it?"

Echloë told her.

❊❊

"I see by your face that you have learned what is requisite," Rodolphe said. "We trust you to be true to your honor."

He and three of the remaining haints faded away, leaving only Queenie behind. She waited in silence while Cat wrestled Echloë's corpse from the coffin and onto her back, then said, "You can see the potting shed from the boulder. The door's never locked. I emptied out a shelf. Place the body there."

Cat staggered into the hall. Queenie followed, locked the door, and faded away.

The lights went out.

"Oh, you bitch," Cat muttered.

It was a long and wearying way to the stairs and up them to the surface and Cat cursed Queenie under her breath with every step of it.

❊❊

When the chore was done, Cat went to her rooms to change into clean clothes. Then she returned to the timelessness of Narcisse's deathwatch.

A mort of soul surgeons was waiting outside the door. They

were thin and albino-pale, and they all, male and female alike, wore white suits, white gloves, white top hats, and milk-glass spectacles. One by one—*pop! pop! pop! pop!*—they doffed hats to her, as if they were so many mechanical toys.

Cat swept past them without so much as a glance their way, recognizing her own rudeness but unable to resist giving in to it. When she entered the sickroom, Narcisse was saying, "—don't understand why you're being so obtuse. What I want from you, Grimalka, is simplicity itself: my name inscribed on the Wall of Martyrs. What's so difficult to understand about that?"

"I understand perfectly. You're hoping to be reborn with higher status than you have now. There aren't that many openings, you know."

"I am threefold bound to the railroad—by birth, by contract, and soon by death. I have earned my place on the Wall."

Looking thoughtful, Grimalka said, "Let me ask you this. When I put in for promotion, why didn't you write me a letter of recommendation?"

"Why, because there was nothing in it for me."

Grimalka's mouth twisted into what might conceivably have been a smile. "Just so. I shall require money. A great deal of it."

"There is a check on the end table. Pick it up and tell me if it is satisfactory."

Grimalka examined the check. Then she tore it in two and let the pieces flutter to the floor.

"Edderkopp said that might not be enough. There is another check in the drawer of the end table."

Grimalka opened the drawer. After a glance at the check, she folded it over once, placed it in a jacket pocket, and buttoned the pocket. "It will do. The entry is yours."

"Good." Narcisse turned to Cat. "Cat, darling, my mother and father are both long dead. I have no siblings. If I don't adopt, House Syrinx dies with me. And House Syrinx is all that keeps

Avernus from sinking into anarchy." She took Cat's hand and stroked it weakly. "My dear, sweet, precious Cat, I can think of no one more worthy of this honor than you. Counselor Edderkopp has drawn up the papers. I want to adopt you as my legal sister and heir. I want you to be the Syrinx of House Syrinx when I am dead and gone."

Cat felt as though she had been hit by a board. "I . . . I . . . can't."

Those dark eyes bored into Cat from the depths of their skull sockets. With the waning of her strength, the glamour was unable to entirely hide her sickly state. Yet there was not the least suggestion of pleading in Narcisse's voice. "You must."

Taking a deep breath, Cat said, "We will speak privately." With an imperceptible nod, Grimalka turned and left. The medical hags withdrew as well. Then, when Josie did not move, she said, "You know too much already. Go."

The haint faded away.

"I cannot accept your offer," Cat said. "I am a fugitive and a dragon slayer."

"The head of a great house is immune to all laws. Surely you know that already."

"I do. But . . ." Cat drew herself together and took a deep breath. "I was hoping to avoid this. I regret that I cannot."

"What are you talking about?"

"I have spoken with your sister, Echloë, and she told me everything."

Narcisse's eyes went wide with shock.

"You only wanted a sister so you could fob off the title and obligations of your house on me. Echloë is weakening and the railroad needs a new sacrifice to replace her. As the Syrinx of House Syrinx, you're it. Unless you can adopt some poor sucker, make her heir to your title, and then die before the soul surgeons get their claws into you.

"And here I, conveniently, am.

"But for your scheme to work, you need my signatures on those papers. And the signatures have to be freely made, don't they?"

The look of terror on Narcisse's face would have been heartbreaking under other circumstances. Now it served only to fuel Cat's wrath. "Thus ends your little scheme. The surgeons will separate your souls from your body, leaving only the spark within it. Your body will stay here, neither alive nor dead. Somewhere, the body that you would have been reincarnated within will be born without sentience. Possibly it will be taken to the House of Glass to serve as a host. Alternatively, it may simply be killed and discarded. All that matters is that you will take Echloë's place and she will be allowed to die."

"Little sister. You cannot be so cruel to me."

Cat discovered that she was shaking with anger. "That was the exact fate you planned for me. How is this any more cruel?"

"You would be raised in estate. Admittedly, it would take some time for you to benefit from it. But when you are, eventually, reborn . . ."

"My mother," Cat said, "is the Dowager Sans Merci of House Sans Merci, an old and noble family. By comparison, the line of House Syrinx is composed of upstarts and parvenus."

Horrified, Narcisse said, "Your mother is really Fata Sans Merci? You're not just shitting me, are you?"

"Dowager Sans Merci, actually. But yes."

"Oh, sweet Kernunnos. Sweet fucking Kernunnos. I owe allegiance to her."

"I am not entirely surprised. Mother seems to have a hand in everything. Which is why, darling Aerugo, I must charge you by your own true name never to speak of these matters to anybody else."

Fata Narcisse frowned, her voice fading. "You weren't quite

the little sister . . . I imagined you'd be. But maybe I was expecting . . . the wrong things."

The last words were almost inaudible. Having completed
them, Fata Narcisse closed her eyes with such finality that Cat
knew she would never open them again.

The door flew open and Grimalka hurried in, followed by so
many soul surgeons that Cat doubted they could all fit in the
room. "Have the papers been signed?" she asked.

"No," Cat said. "Nor will they ever be."

"Then you must leave immediately. The surgeons have a
great deal of work to do and some of it is going to get ugly."

"I'm as good as gone." Cat started out, then looked back at
Grimalka. "Aren't you coming?"

"I must stay and see the work is done properly," Grimalka
said. "The railroad takes care of its own."

⁂

Cat went outside to discover that night had fallen. The servants
had set out flambeaux along the paths in case anyone cared for
an evening stroll. She followed a line of them toward the knoll
at the center of the compound. As she passed by the potting
shed, there came from it a smell so foul that she almost
puked. Echloë's body, she presumed. Which meant that the
soul surgeons' work had begun.

Now she understood why the haints had been so eager to
have the corpse removed from their workspace.

At the top of the knoll, Cat stared up at the stars until they
swam in her vision. At last, having no one else to ask, she said,
"Helen . . . tell me. Did I do the right thing? Maybe I shouldn't
have confronted Narcisse. Should I have pretended to sign the
papers and let her slip away believing that I had been tricked
into taking over her title? Or would that have just made her

coming to awareness anchored to the Bell of Liberty that much more cruel?"

"Who? What? Me? I'm not the one you should be asking. I botched up every relationship I ever had. My parents. My friends. The marriage that didn't make it to three months." Helen grew thoughtful. "Now, though, I wonder if maybe that was a feature instead of a bug. Maybe the purpose of friends and family isn't for everything to go right all the time. God knows, I learned a lot from all those awful relationships. Did I ever tell you I was married three times? I was a slow learner, I suppose. Each marriage, hideous as it was, taught me new truths about myself and the nature of the world that . . . So maybe I was supposed to . . . There was this one time when Jeremy and I . . ."

She fell silent.

Cat did not feel she had the right to pry.

⁂

Esme was wearing her Hello Kitty knapsack with the gooly-doll peeking out of the top. Cat's heart quailed at the sight. No, not now, she thought. Not when I'm drained and sweaty and emotionally exhausted. But duty was as duty did. She let Esme reach up to take her hand and start to lead her away. "How much time do we have?"

"Dunno. Not much. Why do you ask questions all the time?"

With an inner smile, Cat replied, "Dunno."

At which very instant her cell phone rang. "Yes?" Cat said.

"Don't talk, just listen. It's Rabbit. I couldn't reach you any other way than this, wherever you are must be glamoured something fierce. Never mind that. The brass know where you are, and that's not the worst of it. The head of House Syrinx is dead and soon the compound will be visible to everyone. It's right in the middle of the poorest neighborhood in the city. That's where you are, isn't it? It all makes sense now. Listen. There's going to be riots. Don't bother to grab the witch-girl, just run."

"How did you know about Esme? No, forget that. I know how you know. I've figured out everything, Rabbit. How you contact me, how your superiors track me, everything."

Silence.

There comes a time to, as Counselor Edderkopp put it, clear the decks. On the spot, Cat decided that the moment had come to stop fooling around. Emptying her mind of all else, she cast her thoughts northward. "Rabbit," she commanded, "come to me."

So, of course, there he was, standing on the grass before her, shivering with fear.

"I can explain," he said.

"Shhh." Cat touched a finger to Rabbit's lips. "You're my shadow, of course. That's why the other pilots didn't remember you. That's why the brass were able to track me so easily. They just asked you. Didn't they?"

"Yes."

"Well, that's all over now." Cat opened her arms and stepped forward to embrace Rabbit.

For a long instant, she felt the warmth of his body, the hardness of his muscles, the terrified heart thumping within his chest. Then the closeness and solidity and rapid beating melted to nothing. When she opened her arms again, they were empty.

Cat was whole once more.

She didn't feel in any way different. But she supposed that was all to the good. Taking Esme's hand, she headed toward the gate.

⁂

At the guardhouse, the dwarf on duty touched two fingers to his cap and opened the gate for her. "Going out on foot?" he asked. "This might not be the night for it."

"I didn't feel I had the right to ask for a car," Cat replied. "Anyway, I'm not going far."

"Be careful, ma'am. The natives are restless tonight. If you know what I mean."

Then they were out on the street. The same seedy folk who had ignored the limo were staring hard at Esme and her. Somebody shouted something after them. Cat ignored it.

After a few blocks they came to the Greyhound station.

They went in.

A giantess crouched in the corner by the ticket booths, staring at an iPad resting in one palm. Two hummingirls played tag in the air overhead until a lutin, obviously responsible for them, scolded the pair back to the ground. Cat bought tickets on the next bus heading west and casually dropped her cell phone in a trash can. Then, leaving Esme on a seat with some comic books, she drifted to the windows.

This high up on the central tumulus, there was a good view of the inner slopes of the volcano walls. Looking out over Avernus, with its myriad windows burning bright, Cat was struck by the notion that if she could lift up the city, turn it upside down, and then shake it, enough misery would flow out to drown all the world.

Far off in the French Quarter, almost unnoticed, a fire suddenly appeared where a second ago had been a patch of darkness. Then, blocks away, more flames blossomed.

"Hey! Look!" somebody cried.

Passengers surged toward the windows, murmuring.

"Is it starting now?"

"Maybe it's just a fire. Fires happen."

The dispatcher cleared her throat into the microphone. *"Attention all passengers. The westbound coach is now leaving. Please board in an orderly fashion."*

✵

By the time the bus had pulled out of its bay and merged onto
the street, there were fires in at least three different sections
of the city. Dark masses of what might soon be rioters were
gathering here and there and when the bus drove past one, a
rock flew out to strike its side and everybody gasped. Then they
climbed the ramp to the Diamond Sutra Tubes and so left Avernus and emerged onto the Interbahn. The lip of the volcano
behind them was black and enigmatic as the bus disappeared
into the vastness of Europa.

Conspiracy: The pleasant fantasy that somebody, somewhere, has seized the reins of a universe that is self-evidently
mad, malignant, and completely out of control. (with apologies to Ambrose Bierce)

—*Helen V., notebooks*

IF THERE WAS A WORSE PLACE FOR AN EXHAUSTED WOMAN
to be than a crowded bus, Cat did not know of it. Every seat
was taken and the aisle was crammed with crates of piglets and
sphinx cubs and bundles of mandrake roots and a clutch of
migrant gnomes smoking hand-rolled cigarettes and making
snickering remarks in *Niederdeutsch* whenever something
female squeezed past them to use the toilet at the rear. Everybody seemed to be poor and tired. The seat beside her was more
than filled by a blubbergut goblin with curved ram's horns and
embarrassingly large breasts who shoved an elbow into Cat's
ribs, let her head loll onto Cat's shoulder, and promptly fell
asleep, snoring loudly and noisomely.

Cat, who was far too uncomfortable to drop off, envied the
lout and Esme, asleep on her lap, as well. As the bus hummed
down the midnight highway, Cat tried her best to ignore a growing catalog of discomforts: aching muscles, incipient headache,
uneasy stomach, bowels that threatened to send her past the
gnomes to an uncertain refuge in the rear . . .

Lighted buildings dwindled and disappeared from the

roadside. Once, on a long curve, Cat saw the black sides of the volcano behind them and the lights lining the roads descending from it. The interior glowed with a city's worth of electricity. For an instant, she fancied she saw flames, but no matter how hard she stared, she could not be sure. Then the highway swerved again, shunting Avernus firmly into the past. Trees flashed by the window and twin moons chased the bus through the summer night. Blearily, she watched them fade to nothing.

Then there was a bump and a lurch and Cat was awake again. The bus was pulling into a parking lot illuminated by tall light stanchions with harsh white LED lamps, so that it seemed to be a raft afloat in a sea of darkness. A low brick building squatted on the far end of the lot and the stink of refineries was in the air.

"Pit stop!" The driver threw open the doors. "Y'all got fifteen minutes."

⭐

The night was warm with sultry breezes, and Cat's head buzzed from insufficient sleep. A nation of tiny flying creatures filled the air between the tarmac and the lights with their myriad pale bodies. Only Cat was looking at them.

A young man with thick black hair combed straight back got off the bus, cigarette in hand, and said, "Hey, beautiful. Got a light?"

Cat dug out the book of matches she had used to light candle sconces what seemed like an eternity ago in the Blinded Cockatrice. "Keep them."

"Thanks. You're a real hero." The youth lit the cigarette, took a deep drag. Then he threw back his head, shaking out his hair and exhaling the smoke through both nostrils, and in that instant revealed herself to be undeniably female. She started to laugh, coughed, hacked, and recovered. "Oh sweet gods, but I love doing that! You should see your face. You look like a giraffe just popped out of your handbag."

"Very funny."

"It's just my way of breaking the ice." The young woman dropped the cigarette and ground it underfoot. "Name's Raven." She ruffled Esme's hair. "Hullo, monster. Remember me?"

"No."

"Of course not. How could you? You never remember anything, do you, Esme?" To Cat, the stranger said, "Thank you for taking care of her." With which words, Raven was for a second time transformed. She didn't look at all friendly or quirky or harmless anymore. She looked like trouble on the hoof.

Cat's stomach clenched. "You know Esme," she said as casually as she could manage.

"Well, of course. We're family. Esme's my great-great-something-great grandaunt. The genealogy is a little murky, I admit. It's been centuries since you sold yourself to the Year Eater, hasn't it, little grandmother? Or longer."

Esme shrugged. "Maybe. I forget."

"Aeons," Raven said. "Maybe more. Only the Goddess knows and she's not talking. Have you tried looking at Esme through the holey stone? She's a lot older than she appears. And she knows a lot more than you'd think. She may not remember people or events for very long, but she never forgets a skill. Plus, she's lucky—which is something you really need when you periodically find yourself in places like a hobo camp. It helps to have the knack of finding somebody to carry you away from it."

Cat stared hard at the young lady. Who, undaunted, grinned like a cockerel. "You know too much."

"Too much? Pfah! I'm a trickster. Secret knowledge is my stock-in-trade. Knowing things I shouldn't is in the job description. And the stone is kinda the reason I started this conversation with you in the first place." Talking fast, Raven

said, "Way I hear it, you've got a demon on your trail and she
has eleven bloodhounds that are drawn to your presence.
Wraiths can't be stopped. They don't tire. They're incorrupt-
ible. You can draw ahead of them for a few weeks, but they'll
always catch up. You don't dare stop running because if you do
you'll go to bed every night knowing they're a little closer to
you than they were that morning. What terror you'll feel! What
sleep will you get? You need my help. We have a common cause,
you and I: Keeping you alive."

"Esme," Cat said. "Get back on the bus."

"Can I have a candy bar first? I know how to jigger the machine."

"Just go back to our seat. I'll get you some candy and give it
to you in a minute." Cat watched Esme scamper back to the bus.
When the child was safely aboard, she said, "Okay, what's your
pitch?"

"There are plenty of cars on this lot, and I can talk any one
of them into letting us steal it. You want to sleep in a luxury hotel
tonight? It won't cost either of us a penny. Drinks, meals, spa,
and extravagant tips included. Male company if you want it.
More importantly, I can find anything and con anybody out of
whatever you want. I don't know what you're searching for, but
I do know that you're not just on the run—you're looking for
something. I can help you find it. All I want is the stone. In exchange, I'll make all your problems go away. Kapeesh?"

The station, Cat noted, was nearly empty. The last few passengers were drifting back to their seats. If she didn't hurry, the
bus—and Esme and her luggage—would leave without her. She
had to make up her mind fast. "You've got a deal." Cat spat in her
hand, Raven did likewise, and they shook. "I'll get my bag and
the kid. You can hit up the machine for a candy bar for her. She
likes Kit Kats. Or Mandrake Chews. Nothing with nuts, okay?"

"Understood."

Back in the bus, Cat dug through her duffel bag, keeping tabs on the station out of the corner of her eye. She saw Raven step out into the lot and light up another cigarette, head down and hands cupped against the wind. Cat found her clutch and emptied its contents into the bottom of the bag. Then she approached the driver. "How many passengers haven't gotten onto the bus?"

The driver stroked her tusks. "Except for your friend out there, you're the last."

"Good." Cat held up the Chanel clutch. "See this? It's not a knockoff. Worth a tidy bit in any flea market. Trust me, it will make your lady chums real jealous. It's yours if you leave my 'friend' behind."

The driver fingered the clutch inside and out. "Looks okay," she said at last. Then, "Lovers' quarrel?"

"Sure. Why not?"

"Then let's go." The driver put the bus into gear and stepped on the accelerator. Looking back, Cat saw Raven running after them, waving frantically as she dwindled to nothing.

"Where's my candy?" Esme asked.

Time either passed or it did not. Cat had no way of telling. All she knew was that she was brought awake again when a perfectly forgettable woman of no particular age, height, race, or species shook Cat's seatmate out of her stupor. "You," she said. "Leave." The mountain of goblin flesh stared at her in disbelief, half rose from her seat, raised a hand the size of a ham as if to strike down the woman . . . and then meekly obeyed.

The newcomer took the vacated seat. Staring past Cat and out the window, she said, "The world is still out there."

"Shouldn't it be?" Cat asked carefully.

"Now, yes. But someday it will be gone and then my long exile will be ended."

"Exile from where?"

"A better place. Back in the day, I played a minor role in the creation of the universe. I was a servant of the Demiurge—the Goddess's consort. He goes by the unlikely name of the Baldwynn now. But this was before there were names for individual things and we made do with functions. Oh, what a time that was! You have no idea what a rush it was to separate the light from the dark, the water from the land, gold from lead, sentience from inertia. I don't pretend I was of any particular importance. Our number was legion. Some of us were responsible for establishing the properties of gases, others for tectonics, thermal exchange, orbital mechanics, and so on. It sounds dull but it wasn't—just the opposite! I vividly remember the moment when we kindled the stars, setting into operation the forges in which the heavy elements would be created. Or the day we awakened the mountains and taught them to sing. Long, long ago that was and near infinite were our numbers. Yet of them all, only I do here remain."

Cat said nothing.

"Alas for me, I had a flicker of individuality, which expressed itself as something no one had ever had before me—a sense of humor. I was forever joking and japing. The pull-my-finger thing? I invented it. Not that anybody laughed, of course. The Baldwynn overheard my baffled coworkers gossiping about my strange behavior and took me aside for a private interview. 'I think,' he said at its end, 'that my creation needs something to give it a touch of unpredictability. Something that will render it just a smidge askew.' His voice was warm and all-encompassing. I was helpless before his gaze. 'See to it, will you?'

"'Lord Shaper,' I said, 'what possible improvement can I make on your work?'

"'I have confidence in you,' he replied.

"As you can well imagine, I was dreadfully flattered. I sat down and did nothing but think for several aeons. Until the funniest idea imaginable came to me. I would have leaped up and clicked my heels, if I'd had any heels and the gravitational constants had been put into place yet. So when the sequence of matters was exactly right, I made the smallest and most amusing possible change to the way things were, and settled back to await the praise I must surely receive.

"But the Baldwynn was not amused. When he saw what I had done, his eyes burned with outrage and continents went up in flame. On the spot, he condemned me with the worst punishment imaginable. Even as my compatriots were one by one flickering out, like sparks, he damned me with eternal life."

"That doesn't seem like much of a punishment."

"Nor did it to me—for the first billion years."

The woman took off her glasses, squinted at them, spat, and began cleaning the lenses with her thumbs. Cat took advantage of this distraction to draw out the holey stone and hold it up to her eye.

In place of the nondescript beside her was a black flake of night. Cold and starless it burned, a hole into nothingness. Its outline flapped noiselessly, as if in a silent wind. What might have been its head turned toward Cat. Crescent moons swam up out of nowhere to form a jagged, toothy, eyeless grin.

The stone fell from Cat's fingers. Once again, she was looking at an eminently forgettable woman.

The nonentity's voice was soft and mild. She might have been telling a bedtime story to a child. "This is the doom the Baldwynn declared for me: to wander unceasingly through a world I know far too well until the end of existence. But here's

the kicker. He could have undone my work but he did not. Long
have I contemplated that enigma and I have come to the conclusion that he wanted the deed done exactly as it was. Why,
then, did he punish me for it? Because he could. He is cruel, the
Baldwynn is. Don't make the mistake of underestimating that
aspect of him." Cold air washed off of the woman, though all the
rest of the bus was stiflingly hot. Cat found herself staring down
at her own feet, for fear of seeing that grin again. "You want to
know why I'm telling you this, don't you?"

Cat forced herself to look up. "I . . . yes, ma'am. If you please."

"It's because his stench is all over you, child. I could smell
it half a world away. Be wary, little mayfly, for the Baldwynn is
cunning and unforgiving and his ways are subtle beyond our
comprehension." She reached across Cat to yank the bell cord.
"I'll be getting off here."

The bus slowed to a stop. "But there's nothing out there."

"I won't be staying." The woman stood and started up the
aisle.

"Wait!" Cat cried after her. "I have to know: Why were you
punished? What was your offense?"

The nondescript woman turned and said, "When I created
the higher life-forms, I divided them into male and female." For
an instant all the universe surged up into a single hyperdense,
woman-shaped object, so that only Cat and the child she
clutched existed outside of her. Stars and galaxies exploded in
the darkness, burned to ash, dispersed into nothingness. Then
she was of mortal appearance once more. With a wry twist of her
mouth, she said, "My jokes were never very subtle."

When the bus came to its final stop, it was morning. Cat and
Esme got off. They passed through a station where the flower
shop and souvenir stands weren't open yet. Following the smell

of fresh coffee out onto the street, Cat saw a cheap-looking café with a badly neglected thatched roof turning green with moss. Above and beyond it loomed the ancient city-fortress of Carcassonne.

There were hippogriffs in the sky over Carcassonne and banners flying from the battlements. Barges and sailboats were anchored in the canal at its foot. Sometime during the long bus trip, the heat had broken and now there was the slightest hint of autumn in the air.

Esme clapped her hands at the sight. "Look!" she said. "Can we climb the walls?"

"Yes. Later. I promise."

All Cat knew of Carcassonne was that the Conspiracy had its headquarters there. So she bought a local newspaper and perused it at a sidewalk table over croissants and café crème. The news was slow and unremarkable but among the want ads she found a job opening for a clerk-typist position with the Conspiracy. Sipping thoughtfully at the lees of her coffee, Cat decided that—

Liquid noises made her look up from her paper. "Esme, stop blowing bubbles in your milk."

"But they gave me a straw."

"That doesn't make it right."

"I'm done anyway. Can I chase the pigeons?"

"Yes, so long as you don't disturb anybody's breakfast."

—it wouldn't hurt to get a glimpse of her persecutors. She could get a notion of how well funded they were, and whether the organization was at all efficiently run.

Mostly, though, she wanted to see at least one of the rat bastards who had ruined her life. If for no other reason than to give her hatred a face to focus on.

Cat rented a cheap room at the Hôtel de la Gare and was about to go apply for the job when Helen said, "In those clothes?"

"What's wrong with them?"

"Child. I was very briefly not exactly blacklisted but certainly persona non grata in the TV industry and to feed myself accepted a gig directing summer stock in the wastelands of Connecticut. Long story—let's skip it. At any rate, dealing with actors who could only by the loosest of definitions act, I discovered that the exact right costume could alert the audience to what the character was supposed to be like, and often enough that was sufficient. You've never worked in an office in your life. But at least you can look the part."

So, after a long nap and a late lunch, Cat went out and had her hair cut, dyed, and curled. More disguise than that she deemed unnecessary for a quick drop-in. Then she shopped for clothes. "You're not auditioning for *Les Miz,*" Helen said of one outfit, and "Nor *Downton Abbey*" of another, before approving a navy-blue skirt and blazer ensemble with the words, "Miss Moneypenny would approve."

"You're talking gibberish again," Cat remarked.

"I got that a lot in my old life, too."

The next morning, Cat went to the Conspiracy's headquarters on rue Saint-Jean to apply for the job.

The building's exterior was standard medieval stonework. But the lobby was so luxurious as to be a parody of itself. There were coral-pink pillars of polished porphyry, a stone floor with interlacing black granite asps set into sea-whorls of green jade, and a vaulted ceiling of lapis lazuli fretted with golden stars. A *Cyclopsus arges* skull rested in a vitrine to one side of the entrance, and a living Fiji mermaid swam endless circles in a crystal bowl to the other. The twiglady behind the receptionist's desk looked up so welcomingly at Cat's approach as to put her immediately on her guard. "Yes?"

"I'm here to apply for a job," Cat said, faking a confidence she did not feel.

"You poor thing." The twiglady slid a sheet of paper toward her. "Fill this out."

One temporary badge and a dull fantasy of her employment history committed to the application form later, "Kate Gallowglass" found herself sitting on a leatherette chair before the head of Employee Resources. He was a blue-eyed aristocrat in a bespoke suit and Royal Harlindon regimental tie who, she had to admit, couldn't have looked more desirable if he were in shackles and shorts. After a quick glance at her application he said, "Why do you want to work here, Ms. Gallowglass?"

"Money," Cat said.

"Excuse me?"

"Oh, I'm sorry. I misspoke myself. I meant to say that this would be a fabulous opportunity for me to express my talents, unleash my inner potential, spread my wings, drink from the fountain of wisdom, kneel before the lingam of the numinous, learn humility and discipline from the best and wisest, be the change that I want to see, and become something more than anything I could ever possibly be. Unfortunately, at this present time, what with food and rent and such, I require a salary. But rest assured, if ever I were to find myself as wealthy as you obviously are, I'd definitely be taking this job, with its utter lack of career potential and a management culture that is obviously both demanding and condescending, for no money at all. That's how highly I regard the position of File Clerk I. It's something of a dream job for me."

The interviewer stared at Cat. "Was that meant to be amusing?"

"If it were, I am almost certain you would have noticed."

Unexpectedly, the ER manager broke into laughter. Extending a beautifully manicured hand, he said, "You have the job. It is, as you implied, intellectual drudgery. But I am certain you have the inner resources to keep it in perspective. I am

Barquentine of House Pleiades. You may address me as Lord Pleiades before outsiders, or Barquentine in private situations, but never Barkers under any circumstances. That name is reserved for personal friends of a certain class and background. Do you understand?"

A little dazedly, Cat replied, "Completely, sir."

"Welcome aboard."

⁂

"You don't disapprove of my plan?" Cat asked.

"Hell, no. It's mad, impossible, sure to fail, and exactly the sort of thing I would have done at your age. Go for it!"

"Okay, now I'm worried. And my stomach hurts." Cat pulled up her pantyhose, smoothed down her skirt, and donned her flats. Now that she was in battle rattle, the prospect of going to work for her enemies no longer seemed a good idea. "Why am I putting myself in their clutches? Suppose they check my references?"

"Nobody ever checks your references until it's too late. My career arc took a steep upswing the day I realized that."

The day before, Cat had bought two costume jewelry bracelets and paid to have them quantum entangled. Now she placed the larger one on her own wrist and the smaller on Esme's. "Keep this on at all times. That way we'll always be able to feel where the other one is and I'll know that you're safe. I'm going to work now and it would be cruel to keep you locked inside all day. So here's some money for lunch. Stay within the city walls, and try not to kill anybody."

"You don't have to give me money," Esme said. "I know how to steal food without being caught."

"That's a useful thing to know. But humor me here, okay?"

"'Kay."

At work, Cat soon discovered the answer to her second ques-

tion: The Conspiracy was, organizationally, a complete and absolute shambles.

The hen-wife in charge of Clerical Services was a motherly
butterball of a trow named Lolly Underpool, who was extrava-
gantly protective of her "girls," not all of whom were female.
She in turn reported to Missy Argent, the chief of Clerical and
Data Entry, who was answerable to both Annable Frowst in the
Division of Corruption and Raguel in the Division of Persecution. These "dotted line bosses" owed allegiance to the officially nameless (though everyone knew who they were) Acting
Chief Conspirator and Temporary Head Conspirator, each of
whose undefined powers were tempered, they being unten-
ured, by oversight committees made up of different composi-
tions of division and department heads. Since Lolly Underpool
sat on both committees, she had acquired a great deal of in-
traoffice power and was in the enviable position of being able
to countermand any orders given her which she considered
impertinent.

The extreme pinnacle of the organizational chart was occupied by the Chief Conspiratorial Officer, who was, as Cat already
knew, her mother, the Dowager Sans Merci. In recent times,
however, her presence had proved to be as fugitive as that of Her
Absent Majesty, and the Conspiracy had effectively been left to
look after itself.

"We'll start you off on something simple," Lolly said. She
produced a tray with a lump of sugar, a brass key, an unsharp-
ened pencil, and a quartz crystal containing a small fossilized
frog. "Choose any item."

Cat picked up the key.

"Excellent! We've been needing to get started on that project
for some time. See that stack of boxes by the copier?" Water-
warped, brass-bound, and crusted with coral and barnacles,
they could hardly be missed. "That key fits one. The others,

you'll just have to break their locks. I want you to Xerox the documents you'll find within, shred the originals, assign each photocopy a document number—I'll requisition a sheaf of them—and then cross-index them by date, sender, and recipient. If Raguel tries to get you to interrupt your work to make photocopies for him, tell him he has to go through proper channels, and that means me. Got it?"

"Yes, ma'am. Only—I've never met Raguel. How will I know it's him?"

"He'll be the one trying to get you to interrupt your work so you can make photocopies for him. Any other questions?"

"Yes. That tray. Is that how all work is assigned here?"

"How do you think Lord Pleiades got his position? He saw the Mont Blanc pen and snatched it up before my hand was half-way to it. The weasel."

So Cat found the box that the key fit and took it back to the cubby she had been assigned. It turned out to contain bundles of documents wrapped in sealskin and tied up with leather straps that broke into bits when she tugged at them. Opening the first bundle, she saw that it was all business correspondence. So many bales of cotton received. So many barrels of wine shipped. The documents appeared to be extremely old and many were so stained that their Xeroxes were unreadable. But "It's Division policy and there's nothing to be done about it," Lolly said when she suggested that the originals of these be saved. "Shred them all." It took most of the day to copy everything— even without taking into account the many interruptions from Raguel, who periodically came glooming down, trailing darkness after him, with work he wanted her to do, and who seemed incapable of taking "Buzz off" for an answer.

Midway through the photocopying, Cat came upon a clutch of letters tied together with a velvet ribbon. She undid the ribbon, and a square of paper fell to the floor which, unfolded, revealed a lock of coal-black hair.

Puzzled, Cat read the first letter.

My beloved beast,

Too long has it been since I enjoyed the raging storms of your passion, the heave and swell of your body beneath me, the taste of salt on my tongue. Too long since I set sail on the frigate of your lust for the distant isles of the South.

You receive my letters. I know this because you answer them. But you cannot possibly believe what I write, for if you did you would be here with me now. How am I expected to live without you? You are as precious as Oceanus itself to me, as deserving of my love and devotion, and, alas, as capricious in your moods.

You ask me to tell you how I fill my days. I do not, I assure you, waste them languishing away after you. In the morning, I take my small skiff out upon the sea. This I do regardless of all but the most violent weather, for the ocean is life itself to me, even as you are. If the waters are clement, I throw aside my shift and dive deep, deep within them, so deep that at times I am close to strangling on the water and never coming up again. When the waves are wild, I exult in the danger. Then I return to the city and walk the seawall, examining it for weaknesses of all kinds, to make certain the harbor is safe from the tides and storm surges that menace it. In the afternoon, there are court cases to be held, petitions to be heard, ceremonies to be attended, sacred fires to be kept burning. I am a king's daughter. I know my duty and I do it well. In the evening, unless there is a formal banquet, I eat abstemiously, listen to musicians, watch dancers, marvel at jugglers. Or else I practice my calligraphy, write poems, read books. It is only the night that makes me weak with desire for you, but oh, how the nights are long!

You say that it is physically impossible for you to live with me. Then make it possible! You say it was a once in a lifetime confluence of moons and tides that enabled us to meet. Are you not your mother's son? Surely you have power enough to make the tides and moons converge again.

But now I pause and the anger leaves me. In this one thing only am I weak: I cannot scold you as I should. When will you return to my loving arms again?

With all my heart,

Dahut merc'h Gradlon

⁜

Every schoolchild knew the history of the ancient city of Ys. Conquered by the warlord Gradlon, corrupted by his daughter Dahut with orgies and licentious behavior, sunk beneath the waves when the key to its sea gates was stolen by Dahut and given to a demonic lover who seemed to have no name or identifiable personality. It was a tale particularly appealing to teenage goth girls. But faced with physical documents originating in the lost city, Cat had to, for the first time, question what she had been taught. Supposedly, a storm surge had inundated the city, destroying it, and that seemed reasonable enough to anybody who knew the ocean's power. But when the tides had ebbed, Ys had stayed submerged, and that made no sense at all.

Nor did Dahut sound like the sex-maddened wanton the chronicles made her out to be. Certainly, there was no mention of orgies in the letter. Only of her yearning for her lover. Whose identity remained unknown.

When Cat had Xeroxed the lot, instead of shredding the originals, she hid them behind the bottommost drawer of her desk. She would read them for entertainment. She could always destroy them later.

Evenings, Cat reunited with Esme. Sometimes they played board games. Other times they walked the battlements and tried to spot the canal serpents that reared their heads out of the waters at dusk and fed on rats and wharf pixies. Esme was endless fun. There were days when that was all that kept Cat sane. The work she did was varied and easy enough to perform, but the demands for her labor came from all directions and added up to far more time than she had to give them.

One week after she started work, Raguel filed a formal complaint against Cat for insubordination.

"That was fast," Annie Hedgewife said when the news got out. "Took me a month."

"I'm still waiting," Rackabite said, mock-dolorously. "Why does Kate get to skip ahead of me in line? I have seniority."

Letzpfenniger crawled out from under her desk with a stack of newly completed requisition forms. "She's cheerful is why. His kind feeds on misery. Metaphorically speaking, I mean. Literally, he feeds on blood and sawdust."

The clerical pool were located in the basement, where there were no windows and the walls were wet when it rained, and given modular cubbies rather than offices such as the Upstairs Crew (as they were known below) enjoyed. On the plus side, the stairway down was a great beast of Victorian metalwork that boomed and clanged with descending footsteps whenever anyone came down it, looking to impose work upon them. So they always had plenty of warning and, between visits, the freedom to gossip.

"Does he really? Sawdust? Why?" Cat asked.

Annie Hedgewife made her face go wide and bland. "No idea. Ask Istledown, she knows everything. Well, not what you had for lunch or where Her Absent Majesty is now. But facts about things, she knows them all. Just so long as they don't benefit her personally. That's part of the curse that was laid down on her."

"Curse?" Cat said. Istledown was a researcher and as such properly belonged in the Division of Corruption. But somehow—rumor had it that a poker game was involved—Lolly Underpool had gained ascendancy over her position and moved her to the basement, where she had an office—a small one, admittedly—entirely to herself. Now she could be accessed only with Lolly's near-unobtainable permission. "How did she get cursed?"

"It was part of the terms of her employment," Rackabite said.

My darling, my demon, my damnation, my dark destroyer,

I enclose a lock of my hair, as you requested. But why are you content to settle for so little when all of me is yours for the taking? When the tides are high and the winter storms hammer on the seawalls like a great fist, I imagine that thunderous sound is you coming for me at last. Yet it never is.

Daytimes, I do my devoir: talk with lawyers, disburse funds, walk through marketplaces eavesdropping on the mood and gossip of the people, hear the reports of the harbormasters, hold polite luncheons where I chat with grain merchants from the hinterlands, pale-skinned ambassadors from distant courts, mercenaries hoping to interest me in a war with our inoffensive neighbors . . . They all turn to faces in a dream the moment I look away, indistinct in an instant and forgotten soon thereafter. Only the nights seem real, for then I imagine you are there with me. I toss and turn until my skin glistens with sweat. By morning the sheets are damp and rumpled. The servants, seeing the aftermath, whisper that I have taken on an invisible lover. I laugh when my spies report this to me because the alternative is to weep, and if once I started weeping over you, I would never stop.

You villain! Your words are pretty and your sentiments all I could desire, but I would trade them all for a single hour sitting quietly in your presence. I curse you with every foul name I know. Come to me and you will be forgiven.

I have told you about the codex that a dealer in antiquities sold me and the solution I found within it. You respond that the price is too dear. It is not love that hoards coppers when it should be strewing golden suns and silver moons at my feet. Along with your worthless, desirable carcass, of course. Had I the Horn of Holmdel within my grasp, do not think that I would hesitate to steal it and to the Dark Lands with the consequences. Am I more man than you? Then seize the main chance and do what you must!

But now my hopes grow too high and I cannot breathe.

Yours only,

Dahut merc'h Gradlon

Cat was eating lunch—a cassoulet with a glass of wine—in Place Marcou when, as gracefully and silently as a shadow gliding across a wall, Lord Pleiades slid into the chair opposite her. "I thought it best we meet outside of work, where we won't be overheard," he said.

"Are we having an affair? Shouldn't there have been a memo?" Cat kept her voice light and amused, though inwardly she felt nothing of the sort.

"I've been noticing your work, Ms. Gallowglass."

"Oh, that's not good. Work should never come to the attention of the people who assume it somehow gets done all by itself. They're sure to do something unfortunate about it.

Mind if I keep eating? I don't want to be late getting back to the office."

"You are unfailingly punctual. Also diligent, hardworking, and competent. You don't mind it when your coworkers take credit for your work or your superiors for your ideas," Lord Barquentine said. "Even your posture is excellent! You can see why I am suspicious of you."

"I could slump a little, if you like."

"It is true that you are the exact opposite of deferential. However, that only makes you stand out all the more. You are the spitting image of an ambitious young woman on the make."

"Thank you, I think."

"It wasn't a compliment. You're too capable to be real. Where did you come from?"

"It's in my application. I was the secretary of a Teggish land baron. He started paying me late, on one pretext or another, until he owed me three months' salary. Then one day when I was on the edge of starvation, he gave me as much cash as I earned in a month and sent me to deposit it in the bank. It's an old, old scam. But instead of skipping town with a fraction of what I was owed, as I was expected to do, I went straight to the bank and deposited it. Then I wrote out a check for twenty times that amount from another of his accounts. Because the tellers knew me, and because I'd just deposited money, I had no trouble. Which is when I ran as fast and far as ever I could."

"So you had money. What happened to it?"

"I kept it safe. I told you I'd be working this job even if I were wealthy. I am and I will. But I still need to be paid—it's part of my cover."

"You're laughing at me."

"It's possible, I suppose."

"I note that your fictitious employer was not high-elven."

"Oh, now you're just borrowing trouble," Cat said. "Yes, I

spotted you as Teggish when I interviewed for the job. But there's nothing mysterious about that." The Tylwyth Teg were all arrivistes and social climbers. To one who knew the aristocracy intimately, they were easily spotted by their exaggerated pose of sophistication. "As tense as a Teg trying to look casual," her mother used to say. Not that she would throw away her job by telling Barquentine *that*. "It's your haircut. Sculpted to reveal that your ears are foliate but disguise the fact that they're falcate rather than lanceolate. I had a job in a beauty salon once, so I spotted that right away."

"Hmm." Barquentine stroked his chin, almost succeeding in smoothing down a small smile. "One last question, not that I expect to get a straight answer out of you. I'm sure you are aware that Raguel has filed a complaint against you. Mind telling me exactly what's behind that?"

"I'm no snitch," Cat said. "If you want an answer for that, you'll have to call Istledown into your office. She knows everything."

⋇

Clerical Services took up one full half of the basement, with the independent fiefdom of Shipping and Receiving and the exiled colony of Information Technology sharing the other. Istledown being Lolly Underpool's chief trophy, her office was in the corner farthest from the other departments, alongside Lolly's, where she would always be under the hen-wife's watchful eye. She never associated with the clerical pool, but occasionally she flitted through, on her way to the washroom or back from lunch.

On one such occasion, on impulse, Cat said, "Hey, Istledown, what is the Horn of Holmdel?"

Istledown stopped and fixed Cat with a hard stare. "It's a Class Four artifact and none of your business. How did you hear of it?"

"Oh, it was in one of the comic books my kid likes, and I kind of wondered," Cat lied. "That's all."

"Ah. Well. That's different." Istledown drew up a chair and began talking.

The Horn, she said, was a tool left over from the creation of the universe. Once, it had been wielded by one of the Demiurge's flunkies. To what purpose, none could say. There were few such artifacts remaining and, as such, its value was beyond calculation. Never mind that almost nobody knew how to use them anymore.

There was a chapbook, Istledown would lend it to her, that recorded some of the songs that could be played on the Horn and the effects these would have. Not that Cat was likely ever to see the Horn itself. There had only been eighteen confirmed sightings of it in all history, the first of which . . .

An hour later, Lolly came through, saw them, and said, "What's all this jabbering? Get back to your desks. We have work to do."

Gratefully, Cat did so. Later that day, however, Istledown dropped by her desk to lend her the chapbook—"I need it back this afternoon!"—which, as she hadn't time to memorize its contents, Cat was careful to Xerox before returning.

Just in case it turned out to be useful.

A clean and innocent conscience fears nothing.

—Queen Elizabeth I

A MONTH PASSED AND THE YEAR TURNED ON ITS HINGES into autumn. Posters for the Plague Carnival began to appear on walls throughout the city. Meanwhile, ensconced as she was within the metaphoric heart of the Conspiracy, Cat found her situation confining but comfortable. The clerical life was like a madhouse-mirror reflection of the Dragon Corps: The pay was small but adequate to her needs; she always knew what she was supposed to be doing and, thanks to Lolly, whom she had to obey and whom not; and there were objective metrics for how well she was performing her job. But where before she had flown between worlds, now she filed documents in triplicate.

In her cubby, Cat had hung up a map of Carcassonne. The city was in outline shaped rather like a hominid skull with protruding jaw and small braincase. Extending the fancy further, its streets curled like the simplified convolutions of a cartoon drawing of a brain. The Conspiracy she thought of as a tumor within that brain and she as a small black dot within that tumor seeking to undo its workings, a cancer within the cancer.

One morning, after fixing herself a cup of tea but before sitting down at her desk, Cat checked her mail slot and among the usual disposable memos found an unopened letter, so densely stuffed that it bulged and threatened to rip open at the seams, with the name and return address of the Dowager Sans Merci at the top left corner. It was addressed to:

TEMPORARY HEAD CONSPIRATOR

THE CONSPIRACY

7 RUE SAINT-JEAN

C. L. DE CARCASSONNE

For a long, still moment, Cat did not move. There were two obvious options here: To slip the thing into the THC's mail slot and pretend she had never seen it. Or to open it and read the contents.

Instead, she went upstairs to the Employee Resources office and walked in without knocking. Barquentine looked up in mild surprise. "Sir," Cat said, "somebody left a fishing hook with a fat, juicy worm impaled on it in my mail. I'm pretty sure this belongs to you."

She handed the letter to Lord Pleiades and returned to her desk.

Cat was just getting her morning chores sorted out when Lolly Underpool dropped an untidy mound of flimsies on her desk, saying, "Letzpfenniger screwed up the invoices and when I chewed her out, she started crying and crawled under her desk and barricaded herself there with boxes of old brochures. She won't come out, so these are all your responsibility now. I'll need them corrected, retyped, and sent out by this time tomorrow."

"Yes'm," Cat said.

· When Lolly was gone, Helen said, "Maybe it's time you left this job for greener pastures."

"I'm not a quitter."

"Maybe you should be."

"There are still things I hope to find out."

What had she learned so far? Surprisingly little. That the Conspiracy was badly organized she could see with her own two eyes. From unguarded comments made by her superiors, she knew that it nevertheless had tendrils everywhere in Faerie and that some of its operatives, distance limiting oversight, were surprisingly resourceful. That the Division of Corruption not only entangled powerful politicians and businesswomen in scandal but reaped the benefits of this through blackmail. That the Division of Persecution was a tremendous, if necessary, drain of resources. That the Conspiracy had a particular interest in the lost city of Ys (not, apparently, in its location but in its restoration, as unlikely as that seemed), as well as in the railroad, the Dragon Corps, and the changeling industry. That the Dowager had taken an active, though distant, role in overseeing its operations but had of late fallen inexplicably silent.

And that the Acting Chief Conspirator (Lady Jane Iron, though nobody was supposed to know that) had a paper thermometer outside her office, showing 87 percent progress toward some undefined objective, while the Temporary Head Conspirator (Ana Kashalyi, also blissfully ignorant of how universally known and despised she was) had a plaque on her door reading ONLY 843 DAYS TO MISSION OBJECTIVE. Some days that number went down; other days it went up. But on the whole, the number grew smaller, the colored-in parts of the thermometer higher, and "mission objective," whatever that might be, closer.

Cat was mentally assembling this catalog while running the copying machine one day when a haint materialized before her and said, "Lord Barky Bark wants to see you in his office. Stat."

"Oh, goody. How come nobody ever brings me pleasant news?"

"Just the messenger, toots. Whatever's between you and His High-and-Mightiness has nothing whatsoever to do with me. Not my dwarf. Not my fight."

※※

Hanging behind Lord Pleiades's desk were twin maps of Faerie and the sky above it, with ley lines marked on each. The sky lines were more familiar to Cat than the back of her hand, for they were the fastest routes a dragon could travel. The earth lines were less so. Whenever she came into Barquentine's office, she wondered if there were ley lines within the ocean as well, and if so why there were no maps of them. This time, however, she saw with a start that the maps had been taken down. In fact, all the personal items in the office were in cardboard boxes lined up against the wall. Had he been fired?

"Sit," Lord Pleiades said without looking up from a document. "Let me finish this page and my attention is all yours." After a bit, he put down his reading glasses with a sharp *click*. "Raguel has lost his position here."

"Imagine my dismay."

"There were any number of gaffes on his watch—he lost Rabbit *and* all twelve of the Glass Mountain revenants. And of course the dragon slayer is still at large." (Cat did her best to look like she had no idea what he was talking about but was trying to look like she understood every word.) "It was inevitable that his failures would catch up with him in the end. But it was you who pushed him over the edge."

"Me, sir?"

"Or, rather, your suggestion that I ask Istledown about him. I decided to do just that. It took a great deal of wrangling to get Underpool to agree to a supervised question-and-answer session, but I finally managed it. His harassment of you was a trifle—everyone here has done worse this week alone, I'm sure. But once Istledown started talking about Raguel, she couldn't stop. Did you know that there are five woodwoses buried in the cellar of his summer place? He lured them in from the forest, killed them, and drank their blood. Something to do with sawdust, apparently."

Cat suppressed a shiver.

"I also asked Ms. Istledown about you. What do you imagine she said?"

"Good things, I trust."

"Nothing. Underpool immediately shut her down. But not before Istledown favored me with the most extraordinarily knowing smile."

Against all expectations, Cat found herself enjoying this. It was exhilarating to play a part, she was discovering, particularly when there was real danger involved. "Oh, dear. Have I been having an affair with her too? Why is it nobody ever sends me the memos?"

"The point being that there are hidden depths to you, Ms. Gallowglass. Depths I intend to plumb. But that's a topic for another time." Barquentine stared at Cat steadily. "Raguel's position was left vacant so I was promoted into it. Hence the disarray here in my soon-to-be former office. Your congratulations are accepted, thank you. The very first action I took as Division Head was to fire his snotty little dwarf-bitch of an executive secretary. What would you say if I offered you the position?"

"I'd . . . say . . . that I need a little time to think over the offer."

"Somehow I knew you'd be the only individual in the entire

building who wasn't interested in more money and power. All right then. Suppose I offered you a position as my interim mistress? Jewelry, furs, clothing, use of a car, a generous per diem. That's on top of your current salary. Guaranteed minimum of two months, maximum of twelve—though that's not likely. What would you say?"

The offer took Cat by surprise. When she could breathe again, she said, "Thank you very kindly, sir. No."

"I could make you very unhappy."

"Is that supposed to be an inducement?"

"Happiness," Lord Pleiades said, "is banal. I've known women who could be made happy by a glass of Chablis and a paperback collection of sudoku puzzles. A deep, romantic misery, on the other hand, fills one's life with all the ineffable emotions that give rise to poetry: yearning, despair, resentment, furious anger, inconsolable grief, and of course lurid fantasies of revenge. This profound discontent is what makes all forbidden loves so irresistible."

"Who's forbidding our love?"

"You, apparently." Barquentine rose, chair scraping back noisily. Cat leapt up as well. "Be aware: I'm having your references looked into."

"Look all you like. You won't find anything wrong with them." Cat knew this for a fact, because the task had already been assigned and shunted downward as a chore no one wanted, from superior to inferior, until it landed in her lap. For the last three days, she had worked the phones, entering each call in the logs in a disguised hand, listening to the baffled declarations of her supposed employers and educators that they had never so much as heard of a Kate Gallowglass, and then written down the exact opposite of what they had sworn. Being careful (since it would look more convincing) to make their commendations sincere but not glowing. She expected to have the documentation in apple pie order and delivered to Barquentine's desk under the signature of somebody up-rank of her and happy to take credit for her toil by this time tomorrow.

Cat was, she had discovered, the single most efficient flunky the Conspiracy had. Which, given how much time she spent engaged in amateur espionage, wasn't saying much.

"Oh, and as long as you're going that way," Barquentine added, before she'd made it to the door, "take this bundle of etchings to Underpool and ask her to add it to the Ys file, would you? There's a good girl."

✢✢

In the run-up to the Plague Carnival, there was a great deal of discussion in the clerical pool of masks and gowns and underwire brassieres.

"I've never had one where the wire didn't break and poke me in the boob," Misabel said.

"Oh, I know!" said Annie Hedgewife. "Plus they're so uncomfortable to begin with."

The Croaker shook her head sourly. "They're not so bad if you get them properly fitted. You're right about the wires breaking, though."

"It's the troughs the straps dig into my shoulders that get to me," Slugabed Peg groused. "You have no idea how lucky you are not to have tits the size of mine. I tried that weight-reduction talisman you hang between the cups and it only gave me a rash."

"It made my skin tingle."

"I tried it twice and threw it away."

"This is so disillusioning!" Rackabite cried in mock horror. "I'm in the middle of a klatch of females discussing their breasts and it's not sexy at all."

"Welcome to our world," the Croaker said.

"Have you bought your mask yet?" Annie Hedgewife asked Cat.

"I've seen the posters, but I have to say it really doesn't look like my idea of fun," Cat said. "People in costumes dancing and looking moody."

"Oh, it's much, much more than just that. It's called Carnival, but it's actually an orgy of excesses of all kinds: deep-fried Mars bars, pink martinis, so much moondust your nostrils bleed, so much mead you puke your guts out, barely enough brandy to make you decide that maybe just this once you'll take it up the butt and skip the condom . . ." Annie Hedgewife pretended to fan her face with her hand. "*C'est tres* hot, as the swells say. And of course you're wearing a mask, so you can be anything you want: a lady, a slattern, an easily misled innocent . . . Everybody else is pretending to be something they're not, so why not you?"

"At Carnival, nobody knows you have the face of a dog." Rackabite grinned like a hound and licked his furry chops with a long, loose tongue.

"It still doesn't—"

"Anyway," the Croaker said, "attendance is mandatory for all employees. It's in your contract."

Somebody came booming down the metal stairs then and they all scattered to their desks. Where Cat, sorting through the etchings which Lolly had told her to Xerox and then shred, came across an image of the exact same tavern that Fingolfinrhod had disappeared into on the day of their father's death.

⚹⚹

Fingolfinrhod was in Ys. Thus was half her quest completed.

Cat considered coming in the next morning to drop her letter of resignation on Barquentine's desk—just to see the expression on his face when he read it—and then catching the next train to the coast. But payday was only four days distant and the money would be useful in the coming weeks. So she decided instead to wait.

Thus it was that the first night of the Plague Carnival found Cat in a green silk consignment-shop gown and a Columbine half mask alone in the crowd that crammed the public square before the Viceregal Palace, watching the fireworks spread themselves across the sky above the city spires in explosion after explosion after explosion of ecstatic beauty. She bought a corn dog from a vendor and oohed and applauded along with everybody else when the display came to its breathtaking crescendo.

An orchestra had been waiting for this moment and began to play. As it did, a tall figure wearing a Portunus mask appeared before Cat and bowed. "Care to dance with a stranger?" he said. "Who knows? Perhaps we'll fall in love. Unlikelier things have happened."

"I recognize your voice," Cat said. "Not to mention those eyes. How did you find me, Barquentine?"

"Oh, please. I'm the Division Director for Persecution now. If anyone has the resources, I do."

Then somehow, effortlessly, they were dancing. Barquentine led well, so well that Cat found herself having trouble maintaining the sassy, irreverent persona of Kate Gallowglass. So she stopped talking and simply let herself be swept across the slate courtyard, a single green silk leaf in a windstorm of bright flower petals that smelled of jasmine, carnations, lust, red wine, and attar of rose.

There came a break in the music to allow the dancers to catch their breaths. Leaning close so he could be heard, Barquentine held up a hand with an opal-and-silver ring. "You see this? It's the single greatest treasure of my house, a Class Three artifact left over from the creation of Faerie. As you can

imagine, I don't wear it very often." The hand fell away an instant before its nearness would have become offensive. "Anyone
whose skin the ring touches is rendered incapable of lying. Ask
me anything."

"What was the worst thing you ever did?"

"I won't tell you that. It was *very* bad, I'm afraid, and knowing it would make you think the less of me." The music started
up again and once more Barquentine took Cat into his arms.
The night being warm, she wore a scarf rather than a cloak. He
slid his hand beneath it, so that his ring touched her bare back.
"Now we cannot lie to one another. Yet neither are we required
to reveal any truths we do not wish to. Do you think you could
outwit me under such circumstances?"

Cat heard herself say, "Yes. Yes, I honestly do."

"Then let us play. I'll let you ask the first question."

"All right. Why is it called the Plague Carnival? Why not just
Carnival?"

"Because it was only a century ago, with modern medicine
and sanitation, that cities achieved replacement capacity. Before
then, more people died in cities than were born in them. Population was maintained by the influx of immigrants from the
country, seeking better lives for themselves. The chief engine
of death back then was plague—and in Carcassonne, plagues
commonly came in late autumn. Hence the Plague Carnival—
one last fling before the dying season. With the rise of sexually
transmitted diseases, ironically enough, the Carnival itself
became a means of reducing the surplus population. It can't be
helped. Periodically, each of us wants to go off our diets, throw
caution to the winds, and just this once do what we most desire
without thought of consequences. Who's to say no? You'll admit, I hope, that I've answered your question adequately."

"You have."

"My turn, then. Are you a virgin?"

"That's not a question a lady will answer."

"Touché. Next question."

"Since you've wasted your question, I'll waste mine. Just what is the purpose of the Conspiracy?"

"You think I won't tell? Our ultimate purpose is to plunge all of Faerie into an age of unending war. To this end, we are ensnarling the Dragon Corps in an escalating series of scandals that will ultimately break the Treaty of Hyperuranion, thus enabling dragons to carry nuclear weapons without the authority of Her Absent Majesty. The railroads' infrastructure is being systematically sabotaged to weaken their independence to such a degree that the Treaty of Shamayim can be renegotiated, forcing them to transport the souls of children from Aerth in such great numbers that we can import more dragons. All of which, taken together, will be an act so heinous that the ruling class will be collectively complicit and thus immune from transcendence practically forever. You'd have learned all this and more during orientation, if you'd taken me up on the secretarial position. Why didn't you?"

"I don't trust you."

"Fair enough." A dancer with a white mask covering all but her mouth twirled past and her cloak flew open to reveal that she wore nothing beneath. Then it closed about her, so that all that showed of her skin was an ambiguous smile. Lord Barquentine spared her only the briefest of glances. "Your turn."

"Why are you telling me all this?"

"Ah. How much do you know about me, Ms. Gallowglass? Precious little, I'll wager. I have wealth, social position, and have amassed by various means as much power I am likely to wield in this lifetime. The Conspiracy is working to ensure an end to transcendence. Without the fear of which, our owners will have no reason to die and be reborn and thus can stay in their social roles forever. So tell me. What can I aspire to which I do not already have?"

"I don't know."

"You. I know your secret."

Cat could not lie. But that did not prevent her from assuming the Kate Gallowglass persona. "Now you're just fishing." Pushing Barquentine away from her, she said, "Everyone has secrets. Even a dull little clerical drudge like myself. That doesn't mean I have to blurt them out in front of a two-bit bully like you."

Seizing her wrist so roughly that his ring dug into her flesh, Barquentine said, "You are Caitlin of House Sans Merci, runagate and dragon slayer. Deny it if you can."

"I . . ." Cat blushed from head to toe. Her throat seized up, so that she could not speak.

Barquentine's eyes burned tiger-bright. Cat could not look away from them. "We are going to my rooms now. You know what we will do there. Will you go with me peacefully?"

"Yes," Cat said, lowering her eyes. "I will."

�֍

Lord Barquentine's rooms were everything Cat expected them to be: spacious, interior-decorator perfect, and a little too calculatedly opulent to impress anyone who knew what real wealth looked like. There was nothing old or shabby or cherished in them, nor the least trace of his personality. He would have servants to make sure that such things were whisked away and discarded.

Not that there were any servants present tonight. All Carcassonne was at the Plague Carnival and so Barquentine had to go through the rooms turning on the lights and (in the bedroom) kindling the candles himself. "The law forbids the rich and the poor alike from sleeping under bridges, begging in the street, or stealing bread, yet the poor do these things often and the rich never. Have you ever wondered why?"

"No," Cat said, more weakly than she would have liked.

"It is because the rules bind those with power more strongly than they do those without. We literally cannot break them. Only the powerless have that freedom. Which is why Ys is such a problem for the Conspiracy. But let's not bring business talk into the boudoir. My point is that at times such as now, when the rules are held in abeyance, nothing is forbidden me. Tonight I can do whatever I wish to you, and in the morning . . . well, the rules are much laxer about what happens within an already-established relationship."

With elaborate insouciance, Lord Pleiades threw his mask on a nightstand and moved toward Cat with an amorous smile. But she forestalled him with an outstretched arm, saying, "I have to freshen up. It won't take me long."

"The master bedroom's bath is through that door." Barquentine sounded amused. "You'll find that it doesn't lock from the inside."

"Such a reassuring thing to hear," Cat murmured. She used the toilet, then took off her mask and washed her hands. As she did, she stared at her face, pale and expressionless in the mirror.

"Having second thoughts?" Helen asked.

"I know what I'm doing."

"There's a first time for everything, I suppose."

Thin-lipped, Cat systematically scanned the toiletries, dismissing most of them as unsuited to her purpose. She picked up an ivory-handled hairbrush, a heavy thing with a chased silver back, hefted it, and was satisfied. Then she re-donned her mask.

Cat emerged from the bath, brushing her hair. When Barquentine moved to take her in his arms, she said, "Is that my compact on the floor behind you?"

"I don't think—" Barquentine began, turning to look.

Cat hit him with the hairbrush, putting all her strength into it, and he dropped to the floor like a slaughtered ox.

Cat put a finger to Barquentine's nostrils to make sure he was still breathing. Then she used tissue paper to wipe the brush clean of fingerprints, restored it to the bathroom counter, and flushed the tissue.

People always thought of pilots in terms of their primary function, guiding dragons through the sky, as if they could do nothing else. They forgot that pilots were first and foremost career military and that all military personnel were taught a multitude of brutal means of killing or incapacitating an enemy.

It was time she got out of here.

In movies, recovering from being knocked unconscious was a simple matter of groaning and rubbing the back of one's head the next morning. But this was real life. Barquentine would almost certainly have a concussion. Even with the sort of medical care his kind could afford, he would probably have to go through months of rehab to recover full functionality. Parts of his memory might never return to him. Nevertheless, he would live.

Not that he necessarily deserved to. But Cat had never killed anybody and didn't want him to be her first.

※※

Pushing her way through the thronged and torchlit streets, Cat waited until she was halfway home and flung her mask to the paving stones. Then she stomped on it, and kicked the remains into the gutter. The crowds were thicker now and their scent muskier and less floral. Someone upstream must have been selling glow sticks, for she saw increasing numbers of them being used as bracelets and necklaces and hatbands. More and more, as well, she saw shadowy figures coupling standing up in doorways or holding hands as one of them pissed against an alley wall. Whatever curiosity she might once have had about the Plague Carnival was more than satisfied now.

"You could have waited an hour or two before coldcocking Barquentine, you know," Helen said.

"You like Barkers? Ick. I guess there really is no accounting for taste."

"You'll admit he has great eyes. Anyway, I've always had a soft spot for a real bastard. You can play with their heads all you like and not feel guilty afterward."

"Again: Ick."

"Oh, like that banal creature in the green jockstrap is any better? There are so many more lustworthy male creatures in this world. You really ought to expand your horizons."

"This conversation is over," Cat said. "I never heard a word of it. Anyway, I intend to get my commission back and an intact hymen is one of the requirements of the job. So a sweaty little tryst in the sheets with Barquentine simply wasn't going to happen, got it?"

"Yes, but—"

Bickering, they made their way home.

Up the stairs Cat clomped, past darkened rooms with doors hastily left ajar from which emerged the sighs and moans of passion. There were times, and this was one, when she felt out of step with all the world.

When Cat pushed open the door to her own room, she was anything but surprised to find that Esme had just finished packing her Hello Kitty knapsack.

"Tell me something," Cat said as she neatly folded the last

of her things into the duffel. "Do you know how to pick locks? And hack a computer?"

"I know lots of things," Esme said. She thought. "Those too."

"Good."

Not much later, with the Plague Carnival still in full swing, they found themselves inside the unlit offices of the Conspiracy, Esme having made short work of locks, alarms, and security cameras. Cat led the way to the basement with a pocket Maglite and watched while Esme jimmied the door to the IT room with a piece of stiff plastic. There, Cat booted up a terminal and, with a bow to the child, said, "Maestro."

Esme giggled and sat down to work. "Should I delete all the files?"

"No. They've surely got it all backed up on external storage. I want to waste their energies trying to fix things for as long as we can. Would it be possible for you to locate everything they have on Caitlin of House Sans Merci and then swap out every tenth item with the equivalent from randomly selected females?"

"Sure."

"Then do that."

While Esme worked, Cat located the server cage. Then she fetched a squeeze bottle of honey from the coffee room.

When finally Esme sang, "I'm done-done-DONE!" Cat went to work. One by one, she opened the blade servers, squirted a teaspoon of honey into each, and closed them up again. Watching, Esme said with solemn respect, "You'd make a good little girl."

Cat swung the child, laughing, up in the air. "And you'd make a great little dragon pilot!" While the servers sizzled and stank, she wheeled Esme around and around and around until she was shrieking with fear and delight.

And then, as always, they were on the run again.

☆☆

On the highway, it took them no time at all to hitch a ride away from Carcassonne. Truckers, it seemed, were suckers for little girls. This one chatted and joshed with Esme until she fell asleep, and then turned sullenly taciturn. After a couple of futile attempts to engage the trucker in conversation, Cat dug out the last of Dahut's letters and began to read:

Belovedest,

All day long, since receiving your last letter, I have spent alone in my locked room weeping—with joy, my love, with joy. Are we at last to be reunited? And forever? I can scarce believe it. But since you say it is true, it must be so. In my mind, I see you speeding toward me in the distance like a white squall coming off the ocean. As you did—need I remind you?— the first time, when you crushed my boat and, laughing, flung its splintered timbers in the air, and I all but drowned in the cold, dark water while we made mad, passionate love.

And then you withdrew, taking away with you my heart.

Yes, I goaded you to this extreme, as if it were nothing, all the while knowing it to be a wonder such as this world has not seen in many an age. But I am making sacrifices, too! The citizens of Ys would tear me asunder with their bare hands if they knew what we intend. Father would weep but plunge his great sword through my body nonetheless. The old man was always kind to me, the people ever obedient. In all truth, I owe them better than this. But the heart wants what the heart wants and my heart wants you. Always and forever.

When you come, I will open the sea gate so that you may enter the harbor and within it sound the Horn of Holmdel. Then the great transformation will occur. I do not imagine there will be many who will welcome it. There will be, I am certain, numerous deaths. But let them die, let them die, so long as our love lives! I surrender to you my heart, my city, and its people. Drown us all. Whatever happens, I am sure my heart will survive, fixed, as ever, eternally upon you.

Tonight!

Dahut

What cannot be said will be wept.

—Sappho

W HEN THE FINAL TRUCK OF THEIR LONG JOURNEY TO the west reached Whitemarsh on the coast of Cornouaille, Cat and Esme got off and waved their thanks until it was out of sight. The dawn was cool and the sky was palest yellow at the horizon. Cat was exhausted. She rented a room at a motel that served transient workers and collapsed onto the bed. Hours later she awoke to discover that it was dark and Esme was demanding to be fed.

No rest for the hunted, she supposed. Thank all the gods that were or might be that Cat had known to pack food in her duffel. She got out tea bags, oranges, rice cakes, and a chunk of parmesan cheese. Also baby carrots and dipping sauce in a plastic container. Plus a jar of peanut butter and a box of Ritz Crackers. Spreading it all out picnic-style on the bedspread, she said, "Look! A feast!" and Esme applauded.

It appeared that she had learned one thing at least from her travels.

The next day, finally taking Helen's advice, Cat found a job as a waitress in a roadhouse café just off the highway by the waterfront. Sea-elves came there after a long night of drinking to fill up on French fries and cheese curds. She listened to their lies, pocketed their miserly tips, and deemed their flirtations harmless. If the weather was rough and the fishing fleet could not put out, selkies gathered to drink bitter coffee and shout scorn at any river-faring kelpie unfortunate enough to wander in. Because she'd been a seawoman herself, though briefly, Cat knew how to pump her clientele for information. She laughed at their jokes and never commented on politics. Occasionally, she asked questions. Bit by bit, she assembled a mental map of the coastline as it was seen from both land and water. Somewhere along this stretch of a hundred miles or so, Cat was increasingly sure, she would find the drowned and forgotten city of Ys, and with it her brother.

"Admit it," Helen said. "You enjoyed working in Carcassonne and you're enjoying working here. Having a solid job is a hell of a lot more satisfying than adventuring up and down the world ever was."

"I had a solid job," Cat responded. "It got taken away from me."

Just before dawn, if the weather was fair, a swamp gaunt or three would come out of the salt marshes to glumly nurse a cup of coffee before leaving to report to work at the Department of Sanitation, abandoning a copper coin or two and occasionally a half-read newspaper on the counter behind them.

The breakfast rush was over and Cat was leaning against the counter reading the paper one morning when Raven walked in. She sat down on a stool and said, "That was a cute stunt you pulled, abandoning me at the bus station."

Cat put down the newspaper. "I'd do the same again in a heartbeat."

"You never could have swindled my dad like that." Raven shook her head ruefully. "When he hears about this, he's going to laugh until he busts a gut. Gimme a menu and a cup of coffee. Cream, no sugar." She studied the menu, ordered the *pain perdu*. Then, when it arrived, "Tell me something. How'd you figure out I was scamming you?"

"I knew how the brass were tracking me, and it wasn't Saoirse's little pack of Gabriel hounds. Also, my lawyer put pennies on their eyes and sent them to the Black Stone to be judged and reborn. So I knew they were out of the game."

"You live, you learn." Raven gave all her attention to the food. When Cat came to clear away the dishes, she said, "Listen. Esme really is family. I really am a trickster. You really are in a world of trouble. I can help."

"I'd trust you a whole lot more if you weren't so fucking sincere."

Choking with laughter, Raven said, "Oh, sweet Mother of Goats, I love you. I love you so much I'd work for you for free, if I could afford it. Luckily I can't, so that's fine." Then, serious again, "You ever cut a deal with a haint? An important deal, I mean. You know how they phrase the compact?"

"I tell you what I want. When you agree I've earned it, you give it to me."

"Yeah. Most folks won't honor those terms. It's why haints don't make many important deals with outsiders. But they'll deal with me. I'm proud of that. I want that stone you've got hanging around your neck. Now tell me what you want."

"I want the Conspiracy off my back and Saoirse as well. I want my name cleared. I want my commission back. I want to fly dragons again. I want to find my brother, who's living in Ys, an undersea city the location of which nobody seems to know. Find me my brother and I'll give you the stone. All the rest, I can take care of on my own."

Raven dug out her cigarette pack, tapped out a Marlboro, lit it, and took a long drag. She let the smoke trickle out her nostrils. Then, finally, she said, "Done. You underestimate Saoirse, by the way. She may have lost her Gabriel hounds, but she's got a dossier on you three inches thick. That's how I found you—by sneaking a peek. Saoirse's a hunter; she's found your trail and she'll sniff out every inch of it. But I'm a pattern juggler; I figured out the trail's logic and skipped ahead of her. You don't have much time."

"Crap! How much?"

"Four, maybe five days. More if you let me slow her down. So. Do we have an understanding?"

Reluctantly, Cat nodded.

"A'right." Raven dropped a couple of bills on the counter, kicked the stool around, and stood.

"What are you going to do?"

Raven paused in the doorway and grinned that grin again. "If I told you, you'd try to stop me."

Then she was gone.

✕✕

Two days later a woman's naked body washed ashore at Port Salemo. Fish had nibbled away the face and fingertips. But there was a broken length of jewelry chain still wrapped around the neck and a Dragon Corps Academy class ring on the stub of one finger. When the coast guardians hoisted up the corpse, ghost crabs scuttled out of its hair, causing them to drop her in alarm. Raven was particularly proud of that touch. She had strutted into the diner, thrown down a copy of *Le Républicain Salemo,* and, jabbing a finger at the news item at the bottom of page 6, said, "It'll be a week before Saoirse is sure that wasn't you."

Cat, who had been washing dishes, dried her hands on her apron, and read the account. "Where did you get the body?"

"I didn't kill anybody, if that's what you're asking. Let's just say that a certain necromancers' convention will have to use a rubber dummy for one of their demonstrations." Raven lit up a cigarette. "I'll have the same as last time."

"Tell me something. Why do you smoke so much?"

"Being a trickster involves the occasional use of magic. Magic requires sacrifice. The sacrifice has to be sincere. You can't offer up something that's easy." Raven flicked ash into an ashtray. "Giving up these things is a real mother. Now. First order of business is to find your city. After that, you'll need a way of getting to it alive. You've got a map, I presume? Why don't you get it out?"

"It's in my head," Cat said.

"Never mind, I'll pick up a navigational chart and we can go over it when you get off work. Which is when, incidentally?"

"The dinner shift takes over at three."

"It's a date."

⁎⁎

Cat's motel room being overly cramped, they bought two lattes and a Pepsi in the local coffee shop, in effect renting a corner table for an hour.

Cat and Raven pored over the map while Esme sharpened pencils, dispensed drafting tools on request, and ate great handfuls of butterfly chips right out of the bag.

"Okay," Raven said. "*Here* and *here* the currents are so strong they'd knock down any buildings unlucky enough to be in their path. I learned that last time I was in the area, smuggling rifles to renegade korrigans. So they're out. The shallows over here are paradise for sports divers. Wall-to-wall shipwrecks. If your city were there, they'd have found it."

Cat leaned forward and crosshatched several stretches along the coast. "These are sites where watermen dredge up oysters and clams. Lobstermen plant their pots *here* and *here* and *here* and *here*. Esme—compass! Thank you." She drew semicircles before all the seaside towns. "If Ys were on the approach to a port, they'd be forever dropping anchors through its roofs. So these areas are out too." She lightly stippled more open water. "And these are heavily fished. It's not impossible that Ys lies beneath one, but it's not very likely either."

"What's this empty space?"

"I don't have any information on it. Nobody fishes there, apparently. It's one of those spots where they never catch anything and when they try, their nets get fouled."

"Uh-huh. How many of these spots have you found?"

"That's it. When we combine your information with mine, I don't see where else Ys could possibly be."

Raven put her hands behind her head and stretched. "We've made a good beginning. Now tell me how Lord Pleiades wound up in Hôpital Maîtresse de la Miséricorde with a blood bubble the size of a golf ball in his brain."

As efficiently as she could, Cat complied, moving from slow dancing at the Plague Carnival to Barquentine's attempted rape in his flat with an absolute minimum of words. When she was done, Raven said, "A pity you didn't think to swipe that ring of his. I could use something like that in my line of work. But what's done is done. Right now, our big problem as I see it is this: Even if we find your drowned city, how are you going to get in? I don't expect you can breathe underwater—I sure can't. Plus, you're too buoyant for any prolonged interactions with its citizens. Indoors, you'd bob against the ceiling; outside you'd shoot up like a balloon. So you're going to need strong magic. And by strong, I mean Class Three artifacts, maybe even Class Four."

"I keep hearing those terms," Cat said. "But I have no idea what they mean."

"Okay. A Class Four artifact is a tool left over from the creation of the universe. Rarer and more powerful than you can imagine. A Class Three artifact is left over from the creation of

Faerie. Not as rare, not as powerful, still an incredibly dangerous object, still worth a king's ransom. A Class Two artifact is
anything magical from before the Industrial Revelation. Some
are more powerful than others, but they're all antiques. A Class
One artifact is mass produced, probably made in Cathay, and
available wherever fine magic is sold. In any case, we're talking expensive. Very, very expensive."

"You have noticed that I work as a waitress?"

"No problemo. Comes with the contract. Everything's prix
fixe. I just want you to appreciate what a good deal you're getting. Right now, I'd suggest you get some sleep. We're going out
tonight to see an old friend of mine."

☈

A long nap and a quick meal later, Raven led Cat and Esme outside and, slapping a hand on the hood of a midnight black
Highlander, said, "How do you like my new ride?"

"That's a lot of vehicle for puttering around Whitemarsh,
wouldn't you say?"

"Oh, I have plans for this baby. After I've taken care of your
little problem, she and I are heading into some very rough
country indeed. Right now, though . . . Ready for an adventure,
Jill?"

"You betcha," the Highlander said.

"Hop in, guys."

So they did.

Time passed. The sun went down. The SUV hummed its way
along the river road eastward, away from the shore and into the
heart of Caledon Wood, a remnant of the primal forest that had
once covered most of Europa, currently maintained as a wild-
life refuge and game preserve. Scrub pines and dwarf cedars
sped by the windows, then gave way to blackjack oaks, sassa-
fras, sour gum, and holly. Nobody said a word, not even Jill.

When Esme fell asleep, Cat wrapped a blanket around her and cradled the child in her lap.

The river road started out smooth and well-maintained. By degrees it grew ruttier, narrower, and twistier. The occasional glimpses they got of the River Aelph darkened from silver to gray and then black. The forest turned to sugar maple, beech, elm, and birch. It was too dark for Cat to make out the leaves of individual trees, but she had her window open a crack and could identify them by smell.

Jill hit a rough spot and everyone within bounced into the air. "Lady of a Thousand Names!" Raven swore, and downshifted twice. The road rapidly devolved into a dirt track.

"Your friend lives an awful long way from anybody, doesn't she?" Cat said. It had been over an hour since she had last spoken.

"With good reason."

The SUV came to a stop before a stream crossed by two heavy wooden beams as far apart as the distance between its tires. On the far side, the road dwindled to a trail leading to a brick house with multiple turrets and tile roofs and chimney pots only half visible in the trees. Warm light from its windows winked at them invitingly. "I'm not so sure about that bridge," Jill said.

Raven patted the dashboard reassuringly. "Nobody's going to ask you to do anything you can't, old girl."

"I didn't say I *can't*. Of course I can. I was just taking a second to see whether there's enough space to turn around on the other side. So I can get back. I could cross this thing backward if I had to. But I'd rather not."

"We can—"

"It doesn't matter. There's room to turn around, I can see that. But if I had to, I could have crossed it backward."

"Jill, you're astonishing," Raven said. "You're the best."

"Shuddup. I'm trying to work."

Slowly, cautiously, Jill eased them across the beams.

Esme was dead to the world, so Cat said, "Take care of the kid, will you, Jill?"

"Can do. If she wakes up, I'll just slap on *Blinding Nemo*."

The house was softly lit by exterior floodlights so the unlikely passerby could admire its complex brickwork patterns, the green copper drainpipes, and the polished brass sheela-na gig knocker on the front door. Raven led Cat around the back. Then, with a clasp knife, she jimmied the lock.

"You told me this was a friend's house," Cat said.

"She's the kind of friend I want to owe as few favors as possible—and, believe me, she keeps track of everything, even if it's only opening a door for you."

Then they were inside. "Don't touch anything," Raven said. "Half of it's ensorcelled to an alarm system." She flicked a light switch.

Cat froze in astonishment.

The room was immense and tidily cluttered: with taxidermy dodoes in bell jars; with iron swords and bronze spears and stone axes hung on the wall in a starburst; with devotional statuettes of Fascinus arranged between a death mask of Queen Titania and the trophy spine of a Nephilim warrior; with a diorama of the Battle of Mag Itha carved inside a ruby the size of a roc's egg, a framed map of a city with the unlikely name of Perth Amboy, and the carapace of a millipede eight feet long; with what looked at first glance to be a suit of armor but was actually a bronze automaton; with the fossilized scat of (so their labels read) twenty distinct kings; with stacks of 16 mm film cans, reel-to-reel computer tapes, and mimeographed fanzines;

with a glove large enough to crawl inside and an ivory tusk that could only have come from Behemoth itself; with vitrines crammed with magic talismans, rings, coins, pins, twigs, boots, brooches, spoons, pendants, daggers, gems; with Disney memorabilia, Han dynasty vases, and brass serpent horns in the manner of Tubal-Cain; with tiaras, crowns, and shackles; with hand-painted ties; with a rack of aluminum briefcases; with vacuum tubes the size of an ottoman, ocher-stained cave bear skulls, a copper leaf large enough to crush a bystander if it fell over; with a lightning bolt frozen in the instant it grounded itself; with a mountain so small it could fit on a dinner plate and an onyx bowl filled with glass mice; with a granite anvil, a pyramid of beer cans, and the busty figurehead from a wooden ship; with golden apples and bells of lead; with a bust of a dog-headed man in Edwardian garb, a gold-plated electric chair, and a thousand things more, all a delight to the eye and each an invitation to avarice.

The room was also cold as ice.

"We should have brought parkas," Cat whispered.

"We won't be here long. Her office is over there."

Without knocking, Raven threw open the door. Cat followed her in. There, a scholar sat at her desk, scribbling. Her hair was long and straight and as white as her skin, her pearls, and her Oscar de la Renta suit.

The scholar looked up in surprise. Then, standing, she swept forward and took Raven's hands in hers. "Orlando! My darling! You've come around at last. Oh, what a feast we shall have." She raised one of the hands to her mouth.

Raven yanked it away. "None of that now, Sasha!"

"Not yet? Ah well, I can wait. But where are my manners?" Sasha disappeared into a side room and returned with a bowl of mixed apples and bananas. Placing it on her desk, she poured lamp oil over the fruit and touched a match to them. They went up in flames and Cat edged closer to catch some of their heat. "To business. Doubtless, you are here for a reason." She glanced sidelong at Cat. "Perhaps, something to do with the *amuse-bouche* you brought me?"

"This is exactly why your social life is so barren," Raven said, with just a snap of anger. "My friend, never mind her name, has an appointment in one of the undersea cities and it's none of your business which one or why. She needs a means of getting to the city and something to keep her alive while she's there. Surely you've got a knickknack or two that will do the trick somewhere in this metastasized junk shop of yours."

"Don't be insulting, sweetmeats." Sasha plucked a rose from a vase on her desk, stared at it until it was blanched with frost, then bit off the flower and crunched it to nothing. The stem and leaves crumbled to powder and dissolved in the air. "If I cared about your friend's name or intentions or why she wanted to see her brother in Ys, I'd know it already."

Unexpectedly, Raven laughed. "I keep forgetting how shrewd you are when you're sober. So. I told you what I want. You can put it on my tab."

"There was a time," Sasha said, "when I had a key to the ocean and a pennywhistle that would summon help whenever it was most needed. Exactly what you need now. But they were stolen from me. So . . ." She flicked her fingers, as if dismissing a trifle. "I'm afraid there's nothing I can do."

"You wouldn't have said any of that if there wasn't a bargain to be struck." Cat had been staying as close to the flaming fruit bowl as she could, and that helped, but now her teeth started chattering. Raven glanced at her and added, "Let's wrap this up quick. My friend and I are both freezing."

"Shall I get you coats?" Sasha asked solicitously.

"At the rates you charge? Not a chance."

"Then we'll continue this discussion in the kitchen. It's

warmer there." Sasha swept out of the office and, having no alternative, Cat and Raven followed.

The kitchen was not exactly warm but there was some residual heat from the Viking gas stove, so it was markedly less cold. The stove was eight feet long, an industrial model whose surface was covered with burners, grills, and griddles. There was a residual smell—pork?—of whatever had been roasted in it last. Crude metal hooks had been hammered into the brick wall to one side and from them hung dozens of butchering utensils.

"See my knives," Sasha said in a tone that was clearly meant to be seductive. "I keep them so, so very sharp. For you, my darling, only for you."

"Charming," Raven said, "I'm sure."

The opposite wall had shelf upon shelf with jars and boxes clustered upon them. "Behold my spices! Some are very close to being extinct. I would let you choose as many as you wish to make a rub for your sweet, tender body. Guests come and go here. The cooking can get, I admit, a tad perfunctory at times. But when you finally surrender, my squab, the night will last forever. I will linger over your preparation. I will marinate you and baste you and roast you as slowly as ever a meal was prepared. Your shrieks and squeals will add flavor to my art. Oh, Orlando! Why wait? You're here, I'm here, the tools and ingredients are as fine as can be. What better time to surrender to your fate?"

"We have a haint's agreement, remember? When I deem what I've received to be worth the price. We're not even close yet."

"Oh, my tart, tangy, succulent thing! Must you always remain the one who got away? Tsk. Then follow me to the library." And Sasha led them back into the cold.

The first room Cat had seen had been full of things to catch the eye and imagination. The library went beyond that. Its books radiated an inner life. Where other books sat on their shelves silent and mysterious, these clustered like so many boats tied to their docks in a winter marina. If she stared hard enough, Cat was sure, she would see them bobbing in the water. More than anything, she wanted to unmoor one and sail it beyond the horizon.

Sasha snapped her fingers in Cat's face to get her attention, then gestured toward a shelf filled with oversized books. Raven was tugging at the largest of them, a monstrous thing bound in gold tooled red leather. "Stop mooning about and give your friend a hand."

Under Sasha's critical eye, Cat and Raven struggled the book down from its shelf. "Holy dogs," Cat groaned. "This fucker must be four feet tall."

"Fifty inches," Sasha corrected her. "It's a double oliphaunt folio and extremely rare, so please do treat it with respect."

Cat and Raven eased the book onto the ground, kneeling to do so. Gracefully crouching, Sasha ran a finger halfway down the edge of the pages. She tugged open the book just far enough to read the page number, then let two pages slide from under her finger. "Open it here."

Together, Cat and Raven threw back the cover. They eased the pages over onto it so that the book lay flat. Inside, rather than print, was a stairway leading down into darkness. All three stood and Sasha said, "You're looking for a woman with abundant golden-red hair. She's carrying a leather satchel that contains the key, the pennywhistle, and a great many things more. Return me the satchel and you can use the two for as long as you need. The stairway will open for you when you're ready to return."

"I'm holding you to those exact words," Raven said, and started down the stairs.

"Wait," Cat said. "I can't be making any long trips now. I have obligations." She didn't want to mention Esme in front of Sasha.

"You'll be back in no time at all," Sasha said. "I guarantee it."

"C'mon," Raven grunted.

Swallowing back her misgivings, Cat followed Raven downward. After a bit, she commented, "I've been down stairs a lot like this before. Nothing good ever happens to me at the bottom."

"That's because nothing good has happened to you for a very long time. I'll bet Esme has told you she brings luck. Technically, that's true—but the luck she brings is bad. She survives in some extremely dangerous surroundings by eating the good luck of those around her. Now you know. So hush up and let me concentrate."

The stairs were steep and narrow but the air was dry and, for a mercy, warm.

※※

They emerged in a train station crowded with a colorful mélange of commercial travelers, military on leave, haints, dwarves, kobolds, tourists, and excursionists of all kinds. "So we're looking for a redhead," Raven said. "In a train station. This is just swell, this is—" She stopped. "Oh, shit."

"What?"

Wordlessly, Raven pointed to a sign: BROCIELANDE STATION.

For a second, Cat didn't get it. "But Brocielande Station doesn't exist anymore. It was destroyed the first day of the—" She clapped a hand to her mouth. "Oh."

Sasha had sent them far away and into the past. Into a very bad place on a very bad day, if Cat's premonition was right—the day the War for the West began at Brocielande Station.

"Now it's urgent," Raven said. "We've got to find the woman with the hair and the satchel and get out of here before the dragons arrive. You go that way and I'll go this."

Raven started away, but Cat grabbed her arm and yanked her back. "Too late." She pointed to the east, where a line of specks, invisible to anyone who didn't know what to look for, were coming in "low and slow" as her instructors had put it, for an antipersonnel run. Low so the dragons could see their targets. Slow so they could either strafe them or lay down a line of incendiaries with maximum effectiveness. Low and slow to maximize the body count.

This being the day of the infamous Brocielande Station raid, Cat knew for a fact that they'd be dropping the mixture of Greek fire and gasoline that was commonly known as golden fire. It was in all the history books.

Pulling Raven after her, Cat went to the edge of the platform and looked down. The platform was made of reinforced concrete and had a little bit of an overhang. From platform top down to the rails was a drop of six feet. "Do as I say and don't argue," she told Raven. "We're going to jump down there. Then we'll lie down flat as close to the wall as we can. Try not to move. Don't look up. Can you do it?"

The dragons were audible now, a low grumble hanging in the air. Passengers stood transfixed, a scattering of them pointing at the distant specks. Their stillness held for an instant and then broke as some ran inside the station and others toward open ground. Both of which, Cat knew from her studies, would prove to be bad choices.

It was possible now to see more than one line of dragons— there were at least five waves and possibly more beyond the limits of vision, all evenly spaced. At a professional level, Cat had to admire the tightness of that pattern. Those pilots knew their stuff. She shook Raven hard. "*Can you do it?*"

Raven nodded.

"Good." Cat stepped off the platform. To make sure Raven followed, she didn't let go of the trickster's arm.

They landed in a tangle, rolled to the wall, and lay head-to-head alongside it. "This would be a funny time for a train to pull in," Raven muttered.

"The station is under attack. Trains are the least of your worries. Keep your head down! The less of this you see, the happier you'll be."

The dragon-thunder was growing louder. Cat could feel it in the pit of her stomach.

Now at last the air raid sirens blared, so loud that speech was impossible.

Cat waited. And waited. The roar of dragons grew louder and mingled with the sirens. It seemed impossible for so much time to have passed without the war machines having arrived. Yet still the sound of their engines grew.

Raven's eyes were screwed shut and her cheeks were wet with tears. Cat wanted to say something comforting but to her profound disgust found that she herself was shivering with fear. Luckily, it was too noisy for talk anyway.

Then, at last, the dragons were upon them.

⚹

After the fact, the accounts of the raid would peg its duration at anywhere from twenty to forty-five minutes. But Cat knew better.

It lasted forever.

There had been over a hundred locomotives in the rail yards when the raid began. Only three escaped alive. While Cat cowered, the remainder died. As for the civilians, "Bullets and golden fire fell on them all, as impartial as the rain," one historian would later write.

Eternity had no duration. It simply was.

When finally the dragons were gone, there was no sound save for the ringing in Cat's ears. Sometime during the raid, probably when the station's roof collapsed, the sirens had been silenced. Slowly, Cat got to her feet. She reached down a hand to help Raven up. Her friend said something she couldn't quite make out. "What's that?"

Raven shouted, barely audibly, "I said: I hope I didn't piss myself."

"If you did, I don't think anybody here's going to hold it against you."

Together, they trudged up the tracks to the end of the platform, where there was a metal ladder bolted to the cement. They climbed up it.

And found themselves in Gehenna.

The remains of the station house were still burning. Flames and smoke and grit were everywhere. Where the golden fire had fallen, there were lumps of charcoal that had once been bodies. Where it had not, there were yet more bodies. Some of them were moving. Dimly, Cat heard screams and sobbing.

"You know about triage?" Helen asked. "Those who will die whatever you do, those who will live even if ignored, and those who need your help?"

"I'm career military."

"Carry on, then. I'll shut up now."

In a kind of daze, Cat and Raven wandered among the fallen, looking for someone to help. There were others, though not many, doing the same thing. With Raven's aid, Cat improvised a bandage to stop an unconscious dwarf from bleeding out, then tied a tourniquet above an elfling's blasted hand. She was midway through a spell to bring sleep to the wounded girl when, with a shrill cry, Raven disappeared from her side.

". . . by the Labrys and the Orchid and the Mercy of the Night," Cat finished, and was rewarded by seeing the child's eyes close in slumber. Then she stood and saw Raven, not far away, kneeling over a woman with long red-gold hair.

Raven was holding a baby in her arms and, Cat saw with unspeakable gratitude, it appeared to be whole and uninjured, though it was crying vigorously. The poor thing was clearly frightened half to death, but it would get over that soon enough. Its mother had obviously sheltered it with her body. Obviously, she was not going to live.

Cat leaned close to hear what Raven was saying to the woman. ". . . to me. Please! Talk to me!"

Raven's face was contorted with desperation. So Cat said, "Here. Let me." She sat down alongside the woman and, summoning up lore acquired in a military first-aid class, placed her hands to either side of the woman's head. She visualized all her body-energy as a glowing fluid. Then she let a fraction of that strength flow from one hand to the other, invigorating the dying body.

The woman's eyes opened the merest slit. Her lips moved silently. Knowing it was dangerous to them both, but doing it anyway, Cat gave her just enough more strength to speak audibly. "Are you Death?" the woman asked. "Am I dying? Where is my son?"

"She's not. You are. He's right here and he's fine," Raven said. "A little thing like a dragon raid can't harm this fella."

"That's . . . good."

"Listen to me," Raven said. "I have to know. Is your last name Whilk?"

The faintest trace of a smile appeared on the woman's ashen face. "Some . . . times." Then her eyes closed again.

Seconds later, she was dead.

Cat and Raven stood. "What the I-don't-know-what was that all about?" Cat asked.

"I had to be sure she was who I thought she was." With one toe, Raven nudged a leather satchel. "That's the bag we came for."

Cat picked it up. Dimly, she heard sirens. The military had arrived at last, it seemed, with ambulances and real doctors and trained paramedics. For which, she thought, thank the Goddess. Because she was exhausted.

And Cat passed out.

All shall be well and all shall be well and every manner of thing shall be well.

—Julian of Norwich

SOLDIERS SET UP TENTS AND CARTED AWAY BODIES AND PUT out fires and shouted angrily at anyone who was clearly a civilian and not dying. In the ensuing chaos, it was the easiest thing in the world to slip away. Raven commandeered a military pickup truck—"In wartime, it's commandeering, not theft," she explained—and, taking turns behind the wheel, they traveled north and east on winding roads toward the Debatable Hills. The countryside was eerily peaceful. Crops were being gathered in and scarecrows burned to placate the fields for the theft of their produce. But in the country stores where they stopped for supplies, citizens clustered about newspapers and radios and spoke in low, worried voices.

The baby was fed breast milk when they could buy it, cow's milk when they could not, and formula when nothing else was available. He seemed to like all of them equally and he ran through diapers like nobody's business. All things considered, it didn't take him long to get over the loss of his mother. "Who's a little rascal?" Raven said to the imp as Cat drove. "Who's my itty-bitty scamp? You are! Yes, you are."

"So what's the story with the kid and his mother?" Cat asked.

"It's personal," Raven replied.

"Given the situation, I kinda want to know."

"Yeah, well, just because you want to know something doesn't mean you ever will," Raven said, and lapsed into a sullen silence.

They drove through lush and verdant lands with hills so green they hurt to look at them and valleys so beautiful as to make Cat forget to keep her eyes on the road until Raven screamed at her to get back on her side of the line. In the evening, they booked weeklong stays in the finest inns they could find and in the morning they went for a drive after breakfast and never came back. It was all tremendous fun and would have been as good as any vacation Cat had ever experienced if it weren't for the horrors of the Brocielande Station raid and the nightmares that woke her in the middle of the night.

This near-idyllic existence lasted until they came to the Great River and discovered that the bridge across it had been secured by the regional guard, who were stopping all vehicles and examining the credentials of everyone in them. Or so said a hulder who had come from the far side and paused to share the information. There was a backup miles long as a result.

Cat pulled the pickup off the road and Raven lit a cigarette. "We're screwed if they ask for our IDs," she said. "You don't have any and mine were issued years in the future."

"So what do we do?"

"Improvise."

At Raven's direction, Cat wheeled the truck about and drove back to the last town they had passed through. It was clearly a staging point for the Armies of the West, for there were young soldiers in uniform everywhere. "Park here," Raven said when they'd reached the center of town and, leaning out the window, caught the eye of one. "Hey, warrior! You got a spare uniform in that duffel bag?"

The soldier was a woods fey, of a height with Raven, and had an easy grin. He ambled to the truck and put down the bag. "What's it to you?"

"We've got to return this brat to his folks in Garena, other side of the river, and my sister's driver's license is expired. I'm thinking, though, if someone were to lend me a uniform, I could bluff my way across."

"Oh, yeah? If I lent you my uniform would you let me watch you take it off when you return it?"

"I'll do a lot more than that, handsome. You look like you haven't mustered in yet. Are you free tonight? Meet us in the Black Hart in Garena at nineteen hundred hours and my sister and I will give you a night you'll never forget."

Even knowing that Raven was making empty promises, Cat couldn't help but blush. The soldier's grin grew wider at that, which compounded her embarrassment.

"Ma'am, you had me at letting me see you in your undies." The soldier opened his duffel bag, dug out the spare uniform, and handed it to Raven. Who, almost simultaneously, kicked Cat in the ankle.

Cat started up the truck and pulled into the road. Raven blew the soldier a kiss. "Bring some silk scarves," she said, "and I'll let you tie me up."

On the far side of town, they found a barbershop. Raven went in and emerged with a haircut so short and ugly there could be no doubt she was presenting as a male and a military one to boot. "Oh, Raven—your hair!" Cat cried.

"It'll grow back. It always does."

After that they stopped at the hardware store, where Raven bought a dog collar and chain. "Put 'em on," she said and, when Cat had, "Okay. Gimme the wheel. It's showtime."

※※

Two hours of stop-and-go traffic later, they came to the road-block at the foot of the bridge. "Amateurs," Cat said out of the corner of her mouth. "You want to set up the checkpoint a distance from the bridge so if an IED goes off, it doesn't do any damage to the asset."

"If they had any idea what they were doing, they wouldn't be defending a bridge in the middle of their own territory," Raven replied. "They're inexperienced and antsy and they're making it up as they go along. I can work with that. Now. I'm going to spin these guys an ugly little fantasy. Are you down with that?"

"Uh . . . sure."

"I'm holding you to your word. Keep your eyes down and don't say anything. No matter what garbage you hear, show no emotion whatsoever."

A kobold and a pair of tiddy men, all in regional guard uniforms, approached the truck. "Get out of the vehicle, sir," the kobold said.

Raven tied the end of Cat's dog chain to the steering wheel. "Stay!" she told Cat, and climbed out.

Cat stared down at her lap, said nothing.

"What's this?" one of the tiddy men asked.

"War wife," Raven said. "Picked up her and two others in the aftermath of the Brocielande Station raid, but I gave one to my CO and the other to a buddy. Plenty more where they came from."

"War wife, eh?" said one tiddy man.

"That's a new one on me," said the other.

"Yeah," said the kobold. "What's the deal?"

"War wives are like real wives," said Raven, "except more obedient. Plus, they don't have any claim on you. Also, you can have as many as you want. They're property, essentially."

The guardsmen looked at one another. "You say you just picked up three of 'em. How's that work?" the kobold asked.

"You grab 'em, you train 'em, you keep 'em. Simple as that. It wouldn't be legal for civilians. But in times of war certain legal and social protections are loosened for . . ." Talking, Raven strolled out of earshot, pulling the guardsmen after her. Just as well, too, in Cat's opinion. She wasn't exactly enjoying anything she was hearing.

Not much later, the guardsmen returned, opened the door for Raven, and waved her on her way. At no time had they asked to see her papers.

When the bridge was invisible behind them, Raven said, "You can take off the dog collar now."

Cat threw the thing out the window. "Just what kind of ideas have you put into the heads of those assholes?"

"I told them that to acquire a war wife legally, it had to be done in broad daylight with ranking officers nearby for witnesses. Then that their victims had to be driven around real slow to teach them that nobody was going to come to their aid if they called for help. Then that . . . Trust me, if they try to act on my advice—and I'm kinda hoping they do—they'll wind up in the brig so fast they won't know what hit them."

Early the next afternoon, Cat and Raven saw two sand giants digging holes in the middle of a bright-green field of oats, casually destroying the crops around them in the process. Since she was planning to swap out drivers soon anyway, Cat stopped the pickup truck and leaned out the window. "Hey!" she shouted. "What are you doing?"

The sand giantess mopped her forehead and, putting down her shovel, wandered over to the road. Sitting, to bring her face level with Cat's, she said, "War's begun. Our kind's always the first to be drafted and the first to die. Because of our size, you see. On the one hand, we're strong. On the other hand, we're easy targets. Face it, you don't have to be much of a shot to hit one of us with a bazooka, do you? So my hubby and me are going to hibernate for forty, fifty years. We'll sleep through this fuss and dig our way out after it's over."

The sand giant had stumped over to see what was going on. Now he loomed over his spouse, listening.

"Fifty years is a long time," Cat said.

"Yup," the sand giant agreed.

"Tell me about it!" The sand giantess threw her hands up in the air. "Worst thing is, all those years in the earth erode your recollection. After I dug my way out last time, I came to with no memory of my past at all."

"No memory nor hardly no clothes neither," the sand giant rumbled. "They'd all rotted off of her. I could see everything. You name it, I saw it."

"Behave yourself!" The giantess punched him in the shoulder so hard that it would have shattered the bones of a lesser being. "You did a lot more than look."

The giant sat down alongside his wife and clasped her hand. "We bonded."

"Oh, is that what you're calling it now?"

"After we'd been together a few years, we went to the local hag and told her we intended to get hitched. But she laughed and said we was already married. Every time a war came along, we went underground, forgot our pasts, and when we dug out, fell for each other all over again. We was kind of a local legend."

"Course, the hag also said that four or five hundred years ago, loverboy here was married to a slut with hair the color of straw. Only she dug her way out early once and wandered off, never to be seen again."

"No big loss," said the sand giant. "Can't even recollect her name."

Raven walked to the driver's side of the pickup and opened

the door. "Slide over. This has been one swell conversation, but we've got to get moving."

"We were having a nice little chat," Cat objected.

"Were. Aren't anymore. Get your ass in gear."

The sand giant stood and slapped his hands against his knees and butt to knock off the dirt. Then he helped his wife up. "Time we went back to work anyway. We got holes to dig and the draft to dodge."

"That's right," said the sand giantess. "Then, before we bury ourselves to sleep, we're gonna want to bond the living daylights out of each other."

⁎⁎

As they drove off, Cat said, "Are you setting an egg?"

"No!"

"Just asking. Because you were pretty testy with those folks back there." There was something different about Raven today. Abruptly, Cat realized what it was. "Hey. You're not smoking. You haven't had a cigarette all day."

"Gave 'em up after the bridge yesterday. Withdrawal gives me a way to redirect my anger."

"Anger at what?"

"Anger at those idiots at the bridge. At everyone who makes war possible. At anyone who flies dragons. At you."

"My mission is to defend Babylon from her enemies, to keep her borders secure, and to uphold the honor of Her Absent Majesty before all the world."

"You think Her Absent Majesty gives a fuck about her honor? She probably ran off just to get away from crap like honor, borders, conquest, slaughter, genocide . . ."

"The Dragon Corps serves as a deterrent to foreign aggression. It is the single greatest force for peace in the world. If you think things are a mess now, just try living without it."

"Yeah, it sounds real good when you put it that way. Not so much when the golden fire falls on a train station crammed with civilians and the screaming begins. Sounds bad while it's happening and smells even worse afterward."

Cat's face went cold and numb. She clamped her mouth shut.

In tense silence, they let the road glide beneath their pickup's tires until a convenience store swam into view. By unspoken agreement, they stopped and Raven went inside to buy the makings of lunch. Cat spread out a blanket on the grass and, after checking to make sure he didn't need to be changed again, set the brat down on one corner of it. She watched as, with great effort, he managed to catch one foot and then lose it again. Contentedly, he set out to repeat the deed.

Raven came back with sandwiches, deviled eggs, two bottles of beer, and a pannikin of warm rusalka's milk. She thumped one of the bottles down in front of Cat, who (for she was learning to read Raven's ways) accepted it as a tacit peace offering. Then she filled the baby's bottle with milk and guided the nipple into his mouth.

After the imp had been fed and the sandwiches eaten, Cat said, "We've got the bag of magical doodads we came for. Why are we going so far out of our way to find a place for the kid? Why not take him back to the present and find someone there to take care of him?"

"I've got my reasons." Raven bit the last deviled egg in half, chewed, swallowed. "But even if I didn't, there's no way I'd bring a baby anywhere near Sasha."

"There seems to be some history between you two."

"Well, as far as Sasha's concerned, I'm the one that got away. And there's no denying that she tried to kill me and eat me. But you don't hate gravity for breaking your leg when you fall out of a tree. Same thing with Sasha. She can't help being the way she is."

"Tell me everything," Cat said.

Raven swallowed down the last of her egg and settled herself into a storyteller's stance. Touching hands together to make the sign of the yoni, she said:

"I was lost. I admit it. I'd been hired by this schmuck—let's call him Hank—whose heart had been stolen and placed in a glass egg by a bitter ex-girlfriend and then dumped in a thieves' market where it was sold to an itinerant haruspex, blah, blah, blah. You've probably heard this story a hundred times. My plan was for us to hike deep into Caledon Wood, where I'd built a stone altar, and leave him standing watch over it all night. 'Prove yourself true—your heart will return to you.' Which wasn't gonna happen, given some of the frights I'd lined up for him. He was going to soil himself and run off screaming. Come dawn, he'd be so ashamed of his cowardice it would never occur to him to come looking for me. Simple. Clean.

"But either I took a wrong turn or the witch-house moved itself into my path because come midnight there it was, glowing bright as the sun. I couldn't convince Hank this wasn't what we'd come looking for. It was all I could do to keep him from hammering on the door. So I pried open a side window and we climbed in and . . . well, you've seen that place. It's like a candy store for grown-ups, 'miright?

"Hank went apeshit. I tried to stop him, but he saw a line of hearts in glass eggs and made a beeline for them. Guys like Hank have consistently lousy luck. So, inevitably, he grabbed one that was not only ensorcelled but lethal. Whammo! Down he goes, ass over teak-fiddle, dead as a doormat. Tough titties to the poor bastard who bought his heart.

"Out comes Sasha, breathing fire and talking trash.

"Skipping over a lot of tedious exposition, it's established that Sasha plans to cook me in that honking big stove of hers and then do her cannibalistic thing. She's got wards and weapons up the yin-yang. All I've got is a superior brain.

"'I invoke the ancient courtesies,' I said. 'I'm entitled to one last wish, right?'

"'You might be and you might not,' Sasha replied. 'It depends on the wish. Ask for a gun and I'll laugh in your face.'

"'Can't help but notice you've got a world-class selection of liquor here. I know how to make the best Manhattan ever. If I have to die, that's the taste I want in my mouth.'

"Long and short, Sasha let me fix a pitcher. I started with Pappy Van Winkle two-hundred-year reserve and then mellowed it with just a splash of Sir John Falstaff grande champagne cognac, distilled under the supervision of the master himself. To this I added Carpano Antica sweet vermouth—why get fancy?—and minuscule amounts of eight different bitters (if I'd used the full twelve, Sasha would have thought I was stalling) and just the slightest shaving of white truffle, to make the flavors *pop*. 'Frost the glasses while I shake,' I said, and Sasha glared them white with rime. The drink itself, however, I chilled with ice from the living glaciers of Niflheim, which crackled most marvelously as I shook the cocktail cold. Into the glasses I dropped two spiced cherries from the Isles of the Blest. I kid you not, it was a drink that literally was to die for. I poured one for myself and another for Sasha. Then I raised my glass in toast. 'Evoe!'

"We drank. Strange to tell, Sasha finished hers before I did mine. So I poured her another. And kept it topped up. And fixed another pitcher.

"I was hoping to get her so plowed she'd pass out. But Sasha was made of stronger stuff than that. Cast-iron stomach and a bladder to match. At last she cried 'Enough!' and marched me off to the kitchen. She slammed open an oven door, and gestured with her handgun—a Mauser, of course; I've never known a woods witch to pack anything else—and said, 'Climb in.'

"I played stupid. I bent over, stuck out my butt to one side and my elbows to the other and said, 'I can't fit in.'

"Sasha thought I was as drunk as she was, so she tried to talk me through it. 'Just get down on your knees and crawl in,' she said. 'Any idiot could do it.'

"'But if I bend like this, it won't work,' I said. 'And when I lean back, the rest of me sticks out.' No matter how I contorted myself, I just couldn't seem to get inside the oven. All the while, of course, I'm reeling and staggering . . . Y'know, I almost spit in his face when my dad insisted I take mime lessons. But, son-ofagod, the old guy knew what he was doing. I was so clueless I drove Sasha nuts.

"Finally, she was so frustrated with me that she put aside the Mauser and got down on all fours. 'Like this!' she said.

"Quick as a lizard's wink, I shoved Sasha into the stove. Her head banged against the back, and I slammed the door on her butt.

"Oh, did she roar! But she was good and caught. So when she ran out of steam, I said, 'What will you give me to be let free?'

"'Nothing!' Sasha cried. 'I am hunger and winter and famine and drought. I am the night that never ends. I am she who does not give but only takes.'

"'My hand is on the gas knob,' I reminded her.

"Now Sasha began to see what a fix she was in. 'I'll give you your life,' she said.

"That was a good beginning. But I wanted more. So I said—"

"Wait! I know this story!" Cat cried. "You're Clever Gretchen! And Hank—he must have been the original for her brother Hans."

"That's an old, old tale," Raven said. "Whatever truth may

lie at its heart, before the distortions of rumor and time, happened long before I was born."

But she did not meet Cat's eyes.

⸙⸙

At last, they came to a nothing-much village nestled into an almost-valley deep in the Debatable Hills. A river ran by it with ramshackle docks and a few unpainted warehouses at the bank and a marsh on the lower end of town. There were eight or ten brick buildings on the central square. All the others were clapboard or dressed log or even (the oldest ones) wattle and daub. "This is it," Raven said.

"Thank the Goddess." The infant had been cranky all morning, though whether he was teething or suffering from colic, Cat had no idea. "I'll be glad to get this insufferable brat off our hands."

Raven rounded on Cat, white with anger. "Don't you dare talk that way about my—!" She stopped. "About the kid. He's an innocent and I won't let you slander him. Do you hear me?"

Cat had never seen her friend like this. But she didn't back down. "I heard you just fine. You said 'my.' Is that your baby?"

"No. He's not. Over there's somebody we can ask directions from."

Working her way across the cobbled pavement of the town square with the aid of a walking stick was an old woman whose exposed breasts, wide hat, and green sash identified her as a hag. Raven got out of the truck, bowed before her, and said, "Reverend Mistress, your counsel I crave. We're looking for a woman named Blind Enna."

"Blind Enna? There's nobody in these parts by that name. The only Enna we have is Enna of the Bright Eyes. She's light-haired, light-footed, light-hearted, and light-headed. A bubble of a girl. She lives at the edge of town where the marsh meets the river. Not the one you seek, I suspect."

"We'll look her up anyway," Raven said, touching a hand to her forehead, heart, and sex. "Our thanks be unto thee."

The house belonging to Enna of the Bright Eyes, when they found it, was a trim, acorn-shaped cottage with a thatch roof and a brick chimney for the stem. The door was ajar and when they rapped on it, there came no response. Cat strained her ears and heard someone sobbing.

They went in.

Enna was crouched in a lightless room, hands over her eyes, crying inconsolably.

"What's the—?" Cat began.

"Quiet!" Raven summoned a handful of the *lux aeterna* and left it hanging in the air, where it illuminated the young woman, revealing two damp blotches on her blouse, one over each swollen breast. Kneeling, Raven put an arm around her shoulders. "You lost the child, didn't you?"

Without ceasing to cry, Enna nodded.

"Where is the body?"

"There's . . . an island in the marsh. It's where she was conceived. I dug a hole there and placed her within, wrapped in silk. I gave her flowers for the journey: thistles to protect her, wraith buttons to bless the way, hyacinth to keep her steady, hollyhock to give her ambition, groundsel so she'll rise, and yarrow to help cure my heartbreak. Only that doesn't seem to be working. Then, to make sure my daughter would be looked on with favor by the Goddess, I offered her my eyes."

Enna lowered her hands and Cat saw with horror that they were black with blood. As were the empty spaces where her eyes had been.

"Get the bag," Raven said, and Cat hurried to comply.

The baby was still fast asleep in the nest of blankets they'd fashioned for him in the open top of the leather satchel, so Cat brought him along. Inside, she lifted him to her shoulder so she could paw through its contents with her free hand.

Each artifact had been wrapped in linen, tied up with string, and labeled with a neatly lettered strip of paper. "There's a packet near the top marked 'sleep,'" Raven said. "Find it."

Cat rummaged, found, untied. Within was a small silver bell. "Now cover your ears." Raven lifted the bell and shook it by Enna's ear. Then both she and Enna slumped slowly to the floor, one this way and the other that. The baby, already asleep, seemed unaffected.

Enna of the Bright Eyes had been sitting alongside her pallet. Cat lifted her onto it. She groped her way to the window and threw open its shutters, flooding the room with light and returning the *lux aeterna* to the substrate of the universe. Then she shook Raven awake.

"Whoof! Wish I'd thought to bring along earplugs." Raven dug through the satchel. She came out with a misericorde and, leaving it scabbarded, slid it under the pallet. "This will help ward off despair. It's why I fixed the baby nest where I did—to erase some of the trauma of losing his mother."

"I wondered about that."

"The healing-women can care for those eyes and a few courses of antibiotics ought to clear up any infection. We'll get them on the case. Right now, sleep is the best doctor."

"Shouldn't we be looking for the father?"

"He's not here. So he's not worth finding." Raven reached for a pack of cigarettes that wasn't in her pocket, scowled, and said, "Our job is to patch her together so she can take care of babykins here."

"Tell me you're joking."

"She's young, unattached, and lactating. It's perfect."

"She's also blind, heartbroken, and probably suicidal."

"Yeah, well. We work with what the Goddess gives us."

Just then, the baby woke up and began to cry. Cat, who by now understood his moods, hurried to mix formula with warm water from the sun bottle. Behind her, she heard Raven crooning: "Awww. Is oo hungry? Is oo hungry? Don't oo worry, ittybitty, I've got a pair of nice milky tits coming your way. Just be patient for a few days and they're all yours."

※

Back in the center of town, the square was empty. The hag was nowhere to be seen, nor any of her compeers. But Raven gave a copper penny to a passing hummingirl and said, "Tell the healing-women that Enna of the Bright Eyes has lost her child and blinded herself. Go! As fast as you can fly!"

The child lifted into the air and, with a whirr of her wings, disappeared.

"Now for a room," Raven said.

The only available lodgings in town belonged to a two-story brick hotel with a wooden façade on the roofline that wouldn't have fooled a hedgehog. The halls were dim, the rugs running along them smelled musty, and where the front office should have been was a bar. Raven talked to the barmaid and got a pair of keys to 2-B. She booked the room for a month, which told Cat they would be staying at least a week.

※

The healing-women converged upon Enna's cottage. Cat and Raven saw them scurrying in and out as they passed it on their way to Edgemoor Road to show the infant the marsh-flowers in bloom. "That will keep everybody occupied for a few days," Raven said. "In the meantime, you, me, and the rug rat can get some much-needed downtime."

"Speaking of whom, isn't it time we gave him a name? How

about Milkweed? Or Belvedere Electroluxe? Or maybe People's Fertilizer Unit 437?"

"Oh, be serious."

"What is this, a fucking puzzle? I'm supposed to put together the clues and figure out what's going on? You're obsessed with this kid, you're determined to unload him on an emotional basket case, you've gone so far off-mission I can't even imagine how we're going to get from here to Ys, you deny he's your baby while acting as if he were, and you refuse to give him so much as a nickname. What gives?"

"I told you. Just because you have questions doesn't mean you're entitled to answers. That's Theology 101."

Thus quarreling, Cat and Raven passed an otherwise idyllic week. They took long walks and got to know the town and its environs. Sometimes they hired a boat and went fishing. The townsfolk in their turn assumed they were a couple, made it clear they suspected the infant was alchemical in origin, and cheated them at every opportunity. Then one day they saw a lone crone exit Enna's cottage. She poured a libation of wine on the ground to feed the spirits of the land, threw a handful of flour to the wind to feed the spirits of the air, and left a smear of blood on the lintel to feed those spirits whom none dared name. "They're done," Raven said. "We'll give her a few hours to recover and then—"

"No." Cat was carrying the baby in a Snugli (bought for twice its proper price in the general store) in front of her. Now she undid the ties and handed both it and the baby to Raven. "You want my cooperation, tell me what's going on."

"You don't understand. This is an *obligation*. I don't have any alternatives."

"Then spill."

Raven clawed at the side of her face, the way she did when the tobacco cravings were particularly bad. "Awright, awright,

awright." She took a deep breath, looked away, and then looked
back. At last, almost shyly, as if admitting to something shame-
ful, she said, "Don't laugh, because this is serious.

"He's my father."

Cat did a little mental arithmetic. "The timing's about right.
Go on."

"This is the town he grew up in. Perfectly happy childhood,
the old man told me, until the War came and busted things up
permanently. The place shaped him. Important thing is, he was
raised by Blind Enna. There's only one Enna in town and she
just blinded herself. Coincidence? Not a chance. Do you have
any idea what's going to happen if, in direct contradiction of
everything we know took place, this baby isn't raised by her?"

"I haven't the foggiest notion."

"Neither do I and I don't want to find out. It would be like
poking the Goddess in the eye. I don't think the results would
be pleasant."

⚹

Raven bought what had to be a dozen yards of black veiling and
wrapped them around and around Cat's head until she felt like
she was peering through a cloud. Chanting guttural cantrips in
what sounded like the Dawn Tongue, Raven tacked the cloud to
itself with silver pins until at last she said, "It's done."

"Yes, but what is it?"

"A spell of disregard. Unless you speak to them directly, nobody will notice you. They'll see you but it simply won't register that you're there."

"That seems like a lot of fuss to go through when I happen to
know that there's a ring inside the satchel labeled 'invisibility.'"

"Magic always costs, remember. For every action, there's an
equal and opposite reaction. That's Merlin's third law. Use that

ring and it's also going to make visible something that was meant to be hidden—we don't know what and we don't want to find out. Same thing with the spell except I know what it's linked to and I know some young ladies who are going to be very amused by what they see. Now. Enna is going to have a supernatural visitor—you."

"Eh?"

"Let me explain . . ."

It took hours of scripting, objections, overruling, challenges, clarifications, and quibbles that threatened to flare up into arguments before Raven finally said, "Remember: Nothing but the truth. If you don't know the truth, don't say anything. Platitudes are fine. But one lie and the whole thing falls apart."

"It's nothing but lies."

"I know. That's the beauty of it."

※

Unnoticed, Cat passed through the village and up Mud Street to the little lane that led to the acorn cottage. She eased the door open and tiptoed into the bedroom. Enna lay on her pallet, staring sightlessly at the ceiling. Cat stood nearby, saying nothing, until the soft sound of her breathing alerted the young fey to her presence. "Who's there?"

"A friend."

Both waited for the other to speak. At last Enna said in a dead voice, "They told me I'm cured. But all I want to do is stay in bed forever. I feel a little less awful here."

Cat made a mental note to remind Raven to retrieve the misericorde before they left. "You're not cured. You'll never be cured. Cured of memories of your daughter? Who would be mad enough to want that? But the day will come when you feel a little less awful. Now stand up. We're going outside."

Enna retrieved two sticks that were leaning on the wall. She probed awkwardly in front of her with them, managed to make her way through the door.

Gently removing one stick from Enna's hand, Cat said, "Take my arm."

Without further conversation, the two walked down Mud Street and into town. New Street led them to the village square, where, it being market day, a labyrinth of tables had been set up from which farmers could sell roots, fairy fruits, and greens, butcher a fresh chicken or firebird or rabbit plucked from a stack of cages, or offer pies baked overnight by the whole or half or slice. All the air smelled delicious and the cobbles underfoot reeked pleasantly of vegetal rot. This being the first time Enna had been out and about since her self-mutilation, there was a rustle of excitement wherever she passed. "Ahhh, Enna," the old gaffers said sadly, while young matrons hugged her fleetingly and whispered condolences, and children were slapped when they demanded to know what had happened to her.

"I should have worn a cloth over my eyes. Over where my eyes used to be, I mean," Enna said.

"Oh, don't worry about that, sweetie!" a woodswife cried in alarm, and, "You'll do that next time," Cat murmured in Enna's ear.

As they were leaving the square, a cow-tailed hulder in a flower print dress rushed up and gushed, "Oh, Enna. Wandering through the market alone! And the terrible thing that happened to you so new."

"But I'm not—" Enna began before Cat quieted her with the tip of a finger on her lips.

"I just wanted you to know I think you're ever so brave." The hulder gave Enna an impetuous kiss on the cheek and fled.

Marveling, Enna said, "She talked to me as if you weren't there. She couldn't see you. Nobody can see you."

"No. Not when I don't want them to."

"Are you a goddess?"

Cat said nothing.

"You are!" Enna started to fall to her knees. "Tell me! Which one are you?"

"No names," Cat said, hauling her back to her feet. "Revere all, give the Goddess her due, and I will be well pleased. For now, say nothing and think seriously on what you have learned today. I will visit you again tomorrow and then you can ask me what you will."

※

The next day, Enna was waiting in the open doorway. She shrieked when Cat came up noiselessly and said, "I'm here." But she clung to the offered arm eagerly

Cat and Enna walked together up Mud Street to Edgemoor Road. After a time, Enna said, "The pain is so much worse than anything I've ever known. Why is that?"

"You have suffered a loss that is worthy of such pain. That's all."

"Yes." They walked on for some time. Then, hesitantly, Enna said, "Sweet, beloved goddess . . . why? My daughter did no one any harm. All those people at Brocielande Station—maybe some of them deserved what happened to them. But surely not all. There's so much misery and injustice in the world. Why?"

Remembering Raven's instructions, Cat was silent.

"Are you there?"

"I am here." Despising herself, Cat said, "Whether you know it or not, you are never alone."

"Why is it there are so many questions you won't answer?"

Cat was silent.

"Am I wrong to want those answers?"

"No." They walked onward, away from the village. It was a

beautiful day, but Cat paid no particular attention to what she saw. She was listening to the smells and tasting the sounds: A frog plopping into water rich with algae. The almost inaudible scrape of crab-folk diligently widening their burrows in the sulfurous mud and repointing the bricks of their wee chimneys. Pussy willows and dogwoods whispering in the breeze. When she deemed there to be clues enough for an answer, Cat said, "Do you know where we are?"

Enna lifted her chin and inhaled. "I do! It's Hagmere Pond." The tremble in her voice told Cat this was a significant place for her.

"Tell me what happened here."

"There was this boy. Man. No, boy. He was my first. He said I had nice eyes. Everybody said I had such nice eyes."

"You did. They belong to your daughter now."

"Yes. Thank you. They do, yes. Oh, that makes such a difference!"

Cat had been carrying Enna's second stick for all their walk. Now she returned it to her and said, "I'm going to leave you now. You'll have to find your own way home."

"But I can't—"

"You're about to learn that you can. You're not as helpless as you think you are."

The hotel room had a background funk of cigarette smoke and brown soap. But with the windows thrown wide and a breeze coming from the marshes, that wasn't too bad. "I hope your day was better than mine," Raven said. "First the spawn came down with diaper rash and when I got that sorted out, he started teething. Then the barmaid finally twigged that I wasn't male and wanted to impose a 'tribade surtax' on the room. It took me forever to shout her down."

"What do you care? We're just going to skip out on the bill anyway."

"It's the principle of the thing. I don't like to be charged for services I'm not receiving. How was your outing with Enna?"

"Exhausting." Cat threw herself down on the bed. When she closed her eyes, the room spun. "The poor, unhappy creature thinks I'm a goddess sent to her to make everything hunky-dory again."

"That's the script we crafted for her, yes. Making progress?"

"I dunno. I suppose. Remind me again why I'm doing this instead of you? It really does seem more your kind of thing."

"Because more than anything, Enna needs truth and sincerity—and nothing makes my stomach ache worse than truth and sincerity. Anyway, this will all be over with soon."

※

Cat lost track of exactly how long it took. But eventually there came a day when she led Enna out of town and up the meadow trail to the top of Eddystone Hill. "So you can feel the wind coming off of the farms," she'd explained. Their pickup truck, Sophie, who liked dirty jokes, country-and-western music, and lying about her service record, Raven had already sent back to the Armies of the West with a full tank of gasoline and a fresh set of spark plugs. When Cat and Enna reached the top of the hill, Raven was waiting there.

"I brought the diaper bag." Raven dropped it at Enna's feet. "It's got wipes too."

"Goddess?" Blind Enna turned more or less in Cat's direction. "Who is this? What's going on?"

"I have something for you." Cat accepted the baby from Raven and said, "This isn't meant to replace your daughter. Nothing and nobody can do that. But it's an infant and it needs to be protected." Cat placed the baby in Enna's arms. "Everybody has to have a purpose. This can be yours."

Suddenly laden with the weight of a child, Enna made a harsh, bleak noise, like the cry of a seagull. "Whose . . . ?"

Now Raven spoke. "It's your sister's child. You remember your sister who disappeared when you were a girl?" This was a complete fiction, which was why they had both agreed that she should be the one to tell it. "His parents died in the Brocielande Station raid, which makes you his only kin. Take good care of him." She started away and then turned back. "His name's Will. Will le Fey."

Cat unpinned and unwrapped the veiling from her head and let a light breeze unreel it downhill, twisting like an air serpent. There was no one nearby, no longer any need for anonymity. "This is the last time we will meet in the flesh. You will always be in my thoughts, however, as I am sure I will be in yours." She kissed Enna on the lips. "May the peace of the Goddess be always with you."

"But I still have questions!"

"Look inside yourself," Cat said, ignoring the cynical grin that flashed onto Raven's face. "The answers you seek are there to be found."

Silently and without fuss, a stairway appeared in the air, leading up into darkness.

Treads materialized under Cat's feet. Moving cautiously, she began to climb. Raven was already a dozen steps ahead, carrying the satchel they had come in search of so very long ago. Cat looked back and saw Enna, with Baby Will in her arms, head down, already dwindling. With each step she took, the stairs disappeared behind her.

It felt exactly like climbing into the sky.

Pain is never permanent.

—Teresa of Ávila

THE AIR WAS FILLED WITH MICROSCOPIC BLADES OF ICE.
Cat had forgotten how frigid Sasha's house was until she inhaled and thousands of those blades slashed her lungs and made her gasp. The witch-woman didn't scare Cat anymore. As well be afraid of a high-tension line because it could kill you. Well, so could anything. A sprig of holly could kill you if it were fired from a powerful enough gun. Accelerate it to the speed of light and it would hit with all the force of a hydrogen bomb.

But the cold was a problem.

Teeth chattering, Cat watched Sasha extend a hand toward Raven with glacial grace. "I'll take my treasures now."

Raven scratched the side of her face. "Yeah, well, about that. I told you I was holding you to your exact words. You said to bring back the bag. So here it is." She let the satchel fall to the floor with a soft thump. "You said nothing about its contents."

Sasha scooped up the satchel, upended it, shook it. When nothing fell out, she clutched it so tightly that the leather shattered into brittle pieces and fell to the floor. "You dare play word games with me?"

Raven twisted a hand and a cigarette appeared in it. She

stuck the fag in her mouth and snapped her fingers. Smoke curled up. "Trickster, remember? I've got a license to swindle. I could fax you a scan of it, if you'd like."

The two stared hard at one another. It seemed to Cat that they were evenly matched and that witnessing this clash of titans would have been tremendous fun if only it weren't so scathingly cold. At last, Sasha said, "What exorbitant demands are you making for the return of my rightful property? Stolen, I might remind you, by members of your family. Which is, I happen to know, legal justification for me to declare vendetta upon your entire shabby tribe of trailer-camp hedge wizards."

Rubbing her arms with her hands didn't seem to do much good. But when Cat stopped, the results made her redouble her efforts.

"My terms are surprisingly reasonable. First, no vendetta. No reprisals of any kind for whatever actions I may have taken in pursuit of your Big Bag o' Magic. Second, my client gets to use the key and the whistle, as per our original agreement. If they're still in her possession when her quest is done, she'll mail them back—you provide the self-addressed stamped envelope. If they're lost, stolen, or damaged, the cost is swallowed by you. No reprisals for that either. Oh, and all past and present debts I may owe you are wiped out in perpetuity. That's a given."

Cat's feet and the tip of her nose were numb. She buried her nose in the crook of her elbow and stepped one foot on the other, back and forth, over and over, in a vain attempt to restore warmth.

Sasha's face was so white it gleamed. The crystals of ice in the air formed a pale nimbus about her head. "Your debt is zeroed out. But I'm restoring ten percent for every hour that passes before I get my baubles back."

"Deal. They're in a heap on the top step of the staircase you sent us down. I gave Cat the key and whistle and dumped the rest there on our way in. Technically, that's in your house, so they're already in your possession and no penalty applies."

For a long, still moment, Sasha was motionless. Then she said, "You're a cunning little stunt. But you'll be back. Your kind always comes back. My house is like a casino to you. You're not the first to leave it a winner, not by a long shot. But not a one of you is able to quit while you're ahead. You'll keep returning, over and over, until your luck runs out at last. Because deep down inside you want to lose. You deserve to lose. In all the world, the only home you have is here and you know it. When you're finally feeling guilty enough to admit it, my stove and my knives and I will be here waiting for you."

"I just bet you will."

"Am I wrong? Then tell me so. But first, remember what the penalty is for lying in my house."

"I—"

"You ran away from the one place where you ever belonged and you'd rather die than return to it, don't pretend otherwise, I know the whole sordid story. Ever since, you've been going up and down Faerie, causing mischief, never setting down roots. Where do you belong if not here?"

"I'm tired of these games and I'm going to leave now."

"Shall I show you to the door?"

"At your rates? We'll climb out a window."

⚹

A fist thundered on the motel room door. BLAMBLAMBLAM-BLAM! "Open up! Her Absent Majesty demands it!"

Cat opened the door. "Hello, Raven."

Raven sauntered in, pulling off a slicker wet with rain. "Wow. What a storm. Have you been out in it? You really know how to choose a day off, Cat. Hey, Esme, guess what? I brought the makings of s'mores."

"Yaaay!"

With a maximum of ceremony, they made s'mores on one of the motel grills under the eaves of the leeward side of the building. Then Raven produced packets of Kool-Aid and they put a much-needed streak of red in what remained of her hair and half a rainbow's worth of colors in Esme's before the child tired of the activity. Then Esme demanded a story. So Cat told The Moon Is Never Silly and Good Ladybugs Make Good Neighbors and The King Who Was as Dumb as Mud and His Three Sons Who Were Even Stupider Than He Was, Hard Though That Might Be to Believe. Then, when Esme clamored for more, Cat looked helplessly at Raven. Who grinned, cockily of course, and said, "I guess it's my turn."

Sitting cross-legged on the bed, Raven traced an X over her heart to make the sigil of truth and said, "Skipping over a lot of tedious and unnecessary backstory, there I was in wingtips, an ascot with a diamond stickpin, and a three-piece Brooks Brothers suit, looking perfectly out of place on a nude beach. Males only, of course, and ichor-blooded purebreds to boot. Gods forbid a female should see their troublemakers. They had trolls in livery standing guard over their clothes! That's how anal-retentive they were. Their cars, on the other hand, were just sitting there with the keys in the ignitions, a fortune in drugs in every glove compartment, and some very nice guns in clips under the dashboards. So, figuring I was a frazz over-dressed for the occasion, I sauntered over and sweet-talked a Jaguar XKE with a trunkful of stolen antique Atlantean pottery— the smutty stuff—into running off with . . ."

"This is a lovely story," Cat said, "but is it really appropriate for Esme's ears?"

"Aw, she doesn't mind. You keep forgetting how old our little sweetie is. Hey, Esme! You know how to hotwire a car?"

"Well, duh."

"Know how to roll a blunt? How to set up a meth lab? How to field-strip and fire a Kalashnikov?"

"I'm just a little girl," Esme said indignantly. "If I tried to fire an automatic weapon, the recoil would knock me over. Everybody knows that."

"None of that matters. If Esme wants the perks of being a little girl, she's just going to have to act like one."

"All right. Here's something that I know for a fact you'll approve of. So sit quiet and just this once, don't interrupt, okay?" Raven clapped her hands three times sharply, the way a professional storyteller would, to call for silence. She touched her head, her lips, her heart, and her sex, signifying that her every word would be, in some sense, true. Then she said, "This is the tale of Mother Eve and the Policeman."

⁂

Mother Eve went to Tiffany's and stole some jewelry. She had enough money to pay for it. She just didn't care to. But the security people saw her do this thing and sent for a policeman.

When the policeman tried to arrest Eve, however, he was careless and she took his gun. Then she forced him to take off all his clothing. She stripped down to her underwear and put on his uniform and equipment. Then she got into his cruiser and sailed off into the streets of New York City with the siren screaming, taunting her pursuers over the radio.

But that game grew old fast. So she took a shortcut through Central Park and ditched the cruiser in the lake. After that, she disappeared into the crowd in such a way that nobody knew where she'd gone. This was a thing she knew how to do.

That night, Eve saw the police officer she had robbed sitting in a bar, dressed like a civilian. He was very handsome, but he looked sad too. It was possible that he had just lost his job because of her. So she slid onto a stool beside him and murmured into his ear, "I think you should come back to my apartment with me. I have a new pair of handcuffs I haven't tried out yet."

In a better world than ours, he would not have gone. But this is the world that Eve made, so the evening went pretty much as you might expect.

⁂

Esme clapped enthusiastically. Raven stood and bowed, grinning as if she'd done something particularly clever. And by some standards, Cat had to admit, perhaps she had. "Esme?" she said. "Go to the motel office and get us some sodas. Also, if they have candy, you can have as much as you want. Tell them to put it on my account. They can call the room, if they don't believe you."

"I don't have a raincoat."

"You can wear Raven's. It'll be big and floppy and fun for you."

As soon as the door closed behind Esme, Cat said, "Every time I start liking you, you pull something like this. Why is that? And how did you know about Mother Eve? She's just this character that Helen made up."

"Is she? Well, maybe she is. As for how I know, you were being tracked across Europa, remember? A team of investigators interviewed every member of the hobo camp you stayed in that they could find, and the centaurs who busted up the place as well. Did you know that the bullbeggar had the hots for you? You wouldn't want to hear some of the things he tried to convince us the two of you did."

"'Us'?"

"Yeah, I was part of the team. I'm a paid employee of the Conspiracy—just like you were, back in Carcassonne."

Face motionless, Cat thought as fast and hard as she could. It had not escaped her notice that Raven had not asked who

Helen was. Now she said, "So . . . are you still working for them?"

"No! I told you, we're on the same side. I replaced one of their persecutors in order to get the skinny on you." Raven raised her hands as if in supplication to an unseen Power. "Nobody ever believes a word I say! Which is ironic because I'm always right about absolutely everything."

Cat made a farting noise with her lips.

"Yeah, yeah, yeah, yeah. You're a fountain of insight. Fine. Great. Here's the thing, though. If it weren't for the reports I've been giving the Conspiracy putting you five hundred miles south of here, this area would be crawling with agents. Ys is important—and not just because your brother is there. All the big mahoffs in the Conspiracy are obsessed with it."

"Why?"

"Okay, this will take a bit. Ys is older than you can imagine. Ancient. Pre-Cyclopean. Before it was destroyed and rebuilt, its name was Yspra. Big place, capital city of a kingdom that stretched up and down the coast, dominating what later became Brittany. But that city was built on the ruins of a much older one, name of Hysprana. Port city, the hub of your standard mercantile power. Before that came a demonic, wizard-haunted center of power named Hy-Paragnon. Evil place. Destroying it bankrupted the civilizations of its time and ushered in a dark age that lasted for millennia. Read a history of it once and had to go on a weeklong bender to blot out some of what I learned. But before it was corrupted, Hy-Paragnon was a city of learning and justice esteemed throughout Old Faerie. Its name then was—"

"Hyperuranion!"

"Whoa. Looks like you're a step ahead of me. So you already knew all of this?"

"No, but I heard about the Treaty of Hyperuranion. And I know that the Conspiracy wants to break it. So they can—how did the Barkster put it?—'plunge all of Faerie into an age of unending war.'" Cat shrugged. "That's pretty much all I know."

"Well, there's more. The Treaty of Hyperuranion can't be broken. It's binding on all signatories and on their heirs and assigns. It can be renegotiated and even negated—but only at the same place where it was originally signed. Hyperuranion. Or Ys, as it's presently called. With representatives of all involved parties present. Only Ys is underwater now. Dragons don't do water. Fire and air, fine. Land, if they have to. But not water. So long as Ys remains sunk beneath the sea, the treaty is inviolate. See?"

"Oh."

"Which means you're walking into one hot mess of magic and intrigue." Raven's expression was as serious as Cat had ever seen it. "So that's yet another reason why we should get this over with as soon as we possibly can."

Esme returned then, clutching a sopping-wet paper bag whose bottom burst the instant she entered the room, sending candy bars and cans of Dr Pepper scattering everywhere. Cat and Raven got down on their knees to gather them up and Esme joined them and long before their task was done, they were all in a heap, laughing their heads off.

So the afternoon went, until Esme grew tired and cranky and refused to take a nap. Then Raven said, "Okay, here's the challenge: Lie down in the middle of the bed and stare at the ceiling. No wriggling, mind you. See if you can make a picture in your mind from the cracks in the ceiling. Then I'll put my hand over your eyes and count to ten. See if you can remember that picture for that long. Bet you can't."

"Sure I can," Esme said angrily.

"Then prove it."

Esme lay down and Raven passed a hand over her eyes. It was like a conjuring trick: The eyes were open when the hand covered them and closed when the hand moved away. Seconds later, the child began to snore.

"Okay," Raven said. "We've got some final planning to do if we want to leave first thing in the morning."

They spread out the map on top of the chest of drawers. Raven drew a small star in the Bay of Dreams. "Here's where we think Ys has to be. So this is the part of the coast where we should go. It's pretty remote. Dirt roads only, but Jill's got four-wheel drive." She drew a spiral on the coastline. "Over here is the closest point to the city. So that's where we'll be heading. Esme and I will set up a tent and wait while you go fetch your brother. Esme loves camping out, so that will be fun for her."

"Do we have everything we need?"

"We'll buy the camping gear and some food along the way. For your part, you don't need much. The pennywhistle to summon transportation. The key to keep you alive. A small, silver-bladed sickle. That's pretty much it."

"Silver I understand—it's a good specific against magic. But a sickle? Why?"

When Raven told her, Cat laughed out loud.

⁂

Later, after Esme had woken up in a better mood and been put to work making pictures with noodles and glue and they'd sent out for pizza and the child was engrossed in the television set, Raven said, "I'm feeling housebound."

"Well, it's been a long day."

Raven tossed her car keys in the air sitting down and caught them standing up. "You and I are going barhopping. C'mon. I haven't debauched anybody in a long time and I don't want to get rusty at it."

"But what about Esme?"

"Esme's a million years old. She can look after herself for one night. Hey, Esme. What would you say if I asked whether you wanted us to leave you alone for an evening with permission to eat and drink anything in the minifridge so long as it wasn't alcoholic and watch television and stay up as late as you liked?"

Solemnly, Esme said, "I think I would say yes, please."

The first bar they hit was the Djinn and Tonic Tavern. Perversely, they ordered mojitos. The bar was empty except for a lone red dwarf who sat by himself drinking so slowly and grimly that it was obvious he had nothing else to do with his life. "When does this start to be fun?" Cat asked.

"The evening is young," Raven replied. "A few bars from now, after we've gotten a sufficiency of alcohol into you, your standards will lower themselves and you'll begin to enjoy the experience."

"Oh, goodie."

The second bar was Kalki's Roost. There they switched to piña coladas and chatted up a couple of commercial travelers who were in the dream trade. It turned out there was a lot more to the business than most consumers suspected. Far more, Cat learned, than she would ever want to know. The salesmen picked up their tabs and Cat and Raven went to the ladies' room together and never came back.

After that was the Mare's Nest, which turned out to be female-only, where the centauress behind the bar comped Cat a Clover Club and frowned when Raven said, "How come I'm the only man here?"

"Finish your drink and leave," the tappie told her. Then, when Raven held the glass at arm's length and poured her pink lady on the floor, the centauress came out from behind the bar.

Hoisting Raven over her head, she rushed them both through the door and into the parking lot. There she disdainfully set the trickster down and, with a snort and a flick of her tail, turned her back on them both. Much the same thing happened at the Prancing Pony. There, putting on her butchest mannerisms, Raven flirted aggressively with a buff young fey until he was flushed with arousal and then, howling with laughter, flashed him her tits. This time, Cat hustled her outside before the bouncer could reach them.

"You are nothing but trouble," Cat marveled as Jill drove them to the next bar. "That guy was definitely going to punch you out."

"I told you it gets more fun as the night wears on."

The Silent Man was loud, dark, and crowded. It had a small dance floor, a disco ball, and music that had passed its sell-by date decades ago. "I can hardly hear myself think!" Cat shouted.

"Then don't think!" Raven grabbed Cat's wrist and dragged her out onto the floor. They danced with each other at first, and then with strangers. When they returned to the table, they were followed by a satyr, who drew up a chair and sat down without being invited. "So what do you do for a living?" he shouted at Cat.

"I'm an officer in Her Absent Majesty's Dragon Corps. So I guess you'd say I kill for a living."

"Oh yeah? You killed very many?"

"To be honest? None. I did put one guy in the hospital, though."

"Was that in combat or training?"

"Neither. I was having a pleasant night out and he put the moves on me."

"Dang, girl." A grin split the satyr's furry face. "You're hard-core, you know that? It's a good thing for you I'm into rough sex."

Raven stood. "Time for a trip to the powder room," she said in a bored voice.

They rounded off the night in Dies Infaustus. It was a quieter, more genteel establishment with a brass plaque identifying the polished slab of wood used for the bar as coming from the trunk of the world-tree Ongysdrail, which had fallen so long ago that, save for such remnants, it had all turned to fungus and loam. Cat had just ordered two fingers of Johnny Walker Crimson when she noticed Raven scratching the side of her face. "Hey! You're not smoking. Come to think, you haven't had a cigarette for days. What's up with that?"

"I've got something big planned for after we go our separate ways."

"What is it?"

"It's a secret." Raven stuck a finger in her drink and rattled the ice cubes around. She didn't seem to be at all drunk. It occurred to Cat that she did a lot more toying with her drinks than actual imbibing of them. "But as long as we're asking each other impertinent questions, what's with that riff you gave the satyr about killing for a living?"

"Oh, that. Well. To tell you the truth, Brocielande Station shook me pretty bad. I've been kind of rethinking the whole dragon-pilot thing ever since."

"Have you?"

"Yeah. Maybe I never really thought it through when I enlisted. Maybe I thought I didn't have to. Maybe I assumed my superiors had thought things through for me." Cat took a sip of scotch. "Maybe I thought wrong."

"As a trickster, I am legally obliged to challenge any renunciation of your personal value system, just as I am legally obliged to challenge that value system itself. But somehow I can't bring myself to do it. Anyone who flies a war-dragon is a criminal and an asshole."

"Hey! I thought we were friends," Cat said.

"Lots of my friends are criminals or assholes. You just happen to be both at the same time." Raven held out her hand. "Here. Lend me the stone, willya? It's time I took a long, hard look at you."

"You might not want to do that," Helen said.

Cat ignored her. She pulled the chain out from under her blouse. It got tangled in her hair but after a bit she managed to tug it free. "It won't do you any good, though. I haven't been glamoured."

"All the world is glamoured, if you look at it the right way. And tricksters know more ways to look at things than you can imagine." Raven took the holey stone. She raised it to her eye.

A long, long silence ensued. Then Raven whistled. "Oh, man. You are so fucked. I cannot believe what I'm looking at."

"What? What?"

"Not that I want to alarm you, but there's this big, dark, ugly *thing* inside you—like a lizard, only disgusting and deathly malignant."

"Oh yeah," Cat said. "That."

"I've been waiting for this explanation," Helen said. "Make it good."

"It's what we call a memory ghost. You spend enough time with a dragon inside you, its impression remains. You know how it reasons, what it feels. If you play along with it, you can even access some fraction of the dragon's strength. Back in the early days of the Corps, there were some ugly incidents. Retired pilots got swallowed up by their memory ghosts. Nowadays, though, we get biofeedback training to prevent that. So it's really not a problem."

"Imagine my relief," Raven said. Then, holding up the stone, "Hey. Maybe you want to take this thing into the bathroom and look at yourself in the mirror?"

"I know who I am."

"You sure? Might be some surprises there."

"Trust me, I've already had enough surprises for one life-time."

⁎⁎⁎

A rusalka came to their table and refreshed Cat's drink. Every now and then, something male glanced over at her or Raven, but they none of them pleased either. Then—

"Whoa," Cat said. "Look at him."

The object of her attention was as handsome as an incubus. Maybe he was one. In any case, he smiled at her. He reminded Cat, just a touch, of the slave boy in the little green shorts. Well, she thought. If I've given up on being a pilot, why the fuck not?

She felt her body rise from the chair, as if of its own volition. But then an arm hooked into hers and spun her around. Raven, she realized, was walking her out the door.

"Hey," Cat said. "Just what do you think you're doing?"

"Two words," Raven said: "Birth control. Three letters: STDs. One declarative sentence: You are as drunk as two pigs and a cluricaun put together. I'm surprised Helen didn't take the keys away from you."

"Not my dwarf, not my fight," Helen said. "As they say here."

"You know what? You're both assholes. And coming from me, that means a lot," Raven said.

"Wait, wait, wait, wait. You can hear Helen? You guys can talk to each other?"

"I keep telling you. I'm a trickster. You can't hide something like that from somebody like me."

"What's this about keys? How was Helen going to stop me?"

"Forget I said anything." They were outside now. The cold night air made Cat's head reel. It had stopped raining. Smears of neon were reflected in the road.

"No!" Cat shook off Raven's arm, staggered, and almost fell. "Were you implying that Helen can take control of me? Of my body, I mean?"

Raven sighed. "Tell her, granny."

"Yes. And yet I never did. Apparently, I'm a saint."

"I bet she didn't know she could. Until you told her. Just now."

"What a clever boots you are," Helen said. "Now let's concentrate on getting you home, safe and unlaid."

"What's wrong with getting laid?"

"Nothing—and I speak from experience. Far as I'm concerned, you can have all the ill-advised sex you want. In fact, I think it would do you good. But your first time is not going to happen when you're sloshed to the gills. Not on my watch."

"You're a big sboilsbort."

"Yeah. You have no idea how ironic that is."

⁕⁕

Cat was taken home and dumped in her bed. As she was drifting off, she heard a voice in the darkness say, "I have lit three candles. And snuffed out one."

Cat sat bolt upright in bed. Then she lurched to her feet, fell, pulled herself up again, found the light, and slapped it on.

There was nobody in the room but her and Esme, sound asleep.

Inanna came to the underworld. At the first gate, she surrendered the golden crown from her head. At the second gate, she surrendered her sacred necklace of lapis lazuli. At the third gate, she surrendered the twin egg-shaped beads from her breast. At the fourth gate, she surrendered her armor. At the fifth gate, she surrendered the ring of authority from her hand. At the sixth gate, she surrendered her measuring rod and line. At the seventh gate, she surrendered her clothing. Naked and without possessions, she was slain and her corpse was hung on a hook.

—The Descent of Inanna into the Underworld

C AT WOKE UP WITH THE KIND OF HANGOVER SHE HADN'T experienced since she was a doolie in the Academy.

"Here. Drink this." Raven handed her a glass of water.

Cat drank. "What are you doing in my room?"

"Your virtue is safe from me, babe. I'm only here to help. Today's the day you leave for Ys, remember?"

"Oh gods, no."

"It's either that or waitressing. Go take a shower. I'll make coffee."

When Cat emerged from the bathroom, she found that Raven had gathered up all the dirty clothes and sent Esme to the laundry room with them. Taking a sip of coffee, she said, "That's the last time I ever go drinking with you."

Raven was folding blouses. Without looking up, she said, "This morning would have been a lot uglier for you if I hadn't been there."

"Ugh. Yes. My apologies. What are you doing?"

"Getting you packed. My stuff is already loaded and so is Esme's. Jill's waiting outside. Hey, is this the music booklet that Istledown shared with you?"

"It's just a photocopy and I've memorized all the tunes. It can be tossed. Unless you want it?"

"Not my style. You start collecting crap like this and you'll end up as mad as Sasha. 'The Green Hills of Avalon' would be a good summoning tune to play on your pennywhistle. *Don't* try any of the others, though. There's no telling what you'd call up. And be careful with the key. Don't lose it underwater or you'll drown. And be crushed. And suffer the bends, if there's time. Nasty stuff, bends, or so I've been told."

Cat joined in on the packing. After a time, Esme came back with the laundry. Cat folded it and put it all in the duffel and Raven pulled the cords shut. "Okay, ladies, we're ready to roll."

"Where to?" Esme asked.

"Cat's going to a city under the sea. You'd like it there. Anytime you want to pee, you can just go ahead and do it. The seawater carries it away without your having to do anything."

"Neat!" Esme exclaimed.

"You and I, however, are going to wait on the shore."

"Awww."

"But you can pee in the woods all you like."

"Well . . . okay."

Cat opened the door and set her duffel down just outside. When she was done with all this, she decided, she would find a skilled dwarven *boursière* and have it cut down and stitched and made into a purse with silver fittings, the side of the canvas with stenciled letters outward. It had been a good servant and she didn't want to abandon it. To Raven, she said, "I wish you'd change your mind and come with me. You're so much more . . ." Cat groped for the right word. ". . . guileful than I am."

"No can do, babe. Everybody's got their own story, right? In yours, I'm the spunky, wisecracking sidekick. I know what happens to *them*. You're going to have to provide your own motivation. No shedding noble tears of sworn vengeance over my pathetic fallen corpse, thank you! Best I can do is offer you some useful advice: You're walking into Destiny territory. Keep your eyes open. Be careful where you step. Try not to fulfill any prophecies. If you see a sword in a stone or a crown in the open jaws of a jade crocodile, leave it be. That's how they fill positions thereabouts. Pull a knife out of a cake or a toilet brush out of the bowl and you'll end up as Pastry-Chef or Janitor-for-Life."

Cat looked at her.

"Joke. That last line, at least. Seriously, take my warning to heart. Memorize it. Maybe get it tattooed on your arm. Just don't forget."

The day was gorgeous. The rain had washed the air so clean that it sparkled. She could smell the trees beginning to turn. Every bird in existence, it seemed, was singing. Yet Cat only wanted to go back to bed. Her head throbbed, her bowels felt loose, and she wasn't at all sure her stomach was up for a long ride.

Back inside, she lined up, for the umpteenth time, the map, the pennywhistle, and the key beside the TV. Then she touched a hand to the chain around her neck, only to discover that it wasn't there. "Hey. Where's the holey stone?"

"You lent it to me last night, remember?" Raven twisted her hand in the air and there the stone was, chain and all, on her open palm. But when Cat reached for it, she drew it back. "Listen. You'll concede that I've given you everything you asked for? That I took some genuine risks for you? Brocielande Station. Sasha. Coulda died. Wasn't easy. So how's about giving me the stone a day early?"

"I underestimated you, Raven, that's for certain. I didn't

think you could do a fraction of what you promised. But you've come through for me, and you've been a brick throughout. And I owe you so much already. And I really do care for you, honest. But, like you keep reminding me, you're not an honest person. I've learned some hard lessons about trust these past few months. So, no, until you've put me together with my brother I don't dare give you it."

"Oh, argh. Shit. Well, fair enough. Another day is no big deal." Raven put the stone down alongside the map, whistle, and key. Outside, a car horn sounded. "Jill's getting impatient. Give me a hand getting Esme safety-belted in, okay?"

"Okay." Cat carried her duffel to the SUV and threw it in the back. Together, they wrangled Esme into place. "You, young lady, are a handful," Cat said.

"I'm not! I'm two handfuls! Three handfuls! Four!" Esme laughed like a hyena.

"Be still, you demon," Raven growled. She walked to Jill's far side and climbed into the driver's seat. "Okay, go grab your magical doodads and we're off."

"Done and done." Cat ducked back inside. The map, key, and pennywhistle were where she had left them. The holey stone was not.

In its place was a Kit Kat bar.

In a panic, Cat ran outside just in time to see Raven peeling out in Jill, leaving twin streaks of rubber on the road behind them. Taking with her both Cat's bag and Esme.

Something shiny flew through the air from the driver's side window and bounced to a stop on the tarmac. As if in a trance, Cat walked over and, stooping, saw that it was Esme's pinchbeck bracelet, which had been entangled in Carcassonne with the one Cat still wore. For the first time since buying it, she could not feel Esme's presence.

Cat pulled off her own bangle and let it fall alongside its

twin. Emptiness filled her. It was, she realized, time she got to the restaurant and started her shift.

⁂

Cat put in a long, miserable day at work and then hit up her boss for a partial advance on her pay. It came to far less than he owed her, so she felt no guilt when the next morning she called in sick and hit the road. She had barely enough for bus fare, food, and the price of a small silver sickle, blessed by the local battleax. The trip, which originally was to have taken ten hours at a maximum, became instead a days-long ordeal involving missed connections, hitchhiking, and many miles more walking than Cat would have preferred.

But at last, penniless and footsore, she came to the Bay of Dreams.

⁂

The trail twisted through a fragrant pinewood whose trees occasionally opened to tantalize Cat with a glimpse of the gray and choppy ocean and then hid it away again. She walked alone, deep in argument.

"So Raven betrayed you. So what? You knew she was a trickster."

"She was still my friend."

"Stop obsessing about irrelevancies and answer me this," Helen said. "You've given up on your fantasy of ever being a dragon pilot again. It's conceivable that you've even stopped wanting it, though I doubt that very much. You've picked up enough skills along the way to keep yourself out of the Conspiracy's clutches forever. So exactly what the bleeping fuck are you hoping to accomplish here?"

"I don't know. I just feel I have a duty to follow this thing through."

"I give up. I wash my hands of—"

"Hey, look. We've arrived." Cat had picked up a walking stick on entering the woods. Now she laid it down again, along with a copper penny as a thanks-giving to the genius loci of the woods for the loan of her staff. Ahead of her was Oceanus, vast and flat, and over it storm-dark clouds that billowed up into the sky forever.

The shore was where land, air, and water met on equal terms to wage never-ending wars of conquest upon one another. The air sent squalls to scourge the ocean and churn its surface to froth, the water sent waves to assail the earth and carry away its substance to undersea exile, the land sent sand to build up beneath the water and push it away, and both land and water conspired to roil the air with updrafts. When the tides retreated, they left behind a fringe of claws and pincers, shields, armor, broken pikes, and shattered legs to mark the border of the battlefield.

Despite that, Cat's heart lightened as she stepped onto the stretch of sand between the scrub pines and the sea. Drawing in a lungful of air tinged with salt and a touch of sulfur from the marshes to the north, she felt for an instant absurdly happy, as if for the first time in her life she were breathing free. She laughed for the sheer joy of laughing. Perhaps things were going to be better from now on. But even if they weren't, she was going to act as if they were.

Cat carried the key to the ocean on a piece of cotton string about her neck. The pennywhistle she kept in a fist shoved into a windbreaker pocket. She looked to the right and saw the pinewoods dwindling into marshland. She looked to the left and—

"That can't possibly be a coincidence," Helen said.

A long rock jetty curled into the water, forming a spiral that made three circuits before ending in a circular platform at its center. After a moment's consideration, Cat walked out to the platform. There, she lifted the pennywhistle to her lips and played "The Green Hills of Avalon," as Raven had advised. Nothing happened at first. But she kept playing, off and on, until at last a line of bubbles cleaved the ocean as a triton came from the deep sea to swim the spiral to its center. He burst clear of the water before her, scattering droplets on her face and up-raised hands. The hair on his head and chest and groin was green as kelp, his muscles were crisply delineated, and since he wore no clothing, his erection was all too obvious.

Cat put down the pennywhistle and formally said, "I claim safe passage to—"

A jaunty leer split the triton's green beard and he grabbed his crotch. "You want a ride, babe? I got your ride right here."

"See this?" Cat showed the lout her sickle. "Give me a hard time and this will make that ride a lot less eventful than you were hoping it would be." Staring meaningfully at his junk: "If you get my drift."

"Haw!" The triton threw back his head and laughed. "Oh, ouch! I like you, hot stuff. Maybe you have rape fantasies? I can fulfill them like you wouldn't believe."

"We'll never know." Cat tapped her toe. "You here to help or do I have to call someone else?"

"Climb on my back, babe. Second-best way to travel there is. Gonna have to charge you for it, though."

They dickered a bit, settled on a price, spat into their hands and shook on it. "Do you have a name?" Cat asked.

"Pelagius."

"Mine is—"

"Don't care!" The triton bent over. He smelled of semen and raw oysters. Cat climbed onto his back. "You better have some

way to breathe underwater," Pelagius said, "because otherwise
this is gonna kill you something bad."

"I've got—"

"Don't care!" Pelagius laughed and dove. With a swirl of
bubbles, they were below the surface.

First the water was green and as clear as glass with gape-eyed
fish and eels that swam like ribbons twisting in the wind. Then
it darkened and filled with fleeting shadows and sudden pale
shapes that loomed up out of nowhere for a startling instant before falling away back whence they had come. Finally (and this
had to be one of the benefits of the key Cat carried), it grew clear
again and they were flying above wild forests of giant kelp interspersed with straight-edged quilt-lands of cultivated fields
dotted with barns and farmhouses and the occasional small
town with a white marble temple to the Goddess at one end and
a tumbledown scattering of cribs and taverns at the other. She
saw tidy ricks of salt hay and merchildren chasing a whale's
shadow across a meadow. "These are our lands," Pelagius said,
"tilled and settled by proper fish-tailed folk. No walkers allowed." They put on a sudden burst of speed and the towns,
fields, and forests blurred beneath them.

"What just happened?" Cat asked.

"We came upon a ley line and tapped into its energy. See, ley
lines are kind of a cleavage in the natural energies of the world
through which—"

"I know what ley lines are. I aced geomancy in the Academy."

"Well, lah-de-dah. Pardon me for answering a question."

"I just didn't know there were ley lines in the ocean."

"Stands to reason, dunnit? You got ley lines in the land and
ley lines in the sky—and land, sea, and sky are just three sides
of the same coin, right?"

The ocean floor zipped past and the lost city of Ys rose up before them. Cat had expected a fantasia of opalescent towers and rose-red city walls, a cross, perhaps, between the legendary city of Petra and a coral reef. What she saw through a darkening murk ("Pollution," the triton commented and she felt his shoulders shrug beneath her clasp) was great black slabs of skyscrapers and enormous white cranes moving slowly as Calder mobiles in a still room to build more. The city streets curved and curled in upon themselves, thrusting up spiraling coils of high-rises higher and higher. In parks bright with seaweed strolled women with iridescent scales and men whose skin was a brazen green. Unlike the merfolk, they walked on two legs, wore clothing, and held themselves as urbanites.

Downward the triton gyred, coming to a stop with a puff of sand just above the ocean floor. "Here's where you get off, sweet cheeks. I don't wanna accidentally wander over the city limits. Bad things happen to them as do." There was a wicked glint in the triton's eyes. "Guess I shoulda told ya that upfront."

"It wouldn't have made any difference." Cat dismounted. She handed over the last of her coins, then on an impulse added, "Do you want the sickle? Now that I'm here, I have no use for it."

But the triton was gone. So she let the thing fall to the ocean floor, yet another piece of scornfully ignored tribute from the land to its sister domain.

The road leading into Ys was empty of traffic—nobody, apparently, went to or came from the city for any purpose whatsoever—and slick with algae. Walking cautiously, Cat followed it inward. A sign proclaimed the city limits. Shortly thereafter, she was passed by a wagon that rode on pontoons rather than wheels and was drawn by draft horses that were half fish. Pedestrians whose cloaks billowed out behind them appeared by ones and twos, became dozens, and grew to such numbers as would have graced a major market town or regional capital. Not a one of them so much as glanced at her, though it must have been obvious from her clothing that she was an outlander.

Propelled by nothing more than hunch and Brownian motion, Cat walked onward. Wherever her brother went, he would insist on being in the middle of things. So she headed for the center of the city, where the buildings were tallest.

Cat walked for a very long time.

Weary and on the verge of giving up for the day, Cat was about to start looking for a hostel when she realized that she was standing before the very place she had been searching for: the tavern whose façade had been a part of her father's collection of building fronts back in Château Sans Merci. Seen from the street, it seemed a nostalgic fantasy of medieval life. But it was merely one of a run of shops and restaurants built into the ground floor of what was surely one of the tallest and grandest buildings in town. Fingolfinrhod would never lodge in a tavern. But, finding himself in one, he might very well book a room in the nearest appropriate locale. So Cat bypassed the inn and walked into the building's lobby instead.

"Can I help you?" a receptionist said in a tone that suggested she didn't much care whether she could or not. Then, when Cat had told her who she was looking for, "Penthouse suite. Elevators are to your left. Use one of the last three; the others don't go to the top floors."

A swift ascent later, Cat stood in the foyer to her brother's rooms. She rang the bell. It reverberated slowly and prolongedly. After a long wait, the door opened. "Oh," said a butler. He was stout, pale-skinned, forgettable. "A visitor." Then, "Do come in."

An octopus the size of Cat's fist that had been lurking on the elevator's ceiling darted past her, looking for prey. Annoyed, the butler flicked out a pristine handkerchief to shoo it out a window and then waft to nothing the ink cloud it had left behind.

"Wait here, please," he said and disappeared into the suite's interior.

After a bit, the stout nondescript reappeared, gesturing for Cat to follow. He opened a door, said, "The master," and withdrew from Cat's awareness. She stepped into a room suitable for informal entertainments. One wall opened into a balcony. There, an elf-lord stood, hands behind his back, staring out across the city. He was tall, elegantly dressed, saturnine in posture, hauntingly familiar-looking. He turned at her approach.

"Father!" Cat cried in astonishment.

"No," Fingolfinrhod said, smiling sadly. "It's only me."

He embraced her formally. Cat hugged him back so hard that tears squeezed out of her eyes. At last, Fingolfinrhod said, "Well. What brings you here? I haven't much time, as it turns out. But we can go out to dinner somewhere and talk." Then, with a spark of his old self, "Or we could stay in and stare at each other sullenly, if that's what you'd prefer."

"Oh, you. You never change, do you, Roddie? I'm so glad. For a second, I thought you'd changed." Then, "Finn, everybody thinks you're dead. Thought you were dead. I was afraid you might be dead."

"Well. It's only a matter of time, after all."

Holding him at arm's length, Cat searched Fingolfinrhod's face but found no answers in it. "Why are you so gloomy? Stop it! You need some wine. Rustle up a bottle and a couple of glasses and we'll get tipsy and catch each other up with our adventures. Okay?"

※※

They talked and drank and talked some more. From the balcony Cat could see that Ys was laid out in curls and coils so that its obsidian-black buildings, taken together, had a swooping recursive magnificence. At this height, the people in the streets below resembled tiny crabs scuttling across the ocean floor. Once, in the murky distance, Cat fancied she glimpsed a giant serpent or eel twisting its way through the city streets.

"I'm afraid I can't help clear your name," Fingolfinrhod said after Cat had poured out her history and her heart. They were midway through the second bottle. "Father's death created a temporary crack in the world and I made the mistake of slipping through it. I'm adapted to the sea now. Three minutes out of water would kill me. Perhaps a notarized statement would suffice . . . ?"

"No. It wouldn't. But maybe that's all for the best. Tell me about your life here, big brother. Tell me that you're happy."

"You can change the context," Fingolfinrhod said with a wry twist of his mouth. "But not the substance. I am no happier here than I was on the surface. I never told this to another living being save Dahut, but eight months ago the soul surgeons diagnosed me as having early-onset transcendence. A year from now, two at the most, I'll be gone. The only ways I can think of to delay it are so repugnant that I refuse to entertain them."

Cat took his hand. "Tell me what they are, Roddie, and maybe we can work something out. You know that I'd do anything to help you."

He looked at her.

"Oh," Cat said, and released his hand.

Fingolfinrhod began to laugh. After a bit, Cat joined him. They both laughed so long and hard that Cat feared she would be unable to stop.

"Enough," Fingolfinrhod said at last and, with a touch to her shoulder, calmed Cat's emotions. By which sign she knew that, willingly or not, and officially uncertified though his title remained, he had grown and matured into his role as the Sans Merci of Sans Merci. For an instant Cat wondered what Father had been like when he was young. Then, with the easy, racist phrasing of his class, her brother said, "Well, the kobold is in the henhouse now, to be sure. For both of us. You need my testimony while I'm every bit as trapped as ever I was back home. However, it's just barely possible a trade could be arranged. I know some very powerful . . . let's call them entities who are extremely fond of certain antiquities. Do you still have Father's stone?"

"I lost it, I'm afraid. Somebody I trusted stole it from me."

"That's a pity. The Stone of Disillusion was a Class Three artifact and one of the treasures of our house. There's no telling what we might have gotten for it. Well, no use crying over spilt seed or shed blood, as Father always used to say. I'm sure it wasn't acquired honestly in the first place." With sudden decisiveness, Fingolfinrhod stood. "We need a fresh perspective on this matter. I'd like you to meet my landlady."

On a sideboard, a crystal orb sat upon a silver base worked with dwarven craft into the shape of a crashing wave. Fingolfinrhod laid a languid hand upon the orb's surface, summoning light into its interior. With a solemnity foreign to Cat's experience of him he said:

"We were born apart, yet together are we in the undying present.
We shall be together when the white sails of death pass over-
     head.
Let there be a bridge between our otherness,
And let the tides of Oceanus flow beneath."

There was a sighing noise outside, like a gentle wind passing through a pine forest at twilight. Cat spun about and saw the black glass balcony turn to shadows that reassembled themselves into a bridge that reached across the intervening street to touch, as lightly as a kiss on the cheek, the penthouse opposite.

She followed Fingolfinrhod across it.

They stepped into a spacious living area as tasteful and therefore unremarkable as any Cat had ever dwelt in. There, an elf-lady was just finishing arranging a bowl of anemones. Putting down a shaker of krill, she turned at their approach. She had the darkest, deepest eyes Cat had ever seen. They were like pools of liquid sin.

"This," Fingolfinrhod said, "is my landlady and my mistress, Dahut merc'h Gradlon."

-� ᴚ-

All the world swam in Cat's vision. She touched the wall to steady herself. "Are you . . . ?" Cat began. Then, "You're not *the* Dahut. The one who . . ."

"The terrible vixen who corrupted the people of Ys, you mean?" Dahut's lips twisted in a dark and mocking way. "Who made its citizens as arrogant, amoral, and licentious as herself, forcing the Sons of Lyr to smash down the seawall and drown the city in disgust? Look at me—am I any of those things? Beyond the ordinary run of vice, I mean. History is written by those who are anxious to prove that because they are innocent, it couldn't happen to them. It could. It did. To my people and to me. We did nothing to deserve the doom that came down upon us. But when the Goddess conspires against you, where do you go to register a complaint?" She embraced Cat lightly. "I am certain that you and I shall be the best of friends."

"I'm sure that we will," Cat lied.

"You've been drinking." Dahut sniffed Cat's mouth. The action, though offensive, was curiously impersonal, like a Manx queen offering her butt for inspection. "The good stuff, too! Château d'If. Your brother must care passionately for you. You should taste the swill he pours for me."

"What a sense of humor the gal has," Fingolfinrhod said, not smiling. "Be nice to my sister, old thing. She's made of worthier stuff than you and I are."

"Do you see how he treats me? He came here as a refugee and I took him in—"

"In more ways than one."

"Ugh! There is no talking to you." Dahut turned her back on Fingolfinrhod and said to Cat, "You and I will talk instead. You may ask me anything. I will refuse you nothing."

Cat considered the offer. "Very well," she said. "Tell me how Ys came to sink beneath the waves. The true story, I mean."

"No one knows exactly how long ago it was. Time is strange here, where no one dies and no children are born. On rare occasions, there come visitors from the surface. Before they die—for they are not bound to the city as are we, its citizens—I inevitably ask them what they have heard of the catastrophe. Always, it happened sometime in the distant, dateless past. Always, it was my wickedness that was its undoing. Now and then, a sailor drowns and the body is brought to me so I can eat the brains and . . . Oh, do I shock you? Different lands, different customs. I assure you, in my small city-state ritual neurophagy has always been the prerogative of royalty. We ingest the brains of the worthy dead and from this learn not only their deeds but their skills and lore as well. From sailors and visitors alike, I determined that the true history of Ys has been erased and in its place a legend artfully inserted. One involving naked dancing, public orgies, and other crowd-pleasing fantasies that ensure any attempt to set the record straight will be met with resentment and denial.

"You will find the truth disappointing. The sinking of Ys was a public works project. The secret masters of the three worlds came here to choose a city whose buildings and populace would be transported to the very deepest waters of the Bay of Dreams, there to serve as an anchor point for a system of ley lines connecting Faerie, Aerth, and the Empyrean. Knowing what city they had in mind, my father was determined to prevent—"

"Wait," Cat said. "Before your lies grow too elaborate, you should know. In Carcassonne I found a bundle of letters from you to your lover and read them all. The last was from the day before Ys disappeared beneath the waves. So I know something about its doom, and it was nothing like what you say."

"My letters? In Carcassonne?" Dahut grasped Cat's hands so tightly they stung. With great intensity she said, "You lie! But why would you? It makes no sense. Tell me. I sent a token in one of them. What was it? What color was it?"

"A lock of hair. It was black like yours."

"Then Prince Benthos is dead." Dahut released Cat, who drew back out of her reach. "Dead or, worse, unfaithful."

"Enough." Fingolfinrhod came up behind Dahut and massaged her shoulders. "You are scaring my little sister, you terrible creature."

Dahut looked like a wild animal. "I must kill myself—but I can't! Not in this cursed place. What am I to do?"

"You are to calm down. A bundle of letters, no matter how compromising, means nothing. Things get stolen, you know."

"Or misfiled," Cat added. "I was in clerical for a while, and it happens all the time."

Fingolfinrhod threw himself back on a divan, pulling Dahut after him. "Here. Lie beside me. Place your head on my lap and finish the story you were telling us."

Dahut shuddered and closed her eyes. Then, her cheek on Fingolfinrhod's knee, she stared ahead of herself at nothing and said, "Where the ley lines of the air converged, Glass Mountain was already an anchor, as was the House of Glass where the ley lines of the land met. The fire lines were anchored in the

Empyrean by Mount Obsidian, of course. That left only the ley lines of the ocean unanchored and since the Court of Lyr refused to sacrifice any of its own cities, Ys was the obvious choice. To everyone but those of us living there, I mean."

"Strange that three of the locales had similar names," Fingolfinrhod murmured, "but not the fourth."

"Ys means 'glass' in the Dawn Tongue."

"Ah."

"Perhaps with my help my father could have prevailed, for I was well-versed in the law and devious where he was straightforward. But while he contended over obscure clauses in treaties dating back to the partition of the land and sea, I slipped away. Then I ran with all my will to the seawall. You read my letters—you know why. The western sky was black with storm and lightning lashed the waters. At the driving edge of the squall was a small speck that could only be Prince Benthos, my lover, racing straight toward the city. In fast pursuit were three more specks which I later learned were the Sons of Lyr, his brothers. The seas were high and the air cold with salt spray as I descended the stairs on the seaward side of the wall.

"My skiff had been moored to a bronze ring there and was being bounced high and low by the waves. It was a desperate deed to judge its ascent and leap into it at the high point. When I crashed down onto the planking, I almost overturned it. But I managed to keep the skiff upright. I slipped the hawser, seized the oars, and rowed out into the open waters.

"No woman is a master of such seas. The ocean took the oars from me with arrogant ease and flung them away. So I had no choice but to raise the sail. It was madness, but at that moment I was not exactly sane.

"Do you sail? A pity. Then I must skip over feats of seamanship that would have left you in awe of me. In brief: I didn't drown. In fact, I had almost reached the four Sons of Lyr when the foremost of them abandoned his sea-form and bestrode the waters on two legs, godlike, raising the Horn of Holmdel to his lips.

"On the first note, flames danced upon the water. On the second, they raced to either side and up onto the land, forming a great encroaching circle with Ys at its center. But I had no eyes for the flames but only for he that blew upon the Horn, for it was Prince Benthos, all unclad and as beautiful as ever a man has been.

"Then the three other Sons of Lyr reached my love and, grappling with him, tried to wrest the Horn from his grip even as he played the final notes of the spell.

"My skiff turned over then.

"It would have been impossible for me to both sail the boat and bail, so it had been filling with water all the time. A blast of wind from an unexpected quarter and I was flung into the sea to die before my beloved's eyes.

"But I managed to claw my way back to the surface and when I did, I saw Prince Benthos with a mighty surge break free from the arms of his brothers. Seeing my plight, he threw—"

"Oh, please do stop," Fingolfinrhod said. "You have stretched my sister's gullibility so far that I just heard it snap, and as for me . . . Well, I never believed in Prince Benthos in the first place. He's too perfect, too conveniently inaccessible, too obviously somebody you made up to instill jealousy in me so I can be more easily manipulated."

Ashen-faced, Dahut snapped to her feet and strode to a cabinet. With three quick gestures, she commanded it to unlock. The doors opened to reveal a conch shell resting on a small stand. Reverently, she lifted it.

Cat could not take her eyes away from the shell. It was so very real as to make everything and everyone around it, herself included, seem but shadows.

"This is the Horn of Holmdel. It was shaped before the beginning of time and sounded to mark the onset of Creation. Someday, a different tune will be played upon it and all of Faerie will be undone and its history unmade so that none of this ever happened." She placed the shell down on a nearby table. "But that day is a long way off. In the meantime, it is quite possibly the most valuable object in the universe. Think how great the love had to be of he who gave me it."

Cat lowered her eyes. "I apologize for any doubts I may have had."

"Not me," Fingolfinrhod said. "I know you too well. I have no idea how you came by that doohickey. But experience has taught me how wily you are and I know better than to believe anything that comes out of your mouth."

"You should revere my every word, and show me far more honor than you do. Someday, Prince Benthos will come for me, and then I will be the only thing standing between you and his righteous wrath, O second-best beloved."

"Says you, fish lips."

"Air-breather."

"Bottom-feeder."

"Third-rate cocksman."

They glared one another into silence. Then Fingolfinrhod said, "Cat, one of the servants can show you to your room. Anything you need—fresh clothes, food, cocktails, whatever—they will provide. Tell them I doubt I'll be home for dinner."

Cat took the hint and left Dahut's apartment, the bridge of shadows unmaking itself behind her.

⁕

When Cat came to breakfast the next morning, Fingolfinrhod was already at table, looking bleary and bedraggled. Smearing herring roe on slices of sea cucumber, he said, "Dahut tells me she has only a fraction of the energy she enjoyed when she was on land." His mouth twisted wryly. "I'm grateful I didn't know her then."

"As long as you're having fun," Cat said, amused.

"I'm not." Fingolfinrhod put down his fork. "I love her. Isn't that awful? It gets worse. I have no idea whether she loves me or not. She says she does. But she says a lot of things." He spooned a mound of pickled jellyfish onto his plate, then stared down at it with genteel dismay. Lightly, he said, "Don't get me wrong, I love the local cuisine. But you can't imagine what I'd give for a fried hen's egg and a slice of toast right now."

Cat ignored this last. "If you're not happy—" she began.

"How could this have happened? One could hardly say we were suited for each other. She is all impulse and I all control. She's needy, I'm aloof. I'm subtle, she's direct. Her prejudices are at least a thousand years out of date. I reason things out to the point of tedium, or so my critics tell me, and she is a force of nature.

"I never did care much for nature.

"So why does she obsess me? I've had more skilled lovers and more perverse—though I have no complaints about Dahut on either ground. We certainly don't share a commonality of experience. I cannot exist without books and yet I believe that a day with nothing to do but read would kill her. When we're apart, I think of nothing but her. When we're together, we argue. We can't even live in the same building. I—"

The sweet sighs of a soft summer breeze sounded from the balcony. What joy, Cat thought, Dahut has come to visit.

Fingolfinrhod wiped his mouth as he rose to his feet, tossing aside the napkin just in time to receive a kiss that struck Cat as being far more passionate than was called for so early in the day. "Belovedest," Dahut said. "Go away. Go shopping or whatever it is that men do when there are no women around. Your sister and I have serious matters to discuss."

When they were alone, Dahut said, "You know that I love your brother."

"I know that it's a possibility."

"Fingolfinrhod is the only joy I have in this city. You heard about his diagnosis? One year. I want him to enjoy every second of that year. Your presence makes him happy. Therefore you must stay. Say you will."

"I'll . . . give it serious thought." A year was a long time. But Cat had nothing better to do, now that all her hopes and plans had collapsed. Her brother was the only individual in all the world she honestly believed loved her. Stay? She very well might.

"No one could ask for more." Dahut hugged Cat and kissed both her cheeks. "Now that that's settled . . . I showed you mine yesterday. It's only fair that you show me yours."

"I'm not following you. My what?"

"Your amulets of power. Or whatever it is that allowed you to make the perilous transition from land to sea. It surely required a great deal of magic to accomplish that."

Reluctantly, Cat drew out the key to the ocean and dangled it before her. "This is what enables me to walk and breathe underwater."

Dahut rubbed the key between her fingers. "It's a Class Two artifact, but a very early one and extremely well made." She let it fall and Cat realized she had been holding her breath. Hastily, she stuffed the key back under her blouse. "And for transportation?"

"I left it in my room. Wait here."

When Cat had fetched the pennywhistle, Dahut took it from her hands and stroked it slowly and lovingly. "The craft that went into this! So lovely."

Then, with inhuman strength, she snapped the pennywhistle in two. When Cat leaped forward, she stopped her with a hand to the face. With her free hand, she tossed the halves over her shoulder, out the window, and into oblivion.

"There," Dahut said. "Now you have no choice but to stay."

Is it death to stay in Egypt?
is it death to stay here,
in a trance, following a dream?

—H.D., *Helen in Egypt*

HAVING NEITHER PURPOSE NOR RESPONSIBILITIES, CAT took to wandering the streets of Ys, as anonymous as a sultan passing among his people in disguise or a *flaneuse* idly observing the ways of Paris (an occupation and a place Helen assured her really did exist in her origin-world), headed nowhere, talking to everyone, exploring its labyrinthine streets and alleys and cul-de-sacs, opening doors marked NO ENTRY, poking her nose wherever it didn't belong. She discovered a dreaming metropolis whose citizens sleepwalked through the motions of their daily routines. Cooks prepared meals that were eaten joylessly and did not care. Musicians played on street corners, hats at feet, for passersby who never threw in a coin. Police went through the motions of arresting criminals who couldn't be bothered to rob a store. Bankers made no loans. Papergirls slept late and drifted to schools where they learned nothing, leaving their newspapers undelivered. Cat picked one off an abandoned stack and saw that it was shopworn and undated.

Talking to individuals restored them to a temporary semblance of life. But it didn't last.

"I was standing right over there when the ocean drank

the city," a construction worker told Cat. "The sea rose up like a mountain and I thought I was going to die. I wish now I had, instead of being condemned to live this same exhausted life forever and ever."

"You could leave, surely. It's not a long walk to the city limits and the merfolk, though fierce and wild, aren't unfriendly."

The worker lifted her nail gun and drove a nail into the sea-oak paneling she was installing. "Does the nail decide to leave after being driven into the plank?"

"But you're not a nail."

"Then what am I? What are we all? Real? Phantoms? I have no idea. My memories are so very vague. Every day is the same as the one before. All the children grew up long ago. Now there are none. Only unaging, undying adults."

"Tell me something," Cat said. "If there are neither deaths nor births in Ys, why is it under constant construction?" The windows hadn't been installed yet and fish swam in and out of the room without hindrance. "Half these buildings are empty. The rest have only a handful of occupied apartments in them. Surely nobody needs more."

"I don't set policy and I don't ask questions. I'm a builder. I build."

In Shipwreck Park, Cat met two day laborers who were stolidly scrubbing away a large white graffito of a coiled serpent that had been stenciled onto the hulk of the *Lithos Pandoras*. Under the serpent in block letters was the slogan VENIT. "Who did this?" she asked.

"I don't give a shit," one of the laborers said. "I just wish they'd fucking stop."

"This is the first time I've seen graffiti in Ys. All the other cities I've ever been in were crawling with it."

"Fifth one this week," the second laborer said. "Every one in a different style, so it's not just one tagger. Cleaning it away is a real pain in the butt. Still, it beats scraping barnacles."

"Any idea what it means?" Cat asked.

"I don't give a shit. I may have mentioned that before."

"No idea." The second laborer put down her brush. "It's a strange thing, though. I had a dream about a serpent last night. Didn't give it a thought until just now. It was an ugly bastard. As big as the Demiurge's dong and as pale as Lady Nyx's tits. I woke up in a sweat, like it meant something, ya know?"

"Keep scrubbing, jackoff. I had the same dream too, but you don't see me sitting down on my thumb to reminisce about it."

※※

In a brothel with a well-stocked bar where no customers drank and an organ that nobody played, a sex worker said, "I had a lover safely stashed out in the countryside when the Judgment of Dahut fell upon us. She died so long ago that I can't even remember her name. Meanwhile, my wife goes on and on, century after century after century, never changing in any way and thus becoming every year more detestably predictable."

"How horrible for you."

"She gets hers," the prostitute said with a terrible grimace. "I haven't said an original word to her for as long as either of us can remember."

"Have you had any strange dreams lately?"

"Naw. Just the one about the snake. But everyone gets that."

※※

It was lunchtime, so Cat went into a restaurant and amused herself by assembling a meal, a plate at a time, from the trays of passing waitresses. She set the food down on a table where a financier (to judge by her HP-12C financial calculator and the spreadsheets she was working on) was eating alone.

"How's business?" Cat asked, applying wasabi to her sashimi.

"Nonexistent. Ys doesn't have a capitalist economy or even a mercantile economy—it has a curse economy. Everything gets done not from rational causes but because it was so ordained. Thus I have no function. But I was a money changer when the Sons of Lyr fell upon the city, so I am doomed to remain in a useless occupation that gives me no pleasure."

"Why don't you leave the city?"

"I don't know. Have you tried doing it yourself?"

"I . . . Somehow, I haven't. I can't imagine why."

"Well, then." The financier put her spreadsheets in her briefcase. "It's time I was back at the office."

"Did you have a dream recently?" Cat asked. "About a large white serpent?"

"How strange. I'd forgotten all about that. How did you—? Well, no matter." The financier dropped a business card on the table. "If you ever need financial services, look me up."

⚹⚹

Such was life in Ys. Its stoops were swept clean daily and the beds of decorative tube worms planted in public spaces were regularly tended to. Plays were performed in its theaters, and operas in the concert halls. Streets were closed for festivals. Sea bulls and hippocamps were sacrificed on all the high feast days. The city was peaceful, productive, and prosperous.

It could have been a good life had anybody cared. But the plays, concerts, street fairs, and sacrifices all went unattended.

⚹⚹

"What exactly is it that you do all day?" Fingolfinrhod asked one evening at supper. They were dining for a change not in his suite but in the tavern wherein he had first fled into Ys, "from one trap to another," as he now put it. Food was brought by busty serving wenches, tankards of ale were drawn at the taps, and a fire burning merrily in the hearth sent clouds of bubbles shooting up the chimney. In any other city, it would have been jolly.

When Cat told him, Fingolfinrhod marveled, "But *why*?"

"It's a basic military principle: When there's no advantageous action to be taken, gather information. I'm gathering information. When I have enough, it will tell me what to do."

"Will it? I doubt that. I learned long ago that there's nothing to be learned in Ys. Everything and everyone here is exactly what they seem." Fingolfinrhod gestured at the tavern habitués, all niched into their oak, beveled glass, and polished brass environs like so many opportunistic reef-dwellers. "The drunkards drink, the tosspots toss back pots of ale, and the lackeys . . . lack, I suppose. Nowhere is there ever anything new, surprising, or strange to be discovered."

"I saw something strange painted on a wall today."

"Not possible. Who would bother? Incidentally, Dahut is going to be dropping by my rooms in a bit and I know she'd love to see you."

"After what she did to me? Fat chance."

※

Cat went to bed early that night, in part to avoid Dahut's company. As she was drifting off to sleep, a voice came out of the darkness.

"I have lit three candles and snuffed out two."

Cat sat bolt upright in her bed, just as she had once before. But this time she didn't bother looking around. She knew that the source of the voice would not be there to be found. "Who are you? What are you trying to do? You don't scare me. You don't. You don't scare me at all!"

As before, there was no reply.

Perhaps for that reason, perhaps not, Cat's sleep was troubled and uneasy. One dream was particularly vivid: She was swimming in swamp water so brown with cedar tannins as to be almost opaque. Taking a deep breath, she plunged down below the surface, far deeper than should have been possible.

At first there was nothing to be seen. Then, through the murk, came flashes of white, transient as heat lightning, appearing and vanishing in swooping arcs of motion. A serpent's head with eyes as bright as lanterns appeared directly before her, and its mouth gaped wide, revealing row after row of thorn-sharp teeth. So quickly that Cat could do nothing to prevent it, the serpent looped itself about her body. It was not cool and dry like terrestrial snakes, but slippery and warm. When she tried to struggle free, it tightened its coils and all the breath burst out of her in an explosion of bubbles. The serpent's tongue tickled her ear and in a voice that was both male and insinuating, it said, "*Venit* means 'He Is Coming.'"

Which was when she realized she was naked.

Cat awoke gasping and sweaty with revulsion and fear. Throwing on a robe, she went out in search of something to soothe her nerves.

The servants were off duty and all the city was asleep. Not a single window was lit. But in the pantry, Cat found a box of crackers, some cheese, and a half-empty bottle of vin ordinaire. She took a plate and a glass back with her into the common room.

"Looking for me?" Dahut said.

Startled, Cat lurched, almost spilling the wine. "What are you doing here?"

"I was having sex with your brother. But he fell asleep."

Dahut plucked the glass from Cat's hand and took a swallow. "So I thought this would be a good time for you and me to have a chat." She handed the glass back.

Cat put it down on a side table, firmly and forever.

"My parents," said Dahut, "were wed on the day my father conquered Ys. He took her in open view of the assembled populace. She submitted herself fully to his will. The citizens saw that there was no future in rebellion. There was no love involved in the match. He needed to consolidate power and she wanted to live long enough to ensure the continuation of her line. They came to terms. I was born. On the day I first menstruated, there were celebrations throughout the city. Bells were rung and blood-feasts thrown for the poor. Then, as my mother had stipulated when she agreed to the match, she was put to death. Because she was of noble blood and because he had grown to care for her, my father strangled her with his own two hands. That evening, at a private meal, he and I ate her brains. He was weeping openly. I was not. That was when I first realized that someday I might be a better ruler than he ever was.

"You've probably wondered why I am the way I am. Now you know."

"I never wondered and I never asked. So why tell me?"

"Because we have so little time to make peace with one another! There is change in the air, an age is coming to an end. Ys is only a breath away from destruction. Surely you feel it. But perhaps a peaceful transition can be managed. I am not without power and my father is great among the mighty. If we—" She stopped. "Now look at that! I spilled a drop of wine on my gown. I can't go out like this!"

With a snap of her fingers, Dahut summoned up the bridge between her building and Fingolfinrhod's. "Finish your snack and get dressed. We have a long night ahead of us."

�֎

Cat didn't hurry. Still, when she crossed the bridge of shadows to Dahut's apartments, her brother's lover hadn't changed yet. Holding up two dresses, Dahut said, "Ruby or emerald?"

"Emerald."

Dahut turned her back. "Unzip me." Then, when Cat had, she shucked off her gown and kicked it away to be dealt with by someone else.

The Horn of Holmdel, Cat saw, hadn't been put away but lay on a table under a spray of bright sabellids in a barnacle-dotted brass vase. The Horn glowed with an inner vitality that made the rest of the world seem gray. Her fingers yearned to stroke it.

Dahut was adjusting her dress in a full-length mirror. Over her shoulder, she said, "Pick it up, if you like. You can't hurt it. Play a tune on it! No music *you* know will have the least effect on anything."

How was it possible, Cat wondered, as her hands of their own accord lifted the Horn to her lips, for a woman to tempt fate as blithely as Dahut had just done? Her body took a deep breath. Her fingers assumed their positions over the holes. Her lips pursed themselves. Then, without her actually willing it, she began to play. *Jesse come home . . .*

Cat's breath, common and suffused with microscopic impurities as it was, passed through the Horn and was transformed into music of stunning clarity. She closed her eyes to savor it fully.

There's . . . The Horn of Holmdel was slapped from Cat's mouth.

"Who sent you?!" Dahut's nails dug into Cat's shoulders. Her face was so close that Cat could smell her makeup. "Speak or I'll tear your guts out with my teeth!" All Cat could see was those eyes, filled with a savage mixture of hatred and fear. "You couldn't have known to do that on your own. Who was responsible?"

Cat lifted a hand to her lips and felt blood. She said nothing.

Dahut pushed her away—not violently but gently. "Oh, what's the use? It's all over and everything's fucked and there's nothing to be done about it."

"I only blew five notes," Cat said.

"Five! Three would have done the trick. Well, what's done is done. No point in blaming you. You were weaponized, pointed in my direction, and set loose. As well blame the bullet for the assassination of Lord Baldur."

"I'm not following any of this."

"No, of course not. You're as innocent as I was when I caused the original disaster. Now you've released the White Serpent and you probably think you did it on a whim, of your own free will. But this moment has been coming for a long, long time.

"I started to tell you the story of how Ys was sunk beneath the sea. But your brother interrupted me before I got to the good part, the moment many years later when I put all the clues together and saw the cunning of the conspirators who had woven their plot so long and deftly: The sailing-mistress who, in my youth, had instilled in me a love of the ocean waters. The rumor of a sea serpent as white as ivory that had sent me out on a day I would normally have stayed ashore. The dealer of antiquities who sold me the ancient codex which *just happened* to spell out the use that could be made of the Horn of Holmdel at a time when I desired such knowledge most. All worked together to put me in a position where I would seduce Prince Benthos into an act of treachery. Once he stole the Horn, the Emperor of the Tides would have no choice but to imprison him. Just to teach his other sons the price of treason. And as long as he was imprisoned, he might as well be used as the central anchor holding together the web of gates and bridges between Faerie, Aerth, and the Empyrean."

"Umm . . ."

"So, yes, I did it all for love. But, like you, I was also being used. Zip me up."

Cat did so.

Dahut grabbed a purse and dumped the Horn of Holmdel in it. "Let's go," she said.

"Where?"

"To accept our doom gracefully."

⁎⁎

Minutes later, they were out on the streets.

"This is my city," Dahut said. "I know it as well as I know my own body. Better, for I have the memories of all its queens, down to the very first and the female line before that, back to a time when we all lived in burrows and were ignorant of fire or speech. I feel its people coursing through my streets, up and down my staircases, in and out of my tenements. I sensed you exploring my heights and depths, my open spaces and hidden crevices, and had to laugh at your folly in thinking you could understand Ys without understanding me."

They walked past a Coach outlet. Then a Lamborghini showroom with a shark-white Aventador displayed in its window. "A woman can love more than one man at once," Dahut said. "You think otherwise because you have never been in such a fix, and because you believe there can be no one the equal of your brother. But you've never met Prince Benthos. Suffice it to say, it does Fingolfinrhod honor that I could even look at him, much less bed him, after such companionship."

"To be honest, I try to know as little as possible about Roddie's sex life."

"Then you know nothing at all about him either. Yet, armored in ignorance, you hope to discover the innermost secrets of my city. Search quickly, then! There is little time left. Does any of what surrounds you look familiar?"

Cat looked up and down the avenue: Vera Wang, Lanvin, Dolce & Gabbana, Bottega Veneta, Louis Vuitton, Oscar de la Renta. The display windows were as bright as television screens and the walls above them monolithic black slabs. The sidewalks were crowded as she had never seen them before. Mobs of pedestrians spilled into the street, their numbers constantly growing. Every shop and office and apartment building in the city must have emptied itself out to make such a multitude possible. "I've been here before, many times. But the shops were different then. And it's so crowded!"

"At night the bleed-over from Aerth is stronger. Ignore the crowds. Look straight ahead. Those ornate brick arches are the Annihilation Gates." The twin arches were decorated with sea lions and ocean leopards; bas-relief octopi wrapped their tentacles about the columns, staring blindly over the shopping district; and chained to the pier was a merman whose expression was the epitome of misery. "Beyond them is Gradlon Square."

"But I've been all over the city. How is it possible I've never seen the gates or been in the square?"

"Gradlon Square is the heart of Ys. Erenow, I closed my heart to you. But the time has come for reconciliation. Tell me you forgive all that I have done, and I will forgive you the evil you have brought down on me."

Cat said nothing.

A terrible sadness passed over Dahut's face. She raised a hand to the corner of one eye, perhaps to brush away a stray strand of hair. Then—

Somebody pointed to the sky. "Look!" Others were pointing

as well, as if at a skyrocket or a strange bird or a terrifying machine. "He's coming!" Meanwhile others pointed not upward but at Cat, murmuring, "She's here." Those standing nearest her shrank away.

The voices clashed and echoed from the building walls.

There was a sound like the wind as whispers rose up from all twelve quarters. Then everybody was in motion and all moving in the same direction. Cold hands seized Cat, shoved her forward, urged her along, pinched her when she tried to linger, shoved forcefully at her back. It was like when the ghosts of her fellow dragon pilots had forced her onto the stage of the Blinded Cockatrice. Only this time there were hundreds of hands and even the slightest resistance was impossible.

She was running full tilt when she passed through the Annihilation Gates. Then she was in a public square and the hands let go of her. Dizzily, she stumbled to a stop.

Cat stood at the center of a large empty space, though the square on all sides of that space was so crowded that there was a constant flow of individuals swimming upward to perch on the windowsills and pediments and rooftops of the surrounding buildings like so many pigeons. This was the first time she had ever seen anybody in Ys leave the ground. It struck her how much like flight their motions were. All this time she could have flown! Yet because nobody else did, it had never occurred to her to try.

Dominating the far end of the square was a colossal statue of a hoary old elf-lord, overgrown with mussels, sponges, feather duster worms, barnacles, oysters, kelp, shipworms, hydroids, and bryozoans. He was seated upon a throne of granite and though his expression was fierce, his eyes were closed. "My father," Dahut said. Somehow, she was standing alongside Cat. "He was no larger than you or I when first he sat down there."

A murmur passed through the throng and all faces turned

upward. Cat saw a wisp of noctilucent cloud twisting and turning far above, almost like a living creature. Then, as it corkscrewed downward, growing larger, swimming faster, it became the white serpent from her dream.

With a rush like a locomotive coming into a station, the serpent hurled itself down into Gradlon Square, its arrival flinging up trash and making hair and clothing leap and dance. Looping and coiling, the creature came to a stop immediately before the king. Then, with no fuss whatsoever, it transformed into a male figure. He was as beautiful as a statue and equally unencumbered by clothing. His cock swayed lightly in the currents his arrival had set in motion.

Cat blushed and turned her gaze away. Then, because squeamishness was unworthy of an officer and a lady, she forced herself to look. Beside her, Dahut murmured, "Behold the man your song released. For this moment, I could almost forgive you."

Fingolfinrhod stepped out of the crowd and approached the newcomer. "Prince Benthos, son of Lyr, heir of the Worm Oceanus of the line of Pontus, Great Lord of the Waters," he said, "welcome."

"Thank you." The noble lord looked about, saw Dahut, and extended a hand. "My love."

For all her personal loathing of Dahut merc'h Gradlon, Cat found herself catching her breath, anxious to hear what she would say, after so many centuries apart, to the lover for whom she had thrown away her dignity, her reputation, and her city. Theirs was a passion like none other in history. So it was a great disappointment when Dahut walked up to Prince Benthos and said, "What kept you?"

"I was imprisoned and tortured," the prince said matter-of-factly. "It was a small price to pay for this moment."

They clasped hands. Fingolfinrhod stepped forward and all three hugged formally.

A collective gasp rose up from the crowd. Cat looked to where all were staring and saw that King Gradlon was slowly opening his eyes. They were alive and alert, where the rest of him remained still as stone. Their pupils were as large as dinner plates.

"What the fuck?" Helen said.

"Shush!"

Fingolfinrhod stood forth from the others and said, "King Gradlon has elected to speak through me." Then, in a deeper, more resonant voice, "Natural order has been defiled and justice long deferred. The guilty are now assembled and the City and Commonwealth of Ys, in my person, may finally judge and be judged. In what little time we have left, let injustice be undone.

"Dahut merc'h Gradlon and Benthos of the line of Pontus, present yourselves."

Hands still clasped, Dahut and Prince Benthos bowed before the king.

"You stand accused of the crime of dereliction of duty and the sin of selfishness. How do you plead?"

As one, they said, "Guilty."

Prince Benthos then released Dahut and turned to face Fingolfinrhod. In the same resonant voice, he said, "Fingolfinrhod, heir presumptive to the title of Sans Merci of House Sans Merci, you stand accused of the crime of dereliction of duty and the sin of selfishness. How do you plead?"

Fingolfinrhod shrugged. "Guilty, I'm afraid."

Dahut now turned to face Cat. Who glared up into Gradlon's enormous eyes, refusing to let her fear show, and defiantly said, "Not guilt—"

"*Silence!*" King Gradlon shouted through Dahut's throat. "If the witness's testimony is required, you will be called up. The court commands the defendant to present herself."

Baffled, Cat said, "But I just—"

"You were never the defendant, dear," Helen said. "Barnacle Bill here is talking about me." A tingling sensation swept over Cat's body and she found herself exiled to the back of her own brain, watching as Helen stepped forward to confront her judge.

"You are Helen V—" Dahut, still speaking in King Gradlon's voice, began.

"I know who I am. Cut to the chase."

"You were in room 402 in Pennsylvania Hospital when a flight of dragons passed through on a soul raid. Tell us in your own words what happened."

⋇

Helen was dying, to begin with. But she had a plan. It wasn't a very good plan. But it was all she had. When the time came, she almost forgot what she'd intended. Still, at the last instant she remembered.

A flurry of confusion and a desperate leap into the unknown later, Helen found herself nestled safe within the skull of a young dragon pilot, as snug as a maggot in an acorn. A lot of what she saw made very little sense to her. So she kept her head down, her eyes open, and her mouth shut.

The pilot's name was Caitlin. The dragon she flew was an abomination. She had a symbiotic relationship with it. Neither could fly without the other. Dragons and their pilots, while they prepared for war, which was their common purpose, were occasionally sent out on missions to steal the souls of children. Helen had been accidentally snatched up on Caitlin's first mission.

Caitlin thought she was a good person.

She was wrong.

Secretly, Helen watched and learned. That child-souls looked like eggs of light. That such eggs were taken to the House of Glass to be implanted in bodies born without souls of their own. That in time those bodies were impregnated by high-elven lords. That the offspring resulting from this miscegenation were valuable tools of the Governance. That by treaty only half mortals were allowed to fly the dragons on which so much of the power of Babylon depended.

It was an ugly way to run a world. But who was Helen to judge? Her own world had its problems too. Also, she didn't know what might happen to her if she were to be discovered. She was enjoying her second life and would not cherish losing it.

There were, however, wheels within wheels. Caitlin was being framed for a crime she had not committed. When it was made clear to her that she would not receive an honest trial, she bolted and ran. Exactly as her enemies intended.

To save the lives of them both, Helen revealed her existence to Caitlin. Who, savage creature that she was, promptly murdered her dragon and, amid much destruction, eluded her pursuers.

They became fugitives.

Caitlin changed her name to Cat. She lived off the generosity of others, abandoning them as it became necessary. Helen tried to convince her to make a new life for herself. But Cat was determined to regain the privilege that had been taken from her. Somewhere in Europa, alongside a field of rye, the locomotive Olympia prophesied for her. Cat did not understand her words. Helen did. But knowing what use Cat would make of the knowledge, Helen chose not to share her understanding.

"I . . ." Helen shook her head and returned to her narration.

In Carcassonne, Lord Pleiades told Cat that the purpose of

the Conspiracy was to plunge Faerie into an age of unending
war. Because it was not her world, Helen did not feel the need
to act or to advise Cat on what actions she should take.

"I . . . I think . . ."

In Avernus, Queenie revealed the hatred the underclass felt
for the descendants of their conquerors. Because it was not her
society, Helen said and did nothing. In Brocielande Station, she
witnessed the death of hundreds and her chief concern was for
her own survival. When her host suffered a crisis of conscience,
she did nothing to console her. Again, she did not feel obliged
to do anything about the Conspiracy's plans to foment war. Everywhere they went, she tried to keep Cat out of trouble not out
of concern for her but because that was the safest course for . . .
for . . .

"I . . . I've been terribly, terribly selfish." Helen broke down
in tears. "I should have helped the girl. I should have been her
conscience. I . . ."

Thousands of eyes stared at her. No one spoke.

Dahut, speaking for Gradlon, said, "Do you acknowledge
your guilt?"

"Yes."

Then the voice of King Gradlon passed again to Fingolfinrhod. "All are guilty by their own admissions. Here is my judgment. For crimes of commission by Prince Benthos and Dahut
merc'h Gradlon: death, followed by demotion to the lower
reaches of the Wheel of Being. Dahut, you will surrender the
Horn of Holmdel to Prince Benthos, who knows what his last
duty must be. For crimes of omission, which is to say failure to
guide my much-beloved daughter toward the melioration of her
crimes, by Fingolfinrhod of House Sans Merci: death, followed
by demotion to the middle reaches of the Wheel of Being.

"For crimes of omission and the sin of cowardice, Helen of

Aerth, you will be set free and admonished to think long and hard on your failings.

"Finally, for outliving its natural span and for serving the ignoble purposes of the Secret Masters of the Three Worlds, to wit, harnessing the natural forces of Creation for worldly purposes contrary to the will of the Goddess, the City and Commonwealth of Ys is condemned to oblivion and the rebirth of its population into new lands and new eras."

The king's eyes began slowly to close. Before they could, entirely, Cat found herself in possession of her body again. Helen's tears were still coursing down her cheeks. Ignoring them, impulsively, Cat shouted, "Hey! What about me?"

Through mere slits, King Gradlon contemplated Cat. Then, with insulting indifference, the eyes closed.

‑✶‑

The trial was over and the sentences were passed. There remained only one act more to be endured. Silent as owls and as unblinking, the citizenry of Ys watched as Dahut snapped open her purse and removed from it the Horn of Holmdel. It glowed gently in her hands. She presented the artifact to Fingolfinrhod, who in turn presented it to Prince Benthos.

Prince Benthos stared down at the Horn, his face a mask. Then he lifted it to his lips and threw back his head.

He blew.

Much later, Cat would try to recapture the memory of what music the prince played on the Horn of Holmdel and how it sounded. It shook her and stunned her, that much she knew. But not a note of it remained in her head a second after it fell to silence. She could only remember its effects.

All the world swam in Cat's eyes. Dazed as she was by the Horn, it took her a second to realize that this was real and not subjective. Skyscrapers swayed and the ground danced under-foot. A tremendous unending groan, as of continental plates rubbing against one another, rose up out of nowhere. A balcony broke free of its moorings and drifted downward toward the street, tumbling and scattering its occupants as it did. Tiles went flying. Windows shattered and shards of glass fell like snow on those below. Everything happened with eerie slow-ness: The curtain wall of a high-rise disintegrating. Fish scattering madly in all directions. The roof-sitters and ledge-perchers being blown from their roosts by wild currents and tumbling overhead like so many autumn leaves.

Then the water boiled black. Storms of bubbles sped out-ward, blinding Cat to what came next. She could only hear the sounds of destruction: metal being ripped asunder, stone shat-tering, buildings collapsing, and—faintly, faintly!—the cries of the dying. Until all the groaning and crashing and shattering combined into a single enormous roar and the ocean *screamed*.

Terrified, unable to see, lashed by the currents, Cat clung to one of King Gradlon's legs, hoping against hope that she would not be torn away. There was a sick feeling in her stomach as if all the city were a gigantic elevator rushing upward at tremen-dous and ever-increasing speeds. Then, as the black, bubbling waters churned about her, she passed out.

An Agon, or contest, or wrangling, there will probably be, because Summer contends with Winter, Life with Death, the New Year with the Old. A tragedy must be tragic, must have its pathos, because the Winter, the Old Year, must die.

—Jane Ellen Harrison, *Ancient Art and Ritual*

EVEN WHEN ALL YOU HAVE EVER LOVED IS GONE, LIFE GOES on. Or so Cat discovered when she woke up the next morning on the sandy beach between the choppy waters of the Bay of Dreams and the city of Ys, newly restored to land. The ocean was a hard gray and carried on it a single ship, small with distance. Perhaps that ship was steaming her way to investigate the sudden appearance of a city on this previously uninhabited stretch of coast. Perhaps not. There was no way of knowing. Turning her back on the ocean, Cat saw for the first time the destructive work of centuries which time, denied entry for so long by the strength of mighty spells, had visited upon Dahut's port nation, on its return.

In a stupor, she stumbled down debris-covered avenues between roofless buildings and the rusted, half-melted I-beam frames of skyscrapers whose curtain walls had fallen away. Ys smelled of land decay, sea growth, and rot. Death was everywhere in the form of fish, seaweed, and other marine life carried up with the city into a medium where they could not thrive. But for a mercy, the citizens of the city had apparently been caught up in the rush of deferred destruction and their remains were as one with the dust of ages.

All was gray. Everything stank.

A vast melancholy filled Cat. Ruins were only romantic when you didn't remember what they had looked like whole and how their inhabitants had once lived. Yesterday's city had been a sleepwalker. Today's was a cadaver. "I fail to see how this is in any way an improvement over the undersea city."

"It was not a question of making things better, but only of justice," Helen replied. "One reason I never seriously considered becoming a lawyer."

An uncanny silence shrouded the city. There was no wind and no birds sang. There was only the sound of the surf and the tense reverberation of spent magic lingering over the ruined buildings and toppled towers like the after-sound of a great bell that has faded to inaudibility but still vibrates to the touch. When the stillness wore off, the creatures of the land and air would return and tourists come to gawk and marvel. But for now all this belonged only to Cat and Helen.

Following streets whose names and destinations Cat knew only too well, they came to Gradlon Square. All that remained of the king after whom it was named were the bottom of his granite throne and two truncated stone legs. On the paving before the throne lay the bleached skeleton of a sea serpent coiled protectively about two bipedal skeletons with their arms wrapped around each other.

Benthos, Prince of Oceanus, cadet son of Lyr, of the line of Pontus.

Dahut merc'h Gradlon, hereditary ruler, traitor, and protector of Ys.

And Fingolfinrhod.

Cat sank to her knees, but only because she knew that was what she ought to do. Strangely, she found that she felt no grief at all. What kind of monster am I, she wondered, to lose a brother and experience nothing? Then something inside her burst and nothing turned to everything. All the sorrow in the world crashed over her and she threw back her head and howled. A hole had been torn in reality and she doubted the damage would ever be unmade.

When enough time had passed that she was capable of speech again, Cat declared, "All the joy in me has died. I will never laugh again."

Helen, wisely, said nothing.

"We'll have to do something about the remains. I could build a cairn, I suppose. There's stone enough for one, Goddess knows, but I'm thinking it would look awfully punk here." Cat visualized a mound of bricks, ceramic tiles, and broken frieze-work, loomed over by the Piranesian tombstones that its destruction had made of Ys. "So that leaves a bonfire."

"What about the Horn?" Helen asked. In her grief, Cat had not noticed it. But the Horn of Holmdel lay among the bones, golden on the outside, cream and pink within, untouched by the destruction it had called down upon the city. "Don't you want it?"

"That thing? I wouldn't—"

"I have lit three candles and snuffed two," said someone standing behind her. "Now I snuff out the third." This time Cat was fully awake and recognized the voice. So when she twisted about and saw Saoirse standing in the center of the square, though she had not been there a breath earlier, Cat was not in the least surprised. The dragon pilot had an equipment bag slung over her shoulder and a bandage over one eye.

"Not now," Cat said, quietly and without emotion. "I have serious matters to take care of first."

Bitter laughter bounced from the walls. "Who are you to dictate where and when you will die?"

"Fine." Cat rose to her feet. Bleak. Empty. Without hope. "Great. Suit yourself. We'll have it out down by the sea. That way whoever dies, the other won't have to worry about what to do with the body."

⁕⁕

The sun was bright and the surf low. Cat felt half asleep with grief. She sat down on a fallen pillar with Atlantean fluting. "Okay, let's talk."

Standing over her, blocking the sun, one eye a glint of light, the black silhouette of her pursuer said, "I didn't come to talk but to unsheathe a sword."

"Oh, don't be melodramatic." Cat patted the pillar beside her. "Sit."

Saoirse hesitated, then sat.

"What happened to your eye?"

A brief flash of teeth split Saoirse's face in what might be either a smile or a grimace. One hand rose to touch the bandage. "Nothing is free. I traded it for wisdom."

Cat felt the ghost of astonishment. "Really?"

"It might have been vengeance. I have a hard time telling the two apart anymore."

"Ah. That would have been the price of the three-candles trick. I won't ask who you bought it from. You run with a louche crowd." Then, not because she thought it would do any good but because she was sure she should at least try, Cat said, "We don't have to do this, you know. We don't have to *be* this. We have so much in common, you and I. Not just the Academy. Not just our commissions. You broke out of Glass Mountain and I have no doubt whatsoever that you left it burning behind you. I came to Ys and look at it now. You follow your duty as I once did mine. We are reflections of each other. When I raise my left hand, you raise your right. We are sisters, the two of us. Look at my face! Think of yours. We came from the same womb. My admiration of you blinded me to that fact. Don't let your hatred of me trick you into the same mistake."

Saoirse's eye blazed with anger. The fire spread until her whole face burned like molten copper. "You are a vicious little shit, you know that? Once, I believed in justice. You disabused me of that delusion. Then I sought revenge. You screwed that up for me too. At last, I came to accept that power is all that matters in this world. And where could I find power? Within myself. I called upon my dragon, and it told me where I could cut a deal." She stood, glowing with internal dragon-fire. It shone dazzlingly from her good eye and more subtly from beneath her skin. She unzipped her equipment bag, removed its contents, threw it aside.

Two crowbars clanged to the sand. "Choose your weapon."

"Seriously?"

"I failed in my attempt to bring you to justice because I acted unjustly. I failed in my quest for vengeance because I offered you no chance to visit vengeance upon me. Now I'm giving you what you asked for: single combat. A fair fight. Even odds."

Cat shook her head. Even though she could see Saoirse rejecting her every word as she spoke it, she said, "I've been through a lot since Carcassonne. I've learned something, I think. I'm not going to fight you."

Saoirse's expression took on a triumphant cast and—

"The hell you're not," Helen said and, snatching up a crowbar, invoked 7708's true name: "Zmeya-Gorynchna, of the line of Zmeya-Goryschena, of the line of Gorgon, *get your fucking ass up here!*"

"Stop. What are you doing?"

"Keeping you alive, you idiot."

The leaden doors of perception swung ponderously open,

hinges screeching, as Cat's mind was turned inside out, giving control to the creature that had been patiently waiting within her all along.

Her dragon took over her body as easily as Cat might have slipped on a blouse. It flipped the crowbar in the air and, without looking, caught it in its other hand. Then it swung the black iron bar down upon a brick, exploding it into orange dust. It laughed. "Oh, but it feels grand to live again! Even in a body as pitiful as this one."

Cat's body took up position facing Saoirse. Her vision, filtered through the dragon's sensorium, reversed all colors, so that the sea was a milky white with black-tipped waves, the ruins like ivory, and the sky overhead a dull red with dark brown clouds. Each of them raised their crowbars before their faces and then slashed them down and to the side in salute.

A dark, gloating hatred for all things coursed through Cat's mind and flesh. It was every bit as seductive as her instructors had warned her it would be. She enjoyed it even more than she had feared she might. It wrapped itself around her like a cloak. She could have lived within it forever.

Then she had taken the crowbar by one end in a double-handed grip and assumed the horse stance. So had Saoirse. Dragon-Cat raised her crowbar up and to one side. Dragon-Saoirse's motions were the mirror image of her own. They faced each other, two dragon-women perfectly at home in bodies that raged with emotions they had fought all their lives to suppress. For the first time ever, Cat gave in wholeheartedly to the anger, hatred, and resentment she had carried within herself, seemingly, all her life.

Why hadn't she done this long ago?

"Learn well from this experience," her dragon said. "This fight will end in death—yours or your opponent's, I honestly don't care which. But should you chance to survive, I want you to remember how good and right this feels—and then live your life in my image."

Slowly, Dragon-Cat's crowbar began to move. She felt her muscles bulging. With more-than-human strength, she drove the weapon down and inward. Her perception had amped up to dragon speeds: the crowbar barely moved in her vision. Dragon-Saoirse, face contorted with rage, matched her slow-seeming actions exactly.

Minutes inched by.

A larger than usual wave came in from the sea and slowly climbed Dragon-Cat's leg all the way to her knee. She felt her body shifting so it would not unbalance. The crowbars were now halfway toward each other. She saw the sweat steaming from Dragon-Saoirse's shining face, the gleaming drops of water thrown into the air by that same wave crashing into her opponent, the motion, slow as the hour hand on a clock, of their weapons. Somewhere in the back of her head, she registered Helen's irrelevant observation that the seawater had surely ruined her shoes. Meanwhile, she concentrated on unclenching her jaw, lest the dragon-strength shatter her teeth.

More time passed.

At last, the metal bars met. At the speed with which she was perceiving them, the sound they made was low and drawn-out, like whale-song. The metal twisted in her hands, sending shock waves up her arms and down her torso. On Dragon-Saoirse's face she saw an anguished expression that was surely twin to her own.

Her crowbar shattered.

Dragon-Saoirse's did not.

All in an instant, Cat was lying on the beach and the wave was drawing back from her body. She was gasping with exhaustion. Her dragon was gone, back into the recesses of her mind, and all her body was numb. She could not move.

She had lost.

Triumphantly, Saoirse flung away her weapon.

Struggling to breathe, Cat said, "This . . . proves . . . nothing."

"It proves. That I'm stronger. Than you are." Saoirse was gasping, too. She must be nearly as exhausted as was Cat. Nevertheless, she drew a combat knife from a belt sheath and sank to her knees by Cat's side. "I'm going to have to ask you to be patient, now. This will take a very long time indeed."

A gout of pink exploded out the back of her head.

Saoirse fell.

Slowly, achingly, Cat stood. She was filled with wonder and bafflement. Confusedly, she thought, Now I truly have nothing, not even an enemy. Then she heard a crunching of feet on rubble and Raven came swaggering up, a cigarette cocked jauntily in the corner of her mouth, and a rifle slung over her shoulder. When Raven got to the beach, she said, "I think we've just proved one thing: A gal with a pal with a Remington 700 is stronger than any dragon."

Cat stared at Raven, trying hard to believe that she was actually there and not a hallucination.

"Gotta confess. I was planning to stop her with magic but you spent so much time under the sea, I kinda fell off the wagon." Raven took the cigarette from her lips and flicked it away. "You know how hard it is to give up these things? So I went with Plan B."

"Raven," Cat said at last. "I . . ."

"Yeah?"

"I'm going to puke."

※

"You'd be surprised how often my line of business involves watching people throw up," Raven said. She and Cat had gathered driftwood, house beams, rotted wine casks, and other combustibles and built a bonfire on the beach, where the sea caressed the land. When it was large enough, they heaped the skeletons atop it. They then had a brief debate over whether to include Saoirse or leave her corpse for the scavengers, but Cat won and she was included. They made sure, however, that her body didn't touch the remains of the others. Cat cut off a lock of her own hair and placed it among the mingled bones. Then, with Saoirse's combat knife, she sliced open a thumb and dripped blood on each of the three skulls, though not on Saoirse's brow. Finally, she doused all with gasoline from a jerry can Raven produced.

At a safe distance, Raven laid out food and wine on a red-and-white checked tablecloth she spread out on the sand. Then she rattled a box of matches. "Before I torch this mother, it's traditional to say a few words about the deceased. And since I didn't know any of them . . ."

"I can do this." Cat took a deep breath and struck the funereal pose of eulogy. "Prince Benthos was one of the Powers of the sea, noble of character, steadfast in love. Dahut was one of the Powers of the land and protector of her city, passionate to the point of madness, able to love two men equally and truly. My brother . . . well, I honestly believe he could have been the peer of either, given the opportunity. They all did their duty as they saw it. They all loved whom they wanted without shame. They were all great among the mighty. They all fell short of what the Goddess expected of them." Cat paused. and then said, "The Goddess is a real cunt."

"You can't end the oration like that!" Raven cried. "It'll jinx you. Trust me, I know how these things work. Add another line, quick."

Cat considered, then with a wan smile said, "They were three sides of the same coin and they died in each other's arms."

"Better," Raven said. "And Saoirse?"

"Once, Saoirse was everything I wanted to be. The Goddess gave her to me to teach me to aspire to something better."

"That's good. Stand back."

The gasoline went up with a *whoosh*, engulfing all in flames.

⚹

Cat and Raven ate slowly and took only tiny sips of wine with each toast they made, so that when the bonfire died to ashes, they were just finishing up the bottle. "Even now, with Saoirse dead, I find myself still admiring her," Cat said, trying to explain something she wasn't sure she understood herself. "Not the half-maddened fury she became but Saoirse as she had once been. A long time ago, before all this nonsense, she was my hero and my role model."

"Well, there was your mistake," Raven said. "Find better role models. Me, for instance."

Cat laughed longer and louder than the witticism deserved, then said, "I thought you'd run off, never to return."

"Naw. I couldn't do that. Not to you, babe. Y'know, you don't get to make many friends in my line of business." Raven held out a hand, closed it into a fist, opened it again. The holey stone lay upon her palm. She gave it to Cat. "So. Have I fulfilled my commission?"

"You misled me, Raven. This is a lot more valuable an item than you let on. You weren't exactly forthcoming on that front. Had I known its true worth, there is no way in the world I would ever have promised you it. Even now, after all we've been through, it's worth far more than the services you performed." Cat handed back the Stone of Disillusion to Raven. "It's yours."

Raven accepted the stone with a nod and placed it on a block of white marble fallen from a nearby temple. Then, with the stock of her rifle, she smashed it to powder.

Cat drew in her breath sharply.

"Thanks. I've got a major scam in the works, and that was the only thing that could possibly have stopped me." Raven made to throw the rifle into the sea.

"Hey, wait!" Cat said. "I might have a use for that."

❊

It had been a long day. But it wasn't over yet.

For hours, Cat and Raven sat and talked over old times. Which technically were recent times. But felt like old times. Cat told every story she could think of about Fingolfinrhod, even the embarrassing ones, and was surprised to discover that almost all of them were from when they were children and almost none from recent years. Raven had tales to tell that made Cat feel like she was living in a larger, bawdier world than she had realized.

At last, casually, as if the question hadn't been foremost in her mind all the time, Cat asked, "Where's Esme?"

"She's being taken care of by Pop-Pop and my mom. Dad's there too. They told me they were planning on having a cook-out tonight, so you can imagine what that must be like. If it were anybody but you, I'd be with them right now. It's gonna be a regular family reunion. We have great get-togethers. You should hear some of the gossip. It would make a manticore blush."

"I was hoping to see her again."

"Kind of a bad idea, babe. You couldn't take losing her twice in a row."

"Well." Cat skimmed her paper plate onto the embers and watched it flare up. "Tell her not to forget me."

"She will, you know. The little brat never remembers anyone."

"Tell her anyway."

"I will." Raven leaned forward and put her hand on Cat's knee. "But listen to me. You must accept this or you'll never accept anything. Esme doesn't belong to you. She was just under your protection for a while. Sooner or later, she was gonna flee you like a rat out of Lady Hel's furnace room. It was inevitable."

"Okay, yeah, I got it."

"It's too bad you can't join us, though. My family would love you. And I'm thinking you'd get a kick out of the fun we have. Horseshoes. Badminton. Boar hunting. Plus we treat Esme like the grown-up she secretly is. These get-togethers are the only times she's able to hang out with folks who really understand her and will let her have the occasional cocktail."

"You give her alcohol?"

"Only a little. With her body mass, one martini and she's dead to the world. But, the Goddess knows, she does dearly love a good cigar."

"You don't—!"

Raven winked.

"Oh," Cat said. "Oh. You're kidding."

"So far as you know. Not kidding when I say I'm going to miss you, though." Raven stood, slapping ash from her jeans. Then she handed Cat a business card. "Here's the address you want. I picked this up working for the Conspiracy."

Cat looked at the card:

THE HOUSE OF GLASS

10000 ALCHEMICAL ROAD

GINNY GALL

BABYLON

"I didn't know I'd be headed there until yesterday. How could you possibly . . . ?" Cat stopped. "Oh yeah, right. Trickster."

Raven grinned. "I keep telling you."

⁕

Jill was parked on a dirt road to the land side of the ruins of Ys, alongside a forest-green Triumph TR6 that Raven had apparently cajoled into a short-term liaison. "Best you get away from here as fast as you possibly can," Cat said. "The Lords of the Conspiracy are going to be converging on this spot just as soon as they can get their chests waxed and book parking spaces for their Learjets. They've got a treaty to break and runways to build so that ambassadors from Mount Obsidian can sign off on the deal."

Raven lit up a cigarette. "I'd go with you if I could. But from what you tell me, you're heading into Destiny country again. And, like I told you last time you did that, I've got good reason to stay the fuck away from there. You can borrow Jill if you like, though. There's some walking-around money and a train ticket to Babylon in the glove compartment. Just make sure she has a full tank of gas when you're done with her, so she can make her way back to me. She and I have grown fond of each other and we've got plans."

"I will."

"Don't forget what I taught you. Whenever you pay for something by check, overpay. Then, when it's noticed, ask for a cash refund for the difference. Then cancel the check. It adds up."

Cat and Raven hugged, and kissed each other's cheeks. "Nobody else gives me advice like you do," Cat said.

She watched Raven drive away, wondering if she would ever see her again and suspecting she would not. Then the last silent reverberations of the Horn of Holmdel ceased and seagulls came to scavenge the ruins, to bicker and fight, to scream ownership, to destroy all semblance of dignity.

Somewhere, agents of the Conspiracy were about to take note.

"You ready?" Jill asked.

"It's good to see you again, Jill. I probably should have said that earlier, but it's been an emotional day and I was a little distracted."

Jill revved her engine. "I'm used to it. You'd be surprised how little courtesy people show a sub-luxury vehicle. Raven's the only one who gives me any real respect."

Cat opened the SUV's door. There on the passenger seat was her duffel bag, obviously full. Beside it was the Horn of Holmdel.

"When did Raven manage to sneak that in?" she wondered.

"Hardly matters," Helen said. "It just saves me the trouble of having to walk you back to pick it up. What we're planning to do will be extremely difficult. We'd be fools to leave a useful tool like that behind."

Cat turned the key in the ignition. Then, when the motor roared to life, she leaned forward and stroked the dash. "Okay, Jill. Ride like the wind."

"On this road?" Jill said. "I don't think so." Cautiously, she trundled down the dirt track.

She who is favored by fortune has good luck even while sleeping.

> —Giambattista Basile, "Sun, Moon and Talia"

IT TOOK SEVERAL DAYS TO REACH BABYLON. CAT GOT OFF the train at Ginny Gall, three stations beyond the Tower. The land thereabouts was flat and the buildings a mixture of abandoned brownfield hulks and nondescript industrial boxes. In the distance, Babel was a thin scratch in the dust-yellow sky. She got a room at the Marriott Express and the next morning took a cab to 10000 Alchemical Road.

The House of Glass turned out to be a long, low, windowless cinder-block building on a tract of reclaimed land bordered by fields of phragmites and a stagnant old industrial canal posted with biohazard signs. There was nothing about it to make anyone look twice. It was hard to estimate how large the building might be, since there was nothing by it for comparison, but it had to be city blocks long and possibly every bit as deep.

"You don't want to get off here at the highway, lady," the cabbie, a balding kobold, protested. "Let me drive you to the entrance."

"No, this is good." Cat paid the fare, tipping generously for luck. "I can use the exercise."

There was a large ground sign by the driveway reading THG

with 10000 ALCHEMICAL ROAD in smaller letters below. Crouching between this and an ornamental thornbush, out of sight of passing traffic, Cat unwrapped the bundle of blankets she was carrying and reassembled the Remington. Clip in, safety off. More clips of ammunition in her pockets. Though, one way or another, she doubted she'd get to use them. Her purse, containing her wallet, a couple of tampons, and the Horn of Holmdel, she slung over her shoulder.

"Walk in casually or run in firing?" Cat asked.

"That's more your field of expertise than mine," Helen said. "But when you look at the path that brought you here, this day seems fated."

"We'll stroll, then."

Defenses looked to be nonexistent. There were no surveillance towers or closed-circuit television cameras, no fences topped with razor wire, no warding fetishes, not even an overweight rent-a-cop by the door. Even more ominously, there were no cars in the parking lot.

"Could this be a local holiday?" Helen said.

"I doubt it."

It was a long walk down the drive past ChemLawn-perfect grounds to the main entrance. The glass doors opened at a touch. The lobby was empty.

"Hello?" Cat said.

There was no response.

"We make such a sucky commando," Helen said. "I've lost track of how many times I've directed this exact scene: a lone avenger charging in, guns ablaze, roaring defiance down the corridors of power. Mind you, in my day, a well-brought-up young lady wasn't supposed to go to foreign lands to kill strangers and bring home ears and whatnots for souvenirs. Though I have to concede that later on that got better."

"Excuse me? Anyone?" Cat called. The building was eerily still. "Is there anyone here?"

Five panels of corporate photomontage, bleeding one into another, dominated the lobby.

The first panel showed blue sky behind the head of a dragon pilot in helmet and oxygen mask above whom was the word AC-QUISITION.

The second panel showed a hospital with a procedure-masked soul surgeon leaning over a greenish-gray infant, almost goblinesque in its ugliness, lying in a crib and the word TRANSPLANTATION.

The third panel showed neatly dressed changeling girls whose faces were smiling masks at work in an improbably clean factory under the word MATURATION.

The fourth panel showed a Tylwyth Teg wearing a Pulcinella mask easing open a glass coffin in which lay a sleeping changeling woman over the word IMPREGNATION.

The fifth panel showed the soul surgeons again, removing the shadow from a preadolescent half-blood child, and the word EVACUATION.

Finally, the last panel showed a slim dragon pilot in flight suit, helmet, and loosened oxygen mask standing on a runway, giving a grinning thumbs-up beneath the word DOMINATION.

Cat could remember a time when she might have been able to convince herself to find this inspiring.

Beyond the unoccupied reception desk was a hallway. They followed that past empty windowless offices, all indistinguishable from one another save for the framed photographs and clan fetishes on the desks, until finally emerging into a cubicle farm. Offices and cubicles alike were unoccupied. The lights, however, had been left burning. They hummed quietly overhead. All the desks had a memo lying on them, apparently

dropped there immediately prior to the building's evacuation.
Cat picked one up and read:

TO THE ATTENTION OF: ALL EMPLOYEES

1. The House of Glass will be vacated at the end of this Day
of the Labrys, Falling Leaves Moon. You may take with you
personal items but nothing else. Be sure to sign out at the
front desk.

2. The facilities will remain vacant throughout the following Day of the Cat, Falling Leaves Moon. Anyone attempting
to enter the building on that day will be subject to summary
dismissal.

3. Regular hours will resume the following Day of the
Phoenix, Falling Leaves Moon. Restoration of normal operations will then be a priority. Cleanup of any damages done in
the interim will be considered a part of your assigned duties.

4. Anyone who fails to return to work on the Day of the
Phoenix, Falling Leaves Moon, excepting only those with pre-
scheduled authorized leave or those with a healing-woman's
certification of illness, will be subject to internal discipline.

5. Please initial this memo below to indicate that you have
read and understood its directives, seal it with a drop of your
own blood, and leave it on your desk.

"Huh," Cat said. "Looks like we were expected. Any idea
what to do next?"

"Thank God I have done my duty. Admiral Horatio Nelson,
October 21, 1805."

"Umm, yeah. Only, excuse me for asking this but what exactly are you saying?"

"We're supposed to be heroes, right? Let's act like heroes."

"Gotcha."

The deeper Cat went into the building, however, the creepier she found the lack of resistance. Management clearly knew she was coming. They could not have failed to conclude that her intentions were hostile. What did they have planned?

"Bingo!" Helen cried. At the end of the hall was a door with a card swipe lock and a sign reading:

MEDICAL AND THAUMATURGICAL
PERSONNEL ONLY
BEYOND THIS POINT

Cat jiggled the handle. To no avail.

"Shoot out the lock," Helen suggested.

"Too great a likelihood for shrapnel or a ricochet. This calls for a more subtle approach." Cat reversed the rifle and smashed the wood beside the lock. On the third blow, the door flew open, revealing the main factory floor. Row upon row upon row of glass coffins stretched into the distance, too many to count. Inside each coffin was a woman covered by a cheap white blanket so that only her head and toes were exposed.

"Remind me again of the prophecy that Olympia made for me."

"She said: *In a glass coffin/Your mother lies imprisoned/Wake her with a kiss.* Her exact words."

"She didn't by any chance provide some clue as to which specific coffin my mother would be in?"

"No."

"Of course not." Cat had met many prophets in her time; the Dowager had a penchant for them. Always, they withheld crucial information, to provide incentive for the customer to buy into the premium upgrade.

Cat advanced onto the factory floor. The coffins rested on concrete piers. She touched one and the glass was so cold it stung her fingertips. Inside was a round-faced woman. Her eyes were closed and her skin was a soft, warm brown like Cat's. She looked to be asleep. Staring down at her, Cat became more and more convinced that even though she did not breathe, she was alive.

Was this her mother? Her biological mother? Her *true* mother? The face within wavered in her vision as if she were viewing it from underwater. Mother, Cat thought. Talk to me. Please.

Did the woman stir? Or was that just Cat's own reflection in the glass?

"Any of them could be your mother," Helen said. "Keep moving. Gather information. Think seriously about what you've learned. That's what you did in Ys, right?"

Cat lingered, however, by the side of the frozen woman. "I wonder. When my father came here, did they wake her? Did they take her out of the coffin and place her in a room for privacy? Or did they just open the lid and let him have at her right here?"

"Don't go there."

"This woman could be my mother! And if she is, the Dowager stole that title from her and Father stole the daughter that was meant to be hers."

"The odds are against this particular woman being her. Keep looking."

Cat continued onward, all nerves and vigilance, weaving a way between the lanes and aisles at random, peering down at the faces of the imprisoned changelings. She paused before a coffin holding a woman who was obviously pregnant. This time the glass was warm to the touch. Leaning her rifle against a neighboring pier, she lifted the lid. She placed a hand on the woman's belly and felt the baby within her womb kick.

"Exactly what do you think you're doing?"

"The kiss, remember?" Cat leaned forward and kissed the

changeling's cheek. The head shifted slightly. Eyelids twitched. But the woman did not awaken. One down. Hundreds to go. Cat eased the coffin lid back.

"All right," Helen said. "I thought it would be best to let you figure this out for yourself. But I can see that's not going to happen. So—"

Cat held up a hand. "Wait. Something is coming. I can feel it in the pit of my stomach."

There was a low rumbling like cannon fire somewhere over the horizon. It grew louder. A tank passing by the building? Or a convoy of them? It might be a giant headed their way. A big one. The floor was trembling now. A storm! Winds shook the loading dock doors at the far end of the factory. Rain rattled across the roof. Lightning struck and struck and struck again, followed almost immediately by the booming laughter of the gods. Then, as one, the doors all blew open, ripped free, and tumbled away. Into the building, crackling with witch-fire, strode—

"Barquentine?" Cat said. It was indeed Lord Pleiades, only slightly altered from when she had clocked him with a hairbrush in Carcassonne. She had snatched up the rifle but now she lowered it. "What's with the eye? Is this yet another memo I didn't get? Are eye patches the new black? Is everybody going to be laughing at me when I show up at cotillion with unimpaired vision?"

Behind Barquentine, the storm died to nothing. He giggled in a high-pitched, unsettling way. "The Year Eater likes eyes. Om nom nom, can't get enough of them." The eye patch only intensified his roguish good looks. But now not even Helen found him attractive. His mouth was too skewed, his gait too loose, as if he were a marionette being operated by a distant puppeteer. There was madness in his eye. "But we can both do without the Kate Gallowglass persona, Ms. Sans Merci. I know better and so do you."

"The Year Eater is one of the Seven. What would a minor Teggish lord like you be doing hobnobbing with Entropy Personified?" Cat scoffed. She didn't drop Kate's manner. It was the only way she knew to deal with Lord Pleiades. "Also, if you want to stay alive, you'll stop where you are." He was twenty feet away. That was close enough.

With a shrug, Barquentine stopped. He awkwardly drew up one foot and then the other, so that he was sitting cross-legged in the air. It seemed he had acquired impressive new powers during their separation. "A rifle. How amusing. Not the weapon I would have chosen in your situation but *chacun à son goût.* Foot disease for everyone! But seriously . . . have you ever been in a coma? Have you wandered the lands of unending pain?"

"No."

"I have. I know every inch of them. Time doesn't exist there. Only fever and misery. And bees." He clapped his hands three times sharply, then touched his head, his lips, his heart, and his sex.

⚬⚬⚬

Barquentine lay comatose in the Hôpital Maîtresse de la Miséricorde (Lord Pleiades said), though he wasn't aware of that fact. It was Caitlin of House Sans Merci who put him there—but that's another thing he didn't know. All he knew was that he had to keep walking. There were stony hills and he climbed them. There were rocky valleys and he descended into their lightless depths. He did not stop. He did not rest. The very concept of rest was alien to him.

Sometimes he heard voices saying things like "I'm not at all happy with these numbers," or "Levitate this patient so I can change the sheets, will you?" or "We're probably going to lose that eye." These were random dialogue from the hospital but he didn't know that either. Only that if ever he stopped walking the bees would sting him over and over again until he shambled and then ran, screaming, from them and that they would then pursue him for miles before falling away at last.

Was the bird with Barquentine from the beginning of his ordeal? The question was meaningless. The ordeal had neither beginning nor end. Nevertheless, he became aware that there was a bird hovering by his ear, speaking to him.

"I have been sent by the Conspiracy," the blind and black-feathered fowl said or was saying or possibly had always said, "to offer you freedom in exchange for—"

"Anything!" Barquentine sank to the ground, not caring if he were stung, weeping tears of gratitude.

Thus it was that Barquentine, poor fool that he was, came to the Tower of Seventeen Eyes. You've seen its baleful glare in religious icons. Possibly, at a low point in your life, you've stood before it in a sleeting rain at midnight, shivering with dread at the thought of what lay within. Even if you'd had the courage to try the door, you would have found it locked against you. But he, Barquentine, found it open. He was expected. He went inside.

He saw the Year Eater.

How to describe the indescribable? Imagine a traffic light in the middle of a trackless desert. Imagine a horse's head afloat in a vacuum. A single perfect rose growing from the back of your hand. Three plover's eggs on a sheet of vellum resting atop an Erlking XIV escritoire in a burning house. A whisper that can smash worlds. A raindrop larger than the Motel 6 it is about to inundate. Hold all these things in your mind at once and picture something looking exactly like all of them simultaneously and you will have taken the first faltering step toward visualizing the Year Eater.

If he hadn't been insane already, the sight would have driven Barquentine mad.

You may thank the Goddess that you were not privy to the conversation that ensued. They came to terms. Or rather, Barquentine learned that it was too late to alter the terms the Conspiracy had already negotiated for him. The Year Eater will give you anything you want. For a price. But that price is always greater than the value of what you'll get. Everybody does that, of course, whenever you sign a contract—it's just the nature of Capitalism. However, when the Year Eater gives you the short end of the stick . . . Well. Suffice it to say, the eye was the least of the many things that Barquentine lost.

One of those things was his memory.

When he returned from the Tower, representatives from the Conspiracy told Barquentine that you hated him and had good reason for doing so. That you were the source of all his miseries. That since your assault on the House of Glass had been decreed by some dread Power greater than them, they dared not approach you directly. They needed a messenger. That messenger was to be Barquentine. He was told what to say and how to make sure you would listen. He came to the House of Glass. He stands before you now and is about to say:

"The end," Barquentine said with a mad little flash of teeth. He unfolded his legs and lowered them to the ground. "Wasn't that a delightful little fable? Would you like to hear the Conspiracy's message now?"

Reluctantly, Cat nodded.

"Then know this to be true: The Conspiracy has authorized me to make you an offer. In exchange for your gouging out an eye and going away quietly, they will reveal which of these women is your mother. You can take her with you, if you wish. They'll even throw in the blanket. But wait! There's more! For one eye and an irrevocable oath of obedience, they will also restore your commission in the Dragon Corps. You won't be able to fly, naturally, but you'll get an honorable discharge, all criminal actions against you dropped, and a clean record.

"Not convinced yet? Well, hang on to your hat! For both eyes and the oath of obedience—well, we can't give you your brother back. Nobody can. The universe has rules that even the Goddess won't break. Fingolfinrhod's gone forever. But the Conspiracy will throw into the pot something almost as good! Absolutely free! Totally naked! Obedient to your ugliest whim! You can have—Ned!" Barquentine drew a circle in the air with his forefinger and a vision appeared within it of the slave boy, no longer in those ridiculous green shorts, weeping tears of blood from what once were eyes. "Waddaya say?"

"Are you quite finished?" Cat asked.

"In more ways than one," Barquentine said jauntily.

Cat looked at his hands. "You're still wearing that opal ring you showed me during the Plague Carnival, I see. As long as it's touching your flesh you can't lie. So: Are you really Barquentine or is he just a puppet for something too big to interact with me any other way? Just how deep does this thing go?"

"Only the smallest fraction of me is Barquentine. Most of him has been flensed from this body." That high-pitched unnerving giggle again. "As for deep? He's being manipulated, you're being manipulated, it's puppets all the way down."

"I thought it would be something like that. This next question is for Barquentine alone. Whatever remains of him, I mean. Barkers? What is it that you want? Not the Conspiracy. Just you personally."

Barquentine closed his eyes and in the weariest voice imaginable said, "Oblivion."

"It's yours." Cat raised the rifle and put three rounds through his heart.

※※

The cement floor around Lord Pleiades's corpse was bright with blood. He was the first person Cat had ever killed. She hoped he would be the last. But she refused to regret doing it.

"Stop staring at the body," Helen said. "Some of us are more squeamish about such things than you are." Then, when Cat had complied, "All right, now it's time I paid the rent. There are things you need to hear."

"Oh yes. You were just about to tell me something when Barquentine made his grand entrance. What was it?"

"I'll get to that. But first, you need to understand that Lord Pleiades was just a distraction. The Conspiracy couldn't possibly have thought you'd take them up on those ridiculous offers. Barquentine was sent here to push your buttons and, by golly, he did a bang-up job of it, didn't he? He was meant to get you so worked up you couldn't think straight. They wanted you to go chasing up and down the aisles, kissing cheeks, until at last you despaired and went away."

Cat considered. "That sounds . . . plausible," she said at last.

"The second thing you need to hear—and forgive me for saying this, dear, but I must—is that this is not all about you. You want to wake up your mother so you two can hug and sob over each other and say loving things, right? Not gonna happen. Look at it from her point of view. She was a sick and probably frightened child in a hospital when the dragons came and stole her soul. Maybe she was dreaming at the time. She woke into a nightmare. After being implanted in a new body, she was indentured to a factory where she performed manual labor until reaching puberty. At which time she was placed in a glass coffin and removed only for impregnation and childbirth. All her memories are evil ones. Does she love you? Sweetie, she doesn't even know you. At best, she got a glimpse when you were removed from her body. Plus, mentally, she's still a child. Whatever solace you want from her, she can't provide it."

"Then why the fuck have I gone through everything I have? What's the gods-be-damned *point*?" Cat's fists were balled. She was within a sliver of punching herself in the face, over and over, simply because that was as close as she could ever come to physically hurting Helen.

"Deep breath, dear. Calm yourself. I know this is a lot of bad news to take in all at once, but I have reason for it. Okay?"

"I . . . Oh, all right."

"The truth is that there has been a great injustice done but not just to you. Not just to your mother. Every sleeping woman in every coffin in this factory is a victim of the system you yourself were once a part of. They all need to be rescued. And once you think about it in those terms, it'll be obvious what you have to do."

✵

In the hands of one who knew how to use it, the Horn of Holmdel was capable of shaking the universe. Cat didn't want to go that far. But she had memorized the tunes from Istledown's chapbook, and one of them, surely, would accomplish what she needed done. "What should I play?"

"Do you know the bugle call for Awakening?" Helen asked.

"Yes." Cat ran through the tune in her head.

"That's the one. In my world it's called Reveille. I saw it in the songbook. I'm guessing that if it's the same in both our worlds, it's in the calls of every world of existence. It's probably hardwired into the stuff of Creation."

Cat's hands were sweaty on the Horn of Holmdel. She looked down and the Horn made them look insubstantial, like mayflies alighting briefly on a boulder just before a wind swept them away forever.

"Can you do this?" Helen asked.

"I can do this." Cat lifted the Horn to her lips. She knew how to play the thing, of course. She'd done it before. Anyway, conch shells were easy. She took a deep breath and then pursed her lips, as if in a kiss.

She blew the first note: Long, unchanging, pure, and piercing, it seemed to hang in the air forever.

All the coffins exploded at once.

"Daughter of Misery!" Cat clapped her hands over her ears. She saw the Horn of Holmdel go bouncing across the factory floor.

Crystals of snow puffed outward from shattered coffin after shattered coffin, chilling the room and turning everything white. Indistinct forms sat up on the concrete piers, looked about themselves vaguely, and then, floating up into the air, were lost to vision in the mist.

And that one! That one! That one there! was Cat's mother. Cat knew it for a certainty. She ran to the coffin in time to see the woman raise herself from the shards, glance incuriously at Cat without the least trace of recognition on her face, and, raising her arms, lift up into the mist and dissolve.

She was gone.

Tiny specks of glass had flown into Cat's face and when she tried to brush them off, her hand came away red with blood.

⁂

As Cat stood, unmoving, over the remains of her mother's coffin, she heard an electronic *chirp* as a door opened and closed. Footsteps clattered toward her. Numbly, she turned to face the newcomers. Hardly caring, she noted that they were both lawyers and that she knew each of them.

"You can kill me now," Cat said. "Or imprison me for eternity. Whatever you came to do, I don't care. I'm ready to accept my punishment. I did what was right, no matter what the Law or the Goddess thinks."

With a tug at her trousers, Lieutenant Anthea knelt down before Cat. Counselor Edderkopp did not. But he reared himself up and, tucking a stick under one armpit, laid a hand upon Cat's head and said, "You have my blessing, child, and that is something I do not give out lightly."

"Why are you doing that? Stop it." Cat knocked away Edderkopp's hand and tried to pull Anthea to her feet. But the predator-woman only bowed her head more deeply, so that her brow touched the floor.

Edderkopp made that dry rattle of amusement he did. He leaped up, slapped knees, clapped hands, clicked heels. Then he said, "Lady Sans Merci swore out a writ of dowagerhood, shortly before your father died, which left his title to be assumed by his oldest surviving child —Fingolfinrhod, it was expected. Had your brother died in possession of that title, it and all your father's wealth would have, for ill or for nil, passed to a cadet branch of the family. He did not. Which means that now you, as the only living blood-child of the old lord, will, as soon as my young associate here notarizes and files the papers, inherit his estate in its entirety, both tangible and intangible, including goodwill and spite, enemies and allies, entanglements and entitlements, debts and vendettas, stocks and bonds, cash, lands, options, et cetera, et cetera, *und so weiter.*"

"I can't. I'm a criminal. I killed a dragon. I deserted the Corps. I didn't kill my brother, like everybody thinks, but I'm not able to prove that. I was responsible for the destruction of Ys and just now I've probably bankrupted the changeling industry. I . . ."

"Milady," Lieutenant Anthea said, still not rising from her knees, "let me put it simply: You are now Lady Caitlin of House Sans Merci and thus the Sans Merci of Sans Merci."

"Which, legally speaking," Edderkopp expanded, "means you retroactively had a right to do everything you did, from fratricide to dragon-mort. You're not a fugitive anymore, but mighty among the Powers of Faerie. There are forty thousand individuals in this world who are above the law, and you are very nearly at the tip of the pyramid. Everything you did is now as legal as the April rain. I do not pretend it's a fair system. But its unfairness is now weighted in your favor." With a rascally wink, he added, "So I believe I have well earned my fee today." He plucked the opal-and-silver ring from Barquentine's corpse and the Horn of Holmdel from the factory floor. Then he scuttled toward the door.

Cat tried to object and found herself incapable of either sound or motion. Then Edderkopp was gone and her body was her own again. Bewildered, she said, "I have no idea what just happened. I thought you'd come to punish me."

Lieutenant Anthea rounded on Cat with a snarl. "Don't you understand?" she said. "Can you possibly be that stupid? You don't have the *right* to be punished. Edderkopp was nothing more than a mask for the Baldwynn. You have been given the blessing of the single most powerful entity in the universe, short of the Goddess herself. It's like having gravity on your side. Or dark matter. Or mercy. Something like this doesn't happen all that often. But it has happened to you."

"What? Really? No. That's not possible."

"There's a car outside, with a chauffeur. Our first task will be to find a notarized shaman. There's an immense amount of paperwork that has to be done to clear up a record as messy as yours, and it's best we start as soon as possible. We'll begin by filing a quitclaim for your service with the Dragon Corps. Then you must legally assert your title. Leave the rifle. You won't be needing it anymore."

That night Cat had a dream. In it, the Goddess appeared to her
in the form of a Singer sewing machine. It was a top-of-the-line
model with both a foot treadle and an electric motor and a ten-
sioning dial at the front as well. Though it did not look new, it
had no visible nicks or scratches. The black and gold metal
housing gleamed with an indwelling light. Cat could not look
away from it.

Has my child been bothering you? the Goddess asked. Somehow, Cat knew that she was referring to the Dowager.

"Kinda, yeah."

*I am glad to hear it. Sit down and work the treadle for me, will
you?*

Cat did so. The needle moved smoothly up and down and she
found herself pushing cloth beneath it. It was an honor to be
serving the Goddess so intimately and she found her eyes well-
ing up with tears. It did not matter to her that she was stitching
up other people's lives. Somebody had to do it. Why not her?

I know you have questions, the Goddess said. *It will be a long
time before you have such an opportunity again. Ask.*

"I guess . . . if I had to ask . . . I'd ask . . . Why?"

*There was a conspiracy behind the Conspiracy and that conspir-
acy was me. Changes needed to be made in the operation of the worlds,
so I used you to make them.*

"I'm not entirely sure I see. Exactly."

This is a terribly indirect way to communicate, the sewing machine said. *But you're all so small and I'm so large. It would burn
you to a cinder to look upon me directly. The last person I let gaze on
me as I am grew horrible growths on his forehead, and he was much
stronger than you could ever hope to be.*

"I understand," Cat said.

No, you don't. But that's not important.

Gathering up all her courage, Cat asked, "Then what is?"

It's time you returned my daughter to me. Her work here is done.

This time, the Goddess, Cat knew, meant Helen. It was a vexatious thing to realize that all she had been through, the losses, the sufferings—and, yes, the love as well—had been tangential to the real story. That she had been living through not her own tale but Helen's.

Still, having no choice, she accepted it.

Then, without transition, Cat was no longer asleep, but sitting up in her hotel room bed, reading a paperback. She put it down, saying, "I just had the strangest imagining." She could feel the specifics fleeing her memory. But, briefly, she still understood the gist of their meaning. "The Goddess appeared to me and explained that life, death, and dreams were three sides of the same coin. Then she—"

"It's time for me to die," Helen said. "Don't try to stop me, my mind is made up on this one."

You can save somebody's life, but it's only temporary.

—Helen V., notebooks

CAT AND HELEN CAME AT LAST, AFTER LONG AND PERILOUS journeying, to World's End. The out-of-season and mostly shuttered tourist hotels, candy shops, and pachinko parlors that seemed so obtrusive when they walked among them disappeared the instant they stepped onto the beach and turned their backs on the lot. The wind whipping off of Oceanus was colder than either of them would have preferred. But they endured it without complaint. Here, there was no land beyond the ocean waters, no farther shore where the cold waves might finally find rest. Only the endless sea, rising from nothingness, without destination, forever in motion.

Standing on the pebbled strand, listening to the waves crash with a boom and then retreat with a hiss and a clatter, salt spray wetting her face, Cat felt Helen gather herself up, as a lady of her generation might have, in her youth, gathered up her petticoats. With quiet dignity, Helen said, "I am just going outside, and may be some time."

"What in the name of seven hells is that supposed to mean?" Cat demanded.

Helen V. sighed. "Nothing." An abyss of time opened

between the two of them. At last, she said, "You're going to miss me when I'm gone."

Inwardly, Cat thought: *As if.* Outwardly, she said, "Maybe I will." Once the words were irretrievably out of her mouth, she wasn't sure whether she had been humoring the old bat or telling her the plain and simple truth.

"Let me share something with you that I learned when my mother died," Helen said with uncharacteristic gravitas. "Are you ready? Brace yourself. You won't ever be free of me. Never. You might as well imagine yourself being free of your dragon or your nightmares or your dreams or your past. Once you get somebody lodged in your head, she never goes away. She becomes a part of you."

"Eh?"

"Just as I said. I leave to you all my worldly and unworldly goods. Good luck finding them and better luck telling one from the other if you do."

Mentally, Cat rolled her eyes. "I'll tell you one thing I won't miss, and that's your constant yapping."

"Peace, my child. Forget that I said anything. A week from now I'm sure you'll have forgotten me entirely."

"If only."

"Hey, what do you want from me? I say one thing, it's no damn good. I say the opposite, that sucks too. Make up your mind."

"Well, fuck you."

"Fuck you too."

They both laughed.

"So," Cat said when she had wiped away the tears, "how do we do this?"

"Lie down and close your eyes." Cat did so, though the beach stones were even colder than the wind. "Imagine a greensward, just after a rain . . ."

She did. Grass, wet and glistening, sprouted underfoot and stretched gently upslope away from her. Its smell was vigorous and green.

"In the distance, mountains. Big ones."

Mountain slopes, golden with sunshine, shot up before Cat, higher than any she had ever seen or imagined. They were lordly peaks clad in gowns of purple shadow and capped with dazzling white snow. Compared to these, the highest mountains of Faerie or Aerth were dwarfish and low. Something within her thrilled with the desire to climb them.

"The sky should be overcast, a little stormy, and absolutely free of birds. But leave the land underfoot unshadowed. There should be a bit more of a rise. Not enough that you'd call it a hill, but enough to hide the Black Stone behind it. Not a steep slope, mind! I'm in no hurry and I can walk a goodly distance."

The landscape assembled itself in Cat's imagination. There were small white flowers dotting the grass. She caught a faint whiff of their perfume: luminous, like Après l'Ondée. She was about to kneel down and pluck one when a lean, energetic woman strode vigorously past and, with a shock, Cat realized who it must be. She jolted to her feet, watching Helen grow smaller and smaller with distance. Belatedly, it came to her that she had lost her one chance to get a good look at the woman who had been such a major part of her life for so very long. "Wait!" she cried. "Hold on a minute. How did you know all—?"

Helen half turned and looked back expressionlessly over her shoulder at Cat. Distance rendered her face a pale oval with black dots for eyes, a slim line for a mouth. "Stop imagining," she said.

And Cat did.

You die when your spirit dies.
Otherwise, you live.

—Louise Glück, "Averno"

A LL STORIES MUST END. THIS IS THE IRON LAW OF EXIS-
tence.

Helen turned her face to the mountains and she did not look back. She walked toward them without hesitation or doubt and she did not speculate on what might lie beyond. After a time that was neither short not long, she came to the Black Stone and, just as had been prophesied to her so very long ago (for Helen was not above a little dramatic self-editing to her own story), she saw that there were two paths around it. One way was well-trodden and that was the one she understood led to forgetful-ness and reincarnation. The other was barely noticeable, and no living person could say where and what, if anything, that led to, for those few who followed it never came back, nor did there return any report or rumor of them ever after.

She had arrived at last at the end of this bubble of a dream-world, even as she had once arrived at the end of the one before it. Neither had satisfied her. Now Helen was up for something real—even if that turned out to be nothing at all. Whatever may or may not be, she thought—or possibly "prayed" was the *mot* more *juste*—I recognize its dominion over me. I am small and the universe is vast beyond my imagining. Since its workings are beyond my control, why should my life, or my death for that matter, be any different?

Any last words?

On reflection, I think no.

Helen bowed to the Black Stone, which she now understood to be an avatar, and possibly the only one, of the Goddess. "Mother," she said, "I surrender myself to your will. Tell me what to do and I will obey." It was the single most sincere thing she had ever said to anybody. But there was no response.

Story of her lives.

She stood before the Black Stone for a very long time, thinking. At last, she made her choice and passed beyond it.

. . . from that day forward she lived happily ever after. Except for the dying at the end.

And the heartbreak in between.

—Lucius Shepard, *The Scalehunter's Beautiful Daughter*

IT WAS SPRING AND THE AIR WAS HEAVY WITH HYACINTH. Even the limousine had bunches of hyacinth in little vases hung on gimbals for decoration. Caitlin hated the smell of hyacinth. But she endured it for the sake of decorum.

"It feels strange to be back after all I've been through," she commented.

"A good strange, I hope," the chauffeur said.

"Well, at least this time I'm not throwing up."

When she arrived at Château Sans Merci, Caitlin called the servants before her. They gathered, arrayed in ranks, in the grand foyer. (Nettie cringed, blinking and wringing her hands as she tried to pass unnoticed in the very last row.) Slowly, deliberately, Caitlin walked the ranks, looking every one of her employees in the eye, making sure they each knew that she could see them all and would be remembering their names just as soon as she learned them.

"I am Lady Caitlin of House Sans Merci, by rights of primogeniture, survival, and inheritance the Sans Merci of Sans Merci, and thus your liege employer. If any of you doubt the legitimacy of my claim, you are called upon to challenge me now.

First blood, third blood, or to the death, as you choose. Any takers?"

She waited. After a silence, she said, "Good."

Caitlin handed her family's ancestral sword back to the armorer, who accepted it with a curt bow and retired. Then she said, "There are going to be changes made, many of them. Whether you like them or not is of little consequence to anybody but yourselves. How well you thrive depends entirely on how well you adapt to them." Then, to brighten the mood, "All those who have been retainers for three years or more will receive ten percent raises, effective immediately, and six bottles of Lemurian wine each Beltaine. For ten-year veterans it will be fifteen percent and a dozen bottles. For those whose service predates my adoption, it will be twenty and two dozen."

A rustle passed among the servants, which was an accolade as good as a rousing cheer for anyone who understood their professional reserve.

"Th'art dismissed." Caitlin turned her back on the lot and felt them dissolve into their roles and duties behind her.

The rest of that day and the following week, Caitlin devoted to seizing control of the mechanisms of authority. Lawyers and accountants came and went. The chiefs of staff were questioned closely and one, who could account for neither discrepancies in the household budget nor her own newly acquired youth, was fired. A delegation of hobs came out of the deep woods and, in a ceremony that dated back to the founding of the House, presented her with five blue jay feathers and a single perfect acorn. She repaid them with silver, bolts of jacquard silk, and as many of the best and largest flat screen television sets commercially available as they could carry back to their burrows in a day.

After that, Caitlin turned her attention to the Conspiracy. Some of its officers could be fired with cause. Others required a buyout. The office in Carcassonne was shut down and all its assets reabsorbed into House Sans Merci's holdings. That would help offset losses due to the fall of the House of Glass. An employment service was engaged to find comparable work for the clerical staff, and Lolly Underpool was offered early retirement on extremely generous terms. The rest of the employees, Caitlin judged, could fend for themselves.

In what little free time she had, Caitlin systematically searched the mansion, crossing off each room on a map she had drawn from memory as one by one they came up empty.

⁕⁕

In a sunless drawing room, Caitlin found her mother at last. The Dowager had lain down upon a divan to rest and drawn newspapers over herself as a kind of blanket. Doubtless, she had left instructions that on no account was she to be disturbed, for the room had not been cleaned for a very long time. The papers had since grown brown and brittle and were covered with a soft layer of dust that looked for all the world like the mycelium of an imaginary fungus feeding upon the Dowager's dreams.

Despite all the time that must have passed since she fell asleep, the Dowager was still alive.

For a green flash of an instant, Caitlin was seriously tempted to leave her mother there, locking the door behind herself, throwing the key into the koi pond to the south side of the mansion, and setting a geas on the help never to go within. It would have been perfectly legal. But instead, she called in maids to remove the newspapers, dust and clean and vacuum the room, replace the lace curtains and gold velvet drapes, and set out new vases of tulips (which her mother loved) and fresh fruit in cut-glass bowls.

There was no denying that the Dowager had led a difficult life. Nor had she, as a lady of her standing and generation, ever had the option of deciding on a destiny of her own choosing. Caitlin supposed she owed her sympathy for that.

Not that she felt any. But she tried.

When all had been made ready, Caitlin dismissed the servants and lightly tapped her mother's cheek. Then, when there was no response, she tapped again, with more force. Nor did this bring about any results.

Stop now, she told herself. Before you start enjoying this.

Caitlin fetched a glass of water and lightly spattered drops from her fingertips onto her mother's face. Eventually, the ghastly old thing stirred. Crepe-like lids twitched. Eyes reluctantly opened. "Why aren't I dead?" the Dowager asked.

"You don't get to die. I have a lot to do here. I need your advice."

"You never took my advice."

"I never took your advice seriously. There's a difference."

The Dowager began to weep.

"Oh, come off it," Caitlin said. "Nobody's buying that act anymore. Here. Take this."

Sitting up, the Dowager accepted the water glass Caitlin offered, and sipped delicately from it. "You are grown cruel, changeling. I underestimated you."

"You tried to kill me."

"That too."

"Why?"

"It's not that easy to explain. I'd have to go all around the Green Man's barn in order to make you understand."

"Try me."

The Dowager touched the fingertips of both hands together, thumbs down, the rest up, and pushed inward until only a narrow space separated her palms. She stared down into that opening for a long, long time, as if scrying within for something elusive. "When I was young," she said at last, "I had an affair with my father."

Caitlin had thought herself incapable of being astonished by anything that might come out of her mother's mouth. Now she knew herself to be wrong. Horrified, she cried, "Why are you telling me this?"

"For once in your life, just listen. It's important that you do." Fleetingly, the Dowager's lips curled in that forceful disdain that Caitlin knew so well from her childhood. "My father was the wonder of the world—strong, masculine, amoral, mighty. I loved him, of course. He was my daddy, my hero, my everything. But as I grew, he seemed to wither. Where once he had struck down servants for imagined insolence and refused them right of cremation, now he was all reason and persuasion. By the first flush of my adolescence, he had grown so very frail and virtuous! It was obvious that he was close to transcendence. I so dearly wished to keep him bound to the world. I could see that was what he wanted.

"Also, the thought of losing him was unbearable.

"Even then, I knew about men. The seeliest of them could be called back to corruption with a hand job and a promise of something more. I promised my father much, much more. And I delivered on my promises."

The Dowager looked directly into Caitlin's eyes. "Do you wish me to be explicit?"

"No! Dear gods. Please, please no."

"As you wish. The affair passed pleasantly at first. What innocent young maiden doesn't fantasize about being debauched beyond the bounds of all decency? By age fourteen I knew more about sex and passion than all but the most depraved adults.

"By age fifteen, my wrists were a mass of scars from my attempts to kill myself. By projecting my body into my father's desires, I had traded one evil for another. He was no longer the man I wanted to save. I loathed him with all my being.

"So I withheld myself.

"That was when I learned where the imbalances of power truly lay. That was the night I turned from provocateur to victim." The Dowager paused. "Again: Do you wish to hear the details?"

"Let's just assume that every time that question comes up, the answer is no."

"Very well. I fled, he pursued. I hid, he found. He bound me helpless in his trap, I turned the tables on him. He begged me for forgiveness. I gave it and was flogged for doing so. I had a knife. He bled. We both enjoyed that particular game. Are you sure you don't—?"

Caitlin shook her head.

"I enjoyed the game far more than my father did. Thus, he died.

"I remember the smell of his corpse burning on the funeral pyre. Oh, it was foul! The stench filled the air. It has never entirely died away. Even today, it lingers in my nostrils.

"My guilt and pride and disgust at what I had done were enough to keep me rooted in this world to this very day. Was it worth it? Today, I look back at what I did and see only the folly of youth. It is even possible to imagine my actions to have been the kindness they were intended to be, for my father so very much loved the world and desired to remain in it. Even at the cost of becoming something he would earlier have abhorred.

"In the aftermath of the funeral, I broke down and confessed my guilt to my mother. We were both dressed in mourner's white. The ashes had not yet blown from my father's pyre. Can you guess what that wicked old woman did?"

"No," Caitlin said, "I honestly cannot."

"She shrugged and said, 'Same old same old.'"

"Umm . . ."

"I had a very long talk with that evil battle crow, that compilation of sins, that cesspool of bad intentions, that most loathsome of all creatures. Unlike you, I asked for all the details. I was sorry I did for they were all of them familiar to me from experience. This was the story my mother had lived and her mother before her and her mother before her, ad infinitum. Every detail was the same. No one could say how far into the past the chain of incest and guilt extended.

"Somewhere along the way, I met your father.

"Despite all my misgivings, I married him.

"You can imagine how relieved I was when, on first try, I gave birth to a male heir and needed not pass the curse of pity on to a daughter. You can imagine my horror when your father brought home a female bastard—you."

"But nothing like that ever happened to—"

"You're welcome," the Dowager said.

Caitlin bit her tongue, tasted blood, did not speak.

"You think that just because nothing happened, it didn't take tremendous effort to make that nothing come about? Oh, you are every bit the fool I always feared you would become. I thank all the gods and daemons there are that I did not give birth to you! Was I cruel to you in your childhood? Well, who had a better right? Who refrained from strangling you in your crib? Who spared you the doom that has haunted our female line since time beyond imagining?

"Was I cruel to you as an adult? Your entire graduating class was about to be sacrificed by your beloved Dragon Corps. By persecuting you first, I gave you a chance to escape and survive. As, you will note, you alone accomplished.

"Was I right to do the things I did? Was I wrong? It is not your part to judge. I look back now and I would forgive everyone everything, yourself included, if I could. Where I could not, I would offer oblivion were such a thing possible in this world. But, alas, neither forgiveness nor oblivion is in our power to offer. All we can offer is understanding.

"Which I have now given to you."

A long silence hung over the room, so profound as to be a living entity in its own right, a beast capable of sucking the oxygen from both their lungs forever and calmly watching them strangle and die. Caitlin could all but see it, a disembodied creature impervious to any weapons save one—words. Her fingers twitched. But she stilled them. If she was to use words as weapons, she needs must choose them carefully. So she did.

"Are you done?" Caitlin waited. "Here is my judgment upon you: You will live, Mother, until you die. Then you will be mourned, who knows with how much sincerity? Until that time, you must live and I must put up with you." She went to the door. "I shall inform the help that you will expect cocktails at six. As usual."

Caitlin found the note when she was cleaning out Helen's things. She hadn't realized that they were Helen's until she no longer had the old woman in her head. Then, when she poured out the contents of her duffel bag, it suddenly became obvious that some of her possessions had no relevance at all to her anymore. The note was in a plain white envelope, addressed *To Whom It May Concern*. Which, Caitlin thought, after all the two of them had been through together, was pretty fucking cheeky.

The world is choking on old stories, the note read. *Tell new and better ones.*

It was signed *Helen V.*

Caitlin put down the paper.

The room looked very different than it had an instant before. A burden had been lifted from her, there was no denying that. But something had been lost as well. Caitlin was at a loss as to whether she had gained or been diminished by this instant of comprehension. It would take a lifetime to sort it all out. She turned her back on everything that had come before and faced into the harsh sunlight of everything that was yet to come.

Stepping out of the old woman's shadow, Caitlin was astonished to discover that . . .

⁂

"What, Mommy?" young voices clamored. "Tell us!" And, insistently, "*What* did she find?"

"Enough, monsters." Caitlin mussed Amelia's hair and drew her up, along with Natalia and Alana, in one tremendous hug. "It's time for bed."

"But I want to know!"

"So do I!"

"We all do!"

"I want to know, too—a great many things. But merely having questions doesn't mean you're entitled to answers. I learned that the hard way."

"Just tell us what came next."

"Yeah!"

"Pleeease?" Amelia made her most calculatedly winsome face.

"That is another tale," Caitlin said in her firmest there-is-no-appeal voice, "to be told another day when you're old enough to hear it. If you live that long, which given your antics I tend to doubt, and even then probably not, because what could you possibly do to deserve it? Now. Hands, face, teeth, horns! And straight to bed."

Willful as kittens and thrice as adorable, the girls lingered, sulked, argued, defied, and were finally, efficiently, swept away by Missy Tibbs, their nurse. Who, when they were at last abed, returned to report to Caitlin on their doings and sayings, concluding as usual that all was well. At the end of her narrative, Tibbsy added, with the not-quite-insolence of a servant who has been with one house all her life and who knows that no one will overhear, "Why do you tell the children such terrible lies?"

Caitlin closed her eyes to keep her thoughts from showing, and, with an expression on her face that could not have been read by the Goddess herself, shook her head. "Nobody ever believes a word I say. Story of my life."